ONCE HUNTED, TWICE GOODBYE

Once Hunted, Twice Goodbye

ARIANA TOSADO

© Covenaan Press | 2024

Contents

ONE

"Tristan Atera was found dead in Forest City a *week* ago," Jak stated, like I'd actually forgotten, leaning forward in his seat in the gazebo. "I figured you'd be... messed up about it."

That was definitely one way to describe the end of my summer vacation—and my summer vacation in general. It's not like I had "Breanne getting Alexa's magic from the bracelet the woman tried using to extract mine" on my summer bucket list. And as much as I hated to admit it, Alexa had every right to be angry that night in the forest when Opal and I confronted her. Beating us half to death, maybe not—but as a wielder who'd been taken advantage of and had her magic stolen, her fury was justified.

Unfortunately, thanks to the remnants of the concussion

she'd given me that night, I had to play this conversation all the more carefully. After all, Jak couldn't know that Dad had only faked his death to buy himself more time against two of America's best Grand Hunters. Yet another Atera secret we'd have to bring to our *actual* graves. I was surprised that Jak had even asked to meet, let alone on my birthday, after I'd flat out rejected him in the hospital.

"I'm just worried about—you know, her." I lightly shrugged, eyeing the small pink bag sitting atop the white table in front of us. "She's the one suffering. She lost her *dad.*"

I looked up at Jak when he didn't reply. His rich-brown eyes weren't even on me; his thoughts had already taken over.

"Em..." He shook his head, overlooking the vibrant park that sat in front of us. "I don't get... I'm—"

His jaw locked on him, his knee furiously bouncing.

"What?" I caught myself asking. Somehow, this boy had gotten worse and worse at keeping things from me over the past few months. Some of his secrets, I'd learned months ago, were probably best left kept—but the rest were a mistake to bury.

"Nothing," he replied, "I'm just—I didn't expect your reaction because of your relationship with them, that's all. I was confused, it's fine."

Something sinister snaked around the paranoid part of my dizzy head. It was exhausting just to think about chasing Jak's answers, but I couldn't suppress my survival instincts: he was lying. Jakson Bleu's truths are always short and concise, yet he was already rambling.

"What is it actually?" I asked.

His chest deflated with a deep breath, a breeze fluttering the curled-upward tips of his hair. He leaned forward, took the bag on the table, and gently set it onto my lap. "Here."

I hesitantly took the tissue paper out until a small, wrapped box was left. I pulled it out. Its soft yet firm surface under the tissue paper suggested a jewelry box.

Because I wanted to see another one of these so soon after Alexa's stupid bracelet.

Jak took the bag off my lap for me as I tore away the tissue paper, leaving a small black box in my hand. I opened it. Three silver bands sat inside.

"Jak," I said, eyes snapping up to him, "you better tell me this isn't a proposal—"

"No, no," he said, quickly shaking his head. "No, um... just look."

I tried to hide my deep breath (and rib pain) as I took out the thickest ring. An elegant "A" was engraved on the front.

Wait a minute. All of the rings had "A" engraved on them.

What... what is this?

I wasn't brave enough to test my fears with the thickest ring. Instead, I set it back into the box and took out the smallest one, barely thinner than the one in the middle. I slid it onto my right ring finger. Perfect fit.

He guessed my ring size?

Well, he's held my hand a lot.

For whatever reason, regret stood right next to my embarrassment on the pedestal.

Jak stayed perfectly still as he watched me slide off the ring. I forced myself to turn it over. My eyes snagged on the name inside: "Emma".

No, don't tell me, no.

I took out the thickest ring, wanting to rip off that Band-Aid. I wanted it to hurt, anything to shove me back into reality, to make me feel more than the stun infecting my chest.

I turned over the ring: "Tristan".

Sensation drained from my fingers. I gripped the ring all the more for dear life. It wasn't possible. There wasn't any way that he...!

"I got the rings before he died." The boy next to me was dangerously still in my peripheral vision as he spoke, like even he knew how fragile the atmosphere was. "I'm so sorry, Emma. It's hard enough to be surrounded by people who've never gone through the loss you have. But that's not the case with me. You can express whatever you're feeling to me, I understand. I do. I know what it's like to lose a parent."

Despite the evidence in front of me, despite the concussion blaring that I wasn't processing anything in front of me correctly, the last remaining bit of my rationality screamed at me to hold on to my cover for dear life. You never know if you just misconstrued something—I never knew if that middle ring read "Adara", the name I'd told Jak in the passageways the day Redway left Callistro.

"I'm just...." I began in a whisper, forcing my volume up. "I'm surprised, it—the thought surprised me. I guess Tristan kind of felt like a dad to me—"

"You don't have to pretend anymore, Merlin."

That nickname meant something different this time. I just knew it. I made myself look up at him.

He softly smiled at me. "Why else do you think I picked that for a nickname?"

A terrified whisper escaped my breath: "You know?"

He reached a light-brown hand up to my cheek, grazing the peach fuzz with the back of his fingers. "I've always known."

"No, stop!" I snapped, shoving his hand away and just as quickly gritting my teeth against the pang in my ribs. "You chose my birthday, you chose when I'm crippled and can't move, to tell me? Are you kidding me?"

My best friends and I couldn't even attend the annual Capperson Fall Carnival this year because of my and Opal's injuries, with Opal stuck in a wheelchair and me in a walking boot. Going to that carnival had been a sacred tradition between me, Sarah, and Breanne since we were eight years old—yet Jak had chosen today to tell me that he was never *once* the boy I'd thought he was.

I didn't have him figured out, and I never had!

"Okay, I'm sorry," he rushed to say, "I got the timing wrong, but—I just figured my other present to you could be telling you that you have one less person to hide from. I know what it's been doing to you, I just..."

One less person to hide from?

Panic seized my mind. I wanted to kick, to scream. I even wanted to wipe his memory, but I couldn't for the same reason that Alexa couldn't with me: his memory went too far, maybe even further than mine did with Alexa. He'd notice. And it especially wouldn't work based on whatever had told him the truth.

"How?" I hissed, daring to lean in slightly.

"I knew before we met."

"*How?*"

He set his gaze dead ahead. The park was mostly bereft of passerby and people spending the afternoon here. I envied them;

I would've killed at that point to have a life like theirs.

"My mom knew," Jak muttered, casting his eyes down to his fiddling fingers like he was ashamed. "Right before she died, she told me to find Amy Dalbert and protect her daughter, Emmalynn. That was the last promise I ever made her. I wasn't gonna break it for anything."

"You told me you never got a name that night." My body screamed for movement, to remove itself of the confines of my skin and fragile bones. "How did she know? Who on this planet could've told her if not *my* mom?"

He sighed, warning me that I wouldn't like the answer. "I don't... I don't know."

"You don't *know?*"

"I was seven," he stated, shrugging. "Those were my mom's dying words. I probably wasn't supposed to know that young, I doubt I was supposed to know at all."

I opened my mouth, ready to bite back against his strained tone and even his argument—but that night he'd told me the story in Callistro's dorm hall shushed me. Mostly because he was right: Aastha had to have been the only one in the immediate Bleu family who knew about the Ateras. William would've come after me long ago otherwise. If Aastha had needed someone to protect the Ateras on her behalf because she knew she was about to die, Jak had been her only option...

My chest felt like it was collapsing all over again. My lungs were threatening to crumble.

"You told me," I repeated, my body stiffening by the second, "you never got a name that night. You said you didn't even think Tristan *had* a descendant!"

"Up until September last year, I was the only one who knew that I knew," Jak said, his tone steadying with authority. "You had to believe I didn't know so everyone else would, too. My dad and Alexa were following me everywhere I went back then. They were bound to catch us talking about it, and then what? We both end up on the list? They find out everything even faster?"

Wait a second. The pack *had* caught us, last year during the carnival. Alexa debriefed Jak that night about any information I might have given him about the Atera descendant—but the morning I found Dad, she told me that Jak hadn't lied about me not being Tristan's daughter. How had he gotten past the cerebral polygraph?

"Didn't Alexa interrogate you last year?" I asked. "The night of the carnival, about me being Tristan's daughter?"

He took in a tight breath, his eyes slightly narrowing, like he was bracing himself to give me the answer. "Yes. But the polygraph didn't catch me."

"What?"

"It was just me and Alexa. I held out for longer than I thought I could, but I had to answer her eventually. Obviously I was still gonna lie. But the polygraph didn't pick it up."

No way. A faulty machine? That single night was the whole reason I hadn't been taken into custody then and there!

I almost didn't want to believe it. When something is too good to be true, it is, and that's practically federal law in the magic world. What was too good to be true then was the fact that Jak had known the truth all this time without any repercussions; he'd already been at risk for being as big a target as I was. I'd never told him the truth for the same reason I hadn't wanted to tell Breanne that she had Alexa's magic. As much as I despised it, Jak was right.

That's why he's so persistent to help us, I realized. *I knew he had other reasons. He knows.*

He'd always known.

Hundreds of memories, from texts to phone calls to in-person moments, shoved through the fog in my head. Every smile, every flirt, every kiss, he'd conducted it all with the truth in his head. He knew that he'd been kissing Tristan's daughter. He knew that he'd been talking to Tristan's daughter. He always had.

"Whatever happened with the machine, I don't care," he told me, turning to face me better. "I'm just glad it happened. Because my mom had it right, Em, the difference between you and me doesn't matter. My goal has always been the same, it's never changed."

I met our eyes. My resolve threatened to buckle under his tenderness.

"I want to help protect you," he murmured. "I'm so sorry I couldn't do the same for your dad."

Those last two words stirred another round of nausea in my stomach. I hadn't been ready to hear them from Jak so soon. Frankly, I don't think I'd ever been ready to hear them from him. And I especially didn't want to hear them when he believed a lie.

I wanted to be furious with him for lying to me for our entire friendship—just like I'd done. I wanted to be furious with him for lying just to protect a friend—just like I'd done. I wanted to hate him for being right, for shoving my actions right back in my face. For verifying that my best friends probably *would* be furious with me for doing what Jak had done.

But he'd also verified that the smallest part of them deep

down would understand. And that understanding would only continue to grow with each second of remembering the kind of world we lived in. If I'm being honest, if I were any other magician's daughter—maybe even any other Hunter's target—I would've told them by now.

If Jak is starting this honest of a relationship with me... I didn't want to step into it with another lie.

"He's not dead."

It was Jak's turn to pause, almost like he had to be careful because I wasn't capable of telling the truth.

"He faked his death to buy time."

Maybe now the pieces were all fitting together—how I hadn't said a single thing about it when the news first made headlines, how I hadn't shown up this afternoon in tears—because Jak's brows eventually straightened and he closed his mouth.

"Wow. Um—how?"

"Long story that my head *cannot* give you right now." I exhaled, part of me ready to jump into this new reality where I didn't have to hide from him, because I was *exhausted* from that life. "The short version is that we stole some of this serum Breanne's been working on. She calls it her 'Juliet serum'. It made—my dad—seem dead. Mr. Dawson went under an appearance spell to look like an FBI agent, and 'found' him in Forest City. My dad woke up in the morgue freezer, and Dawson sneaked in with an invisibility cloak for him and a dummy under an illusion spell. The dummy's getting cremated, and Tristan will never see the news again."

"Wouldn't they wanna do an autopsy on a powerful sorcerer like him?"

"There'd be no point. There was an obvious bullet wound in

his neck and head, and a magician's magic dies with them, so there isn't anything to get from an autopsy."

He tilted his head. "I think you still have a few plot holes in your plan, Merlin."

"That's what I said. But they planned everything—Mr. Dawson is using an appearance switch spell to impersonate a few authority figures. They took care of it."

His brows furrowed with curiosity. "Why now? After this summer?"

I dared a scoff. "Yeah, apparently, they've been planning this since a couple of months after we found my dad last year. I woke up last week thinking he was dead. My mom came barreling into my room to tell me it wasn't real. We had no idea my dad and Mr. Dawson were planning it—they figured, if we believed it for even a second, we'd be able to use that memory whenever we have to act it out in the real world."

Jak shrugged. "Makes sense."

"We'd rather have the world think he's dead and cut off all potential future trails, seeing as Alexa definitely isn't gonna let us go that easily. We can deal with one pack, not every pack in the country."

Jak nodded. "Cool. Then I'll pretend I never heard anything."

Or I could wipe your memory and make that true. But after this summer, I wanted to stay as far away from memory-wiping spells as possible.

There *was* one spell I could put him under. I trusted him, but I wasn't as stupid as I'd been the night we met.

I closed my eyes. *Veritatem dicere.*

"You've really known the truth this entire time?" I asked. "Because your mom told you?"

"Yep," he replied, "but I've never told a soul. I've kept it to myself since I was seven. I promise."

I forced a soft smile. "Thank you."

He returned it, looking back out at the grass. I closed my eyes to release him from the truth spell. *Converte.*

Staring down at the sundress covering my lap, I took a deep breath against my ribs' warning. Our junior year of training to expel magicians from the face of the earth lay ahead of us, and yet in that moment... admittedly, I could breathe. For once, I only had the everyday routine to commit to. Now whenever I was around Jak, all I had to do was continue breathing.

"Thanks for the rings," I told him. "It's gonna be a long conversation, but I know my parents will really like them."

"I'm glad."

"Nobody was suspicious when you asked for 'Tristan A.' on one of them?"

One corner of Jak's mouth lifted. "I said you guys were my cousins, the Adams."

CHAPTER

Two

I kind of didn't want to admit it, but Jak *had* given me the gift of having one less person to worry about. Maybe even another person to confide in once I got over the whole lying-to-me-for-a-year thing—but I wasn't sure how much room I had to be mad at him when it came to that.

Dad and Aunt Becca's apartment Mr. Dawson had gotten them this summer was tiny, but safe. And it didn't affect my excitement as I walked into the living area that evening and saw the HAPPY BIRTHDAY! sign draped in front of the window, the small pile of presents on the sofa, and the balloons sitting in the corners of the room.

"Happy birthday, kiddo!" Dad exclaimed, his strong arms mindfully wrapping around me. "We missed you!"

"I missed you, too!" I broke away, careful of my sticking-out walking boot. "It looks amazing, I love it!"

"You're welcome," Aunt Becca said, leaning against the black entertainment center. She grabbed her coffee mug sitting on top of it. "I'll hug you once you sit down, I don't wanna break you."

"I missed you," I told her as Dad kept me balanced.

"Duh."

I turned my head at the sound of Mr. Dawson setting down a plate in the kitchen. He smirked, nodding down at the chocolate-frosted cake. "Got your favorite," he said. With Momma and Dad's help, I took a seat at the island. "Even has the semisweet chips you like."

I hummed in fake thought. "Thanks, that *almost* makes up for things."

He rolled his diamond-blue eyes, Dad coming to stand beside him. "It's *not* our fault that phones were banned from the school. And you know why you were kept in the dark about your mom."

That doesn't mean I have to like it. Apparently, being the headmistress's daughter doesn't constitute grounds for *telling* me that I was going to be the headmistress's daughter. I was choosing not to focus on Alexa at the time, but the adults in my life were on a better page: they'd decided that if the pack was going to retaliate in any way, a head who *wasn't* a magician should be the one to handle it. Honestly, I think they were just having fun keeping *me* in the dark for once.

"That's not the only thing, you know," I muttered. Despite having a relatively successful recovery period so far, my family had decided that I still wasn't worthy of knowing whatever my parents and Mr. Dawson were keeping from me about my identity as a sorceress. I'd overheard Momma and Mr. Dawson talking about it in the living room this summer, and he'd sworn to me that the only reason he wasn't telling me was out of respect for my parents—who thought I "wasn't ready" to hear it.

"Well, we're definitely not telling you as long as you have that attitude," Momma said all too gingerly. "Tell you what: prove that you can last the rest of the year surviving and *not* questioning my parenting decisions, and we'll tell you on New Year's Day."

That almost sounded doable.

"And it doesn't matter if you like it or not," Mr. Dawson added, like he was reading my mind. "That's how it is."

Dad chuckled at him. "You're good. No wonder she turned out so well."

Behind me, Momma contently exhaled as she smoothed my hair. She kissed the back of my head. "I can't believe my baby girl is almost grown up. Seventeen. *Seventeen*, Emmy."

"I remember," I teased, resting my hand on the granite-top island.

Her amber eyes traveled down to it. A divot formed between her brows.

Oh no—

"Hey," she began curiously, "where'd you get that ring?"

As if my chest needed more tension, my ribs tightened with an anxious soreness. Out of everything I'd had to tell my family since last September, this was the absolute hardest—and that says a *lot*. I guess that was one reason to be grateful for this summer: I'd developed a bad habit of telling the truth.

I reached into the pocket of my dress and dug out the small black box holding Momma's and Dad's rings inside. My heart skipped another giant beat as I opened it.

"It's a birthday present," I began, staring at the rings in fear of making eye contact with anyone. I took them out and handed them to my parents. "A set of rings for our family."

"This is beautiful," Momma said, coming to stand beside me. In front of me, Dad speculated the engraving of his name on the inside. "But you're not the one that's supposed to be giving gifts today."

I swallowed. *Rip off the Band-Aid. Don't wait.*

"They're from Jak."

A time bomb seemed to explode, fossilizing the entire room. And with my heart thumping all too loudly in my concussion-possessed head, the last thing I wanted was to shatter the silence just for the shards to cut me.

Momma shifted her weight to one side. I could already feel her eyes tacitly demanding mine to meet them, but I wasn't brave enough. "Jak got these rings?"

I almost wanted to tell her that she couldn't hit me because I was crippled. Why was I so afraid? It wasn't like I'd kept this from them during the entire year Jak and I had known each other. It wasn't like I was actually to blame this time.

But what if they stop me from ever seeing him again because he's dangerous—?

Oh. There it was.

It was too late to turn back, so I finally made my gaze meet Momma's. "He's known the truth the whole time."

Never in my life, even to this day, have I seen rage grip Momma's face like it did that evening: every muscle twitching, a subtle tremble in her lip, eyes hardening to stone as her pupils doubled in size. Her whisper practically slashed me as she asked, "You told him?"

"No!" I immediately said. "I never told him, he knew before he met us—"

"You better have a *bestseller* of a story lined up, Emmalynn, and I sure hope you can give it to me in the next ten seconds!"

"His mom was the one who knew, she told him before she died!"

"That's a *lie*," she growled, slamming her hand down onto the island. I was the only one in the room who flinched. "Before last year, the *only* people who could've known I ever had a daughter were people I'd actually met and *allowed* to know. William is the only Bleu I've ever known, Jak is lying and you believed him!"

Anger carved out my words. "He wasn't lying. I used a truth spell on him. And I know what it looks like when he lies."

"That's how you knew he was lying every time he referenced Tristan's daughter like she was a separate person, right?" Mr. Dawson said, cutting Momma off.

—*Whose side are you on?*— I hissed, glaring at him.

His deep-set eyes kept their authority. —*The side that keeps you and your family alive.*—

"He was telling the truth," I said again, glimpsing Aunt Becca coming to stand at the island with her coffee. "He told me, verbatim, under the truth spell, he never told a soul, let alone his parents. He's kept this since he was seven years old."

Anger was still all too present in the air, but for once, I was the wrong person to be mad at. Actually, Jak was, too; he had lied for all of the same reasons. For every lie I had about being Adara's friend, he had one for believing it. And somehow, we'd lied for the same cause: my family's survival.

If anything, I think we were all mad at ourselves for never figuring it out on our own. Especially me, the girl who'd spent the most time with him and let a crush blind her to the most crucial secret about her target. Again. But it wasn't like he knew who Adara actually was—

I froze.

"What?" Mr. Dawson asked across the island.

I anxiously chewed on my cheek, scolding myself. *Couldn't hide it in time. But I can't tell them this, I'll never hear the end of it.*

It's fine, Jak isn't a magician. There's no way he'd know who Adara actually is, that day in the passageway was probably the first time he'd ever heard the name.

But won't he wonder where I got it from? He knows me, isn't he gonna ask why I picked something so unique?

"Emma."

I looked up. Next to Mr. Dawson, my father was staring at me with a similar quizzical gaze. His sister next to him had one brow arched high over her icy-blue eyes.

"Sorry," I said, more quietly than I'd intended. My brain desperately grasped at whatever excuse presented itself first amidst the fog. "I'm... I got scared."

"Well, if he was telling the truth, you have nothing to be afraid of," Dad said simply—like he knew I was hiding something worthy of being feared.

I tried to maintain stolidity as I said, "He never told me because his parents were watching too closely back then. But now that I know, they might pick up on that. They might... hurt him."

Aunt Becca set down her mug on the island. "No, they

wouldn't. They might debrief him, but I doubt even William would go so far as to resort to torture."

"And Alexa has a son of her own," Momma added, more calmly than I'd anticipated. "Jak's not related by blood, but she probably wouldn't resort to authorizing his harm just for an answer he shouldn't have."

Yeah. "Probably". Because this was the same woman who had lured me and Opal Dubois into the Callistro Forest and potentially tried to kill her while leaving me defenseless so I couldn't blabber the truth about her family. I didn't know how far she'd travel for certain things, but I did know that she wasn't afraid of the distance.

"I don't want anyone else getting hurt because of me."

The words were out before my brain could even realize that I'd spoken them.

"Honey..." Momma murmured, rubbing my back.

Dad walked around the island and to my other side. "Nobody's getting hurt because of you, kiddo," he told me softly, leaning on the granite and folding his hands together. "You're forgetting that you were the one *most* hurt because of who's really responsible."

No. Opal was the most hurt—physically *and* emotionally. But I was too tired and fogged up to argue.

"We're dealing with a wicked person," Dad said next, his icyblue eyes that matched mine consoling me. "The people around you are hurt because of her. *You've* been hurt because of her. Look at you: in a walking boot, waiting for your ankle and ribs and head to heal, one of your best friends stuck in a wheelchair, and you both have to start the school year like this. You're not the cause of this, sweetheart." He placed one hand on the back of my head, pressing a gentle kiss to my forehead. "Promise me you won't think like that."

I carefully nodded.

"Okay, happy day," Momma said, clapping her hands together as she walked into the kitchen. She opened the drawer between Auntie and Mr. Dawson and grabbed a package of pink, gold, and white birthday candles. "We can talk about this later. Nobody gets to say another word about it for the rest of the day."

That was fine, I thought as the four of them gathered around the cake and started placing what would total to seventeen candles. They couldn't access my head, where I was tormenting myself about Jak potentially putting the pieces together about Adara. Maybe I could trust him with the truth of my real family, but I couldn't trust who could get that information out of him. Especially after I'd exposed Annisa's identity as Morgana to Moren a couple of months ago—I wanted all of us as hidden as possible. I'd witnessed firsthand the damages of being an open target.

CHAPTER
THREE

Mr. Dawson had been our Hunter instructor for over a week by now, but walking into class that Thursday felt like the first day all over again. We knew the routine well already, though: come to complete silence the second we stepped inside, take our seats, and wait for the man at the front of the room to begin his lesson.

But even after the bell rang and the room was left in dead quiet, Mr. Dawson stayed leaning back in his desk chair at the front of the room. One leg rested on his other, his hands folded in his lap. We knew to maintain perfect posture until he said something—to never break eye contact, to not be the first to speak.

According to the clock mounted above his head, a solid five minutes passed before he rested his other foot on the floor and sat up straight. "Sometimes you'll have to wait *much* longer than that before your target is in a position for you to catch them," he said, speaking with the confidence of a man who'd spent even his teenage years teaching. "Especially when you're undercover. So before you master the art of disguises, you *must* master the virtue of patience. So far, nice job, ladies.

He stood from his desk, coming to stand beside it. "All that said, let's start our first real lesson of the year: going undercover. You touched on this briefly with Headmistress Marie last year, but we're fully indulging in it this semester. It'll be one of the most difficult things you'll have to do in your career, but that's because it can make or break an entire hunt."

Even Alexa had demonstrated that with her Julia cover this year.

Mr. Dawson sat on the edge of his desk and crossed his arms. In his navy-blue blazer, he almost looked like he was revisiting his Redway days. "Going undercover opens up a world of opportunities otherwise unavailable as a Hunter working in the shadows: you're able to blend in with their environment. Gain their trust without suspicion. Gather more intel without anyone asking questions. The sooner you get it down, the better."

He opened one of the drawers in his desk, taking out a thin stack of paper. "Miss Holland," he said, strolling up to Kimia's seat in the far-left corner, "thank you for passing these out."

Kimia didn't hesitate to take the stack and stand. She started with Hannah Lowe in the seat next to hers and then worked her way down the room.

"As I said before,"—Mr. Dawson sat back down in his chair— "to master going undercover, patience needs to be your number-one priority. On your paper, I want you to write a five-paragraph essay summarizing the founding of the Callistro Academy and what you deem as its most significant contribution to society's well-being. Give as many details as you can remember, like you're writing the textbook itself. After all, it's a story you know well."

It doesn't *sound* terrible—but writing a detailed essay about a story that was practically a nursery rhyme to us at this point, and its significance that society had drilled into our heads since birth? Talk about patience (and self-control, if you're anything like Sarah, Elizabeth Moody, or Teresa Darci, who take advantage of the secret passageways way too often and use them as shortcuts to get to class).

Kimia placed a clean sheet of binder paper in front of me. I picked up my pencil and glanced at Breanne sitting next to me. Within seconds, she had her heading, her title, and the first few words of her introductory paragraph.

I lifted my pencil after writing "Dawson" in the heading and couldn't help but steal a glance in his direction: he was already typing away on his laptop.

I exhaled, setting down my pencil. It was pretty cruel of him to make me write a whole essay during the tail end of a concussion.

Sheer curiosity let me risk a glance at Sarah behind me, in the corner of the room. I paused in remembrance yet surprise: there her copper hand rested on her cheek as she tapped the end of her pencil on her paper. Elizabeth Moody wrote furiously beside her. Sarah glimpsed her scribbling pencil before blinking back to her own page. Her nose wrinkled in a nearly silent sniff as she slowly started writing.

If only that sight weren't so familiar.

⚓

"I hate that I actually *have* to use the elevator," Opal grumbled as Sarah wheeled her into our dorm after school. "So stupid."

"You had surgery for a spinal fracture," Sarah deadpanned, stopping Opal in the middle of the room. "How about focusing on how cool it was that you survived without being paralyzed?"

I made my way over to my bed, survivor's guilt (and my walking boot) weighing on me like an anchor. Plopping down, I stared after the purple-eyed druid in the middle of our room, a young woman meant to be a high priestess one day, trapped in a wheelchair until the end of this month.

"I'm sorry" was ready to fly out of my mouth again, but she'd made it painfully clear that that was the last thing she wanted to hear from me; in her eyes, I wasn't the person responsible for that night, and she didn't want me sharing the blame with the person who was.

"Of all things magic can do," Sarah began from the bathroom, brush already in hand as she moved it through her long black hair, "there isn't, like, a spell for healing or something?"

"No," Opal stated, cutting off Breanne with a glance as she opened her mouth. By the desk in the corner of the room, Breanne hugged herself tightly in her crimson blazer, her mouth clamping shut. Her role was identical to mine now: pretend that she knew little about magic because she wasn't a wielder. Her light hands picked at the blond hairs on her wrist instead.

"And please don't talk about it," Opal softly added, fiddling with her thumbs in her lap.

I swallowed down "I'm sorry" again.

"At least you're stuck with people who know what happened," Sarah said with a snarky grin. Telling her about Opal in the hospital did have its perks; it was one less lie to keep up with, one more topic to openly meditate on.

"Yeah, and it's not like your uncle's going any easier on us because of it," Breanne remarked, sitting down at the desk. "I had *no* idea how to write about the societal benefits of hunting after... what happened."

Breanne Shaw had just confessed that she didn't know how to write an essay. Alexa had messed her up way more than I'd originally thought.

"Same." I sighed, careful of my ribs. "The concussion didn't help. I kept accidentally writing about—"

—how Caralyn Callistro's father, Henry, stole magic from his prey and that's why Caralyn built the school.

I'd almost just said that—and had it not been for *how* I'd uncovered that truth (by sneaking into secret underground passageways built for the "soul of unity"), I would've actually been able to tell these girls.

Stupid brain fog.

"About what?" Sarah asked, leaning against the bathroom doorway.

"Sorry," I said. "I totally lost it just now."

She pouted at me, meandering back into the room. "Just a couple more days, Emmy."

And three more weeks for the sprain. And five more weeks for the two ribs Alexa broke.

Maybe we *should* have been talking about it. Maybe we shouldn't have been suppressing the topic of this summer under all the homework and anticipation of what the big junior class trip was going to be this year. Maybe we should have talked more about how the gash across Opal's stomach was healing, about how Tristan Atera was "dead" and none of us had heard from Alexa or the pack since she and Anthony disappeared. Maybe we *shouldn't* have been pretending that this school year was normal, no matter how much easier it was.

Maybe that was how Breanne knew to change the subject, because the moody atmosphere was no stranger to any of us by then. "I need a muffin." She stood from the desk. "And I think they have double chocolate chip today. And raspberry Danishes."

Hyperactive sweet tooth: she was anxious.

She reached Opal in the middle of the room, her dainty hands taking the handles of the wheelchair.

"Let's yell at Uncle Thomas while we're at it," Opal said. "I hate having to sit at his desk to do assignments just because the tables are too high."

Sarah heavily exhaled, running her hand through her hair. "You know what, you guys go ahead. I'm gonna take a nap."

I actually would've believed her—had it not been for third and last period. Mrs. Shenley's project introduction on our research proposal due next week had left Sarah in a hunched-over position at her desk. I was struggling to keep up with comprehension over the second week of assignments, too—but not in the same way she was. Ninety percent of me was sure of that, and that was enough to keep me glued to my bed.

My roommates' eyes fell onto me. I chewed on the inside of

my cheek, my fingers subconsciously around my locket.

"Are you coming, Em?" Breanne asked.

There was a plead pulling down Sarah's pear-green eyes when I looked at her; she wanted me to go. I didn't really doubt that a nap was what she intended to do, but I did doubt that it was the first thing on her list. A Hunter knows their targets—and not even my still hazy brain could make me doubt how well I knew my best friend: she needed a friend.

If she can't handle one right now, I'll leave after.

"I'm gonna rest for a bit, too," I replied, playing on a tired sigh.

"Don't let me keep you, Em," Sarah chimed, shooing me with one hand as she plopped down onto her bed in front of me. Anticipating that I was staying because of her to begin with. She had overshot the assumption, and now my theory was confirmed.

"It's fine," I told her, gesturing to my boot. "I'm tired."

With a quick glance at it, she nodded and smiled sweetly at our friends. "She'll be with you momentarily."

Breanne and Opal walked out and closed the door behind them, leaving the air fuzzy. Sarah leaned forward on her bed, an inviting smile on her mauve lips.

"You, too?" she asked. "How are you feeling?"

"I'm fine, but what about you?"

Her arched brows scrunched together, defined eyes stuck in a question. "Why are you asking *me* that?"

At least there were *two* reasons for it: "Nobody's asked you that since all this happened. It's been about me and Opal, but you're involved, too. You were dragged into it, too. Who's been checking in on you while that's all you've been doing with us?"

"First of all, it's my *job*." She chuckled, then shrugged like she didn't know what to tell me. "And I don't see you asking Breanne that—she's much more ready to fall apart at the seams than I am."

"I did, it was just private." Lie.

Her smile grew taut. "It's sweet of you to ask, but I'm okay. It's an insane adjustment, to say the absolute least. But we help each other adjust. That's how it works. I'm okay as long as you are."

My heart thumped harder in my chest. But I *wasn't*—that image from the essay today churned in my head, and all the other times before that. I felt like I was betraying my pact with Breanne to not ask Sarah about it, but how was I supposed to let my best friend suffer in silence? She'd flung her textbook off her lap last semester when we were studying for finals after I'd asked! I wanted Sarah's full honesty about how she was doing. I wanted her to know that even if she had a secret as dark as magic, I'd be there for her. Nothing could scare me away from her; I was her best friend.

"What about school?" I asked faintly.

Asking the right question was far from the relief I'd thought it would be. For a fraction of a second, her smile faltered and couldn't return to what it was. Even her eyes searched for an escape, softening with vulnerability.

"It's fine," she chirped, batting her eyes. "I'm okay."

I swallowed, bracing myself for impact. "Are you sure?"

In the second that her eyes narrowed, I read it as clearly as a book: she wasn't confused about why I was asking, she was trying to figure out how I'd seen right through her. And I think the weight of that question crushed her, because she seemed to forget to hide how her eyes glistened with tears I'd only seen from her three times in my life before. That third time had been when she was sitting on her bed, ruthlessly studying to get up her three C's.

Momma's was the only class she wasn't struggling in.

Sarah looked down at her knees—and sniffed.

She does *need someone.*

Before I could reach out to her, my best friend sharply inhaled and pressed her hand against her nose. "I wish—I'd tried harder to hide it. Couldn't do it."

My mistake started pressing down on my chest, pushing the words straight through my mouth: "You don't have to tell me anything you don't want to—"

"No," she stated, sitting up with reddening eyes, "no, I just— I want to know—why my parents sent me here. I don't know why they weren't—*smart* enough to send me anywhere else. This school is for the most intelligent girls in the state, and they sent *me* here."

I didn't dare insert my thoughts along the way; Sarah was finally letting herself unravel like I was sure she had to, and she needed my ear and nothing else to do it.

"Even though they knew—I'd struggle." Her hand balled into a fist. She pressed the back of her fingers to her lips as she looked away, breathy cry after breathy cry. "I always have in school and they got me tested to help—but it didn't help, it just..." She looked up at the ceiling like it would stop her tears, and exhaled. "It made me hate myself."

Her words pulled the oxygen straight from my lungs. Sarah Duncan was the girl every girl wanted to be, the girl every guy wanted to have, the girl a runway model could take inspiration from. And she *hated* herself?

"I hate saying it even more," she muttered, slouching and looking back down.

Come on, I snapped at myself. *Put it together: thrived in Mom's Hunter classes, struggles in academia, was tested—*

I bit down on my lip, scolding myself for never figuring it out sooner. "Dyslexia?"

She didn't even nod. Like she refused to claim the word with even so much as a gesture. "Never," she whispered, "say it again."

There was so much I wanted to tell her, so much I wanted her to know. None of it would do any good if she heard me but didn't *listen,* but how else could I stop her from hurting? How could I make this easier?

"No, that's..." I said, praying that my mind could recover enough to find the right words. "You can't blame yourself for that, that's not your fault—"

"But it happened to me," she said, her harsh eyes almost pushing me back. "It's not my fault, but it's mine to deal with. And I had no choice with it. I have to fight it every *single* day!"

My breath tightened. I was terrified of the voice telling me that I didn't have the words. I'd opened up Pandora's Box without having a way to close it.

I can't back down—she needs someone right now. Her opening up to me at all was proof that her box had been jammed shut for too long. I needed to let her pour out as much as she needed.

"I got the lowest grade in this school's *history* with a C last semester. Do you know how stupid that makes me feel?"

"No," I snapped, fighting to stay in place for the sake of my ribs. That was the final straw for me, but at least she'd given me the words with it. "Okay, I'll never say that word again, but you don't ever get to say that about yourself."

"What else am I supposed to—?"

"Anything but that because it's not true. How did you end the year? With two B's? In *this* school and with *that?* Are you kidding me, that's—amazing! That's incredible, and you can't argue that because I ended the year with that, too."

Unfortunately, Ms. Perketti's physics final took my A minus out of the game at the last second. And after seventy-five multiple choice questions about the year's reading, I wasn't able to write a three essays of redeemable quality in a row for Mrs. Durrett.

I couldn't understand why this was affecting Sarah as deeply as it was—considering it was anything but uncommon—until I remembered that she had been carrying this for I didn't know how long, I didn't know how many years, alone. Right now, Sarah considered dyslexia as an integral part of her identity and something she couldn't share unless she wanted to permanently alter how people viewed her. And I understood that on a level that went beyond even the nine years we'd been best friends.

I forced the words through the remaining haze of my mind: "And you passed your other classes—with a C instead of a D. You did all of that *despite* what your mind tried to do to you."

She looked away from me, wiping away a stray tear. "I worked so hard. For the whole year. And I barely managed to pass."

Her thoughts were brewing, I could feel it. I needed to give her the time to solidify them.

She took in another sharp breath. "Do you remember when we talked about what to do this summer? I said we could visit colleges, and you guys looked at me like... like I'd spoken Chinese. Or like you doubted I could take academics seriously. And I had to go back to the girly girl everyone's used to."

Shame twisted my stomach, straining my words. "Sarah... I'm so sorry, that wasn't how we meant it."

She shook her head dismissively. "It's so hard not to think sometimes that... I'm good for everything else. People tell me I'm pretty, I have confidence, I pick things up quickly, I'm great with people—everybody thinks I'm good at everything, so I have to be. I have to be because my brain mixes up letters and entire words, sometimes whole lines, and I remember the version my brain messed up, not what's actually printed. I have to compensate for that, I have to be smarter than that."

"Intelligence has *nothing* to do with—that condition," I told her, the tip of my nose burning. "And your grades don't reflect your intelligence. They reflect what you *did* manage despite a handicap. They show you how hard you worked to pass and how you fight harder than everyone else here and *win*. You're right, you deal with it all the time, you fight it every single day, but that just means you earn your place here every single day. *That's* why you're a Callistro Girl, whether you feel like it or not."

She brought her hand to her other red eye, wiping it dry. This time, though, another tear didn't follow.

"You're not stupid, Sarah." I waited until she met my gaze. "You're bright. Because you do it despite everything."

Her face scrunched back up with her tears as she leaped from her bed. Somehow, she managed to cautiously throw her arms around my neck. My heart reached for her as I squeezed her as tightly as my chest would let me.

"Thank you," she cried. "Nobody's ever said—anything like that to me."

"Breanne and I wanted to," I told her. "But we didn't want to force you to say anything. I just—I was worried. I saw you in class today, and..."

She broke away, her sweet perfume wafting into my nose. "Yeah," she said, running a hand through her waves, "imagine my sheer horror when Dawson pulled that out on us. I thought I was better at hiding it."

"The only thing that would've given you completely away is if you started breaking out on your face."

She breathily chuckled. "Yeah, no. I take preventative measures for a reason."

"Okay," I began cautiously, gesturing with a loose hand around my face, "then if you don't want Breanne and Opal to know, I'd touch up in the bathroom."

Which wouldn't take much—the girl's waterproof mascara is *strong.*

Sarah paused, looking down at the carpet. Her heel dug into it as she asked, "If all of you knew, would you look at me differently?"

"Never," I said instinctually. "Of course not, we'd be here to help however you want us to. Ha, especially Breanne."

I thought back to how Breanne had offered to tutor Sarah in math so many times, how Mr. Hartman had once determined that Adrien was the problem. Maybe he'd been *one* of the problems, but realizing that Breanne and I had been right since that semester... I couldn't be mad at Sarah. Especially not after knowing everything I did about her now, dyslexia and insecurities and all.

"If I get any help, I want it to be because I asked for it," Sarah told me. "No offering, no asking, only if I want it."

"I know they'd agree to that."

Breanne had gone through something similar after what had happened with Ethan, her ex-boyfriend from freshman year. The poor girl had wanted to block out any and all memory of it, and nobody blamed her. We all chose to forget with her unless she reached out. There was no doubt that Breanne would understand, and so would Opal.

"Then," Sarah said, nodding gently like she was persuading herself, "I'm gonna tell them. When I'm ready. Will you do it with me whenever that is?"

"That's not even a question." I smiled at her, carefully standing with her. She walked ahead of me and to the bathroom on the other side of the room.

Those green eyes are bright enough on their own, but it wasn't until that moment that I realized how heavy they'd been for the last year—and how much lighter they looked now.

C H A P T E R

FOUR

R umors buzzed around the junior class for the entire weekend. We'd spent more than half of last semester hearing about the amazing, mysterious class trip planned for this year, and Mr. Dawson was supposedly going to reveal it on Monday. Which was an interesting theory, considering that if he was telling us in mid-September, it probably meant that we'd need over two weeks to pack for it.

Where were we going that would require two whole weeks to pack?

"How many of you have always wanted to travel across Europe?"

No way. He's kidding. There's no way.

Half a dozen hands went up into the air. (For a class of nine, that's a lot.)

Mr. Dawson didn't let so much as a smile crack on his face as he leaned back in his desk chair. "All right. Where exactly in Europe, Miss Lowe?"

In the front-left corner of the room, Hannah took a second to think about it. "Anywhere in Italy."

"What about you, Miss Walker?"

From the table next to me, Caroline's brown eyes glazed over with fantasy. "Paris."

Mr. Dawson nodded once. "Miss Moore?"

"London," Sloane answered from the back.

"Then I have brilliant news for all of you." Mr. Dawson stood from his desk and then stepped off the platform. He started strolling down the right side of the room. "I wouldn't be too envious of last year's junior class's grand tour of Australia. But that depends on your taste." He calmly walked down the center aisle, right by me without so much as a glance or telepathic thought in my direction.

When he stepped back up onto the platform and leaned against his desk, a smile that not even he could hide was playing in his deep-set eyes. "It sounds like a cruise around Europe is the perfect trip for this class."

Gasps and accidental squeals erupted around the room. Breanne and I instinctually locked our stunned stares with each other, tacitly asking the other if we'd heard the same thing.

"We're going on a cruise?" she whispered. She turned forward and raised her hand.

Mr. Dawson nodded at her. "Miss Shaw."

"Where exactly in Europe are we stopping?"

"Athens, Barcelona, Paris, London, you name it."

Some Callistro Girls couldn't contain their squeals and excited laughter, but Breanne fell to silence as she turned back to me.

"All around Europe..." I said, dazed with disbelief. "For—?"

I shot my hand into the air.

Mr. Dawson quieted the room by simply holding up his own hand. "Yes, Miss Marie?"

"How long will we be gone for?"

"Great question." He walked back to his chair and sat down. "We leave for the airport to Athens mid-October. After that, we fly back to North Carolina on Halloween."

A two-week cruise around Europe. That left a month to pack and get documentation in order.

Is this partly why every student needs a passport before they enroll here? I couldn't help but wonder. Junior and senior trips have always been Callistro tradition even when the school was nothing more than an advanced self-defense school; it was almost like they wanted to prepare us for any impromptu international adventure, Hunter training or not. Which was all the more ironic that I was here to begin with: the amount of magic it takes for a wielder to snag a legal passport (or, well, sometimes a fake one) without getting caught is concerning on more than a few levels. Knowing two ex-Master Hunters was considerately convenient last year when Momma enrolled me.

They definitely knew that I'd be taking an international trip next year. Did they know exactly what it would be?

Excitement still buzzed around the room like bees at the hive, but Mr. Dawson seemed to have read my mind again: "It won't exactly be the vacation you're imagining. This is what we're calling a 'destination classroom'—you'll be continuing your training throughout the trip under my and Headmistress Marie's supervision."

Hang on—Momma was coming with us? But what about—?

"The administrative board has already scheduled our substitutes, which means you'll be with us at all times and expected to be on your best behavior despite being out of uniform. Don't worry, you'll be given plenty of time to enjoy each city we visit. But we also expect your one hundred percent when it's time to hunt around these cities."

Okay, this was starting to sound more and more promising.

Whispers of thrill and anticipation swam around. Breanne furiously picked at the hair on her wrists, her eyes staying forward.

"Are you okay?" I whispered.

She snapped her head to me, her straight blond hair swishing. Her thin lips were stuck open as she tried to formulate her next sentence.

"I..." Her stare switched between me and Mr. Dawson before settling on him, like he wasn't supposed to hear her when she leaned in toward me and mouthed, "Magic is legal in some of those cities."

To her, it was probably relief; to me, it was nothing but a cruel reminder. My family and I would have moved overseas years ago if it weren't a suicide mission (considering Canada and Mexico have magic outlawed, too, and it wasn't like we could teleport anywhere safe). In the United States alone, magicians who try to move internationally are killed about as often as they are in a hunt. Traveling with a passport is one thing, but getting a visa and citizenship—on top of the fact that Interpol would more than likely be involved—is a fatal game few wielders dare to play. That was why Dad's fate had been impossible to predict after he'd left the country before I was born.

Wait. Dad and Aunt Becca—we'd be overseas for two *weeks*! What did this trip mean for them? Were we really leaving them behind for that long?

I looked at Mr. Dawson, but he only met calm, knowing eyes with mine before sweeping them over the room. "One more thing, ladies," he said in a louder voice that settled us again. "You have a reckless, dangerous habit of letting your excitement draw you out of your training. The next time I give you news, I should be able to hear a pin drop."

⚓

Needless to say, when Momma, Mr. Dawson, and I went to Dad and Auntie's apartment that afternoon to tell them about the trip, Auntie was *not* happy. In fact, she hadn't even taken a single sip of her coffee since Momma started talking.

"Why do they need you, too, Amy?" she asked, so exasperated that she'd even stood from the recliner in front of the window. "Or why can't it just be one of you that goes?"

"Thomas is the junior class Hunter instructor," Momma replied beside the kitchen island, hand on her hip. "It wouldn't make sense for him to stay behind, but we're not leaving one man in charge of almost fifty girls. And should anything happen to the girls or Emma and her friends, it makes sense for the headmistress to be there to address it—someone who *doesn't* have magic."

"So, what, are we supposed to stay under an invisibility cloak the entire time you're gone?" Aunt Becca asked dully, loosely gesturing to her brother sitting next to me.

"You have options," Mr. Dawson said in the kitchen, closing the fridge. The last slice of my birthday cake was in hand. "Keep moving. Always have the cloaks, but stay with Ingrid for a bit. Or Moren—better yet, Cara and Steven. And you'll always have the safe room in my basement if one of them will give you a ride."

It was a miracle that his house hadn't been swarmed after being compromised this summer. I couldn't help but think that we had Alexa to thank for that; after she'd lost her memories and probably fallen back in love with Mr. Dawson, I feel like part of the reason she'd been so angry was because she still couldn't bring herself to sabotage him.

"So take the cloaks, Tristan," Mr. Dawson said, cutting a bite from the cake, "and if push comes to shove and you need to be *really* hidden, use that."

Momma nodded. "Keep moving and use the safe room for the last few days, and you should be good." She walked to the sofa, plopping down next to Dad on his other side. "Isn't this why you're dead, honey?"

He grinned, wrapping his arms around our shoulders and squeezing us both. "Exactly why."

After all, the Tristan Atera case had officially closed, and we already had a plan to put Aunt Becca's to rest (morbid pun not intended) in December. In the waiting period, though, at least we had allies in town that could keep them safe when we weren't there.

Auntie rolled her eyes and walked into the kitchen. "Good

to know I'm the only one who still thinks caution is a worthy investment."

"Caution is one thing, paranoia is another," Mr. Dawson said.

I knew Aunt Becca was *mad* when she dumped her coffee down the kitchen sink. She whirled on Mr. Dawson, her platinum-blond hair flying. "It's not paranoia, Thomas! I'm *so* sorry that after I had my baby brother stolen from me for *seventeen* years, I spend every waking moment scared I'm gonna lose him again! Sue me!"

Mr. Dawson rested his hand on the granite top, his fork hovering above the plate. Dad's hold on my shoulder tightened. Even though he'd come home over a year ago, the memories of his absence, let alone that early morning in the beach house basement, were still too fresh to gloss over.

"You don't *have* to go on this trip," Becca said. "Tristan and I *have* to stay alive."

She sped past Mr. Dawson and walked across the hall, into the bedroom. The door slammed shut.

A fuzzy silence trailed behind. Dad started rubbing my shoulders.

"I'll talk to her," he murmured, standing. "She'll never like this, but—I'll calm her down."

We took his word for it; he was the only one out of all of us who could.

I looked down at my phone in my lap, at the black screen. I wondered how Jak would react to not having the option of seeing each other for two weeks. The scared part of me actually wondered if he could keep my secret while I was gone, like he hadn't been doing that for the last ten years.

Geez... He carried that for over half his life.

I unlocked my phone. The apartment was tiny, but at least the Wi-Fi was fast. (Momma didn't want to pay a monthly phone bill for a phone I'd barely get to use throughout the school year, and Wi-Fi was cheaper per month.)

E: I have news

J: Not good news and bad news?

E: Kind of both. That trip for the junior class is a two-week-long cruise around Europe, we'll be gone for half of October

I made him mad. At least, that was what I was left to think when two minutes had gone by and I still hadn't gotten a text back.

Or he had to hide his phone from his parents. Or his parents are tracking his texts. Or–

A hand was waving itself in front of my face. "Emmy."

I blinked and looked over at Momma. "What?"

"Who's making you nervous?"

The woman still scares me sometimes with how good she is at her profession.

"I think Jak's upset that we're leaving next month."

As though to embarrass me, my phone dinged with his response.

"Well, if he is," Momma said, leaning forward, "remind him

that now there's nothing stopping your dad from trying a trick or two on him."

That was exactly the courage I needed to smile and look down at my screen.

J: Would you wanna meet me at the fountain in
the square on Friday?

Okay. Definitely not what I'd expected as a response to *that.*

E: You're gonna drive all the way over here?
Why??

J: Ur just gonna have to trust me on this, Merlin

Is that a yes?

E: Sure...

J: Cool :) Then meet me there at exactly 6:00.
Do not be early. You can be a couple minutes
late, but do NOT be early.

A period at the end and everything—he was serious.

E: Lol okay, won't be early

"So?" Momma asked, arching a brow. "Everything okay? Still hasn't turned us in?"

I scoffed, cursing the fact that I couldn't nudge her (or, rather, I was too scared to). "I told you, I put him under a truth spell, he's on our side."

"And that's all good and fine and dandy," she replied, mocking my casual tone. "Doesn't change the fact that he has two Grand Hunter parents who could put a discreet wire or camera on him and he just doesn't know it. Don't be so quick to trust that your *interactions* are clean. Maybe you can trust him, and I'm not even entirely sure that you can—but you can't trust his environment."

I wanted a response to that just for the sake of replying; the concussion had dissipated by now, but it takes a much stronger mind than mine to beat Momma in a battle of wits.

"That doesn't apply to just Jak," Mr. Dawson added from the kitchen, resting his arms on the island. "Becca did bring up a good point: you know Alexa isn't going to sit back for two weeks just because we're gone. She may not be able to do anything overseas, but all you need is a mind to have a plan."

Momma exhaled, leaning into the sofa. Part of me couldn't help but curse that I knew the truth to Mr. Dawson's words all too well. If anything, it was obvious that the only reason Alexa would find herself on that ship would be *because* she had a plan.

"I'm just saying that we shouldn't pretend we'll be safe because we'll be international," Mr. Dawson said. "The woman isn't stupid or desperate enough to do that without a plan. No matter how unlikely we want to think her following us onboard is, we need to think it's just as likely."

"What if we *do* find her there?" I couldn't help but ask, hoping my expression communicated something more mature than fear. "She can't do anything, but neither can we."

"Not outwardly," he replied simply. "Inwardly, though, a Hunter's entire arsenal is at their disposal. You know that, Em."

I did—partially because Alexa had indirectly taught me that herself last semester. Irony can be sinister.

"I see," Momma said slowly, like she was catching on. Her lighter tone expressed her approval. "Use it against her."

"Reconnaissance." Mr. Dawson nodded his verification. "Which was, funnily enough, my lesson plan for November. But I don't mind if Alexa wants to move things up a bit. It won't be a hunt this time." His stare shifted to me. "Just a matter of who blinks first."

The Hunter game is probably the only one where you can fight fire with fire and win; it depends on who shoots the bigger fire. Me, Momma, Mr. Dawson, Sarah, Breanne, and Opal against—worst-case scenario—Alexa, William, and maybe even Anthony?

To be honest, that playing field felt kind of even.

Momma rested her elbow on the arm of the sofa, her cheek sitting on top of her fist. "Better to be prepared for the worst than expect the best. Even my instincts are warning that she *is* crazy enough to try it. Unfortunately for us, I doubt she'd let her trusty stepson in on it if she were..."

Her eyes fell onto my right hand, onto the silver ring Jak had gotten me for my birthday. She exhaled like she didn't know what to think. "You have to give it to the kid," she said, eyes jumping between the ring and my locket, "he has good taste in jewelry. Like he's known you your whole life, Em."

I traced the "A" engraved on the top of the ring. Mom and

Dad had left theirs in the box; they needed a more concrete reason to trust Jak and symbolically accept him with the rings, and I couldn't really blame them for it.

I think that was why an uncomfortable shudder slithered through my chest as I carefully nestled deeper into the sofa. "Kind of feels like he has."

FIVE

Friday night, I tried sorting through any last thoughts, and feelings, as Momma drove me to town square. As I stared past the main road and over the tree line on the edge of town, where the Capperson Forest lay, my fingers fiddled with the folded permission slip I'd gotten from her to go off campus. A familiar sunset of orange and pink was at least some comfort.

"Have fun," Momma sang as I opened my door and climbed out. "But not too much fun. And if he starts acting stupid, kick him with your good foot."

That won't be hard. He may be suave and romantic, but Jakson Bleu hasn't been the brightest when it comes to reading a room.

"Thanks for taking me." I leaned in the window frame of the

passenger door. "I'll text you later."

I watched Momma's car drive a little farther down the road. She'd be watching me until Jak got here, which was partly why I was brave enough to meet him tonight.

I faced the square in front of me, where the déjà vu nearly knocked me over. Tonight, I'd picked a flowy blue top with jeans—close enough to what I'd been wearing the night I met Jak—and I'd even forgotten my jacket like last time, too. The walking boot was new, though.

My breath stopped short once I processed the full scene in front of me: short white candles sat on the ground, on both ends of the four benches that surrounded the fountain. Their flames flickered in the lack of a breeze, despite fall being only a few days away. It was a good thing that the feet of the benches were metal and not wood.

Look at that—the fountain is off like last time, too.

A remembering smile pulled my lips upward. I'd wondered last year if turning on that fountain would be my last opportunity to use magic. I internally laughed at how that had turned out to be nowhere near true.

Thanks to the deserted square, I had the perfect opportunity: *Interfluo.*

Seemingly in slow motion, water rose from each spout across the concrete basins. Shy waterfalls poured over the edges, overflowing into the bottom of the fountain.

I smiled to myself and made my way over to the front bench, the one that faced the main road. But I couldn't sit down. The whimsical part of my curiosity led me to the bench across from the front one, the one facing the line of stores.

A small note sat on the wooden surface. I bent down and picked it up, instantly recognizing the neat handwriting:

If you're wearing a jacket right now, take it off

I couldn't help a giggle—because if I hadn't known that this was Jak, this would've *definitely* come across as a threat.

Guess it's a good thing I'm not wearing one.

I sat down on the bench and checked my phone. I was a couple of minutes late, like he'd told me I could be, yet Jak was nowhere in sight. For a second, a split second, part of me wanted to think that it hadn't even been him asking me to meet him—like his parents had taken over once I'd given him the news about the cruise, and asked me to come here so they could kidnap me.

Momma was the only reason I wasn't too worried this time; I could feel her eyes on me even now.

Something black slid down my bare arms, and I whirled around. Jak stood behind me as a sharp pang jabbed me on the side of my chest. I gasped, and concern instantly etched Jak's features.

"Whoa, whoa, whoa," he said, his black jacket in hand as he leaned down, "are you okay?"

"I'm—fine," I said, the fading deep breaths of adrenaline contributing to another sharp jolt in my ribs. My hand hovered over them like it would help me breathe less painfully. "You—scared me. My ribs are—still healing."

Jak sighed in remembrance, his jacket falling to his side. He came out from behind the bench to take the seat next to me. "Wow, I..." he began, shaking his head, "I really can't get it right with you lately."

The pause helped my breath recover, but then I remembered our last hangout: the rings. How horribly he'd gotten the timing.

He's right—he's been having trouble getting it right. But why? This has never happened before...

Then again, the boy kissed me for the first time after telling me about the harrowing morning of his mother's death. Then he flat out confessed his feelings for me (again) right as the Redway Boys were leaving the Callistro Academy. Then he picked the underground hideout where we'd *both* suffered a traumatic spring final for a date spot.

Huh. Evidently, this *had* always been an issue. I guess fantasy isn't as easily blinding the worse things get.

"You're learning," I finally said, trying to let the soreness in my chest fade. "You won't always get it right. Have I?"

He snickered. "I don't think I'm allowed to answer that."

I couldn't help but bite my lip, smacking his arm with the back of my hand. "You're right. But that wasn't the right answer, either."

Silence rested between the two of us, letting the tepid air settle. It was a relief to finally start leaving behind the eighty-five-degree nights. Now we just had to wait a few more days to welcome fall in full swing. Until then, the dusk-blue sky above us and glowing streetlamps in front of the stores were just the right amount of summer.

"No, Em, it's different this time," Jak said, leaning back. "I wanted this to go perfectly."

"By sneaking up on me and trying to put your jacket on me?" I resented the pain in my ribs as I giggled. "Again?"

"I wanted to recreate that night. I wanted to do it right this time."

My heart let itself melt, my smile expanding.

"I wanted to do it the way I'd *wanted* it to go that night."

I nudged him. "Then take it away."

He turned to face me completely, pressing his lips together and draping an arm across the top of the bench. A rare sight flickered across his face: lack of eye contact. Then, a nervous breath in.

How many times has he rehearsed this? I kept my chuckle to myself.

"Emmalynn... Marie?"

My smile instinctually fell as if we *were* having this conversation for the first time. Except this time, he knew the truth.

"Yes?"

"I'm Jakson Bleu." Whatever confidence he wanted me to believe he had struggled to ride the wave of his voice. "And I have a sworn mission to protect you and your family from a famed pack of Grand Hunters. If you'll have me."

There. This time, it felt so much better. This time, it did feel right, because this time, there was no trust spell. There was no stranger, and there was nothing hidden between us. There was just us, who we were fully disclosed unto each other, and nothing but what was real—no lie of magic to fall into.

This felt infinitely better than it had the night we met.

"Well, thanks for the offer," I told him with a wide grin. "We'd love your help."

"Then can I say something completely crazy for two people who 'just met'?"

Oh boy. Here it came: the flirting, his romance. But now that we both knew where the other stood, that guilt had nowhere to stand anymore.

"What?"

"I don't know"—he scooted closer to me and brushed a brown strand of my hair out of my face—"if it's the lighting or summer air making you look prettier than you already are. But you look beautiful. And I've been falling for you for the last year. All I know is that I wanna keep you safe—not just for my mom, but for myself, because now I know you, Merlin." His thumb gently rubbed the top of my hand. He looked down at it as he said, "Now I know what you mean to me. And I know we work." His eyes rose to mine. "As long as you want us to."

Stunned into silence, left to mentally wander the grounds he'd laid down, I screamed at my head to come up with anything to say in response. Even one word. Just one word!

Nothing.

"And if you do,"—Jak's thumb slowed on the back of my hand—"then I'd love to know if... you would be my girlfriend."

He'd said it. Jakson Bleu had actually *said* it for the first time ever.

"Too much buildup?" he asked, breathily chuckling. And I realized that silence was *not* an option right now.

"I'm just—" The air in my lung was scarce, like I was afraid to breathe it in. "I'm... I'm sorry, I don't—"

My throat finally released a laugh, but at least part of it stemmed from, well, joy. "I'm surprised, I don't know what to say!"

No more teases or possibilities or even fun for the sake of

danger. It wouldn't be "what if", it'd be "it is". From a carnival ride together one year ago to wanting to make things official... Needless to say, this definitely compensated for the fact that my friends and I hadn't been able to go to the Capperson Fall Carnival.

Thankfully, Jak shared my laugh. "Well, at least your immediate instinct wasn't 'no'."

Part of me was surprised that my immediate instinct also wasn't a yes. Maybe there was a reason for that; I couldn't help but think about how this was really where we were finding ourselves after our second-to-last interaction, where I'd blatantly shot him down in the hospital for *any* chance of us happening—

Wait.

"Is this why you told me?" I asked carefully. "You knew that I rejected you because of who I was, so you confessed that you knew so you could ask?"

"No," he said quickly, dropping my hand like he wasn't worthy of touching it. "No, not at all, I really did see what keeping that in was doing to you. Correct me if I'm wrong, but when I kissed you back then—it felt like you wanted it, too. And then when you told me it couldn't happen, you weren't just upset about it, you... you were too tired. It wasn't *just* keeping it from me that was eating at you. It was keeping it from Sarah and Breanne and Opal, it was facing another year where you'd have to hide it all over again from the entire school. I wanted to shave *something* off. I know I'm not the biggest weight off your shoulders, but—it was something. It was at least something, wasn't it?"

Like he'd just said, Jak knew me. In fact, he knew all of me now. And somehow, *that* was what made me trust him more than

I ever had before.

I nodded. "Yeah. Bigger than you think."

Because he meant more to me than I wanted to admit to myself.

Here I was, ready to scold him for using his knowledge as a way to finally make us happen, when I was ready to use it to convince myself that him knowing was exactly why we should happen. But it was also the very reason it couldn't.

Please don't let this turn out like how it did with Nolan. I was pretty sure that not even a memory-wiping spell could bury his words from that night. He'd asked me to meet up with him, too, to clear things between us once and for all. And it had quickly spiraled into a conversation about how selfish and ignorant I'd been—with him and the boy sitting next to me right now.

"You strung me along... you enjoyed it enough to let me keep going!"

"Part of me wants to forget you completely."

And I'd granted his wish. Accidentally—that was what I'd always convinced myself of. But intent means nothing in light of action.

"Jak..." I let myself sink into the bench, dropping the memory from my mind. "Do you know why I still haven't told my own best friends who I really am?"

"I don't think it's because you're scared anymore."

"That's not the main reason anymore, no." I looked down at my hands in my lap, trying to figure out the clearest delivery. "For one, they're—"

Wait a second. He didn't know *anything* real about the Delphines. Telling him that two of my best friends were on their list just for knowing their secret—that would be a long conversation...

There was no predicting how he'd react to a magic secret that he actually *hadn't* known for over half of his life. Was I even allowed to tell him?

I feel like Momma and Mr. Dawson wouldn't approve. But why not? If anything, Jak would be all the greater an ally if he knew about the Delphines, wouldn't he? At the very least, wasn't that piece of information owed to him as Alexa's stepson?

"They're what?"

I forced myself to push the notion away. It didn't matter: we weren't ready for that conversation yet, but there was still one part of the truth he could know. "If they knew, they'd end up on Alexa's list of targets. They'd become direct leads to me if the pack ever found out that they knew. And then they become three more leads to my dad, my entire family. That became a big part of the reason why I never told *you* the truth on my own."

Jak nodded once after a second, eyes moving to wander the scene in front of us.

Great... How could I form this in a way that wouldn't sound like I secretly didn't want this?

I took his hand, gaining his eyes. "I *do* want this," I told him, riding the sudden wave of courage that had come to save me, "but I also want you to be safe."

"I live with them, you know," he teased. My biggest fear was that that small smile was fake. "And I know how to avoid them."

"Jak."

Just like that, his smile dissipated. He knew me: he knew exactly where I was going with this, but he let me say it anyway.

"You're just like my friends: they're already in the crossfire just by knowing me. You know how big a risk you took in taking an interest in me at all while knowing the truth. And you threw what security you did have away by telling me that you knew. If we were together, I don't think even you'd be able to hide those signs. The pack's curiosity would be piqued, at the very least."

That teasing smirk went back onto his lips. "We wouldn't be doing anything different than what we usually do, Merlin. It'd just be official."

"That's the problem. *That* would be their smoke signal."

"How?"

"Because they know me, too. They know I'd never get into a relationship unless the guy knew."

So that's *why I'm hesitant to tell him.* He'd managed to keep knowing about me a secret, but, call it intuition, something told me that the Delphines wouldn't be exempt from his resentment. Emotions cloud rationality, but rationality paves the way for action. If Jak wasn't ready to act above that yet, he could sentence us all to the punishment of Caldwell's law.

We'd have to not just tell *him—we'd have to* talk *to him about it. I think he deserves to know.*

He pressed his lips together with his hand resting in mine. I was glad he wasn't taking it away. At least he understood. At least he knew that I was right. It looked like I was safe from another night like the one where I'd made Nolan completely forget everything. I'd made him forget because I couldn't handle the reality of what I'd done to him for the last year.

Which reminded me, Jak was owed an apology of his own.

"I'm sorry," I whispered. I forced my volume up because he deserved that, too. "For leading you on for a year and making you think I was gonna let this happen, it was just a giant tease—"

"Okay," he said, sitting up straight, "first of all, remember where I was coming from the entire time: I knew who you were. I knew what I was getting myself into. If anything, I was teasing myself. You're right, even I know you'd never get into a relationship unless the guy knew."

"That doesn't mean what I did was okay."

I thought back to Nolan's words that night in the back area of Dom's Bakery. Nolan didn't remember saying them, but I'd all *but* forgotten. Because he was right: I'd hurt him.

"Okay," Jak said again, a little more accepting this time as he nodded. "I get that. You're right on some fronts."

"'Some'?"

He leaned forward in his seat, resting his forearms on his knees. "We both handled this the wrong way. We were having fun in a world that's banned it, at each other's expense, and it just finally caught up to us. But you only have to apologize if you wronged me. I don't feel wronged."

When he put it that way, I didn't really feel wronged, either. I felt like I'd been a teenager being stupid and having fun in areas I shouldn't have been testing. I felt normal. Like I was dumb enough to make the mistake but fortunate enough to have avoided the consequences.

I nodded in understanding.

Huh. Seventeen looks good on us.

"So," Jak said after that, sitting up straight again, "are you still cold? Because I know a great coffee place nearby."

CHAPTER

SIX

The streets of an ancient, foreign city whizzed by my vision, flashing every few half-seconds until I looked down at my feet pounding on the cobblestone.

Someone was... after me.

Flash.

"Emma!" Mr. Dawson said through my earpiece as I bolted down another cobblestone street. "What're—?"

Flash.

I felt the absence of my earpiece now as I stumbled against a shop's brick wall. Furiously panting, I rested at the corner for only a second.

All went to black as my eyes rolled backwards.

Flash.

"So you're her," said a male voice in Spanish.

When I looked over, a boy with spiky black hair and eyes the color of dark oak sat next to me in a black car. His hands were on the steering wheel, on the right side.

Did he just kidnap me?!

Flash.

"—you?" I heard myself asking a question in Spanish, never catching what was in front of us.

The car was still. The boy's hands were off the wheel as he ran a hand through his hair. "I'm the mage."

Another flash, and my world black.

Ow, ow, ow!

A familiar pang in my ribs stopped me from springing up all the way in bed as my eyes shot open. The darkness of my dorm room all but swallowed me whole. The sleep remaining in my system was so thick that Sarah's and Breanne's mild snoring was muffled for a couple of seconds.

Stupid ribs! I screamed in my head as I tried to regulate my breathing.

The silence pursued my breaths. It was familiarly strange.

Opal's quiet again. I'd only been living with her for three weeks, but I'd learned in that time that she does snore—more often than Sarah and Breanne. Whenever I randomly woke up in the middle of the night and didn't hear her, I was almost afraid that she wasn't actually sleeping.

Tonight, though, was the first night I'd woken up from a vision—something that caused mild gasps as I tried to recover from the pain in my chest. I'd made a noise.

"Emma?" a sweet voice whispered from two beds over. "Are

you okay?"

For some reason, I didn't even know if I was supposed to reply. Part of me couldn't help but think that Opal deserved more than that. I still had no idea why she'd lied about being a target in last year's hunt for my dad's descendant, but right now, she deserved more.

"I'm okay," I whispered back, stuck in a firm position on my back—like she was. "Bad dream."

"I'm sorry."

Sarah released a loud snore. Apparently, though, both of us were too tired—or disturbed by our minds' terrors—to find it funny.

"Are you okay?" I whispered.

"Yeah," she said in a high-pitched whisper.

I wish she didn't feel the need to lie to me about that, of all things. "Are you actually?"

Silence rang for a couple of seconds. "Same. Bad dream."

The high-pitch airiness that gave her lies away was still there. Granted, though, she was a *lot* more restricted than I was in this position. The nights were probably five times as tortuous for her: her spine was still healing from the fracture, her back was still healing from the surgery, and the deep gash across her stomach was still sore.

I wanted to be anywhere *but* Opal Dubois's head that night. At the same time, the last thing I wanted was for her to be in there alone.

"You can tell me," I whispered. "No matter what it is."

Another couple of seconds of nothing until she replied, "It's—the same thing."

No high pitch.

The same thing that had kept her up all those other nights.

"I wish I could..." I said, "take it away."

A breathy chuckle. Then a sniff. "Me, too."

I desperately fought the heaviness of my eyes as I said, "I'm here. I'll be here for as long as you need me."

Another sniff whispered in the darkness. "Thanks."

I wanted to be there for her as a wielder, though. I wanted her to feel less alone in at least that way. But she was suffering like this *because* she had chosen to be my ally in magic after finding out the truth. As soon as my best friends knew the whole truth, as soon as they got one step closer to Emmalynn Atera and then Adara, they wouldn't just become Alexa Delphine's targets: they'd become the world's.

You will be feared, hunted, and betrayed. Mr. Dawson's Adara prophecy replayed in my head. I knew that that part of it didn't apply to just the Delphines.

With Opal leaving me in the quiet dark, frames of my "dream" were able to flash in my head, calling back my attention. I needed to sort through that vision. I'd been running through the streets of a foreign city, kidnapped by a Spanish boy, and he had been a mage—no, THE mage. What had he meant by "the mage"?

My eyes shot open in realization.

Sorceress, druid, nore, mage.

The most powerful druid to ever live.

The magic world's nore.

The mage.

Was this boy just like me, Annisa, and Kamose? Who *was* he?

What if there was a chance that I'd meet him during the—?

"Emma?"

My mind snapped back to the present, instantly switching to Opal as its focus. "Yeah?"

She released a relieved yet quiet exhale. "Just checking."

"I'm here."

I mentally prepared myself to get out of bed at a moment's notice. I hadn't been able to do anything the night this had happened to her—but I definitely wasn't going to let a walking boot stop me from getting out of bed and being there for her now if she needed it.

Despite his gift, the only present circumstances Kamose *doesn't* know are our magic identities—the ones of those still hidden, however many there are. That meant, with no phones, I had to email Annisa instead and ask her to let me know if she ever had any visions about him.

I didn't get an interesting email until almost a couple of weeks later, in the midst of the junior class's final preparations for the cruise. Because Jakson Bleu has always had phenomenal timing.

To: Emma Marie

From: Jak Bleu

Maybe you were right. I just found out that the pack has *officially* dropped you. Which means they AND Caldwell are in agreement that the case has gone cold

Okay, I get it: I should've been jumping out of my skin with sheer joy—and the Emmalynn the pack had hunted last year would have. But I knew too much now—I'd seen too much by now.

I wondered exactly how many emails we'd immediately have to delete after tonight as I typed my response.

To: Jak Bleu
From: Emma Marie
I never thought that message would scare me more than relieve me. Why? Did they say? How'd you find out?

To: Emma Marie
From: Jak Bleu
Dad came up to me and went "Congratulations, Tristan's descendant is a no-go after all." Then he asked if I wanted to participate in the next big hunt, kinda sarcastically

But... but William knew that that wasn't true. I'd confessed to *him* that I knew where that descendant was hiding while under a truth serum! Why would...? How could they...?

To: Jak Bleu
From: Emma Marie
I don't like this, he knows that's not true

To: Emma Marie
From: Jak Bleu
Yeah that's why I was so confused. Unless, does he somehow *know* about you?

There were too many ways to answer that, and I somehow wanted all of them to be the truth. I'd been mulling it over the last couple of weeks and come to the same conclusion: Jak deserved to know. If not as a stepson, then as our ally—because the only way William would know about me would be if he were somehow *helping* the Delphines with their goal for the Ateras' magic. But Jak couldn't know that. Yet.

"Em?"

I looked up at Sarah's voice. She was fishtail-braiding Opal's hair in front of Opal's bed, looking at me. Breanne worked away at the desk in the corner of the room, ignorant to us.

"Are you okay?" Sarah asked.

"Yeah," I said, my fingers finding the locket around my neck. "Emailing Jak."

Sarah's eyes relaxed, cautiously skeptic as her braiding slowed and even Opal turned her head to me. "Did something happen?" Sarah asked in a warning tone.

I tightly, quietly exhaled. Telling Jak the Delphine business, I'd already realized, meant telling him about Opal and Breanne, too—which I couldn't do without their permission. I was already betraying their trust about my identity; I refused to cross that line when it came to theirs.

"I didn't tell him anything." I sighed, the words already heavy on my tongue. "But... what if we did?"

This, even Breanne looked up for. "What?" she asked. "You can't, what if he turns Opal in?"

"He wouldn't. He's on our side."

I hope he still is after I explain why I had to keep the Delphine secret from him for a year.

"How can you be sure?" Opal asked cynically, pale hands lifelessly resting in her lap. "Wasn't his mission last year to protect you from his parents because you were innocent? He wasn't protecting you because you had magic, he was protecting you because you didn't."

I scolded myself for almost letting a smile poke through—because that statement was wrong.

I searched for what to say, how to reply. If I was going to do this right and convince my friends, I needed to trust them with the right part of the truth: "I know because he wants to protect Tristan's descendant."

I hadn't expected the scoffs from all *three* of them—Sarah, definitely. Opal, maybe, but Breanne was a blatant surprise.

"You mean the one they ruled as nonexistent?" Sarah said, holding Opal's finished braid in one hand and a hair tie in the other.

"No. That's what they want you to think."

A little more.

"That's why the case went cold this year. But Jak told me everything. His mom's dying wish was for him to find them and protect them. That's partly why he wanted to prove my innocence last year. Even if he can't do much, he wants to do something. He wants to at least try. He's on their side, and I *know* he'd be on ours if he knew about Opal and what we're doing, especially if he knew about the Delphines—that could even help him achieve his goal."

I did it... I did it. I didn't dare move on my bed as I prayed for the best, watching all three of my roommates for their reaction. *I hope I did it.*

"So now," began a feeble Breanne, her brows scrunched together, "we're protecting—Tristan's descendant?"

"No," I stated, "no, we're *not* getting involved in that. Jak can do whatever he wants with that, but we need someone on the inside to help us stay ahead of the Delphines as long as things are— like this. But he can only help us if he knows. Which would kind of be like us helping him."

Sarah pressed her mauve lips together, tying the end of Opal's braid. (Her lipstick is as strong as her waterproof mascara.) "I say Opal secretly puts him under a truth spell. Then we tell him if he's trustworthy."

It was a wise plan, but one that Jak and I would have to pretend to follow through with; I was definitely telling him everything with my family.

Opal fiddled with her thumbs in her lap as Sarah loosened her hair in front of her ears, then coming to stand in front of her to admire her work. Opal looked up at her, landed on Breanne next, and then turned her head to meet me.

"If he tells anyone, I'm flinging him into the sun."

The relief of laughter was sweet but short. After deleting the email thread, I stood from my bed and set aside my laptop.

"Where are you going?" Breanne asked.

I briefly turned to her on my way to the door. "I'm gonna go tell my mom."

C H A P T E R

SEVEN

I t wasn't like I was getting *called* to the head's office, but that didn't erase the fact that it was always five times scarier going into my mother's office than it ever had been with Mr. Dawson. Her being the one to open the office door was a sight I wasn't sure how long it would take me to get used to.

"Pleasant surprise," she chimed. Then, within a blink, her smile dropped. "What did you do?"

"You'll be proud of me this time," I said, strolling into the brightly lit office. "Remember when Jak asked me to meet him a couple of weeks ago?"

Momma shut the door behind her, planting one hand on her hip. "Yes..."

I sat down on the white couch against the right wall. Probably every mother wanted to hear this news from her daughter during at least one point throughout the high school years, but I wished the circumstances weren't so... unideal: "He asked me to be his girlfriend."

The woman once caught a target hiding in a toy store's display of stuffed animals with dog ears on and didn't bat an eye, but *this*, her brows shot up for. "Really, now?"

"Don't say it like that," I said, picking at the threading on the couch's arm. With Jak, the moment had felt like sparkling butterflies were fluttering all around; with Momma, it felt like I'd just accidentally run them all over.

"Wait," she said, crossing her arms and wearing that all-too-familiar scolding tone, "are you really about to tell me that you've had a boyfriend for two—?"

"No, Mom, I said no."

"You did?"

I shrugged. "It would've been stupid to say yes. For the same reason we haven't told the girls anything."

Momma gently nodded her head, leaning against the door. "All right. I'm proud of you."

"Told you."

"A little less so." She meandered to the couch across from me. "So what do you need to tell me?"

I took a discreet breath in, like she wasn't allowed to see me mentally prepare for this conversation. "I couldn't tell him part of the reason I said no because it would've exposed the Delphines. And I've been thinking about it for the last couple weeks, like... if he kept my identity a secret for as long as he did, even after years of living with Alexa Delphine, of all people—can't we trust him with the Delphine truth?"

I knew it: I knew Momma would freeze like that, I knew the gears would start turning in her head when she began processing every mountain this choice could tumble down. And I couldn't blame her—the issue was if she'd allow me to help her fill in that process.

"You want to tell him that the Delphines are magicians?" she asked steadily. "Is that all?"

"No. I think we're safe to tell him exactly what we're fighting for: the girls' safety and not just ours. He needs that perspective if he's gonna give us everything he can. He needs to know what his targets are really after if he's gonna have any chance at intercepting it."

Momma sighed, her arm falling to rest on the couch. "This is assuming we can completely trust him."

"We can—"

"You know I'm not talking about his intentions, Emma."

To my disappointment, my mouth clamped shut. I didn't know how to immediately argue that.

"Can we trust him to not be found out?" she said. "Can we trust him to set aside his personal feelings toward them for deceiving his father like this? Can we trust him to act well enough in *all* circumstances?"

I couldn't answer any of that. I wanted to believe in Jak for all of it, but I couldn't trust him with any of it.

"Can we?" Momma asked.

"You haven't even been able to trust *me* to not get caught," I said against my own pride. "But I have you and Dad and Mr. Dawson to help me do damage control and get me back onto the right path. If Jak knows, he'll have us, too. He and I have kept the same secret all this time, and he's arguably done it better than I have."

Momma chewed on her thumbnail, honey-colored eyes pensive in the fluorescent lights. I could almost hear the gears in her brain grinding.

"I think he deserves to know," I finally said. "If nothing else."

"You realize you're doing exactly what makes you such a big target to Alexa, right? You're not keeping quiet."

No... that didn't sound right. I shook my head. "We know why she's actually after me. The secret thing is just a cover."

Momma eyed me carefully, like it was her responsibility to make sure that I didn't move from the couch. "How do you know you can trust Jak?"

"Truth spell, search him for bugs, we'll make sure he never meets me or any of us to discuss incriminating evidence without knowing he's clean."

I counted the seconds until Momma finally started nodding. Slowly, and then like she agreed.

"You've been thinking about this since that night?"

I nodded.

"I still can't say that I trust him completely. Only because I didn't train him. I trained you, I know your mistakes and weak spots. I need to get a better assessment of him, and so does Mr. Dawson, before we trust him completely."

I waited to hear her next words like it was a court sentence.

"But—I do think there are grounds in telling him. It's probably wisest for what we need from him, and for his new role in your life. But we need to tell him collectively. All together. It won't be an easy conversation, and we need to anticipate any and all routes that we can."

I nodded again.

"It may be wisest for his sake, too," she said with a firmness that convinced me that she actually agreed with me. "Then he'd have leverage against the Delphines, because if they ever found out that he's been hiding the intel he has…"

That was when I stopped staring at her and started looking at her—really looking at her like she had every answer to the sudden fears and paranoia that had sprung up with that one sentence. If Alexa ever found out… But if William found out… But would they…?

"No, they wouldn't—" I began, realizing my words as I spoke them. "They can't do anything to him. They wouldn't hurt him, right?"

"No, I don't think even Alexa would let the pack go that far." Momma rested her hand on the arm of the couch again. "But he *is* subject to the law, and they're the law. I don't know what they'd do to him, if anything at all. But he'll have something to throw back if they try to pin him."

I stopped fidgeting with the threading. I couldn't waste time being afraid of the possibilities; I had to prepare for them. Alexa had immobilized me and almost killed Opal in the forest as if to punish us for knowing, but Opal and I *weren't* simple solutions because our memories went too far back with the Delphines. Jak, on the other hand, *could* be solved with a simple spell since he'd only know their secret for a day tops…

Could I take that big a risk on his life?

No—it wouldn't matter. His life was already in danger because of his information, not ours.

I slowed my thoughts, repeating Momma's words in my head. "What do you mean by 'tell him collectively'?"

"Your dad's the one who spent years with them. He has a side of the story Jak should know. Plus, he's always wanted to meet the boy interested in his daughter, and now Jak is a much bigger part of your life. On top of all that, I *know* you don't want to tell him about the Delphines alone. This is your chance to tell him with support and prove he's not dangerous—if he isn't."

I paused. "You don't think he's dangerous?"

"I didn't say that. He's dangerous until he isn't, so as long as he has nothing on him, he's harmless. Like you said, we make him our mole. And if he's going to be our mole, he should meet his headquarters. Meet us *formally*, at that."

Had I just stepped into an alternate reality? Was this really happening? I'd hoped for a positive reaction, but this was practically optimistic!

I carefully nodded like it would undo Momma's entire decision. "Okay. I want him to meet my family."

CHAPTER

EIGHT

Standing in the living room of my childhood home with my family, I wanted to rejoice at how the pack had finally officially dropped me as a target. But I knew there was a catch, some kind of consequence. In the magic world, believing something that's too good to be true is often a death sentence.

It angered me to a fault that *this* was the first move the pack had made since what had happened in the forest. William was potentially in on it this time, but we couldn't say for sure; he knew that Tristan had a descendant, I was the one who'd verified that for him. But I wasn't sure if even Alexa could pull off convincing him that the case was actually cold. Unless she put William under a forgetting spell...

Being fully honest with ourselves, we had no idea if William

Bleu knew the truth.

Standing at the front door, I looked at the clock mounted on the wall above the dining table. Jak would be here any second. The only reason we were even doing this at my house was that Momma and I could find somewhere else to live a hundred times more easily than Dad and Aunt Becca if we were caught. And Mr. Dawson's house was the only place that had a secure safe room, so we couldn't compromise it any further.

"Be. Nice," I told Dad and Aunt Becca. Dad, I could trust to stay civil, at the least; it was Aunt Becca I had to worry about.

"I'm always nice, Mom." Auntie rolled her eyes from the sofa, a mug of coffee in her hands. Mr. Dawson had filled it to the brim to stop her from making any "wild gestures", and he stayed right beside her with a full, hot pot on the coffee table to fill it back up when she drank too much. Dad stood, arms crossed, in front of the living room window with the blinds and curtains closed. I couldn't help but wonder what he was thinking, if he was secretly disappointed in me wanting to do this.

I looked at Aunt Becca again. "He's not the problem," I said. "It's his parents we're fighting."

"It's also his parents who probably put a camera or recording device on him without him knowing."

"Becca," Momma snapped, setting her fierce eyes on her. She dug in her jacket pocket and then pulled out a black, rectangular box the length of her hand. A speaker was installed in front of it. "I brought this for a reason."

The omnitracer—I'd seen it on display down in the Hunter's Room a hundred times. It has a metal detector, a GPS sensor, and a loudspeaker to create microphone feedback. If someone has a microphone, camera, or tracker on them, an omnitracer will pick up all three.

"Okay. Good," Dad said, nodding slightly. "And if he has nothing on him, then we make him feel welcome."

I couldn't help a soft smile at his willingness to not, well, instantly declare Jak as an enemy. And he'd styled back his chestnut hair and shaved his stubble for this, even put on his ring Jak had gotten for my birthday. Not even Momma and I could wear ours because we'd just have to take them back off once we got back to the school, so we kept them in the box on her nightstand. But Dad wore his today. I wondered how he had so much respect for people he'd never even met before.

Aunt Becca had nothing to say. Mr. Dawson refilled her half-empty mug. I would have giggled had the doorbell not rung.

"Okay," I whispered to nobody but myself, my fingers already around my locket. Momma nodded a confirmation at me, but the little girl in me wanted to bolt out my bedroom window.

Okay, I thought, trying to stop the squeezing happening in my stomach. Sweat was already gathering in my palms.

"Em," Momma whispered. "Do you want me to answer?"

I love you.

I nodded and stepped aside, positioning myself behind her. She looked through the peephole on the other side and then twisted the doorknob.

Please don't have anything on you.

Momma cracked open the door, revealing only her face to Jak. For the first time since we'd known each other, I couldn't bring myself to look at him.

"Hi, Jak," Momma said quietly.

There is no way this is happening.

Knowing it is one thing, but seeing it... What if he changes his mind?

What if it all hits him that he's protecting someone he shouldn't be?

Hasn't he always known that?

"Hey, Mrs. Marie," I heard him reply. My heart was ready to burst out of my chest. "I double-checked before I left, nothing's on me."

"I'm gonna have to triple-check for you, honey," Momma said gently. "I think you understand why."

"Yes, ma'am. No problem."

He wouldn't change his mind. He'd never turn on me like that.

I trusted Jak, but that didn't mean that I wasn't scared about the aspects I couldn't control.

Momma slid out the front door, careful to not leave even a crack of extra space as she went.

"Honey?" Dad said softly from behind me.

I turned. There he stood against the windowsill.

"Are you okay?" he asked, his icy-blue eyes softening.

I nodded. I was too tired to be honest.

Aunt Becca eyed the coffee table in front of her with her mug close to her lips. Her natural brown hair was visibly growing from her roots again, bleeding into the platinum blond. Dad was doing a great job at trimming her hair and making sure it stayed shoulder length like how she liked it.

—*Are you actually okay?*—

I looked at Mr. Dawson. —*Nervous. This is the most vulnerable I've ever been with him.*—

—*Are you scared he hasn't proven himself like you thought?*—

No, because Jak had more than proven himself. But after

Breanne's anger upon finding out that she had Alexa's magic and Opal's hurt when Alexa had exposed me in the forest…

—I'm scared he'll turn on me.—

I remembered then that I'd been scared of that with Jakson Bleu since the day we met. And I don't think I ever stopped.

The front door behind me clicked open. I turned. Momma opened it widely now, Jak standing right behind her in a black hoodie.

"He's clean," she told us, stepping into the house.

Jak now faced me in full. The purple rose wasn't there.

"Wait!" I exclaimed, grabbing the edge of the door and standing in the small gap I provided between it and the doorway.

His brows furrowed, brown eyes puzzled as Momma came to stand behind me. "What's wrong?" she urged.

"The purple rose hoodie, where is it?" I asked him, trying to pull my rationality above the sea of my fear. I wasn't sure if I'd be able to handle this situation again, let alone if this was worst-case scenario and my enemy had almost every last target she needed in front of her right now.

"It's dirty," he told me simply, his confusion deepening. "Why?"

Too easy of an excuse. "Tell me your nickname for me."

"'Merlin'," he said, glimpsing Momma. "Which I'm questioning if I'm allowed to use right now."

I tried to find something that obviously *wasn't* Jak—Alexa could've easily figured out that nickname.

My eyes fell to his chest as if daring the purple rose to fade into existence. I needed my rationality right now, my instincts that I'd spent my whole life building up and the last year training.

Okay—a truth spell. He knew about me, and if this wasn't him, he'd just need to forget.

I closed my eyes. *Veritatem dicere.*

"Are you really Jak?"

"Yes..." he said warily, something shifting in his eyes—softening them. Like he was suddenly aware of all of my doubts. "It's me, Merlin."

With those words, that tone, he'd reduced my worries and fear to honey. And only Jak could do that.

"Why?" he asked with a gentleness that deflected all accusations.

I almost forgot that Momma was standing behind me as I released him from the spell. So help me, he barely managed to suppress a smile in time when my eyes flashed. "I used a truth spell. To make sure it was really you."

That wonder instantly melted into bafflement. "Why would you need to make sure it's me?"

That was it: the cue to start this conversation. "Just—come in."

I waited until Momma stepped out of the way, back into the house, before turning around and following her. Jak's steps came in after mine before stopping on the wooden floor of the entryway. I turned around.

His eyes were frozen on the man standing by the window, his jaw slightly agape.

My gaze jumped to Dad. The two were locked in a staring contest, studying the other as if their entire personalities were written on their shirts.

I looked back at Jak. His mouth moved enough for him to

say, "Hi."

I would've chuckled had my heart not been rocking my chest so hard that even my ribs felt it. What *do* you say to the supposedly dead most wanted man in America when you meet him for the first time?

"Hello, Jak," Dad said with a small, kind smile. He uncrossed his arms and stepped across the living room, holding out his hand. "I'm Tristan."

Jak blinked a couple of times before taking his hand. "It's an honor to meet you."

Dad smirked. "Don't say that because you have to. What're you actually thinking right now?"

Jak licked his lips, staring intently into his eyes. "That... I've never seen a dead man walking before."

They were the only ones in the room that chuckled, but Momma smiled next to me.

"And," Jak added as Dad released his hand, "that seeing my mom's last wish finally fulfilled *is* an honor, sir."

Wow, this boy knew how to charm a room. Thankfully, I knew all too well how much he meant it.

Dad patted his shoulder. "You and I have a lot to talk about."

"Dad—"

Jak's laughter cut me off. "You got it, all of it."

If I'm being honest, this whole scene felt like a fever dream.

Dad stepped out of the way, revealing Mr. Dawson and Aunt Becca on the sofa. Mr. Dawson was refilling her mug again.

Her icy eyes were trained on Jak, a strained smile pulling her lips taught. "Hello, Jak."

"Hi—Ms. Atera."

Now the moment was awkward.

—*He's clean,*— I told her. —*And he's part of the reason we're all here in the first place. You can trust him.*—

Auntie took a giant gulp from her coffee, set down a half-empty mug on the coffee table, and then stood up.

Mr. Dawson immediately set down the pot. "Becca—"

"I'll be nice," she told him sweetly.

Jak's eyes shifted between the two as she walked over to him and held out her hand.

"It's nice to finally meet you, Jak," she said. "After a year of hearing about you."

She wouldn't dare.

Jak accepted her hand, tilting his head. "A year?"

"Yeah." Becca's smile grew, melting with sincerity. "When Emma told us about you asking to meet her in the square and she had to ask if it was a date."

"I cannot believe you," I spat, crossing my arms.

"What?" she asked defensively. "Stop being dramatic, he likes you, too."

So much for worrying about if she'd be nice to Jak.

"Tease them later, Becca," Momma said, taking Jak's shoulder. "More pressing matters right now."

Auntie cocked her brows as if to say "if you say so", stepping back and turning to the sofa.

That seemed to remind Jak that Mr. Dawson was here, too. "Mr. Dawson," he said shyly, rubbing his hands together. "Are you, um, also—?"

"Yep," Mr. Dawson said, nodding. "Druid, though, not sorcerer."

"With all due respect, I would've never taken you for—a magician."

"Good." Mr. Dawson smiled as Aunt Becca sat back down next to him, grabbing her mug. "That means I've done my job."

"It's not a bad word," I assured Jak. "You can say it here."

He met me with wary eyes, his mouth opening but words struggling. "Right, yeah, I just—" He glanced back at Aunt Becca and Mr. Dawson on the sofa before looking back at me and my parents. "I'm not used to talking about it so openly."

"You're gonna have to be," Dad said, reaching for him. Jak let him guide him to the spot on the sofa next to Mr. Dawson. "Because that's why you're here."

Dad turned around to face me. "I think he should hear it from you, Em."

Great. Which meant remembering what I'd done this summer—remembering everything I wanted to forget.

I took a deep breath in, because no matter what, I had to do this. "You know I'm still being hunted. But it's not just because I'm Tristan's daughter. Alexa's making sure I stay silent about her family's secret."

Jak paused. I could bet my magic that the truth was already running through his head, but it was too crazy for even him to believe. "What secret?" he asked.

"I needed that truth spell to know if it was really you because... Alexa came after me this summer. Using a spell to disguise herself as you, in the same hoodie. I figured out that it wasn't actually you, she got mad, and I—accidentally wiped her memory in self-defense. That's why she went missing for a month."

His eyes were trained on me, forearms resting on his knees.

Like he was daring me to give him another example of her using magic, because otherwise this was just a sick joke.

"And that's why I couldn't remember Anthony when you first asked me about him." I swallowed down the wrong words, my throat already strained from tension. "Because he *did* come after me that day. He took me into the Callistro Forest with telepathy and then used his magic to choke me. But he wiped my memory of the whole thing."

Jak's eyes fell to somewhere straight ahead of him. "So, the Delphines—have magic."

"They're warlocks. Alexa's really after the Ateras' magic."

A sizeable lump passed in his throat. With his fingers fiddling with each other, his jaw was locked so tightly that it rivaled Mr. Dawson's in sharpness. I had to wonder what it felt like to have so many eyes on you as you tried to process one of the biggest bomb drops of your life.

"It's a lot," Dad said, crossing his arms again, "but things have only gotten crazier since. And we want you to know what you're really up against while you're with them, especially since you know about Em. And we could really use someone like you."

Jak looked up like something in him had clicked. Then he looked at Mr. Dawson and Aunt Becca beside him, then at Momma, and then at me—whom he stared at the longest. I wanted more than anything to translate what was going on behind those eyes. Aunt Becca was the only one in the room who hadn't gone through Hunter training, but even she was observing Jak like a hunter observing its prey, anticipating its next move.

As if he knew this, he suddenly cleared his throat and stood up. "I'm sorry, I need—I need a minute."

He briskly moved to the front door, a cologne-scented breeze passing me. Nobody stopped him as he turned the knob and slipped out of the house. The door firmly shut behind him, placing me and my family in an unsettling silence.

Did we just break him?

I wanted to talk to him about it, to comfort him in case he felt betrayed somehow or disturbed or lied to—but I also couldn't stand even imagining the look on his face right now. The hurt.

"What does he like to eat, Em?" Momma asked me quietly.

My mouth didn't even open to answer; not only did we not have pineapple pizza (nor would I ever let it in my house), but I also couldn't stop wondering if Jak wanted to be alone or if that had been code for me to follow him outside. The rational part of me knew better: he needed alone time and was taking it. The other part of me was thinking of every reason possible to justify walking out that door.

"He's fine with whatever," I said, turning to it. Not nearly enough time had passed, but I needed to know that we were okay.

"Em," Momma said, "you need to give him his space. We just dropped a wrecking ball on him. Let him process it."

I wanna process it with him. I wanted to be there for him.

"There's so much to explain," I said, torn between which side of the door to take.

"He's sorting through all of that right now," Momma replied. "I know you want to help him, but you won't do that by cutting his processing short."

I caught myself taking a step forward anyway. For all Jak knew, his father had emotionally detached from him for the same reason he was now helping the Delphines—if I was right about him helping them. Jak probably felt like his father had abandoned one family for another when William, as rocky as their relationship was, was the only family Jak had left. I had to at least *offer* comfort, right?

I put my hand on the knob.

"Em," Momma stated behind me.

"I need to make sure he's okay," I said, opening the door before anyone could protest.

There Jak sat on the ground and against the wall of the house. The sudden dart of his gaze as the door shut behind me made me second-guess coming out, like I *had* cut something short. I'd read his "code" wrong.

"I wanted to make sure you're okay," I said, hating that I didn't have the right words—because "okay" was the absolute *last* thing he could've been right now.

Not a word.

I slightly nodded to myself, accepting that I'd been wrong. "I get it." I turned to the front door. "I'll give you space."

"How long have you known?"

My fingers froze around the doorknob. That question alone burned me with anxiety, but I had to be honest with him. He deserved that.

I faced him again, keeping my hand on the knob like it was a safe space. "Since my birthday—last year."

His head rose to look dead ahead of him. That had *definitely* been the wrong answer. Was the truth ever wrong?

"For over a year?"

Betrayal clawed at each word; the truth had *definitely* been the wrong answer.

"Yeah."

"Why didn't you tell me? How did you go months without ever telling me?"

This was new: Jakson Bleu's lack of understanding was way too new, and I didn't like it one bit.

"You know why," I said. "I *couldn't*. I never even told the girls."

"So they don't know?"

I took in a breath and then realized that I didn't have the words yet, but Jak didn't give me the time to find them.

"Got it," he said, nodding to himself. "I was the only one you didn't tell."

"Don't start," I stated. "I never told them because I wanted to, they found out."

He sneered. "How did they possibly 'find out'?"

"Your crazy stepmom lost her magic to an enchanted bracelet she wanted to use on me, and Breanne put it on!"

Okay. I wasn't sure I was supposed to reveal that part *just* yet.

Jak froze like he was processing the world in front of him all over again, his eyes narrowing with thought. "Alexa doesn't have her magic? *Breanne* does?"

I exhaled, accepting reality before it could wash me away. "Yeah."

"Sweet, shy, innocent little Breanne has Alexa Delphine's magic?"

"*Yes.*" I crossed my arms against the early-fall heat. At least he was still rational enough to keep his voice low. "Sarah's the only one who doesn't know."

"What?"

"We didn't think the hospital was an appropriate time to tell her, and Opal only knows because she's a druid—"

I mentally facepalmed. Did my mouth have *no* limits?

I may as well go all the way. "Opal's Mr. Dawson's niece."

Jak pressed his lips together like he was trying to stop a reaction. "Wow. I missed a lot just for 'not knowing'."

"I wanted to ease you into that part," I told him, negligibly kicking at a pebble on the concrete porch. "The Delphine secret shook me when I found out, let alone why I was actually being hunted. Let alone when my best friend got the leader's magic... You're not buckling under the pressure like I did, and it's kind of weirding me out."

He bit his lip as it stretched into a sarcastic smile. His head fell back against the wall of the house, and he closed his eyes until that smile released itself into a grin. "Why didn't you ever tell me sooner, Em?"

Rhetorical—a regretful question. He knew the answer to that. And I couldn't blame him for asking it because there was a lot about the past that I regretted but couldn't change. Not even Annisa's time traveling can alter the past.

"You know you have to act like you don't know," I finally said, my fingers running home to my locket. "Like you don't hate them."

"Right," he said, standing up and not bothering to dust himself off. "Because they're not the biggest hypocrites God's ever seen, right? Because they can get away with stringing my dad along and taking him from me just to make him do everything he ever swore against. Ignore it, that's what I have to do, right? Pretend they're not magicians, they're *not* the reason my mom's dead and my family fell apart when I was seven years old!"

"Jak," I said lowly, trying to remind him that we were outside. My heart raced with a crack down the middle of it. "Magic didn't kill your mom."

"No, magicians like *them* did. They're the magicians Hunters think they're after. *They're* the magicians Caldwell wants to get rid of, the reason anyone was ever sent after her, and they get away with staying right where they are."

My lips glued themselves shut, silenced by truth and my damaged pride. I hated that my swallow was probably visible to him, that he could read my eyes so well, that he most likely knew exactly what I was thinking right now.

"I check myself for bugs and wires every time I go out to see you, I double-check every single time," he told me. "I've never found anything and we seemed to be okay—but now I know I wasn't being overly cautious. They just gave me a reason to *have* to do that, they just made me all the more of a liability. And that's probably what they want, so I'll have to stay away from you."

I looked to the side, at the front door next to me. I wondered if my family was piled up against it, eavesdropping. I wondered if any of these words stung them like they stung me.

I held myself tighter. "I'm not happy about it, either. But if we expose them, they expose us. If you wanna help protect us, stay silent. Please."

His jaw tightened as he looked away, clenched. He lightly shook his head. "I hate them."

I wasn't brave enough to say it with him. Part of me questioned if I could bring myself to make those words true. I knew part of Alexa's story but probably nowhere near even half of it; all

I knew was that something was fueling her actions, and her family members weren't blind followers.

Jak knew that Alexa had been a teen mom, but did he know how she'd gotten there?

"Do we have your word?" I finally asked. "Can we trust you to pretend that you don't know?"

He licked his lips before tightly pressing them together, like he was caging something. When those warm irises finally met me again, they were too tired to be Jakson Bleu's eyes. "Yeah. I've been doing that for a long time."

NINE

That was just about the *last* way I wanted my last time seeing Jak before the cruise to go, but thanks to Momma ordering pizza and making smoothies for dessert, we didn't end on the worst note. And then it was a final hug goodbye before mid-October rolled around and the junior class got onto a plane to Athens—which doubled as my first flight ever.

For once, though, there was no trauma waiting for me at the end of the journey. Even the take-off turbulence was more surreal than scary. We were leaving Capperson. North Carolina. *America*.

Sarah, Breanne, and Opal had too much fun telling me all the moments to look out the window, like when we could actually spot our school in the middle of the Callistro Forest, and when we were officially above the clouds. But none of it stopped my anxious fiddling with my locket as I repeated to myself for the entire flight, *Dad and Auntie are safe. They're fine.*

After the monumental hassle of landing and getting to the hotel (since we weren't embarking until early tomorrow), the best part about vacation so far was settling *into* said hotel. The Callistro Academy is funded fairly generously under Homeland Security, but eight cabins that housed six each for two weeks was a pretty penny, and I couldn't imagine what the hotel added. It was no wonder that every junior who wanted to go had to pay an eight-hundred-dollar deposit, but I think deposits are a normal thing for school trips. Sadly, three classmates opted out—but that was three fewer girls to hide from.

"Finally!" Breanne exclaimed as we stepped through the door and faced a clean, organized room. "I want a catnap and then to go right back out to explore before tomorrow."

A wide window with a view of the city lay in front of us, streaming sunlight onto the credenza and TV. Opposite of that were two king-sized beds. I almost made the joke of magicians in one bed and mortals in the other.

Sarah set down her suitcases next to the bathroom door, Opal next to her. "Good, because we only have this afternoon, and I *need* to visit this boutique we passed at—"

"*Sas efcharistó,* Albert," Momma said, appearing in the doorway. A young man in a white uniform followed her inside, carrying three suitcases while Momma carried her own. "*Boreíte aplá na ta thésete edó, tha to frontísoume.*"

My friends and I shared a confused look with each other.

"*Nai, kyría.*" Albert set down the luggage against the wall and then turned to Momma. "*An chreiázeste káti, parakaló kaléste.*"

With a professional smile at me and my friends, he nodded curtly. "*Anvtio sas, kyríes.*"

We returned the gestures, having no idea what he'd just said. He walked out and closed the door behind him.

"Was that Greek?" I asked, strolling farther into the hotel room.

"Good ear." Momma pulled her suitcase to the bed closest to the door. "You usually learn it when you join a Master agency. I agree with Breanne, a nap sounds great before we head out."

Breanne perked up beside me. "I already booked us an Athens sightseeing and museum tour that starts in an hour—"

"A *museum* tour?" Sarah groaned. "Museums are—"

"—one of the greatest gifts to mankind!" Breanne gawked at her in disbelief.

"It's, like, 6 A.M. in Capperson!" Sarah argued. "And *you* kept me awake for most of the flight talking about the aerodynamic logistics of a jet's main—"

"Girls," Momma stated, clapping twice. Sarah rolled her eyes and Breanne muttered a quick apology. I saw why Momma wanted them to stop when she looked at the girl standing timidly next to Sarah. "Are you okay, Opal? You've been quiet."

Her purple eyes, a little lighter because she had been out of the wheelchair for over a week now, looked up at Momma. A soft smile graced her thin pink lips. "Yeah, I'm okay," she said in an airy, high-lilted whisper. "Settling in."

Momma nodded, pretending to believe her. Finding out Opal's tell had made me realize exactly how many times she'd lied with that question in the past. I'd figured that getting to go on the cruise and only needing to be careful about how she moved her back would've shoved off some weight—but I don't think I knew Opal Dubois as well as I'd thought. She was my best friend, but she was still my *new* best friend.

I wish I could tell her telepathically that I'm here for her.

"Okay," Momma said gently. Her gaze swept over the four of us. "Rest up. Then we'll grab Mr. Dawson and do that tour."

⚓

Sarah couldn't deny one thing about the museum: it was exactly what she needed to work up an appetite for dinner. The hotel restaurant's food only made me all the more excited for what the *Elina* would serve for the next two weeks, and it was more than enough to keep us awake when the jetlag started settling in. It was only past noon back in North Carolina, but we'd been awake since the middle of the night there.

The restaurant dining room was fairly elegant, slightly more old-fashioned than the Dining Hall back home: dark-oak wall paneling, white tile, and bright pendants scattered across the ceiling. Despite that, poached salmon with mousseline sauce and sauteed asparagus was the last thing I was expecting for hotel cuisine, in full honesty.

"Em, pay attention."

"What?" I asked Sarah as she gently nudged me, glancing at the seven other girls around the table. "What's happening?"

"*Orientation*," she mouthed.

My chest sank in disappointment as I realized that I'd missed half of Momma's introduction speech already.

"...which means even though it'll be after-school hours, we'll still be grading you accordingly," she said from three tables away.

Okay. I'll figure out what that means later.

"And finally, we need to address the elephant in the room." She gazed over the nearly fifty Callistro Girls sitting across six round tables, eyes all on her. "Magic is legal on the ship and most of the cities we'll be stopping at. If you see a magician using magic, I expect you to regard them as another law-abiding citizen. Understood?"

We nodded. I couldn't believe she even had to speak the words.

"All right, then." My mother nodded with a professional smile, resting her hands in a steeple position on her stomach. "Enjoy dinner, ladies, and be prepared for your first day of classes tomorrow after we embark on the ship."

Unfortunately, that had been the only reason we'd been allowed to pack laptops; lectures and assignments had been posted online for the junior class with rather prompt due dates, but at least we only had to dedicate four days of the week to those lessons.

"If the hotel is like this," Sarah began as she stuck her silver fork into her salmon fillet, "imagine what the ship's gonna be like. What do you guys wanna do tomorrow after class?"

Opal shrugged, brushing a straight lock of black hair behind her ear. "Anything that makes me forget everything. I just wanna feel like I'm in Athens."

I glimpsed Sarah and Breanne on either side of me, both of them quiet with agreement. The last thing the four of us wanted was a reminder of what we'd left behind in Capperson despite the banes of our existence being an ocean away. I tried anything, any distraction, to remove that red hair and those emerald-green eyes from my memory, relying on the normal people sitting across the restaurant when my food didn't do the trick.

The first thing my eyes landed on was the profile of a red-head.

I nearly dropped my fork until she turned her head, laughing with the blond man sitting next to her.

Not Alexa, and not William.

I swallowed the lump stuck in my throat and went back to my plate of food. I had to nod to myself in reassurance. Alexa and William were nowhere in sight.

Yet I couldn't shake the feeling that we'd never been closer to each other.

The second we stepped into the *Elina*'s dining hall after settling into our (minuscule) cabins, I don't think any of us wanted to leave. If the gold trim, chandeliers, and waxed floors didn't say enough about what the food would be like, the red-padded chairs and gold-plated eating ware probably did. Few passengers roamed the hall as people continued embarking, which made it the perfect place for us to receive our first mission of the trip.

"All right, ladies," Mr. Dawson announced at the head of the table, temporarily re-entering headmaster mode. His diamond-like eyes sharpened, his clean-shaven jaw set. "For your first mission overseas, you're on the hunt for what we're calling a 'Minotaur's Ring'. In partners, you'll be tracking your target on a GPS as they lead you to your final destination, where a ring will be hidden for you to find and bring to me there. If your target catches you while you're following them, you're out of the hunt."

Breanne, next to me, raised her hand. "So our targets don't have a ring on them already? They'll be leading us to our final destination, where a ring will be?"

Mr. Dawson nodded once. "Correct. There's a Minotaur's Ring for all of you."

Sarah raised her hand next. "Who are our targets this time? Hired agents again?"

"Yep," Momma said. "You haven't seen these agents yet because they're only meant to be seen during your missions throughout the trip. Today, you'll hunt them until they drop their tracker at the final location—unless they catch you first, of course."

Target tracking and object recovery? Easy. We were just dipping our toes into the water today.

"No further questions?" Mr. Dawson asked as another couple left the eating hall.

Just like he wanted, you could hear a pin drop on the waxed floor.

"Then partner up. Once we give you your GPS,"—Mr. Dawson set his smile on me—"set off in Athens."

⚓

"Please." Sarah scoffed as she placed her hands on her hips, standing next to me beside the cobblestone street. "*Shopping* is the first thing we're doing once we're off the clock, not another museum. I'm getting a jacket just for this trip!"

The girl was definitely having fun with the free dress code of the cruise.

"Our Hunter isn't gonna be focused on what jacket you're wearing," I teased, looking down at the black GPS device in my hand. "They're still stopped. It's like they're *trying* to distract us with the stores."

Which was a great way to keep us awake—it was past 2 in the morning in North Carolina, and I wasn't doing well with the jetlag. Sarah, on the other hand, had spent more than a few trips abroad—and the girl is used to staying up until ungodly hours of the night when she doesn't have school (a terrifying reminder being that one sleepover in seventh grade where she had the three of us take turns being tied up in shoelaces and scrambling to get loose in under five minutes).

Greek conversation faded into the cold air as Sarah strolled closer to me. I couldn't remember the last time I'd been surrounded in foreign conversation I didn't understand. It was almost comforting—nostalgic.

"They're moving." I eyed the red dot on the GPS's dark-gray screen. "Up the street, go."

We moved down the cobblestone road, free of cars and allowing tourists to travel along and provide us cover. The aroma of freshly brewed coffee and cinnamon-sprinkled pastries floated down the street with us as we passed a couple of local cafes. In a blink, our target turned down an alley and froze. Sarah and I stopped at the window of an antique store, sitting down on the cold bench in front of it.

"Wow." I sighed as my gaze settled onto the small building on the other side of the street, then the ones next to it, going all the way down the direction we'd come. Three-story buildings stood on both sides of the street for each business, whose doors stood out in either a stark white, bright blue, or yellow.

"Yeah. I'm kinda sad we're leaving tonight," Sarah said. "This place is a perfect combination of old and new. The history is so... layered."

I chuckled. "You sound like Breanne."

"That's a compliment," she said cheekily, nudging me. Her ebony waves gleamed in the sunlight, her bronze skin aglow. Egypt had loaned Greece one of their goddesses, and she fit in perfectly. "You're not just... saying that because of what I told you, are you?"

I quickly shook my head. "No. I told you, that doesn't define you."

She gave me a light smile. Just as quickly, her eyes lit up, her jaw dropping. "No, seriously, did you see all of the ceramic plates on display a few doors down? My dad would *love* one of those. Oh, and my mom would love the beaded—"

"Remember that and get up," I said, standing and treading farther down the curving street. A four-way intersection sat ahead with another business on the corner. An alleyway lay only a couple of steps away.

I turned my head to look at Sarah behind me. "She's going down the alley."

"Let me see," she whispered. I handed the GPS to her and took a baby step, leaning my head around the corner of the building. Our Hunter walked down the frigid alleyway in a flowy dress, her sandals muting her steps.

How is she not wearing a jacket? Are Hunters that cold hearted?

"Got it," Sarah whispered, handing me back the GPS. I

glanced at her, waited for Hunter to reach halfway down the alley, and then finally rounded the corner. "The Acropolis is our ultimate destination."

I looked back at Sarah before setting my gaze in front of me. "How do you know that?"

"This alley turns east and then winds down," she said. The crème buildings sandwiching us stood tall on both sides, potted bushes and plants scattered across the edge of the wall. "Heading south takes us to the edge of the urban area. The only area beyond that is the Acropolis—conveniently where the Parthenon is at."

I wanted to turn around to face the girl completely, to just marvel at the wit and instinct I'd seen from actual Hunters, but my focus on executing Belov's Crawl properly couldn't be broken. (I hadn't earned a sprained wrist mastering it during the practice hunts last year for nothing.)

Sarah proved to be right as we left the alley and broke out at the edge of the last few buildings. The towering hill in front of us came into view. Hunter weaved through the crowd that was both approaching and coming from the Acropolis, and Sarah and I weren't far behind.

A museum was the last thing behind us as we drew farther and farther from urban Athens. Acropolis stood majestically ahead, challenging us to follow our Hunter up the limestone steps of the hill. Dusty stone wafted into my nose, and I had to suppress a sneeze.

"If only we could do a phantom circle like we did for our final," Sarah whispered, leading the way.

I mentally shivered. After *why* we'd had to do a phantom circle, that was the last method I wanted to use.

Sarah and I continued our casually cautious climb. With my target locked in sight, the only hard part now would be finding one small ring amidst a labyrinth of history. But that was a problem for later. Right now, Hunter was taking her next step up as a woman came down next to her—

The woman's short, strawberry-blond hair shone in the sun as she passed. Emerald-green eyes beamed at Hunter and then landed on me.

"Stop!" I hissed, grabbing Sarah's wrist and twirling us behind a group of tourists.

No. No, no, no. There's no way she's here. She wouldn't've actually—

I held up my finger at Sarah, slightly turning my head in the direction of my targets. With her back turned to us, Hunter's eyes moved all the way to the side even though she couldn't see us.

I kept myself frozen, controlling my breath and eyeing the red dot on the GPS. Hunter remained stopped.

"Her steps slowed at the last second," Sarah whispered, wary. She stared down at the GPS as if we were trying to map out directions. "It would've been over for us. Good eye, Em."

I couldn't tell her that that wasn't the reason I'd turned us around. Especially because no matter where I looked all over the steps of the Acropolis, Alexa was gone.

I know I saw her. That had to be her. I know I...

Right?

Sarah looked out over the hill, and I tilted my head to look at her. "You were right. Nice job on the Acropolis theory."

Frankly, at this point, I wouldn't put anxious hallucinations past myself for a second. And if that was what it was, I refused to worry Sarah about that right now. I needed evidence, not fear.

There were lots of redheads with green eyes in the world.

Sarah smiled at me, the only genuine part of her act as a tourist. We stayed in the same spot for a few more seconds.

After one final scan around for a potentially phantom Alexa, I looked back down at the GPS. "Target is moving," I said as Sarah peered around the group of tourists.

She stepped out from behind them and walked up the next few steps. I closely followed, our Hunter moving faster.

We passed the scenery, the red dot leading us straight toward the Parthenon. The second we began to approach the ruins, the dot disappeared.

"We did it." I grinned at Sarah, high-fiving her. "Arguably, the hardest part is over."

"Not arguably." She smirked, placing her hands on her hips. "Leave finding the pretty ring to me."

Which I actually would've done if Momma and Mr. Dawson weren't monitoring my progress on this hunt, too.

The two of us advanced as close to the ancient marble of the closed-off Parthenon as we could go. Massive columns upheld its two layers, piles of rock and limestone littered across the ground. A gentle wind blew my hair back as I turned with Sarah to face the world we stood on top of. The city of Athens lay before us in a panoramic view, stretching out farther than our gazes could match. Athens seemed to smile under the Greek sun.

I turned back around, walking toward the corner of the Parthenon and peering past the edge of the hill. Barely a sliver of the Aegean Sea was visible from this far inland. The thought of the waves lapping against me increased the chill in the air, and I shivered.

If only the move here wouldn't kill me before I could make it past where the Titanic sank.

"Em!" Sarah exclaimed from somewhere behind me.

I spun around, broken from the trance of Greece. "You already found it?"

She came out from the border of the Parthenon, holding up a thin silver band. It reminded me of the one I had back at home—I would've worn it if my last name didn't start with an "m" to the rest of the world.

Sarah's eyes, even lighter in the sun, glanced all around the top of the Acropolis ruins. "Would you look at that: we're the first ones here."

"You are," a familiar voice chimed, turning me and Sarah toward the Aegean Sea. Momma and Mr. Dawson approached with proud smiles, and he reached out for the ring. "In a rather impressive time, I'll add."

Sarah beamed next to me, and I was right there with her.

"Mr. Dawson!"

Beside us, Ava Baleen ran up with Caroline Walker. Ava held up a silver band. "Second-best time!"

Mr. Dawson smiled, taking the ring. "Congratulations, Miss Baleen and Miss Walker."

Momma stood behind him, mindlessly twisting the golden band on her left ring finger. Her silence felt out of character, but I wanted to think it was because she was observing us as the headmistress and making sure we were "upholding standards".

Ten minutes later, the Callistro Academy junior class stood atop the Acropolis. After that, we were allowed to roam the city for the next hour—but we had to take notes on what our Hunters did with their time off after the mission. They were no longer tracking us and were off the clock, but we weren't. And if we were caught, our notes would only count for half credit.

This kind of class time was arguably worse than our normal ones.

After having to (literally) hold Sarah back from exposing us when our Hunter bought the last white Greek-style coat she wanted from the boutique on Athinas Street, our hour was up and we made our way back to the *Elina*. Sailing away, watching the ship break from the port, is another first-time experience I'm grateful to have in my memories. And it was like Steven knew where I was in that moment and wanted to make it even better, because he chose that evening of all times to call me.

Thank goodness for Wi-Fi calling.

By the time I managed to escape from deck and down into our cabin's hallway, I'd missed his call and had to call him back. He picked up immediately.

"I'm so glad you're there!" he chimed on the other line. "I know you're on your cruise right now, um, I'll make this quick: Cara and I just got to the hospital, she went into labor today!"

My jaw dropped, excited goosebumps tingling on my arms. "Really? Can I talk to her?"

In the couple of seconds Steven spent handing Cara his phone, even as I opened our cabin door, it was hard to believe that I was on a ship floating farther and farther away from Greece. I almost felt like I was back in North Carolina with them.

"Hi, honey! How's your trip?" Cara asked. There was no way to tell that she was lying in a hospital bed right now. "What've you done so far?"

"Athens was great, but what about you? How are you feeling?"

"Everything's good, the pain isn't too bad yet. I'm just preparing, in all senses." She chuckled giddily. "We're obviously really excited. You have no idea how long we've wanted this."

I plopped down onto the small couch in the main area of our cabin, fiddling with my locket. "I'm so upset I'm not there, I really wanted to meet the baby."

"They'll only be a couple of weeks old when you get back, don't worry."

"Still—I wanted to be there for you guys... I'm really happy for you. You'll do great."

"Thank you, honey. Okay, I don't want to keep you away any longer. Where's your class right now?"

"Up on the main deck, celebrating the sail-away party."

"Oh, right," Steven said, faint in the background. Background noise rumbled on the other side of the phone. At the same time, the door to the cabin opened. "We won't keep you from that, we love you!"

Perfect timing, I thought, looking up at my best friends coming in. "I love you, too!"

Sarah tossed her hair behind her shoulder, hands on her hips as she smirked. "Was that THE l-word I heard?"

I rolled my eyes, standing from the couch. "That was Cara and Steven. They're having their baby!"

"No way!" Opal squealed, her face lighting up in a way I hadn't seen since before that night in the forest. "That's so cute, tell them we said congrats!"

All the girls knew about Cara and Steven was that they were "not-so-distant relatives", which was basically true at this point.

Still, I wondered every day if I'd ever get to share the truth with them so that they could be happy for the real Cara and Steven. But keeping my identity a secret wasn't about me anymore—it was about my family and friends in the magic world. If I involved my best friends in my magic life, I involved them in everyone else's. I needed to keep them all on the safest side of the war: my friends on the mortals' and my family on magic's. Sometimes division actually makes for the best defense.

CHAPTER

ELEVEN

Barcelona, Spain: my one chance to meet the mage from my vision. He definitely spoke Spanish and had Spanish genes, so this had to be the place I was destined to meet him. After a calm and brief stay in Venice, Mr. Dawson even announced that we didn't have a mission this time, either.

The only problem was, Spain was a lot bigger than just Barcelona, and it wasn't exactly like I could teleport to the boy. My only option was taking advantage of the twelve hours we'd be here to explore the tabernas, stuff our faces with tapas, and tour the historical sites and cathedrals (and support Sarah's lucrative spending on whatever piece of fashion her eyes caught).

"*Yes!*" she squealed, grabbing a pair of dangly golden earrings from the stand in front of the local store she'd dragged us to.

"These, these are what I need with my new coat!"

"They're perfect!" Opal chirped, stiffly walking to the booth and taking a matching arm cuff decorated with small golden chains hanging off it. "This would look *perfect* with the entire outfit."

Sarah gawked. "I love you," she said, like she was stunned with the mere imagination of what it would all look like.

"Guys," Breanne rasped, shifting the position of the cardboard box in her hands and her blond hair falling into her face, "these plates are getting heavy."

I brushed her hair out of her eyes, pushing it behind her ears. "Are you *sure* you don't want me to take those for you?"

She shook her head. "Got it," she whispered with strain.

She didn't have it, even though she'd just gotten those plates from the ceramics shop two doors down.

I couldn't grab them anyway because my phone was buzzing with a new text—and I was a little too excited every time I heard this notification sound assigned to a specific person. Okay, boy.

Taking my phone out of my back pocket, I realized that it was 6 A.M. in North Carolina. Jak had a more messed-up sleep schedule than I thought.

J: I wanna be in Barcelona too :(

E: It's definitely better than being around your parents, get a plane ticket

J: That'd be a lot of plane tickets. Even a Hunter kid's allowance doesn't stretch that far, Merlin

The woman running the stand told Breanne that she could set her box down onto the corner of the table. Breanne told her a thank-you in Spanish, and I looked back down at my phone.

E: Speaking of, are they still around?

J: Lol what? Wdym?

E: Your parents, what've they been up to?

J: Same old same old, why?

This was tricky: if I told Jak that I was pretty sure I'd caught a glimpse of Alexa in Athens a few days ago, would he believe me? I didn't even think I believed myself at this point, considering I hadn't seen a single Delphine or Bleu since.

E: I think I saw Alexa when we were in Athens
but I honestly don't know if I did or not

J: That'd be pretty concerning considering she
just said hi to me yesterday

Call me crazy, call me absolutely insane—but it turned out, that wasn't the answer I wanted to hear. I think it was because if Alexa and William were back at Redway, it was physically impossible for me to keep them locked in sight.

My muddied memory of Acropolis flashed in my mind: the red hair, the green eyes, the knowing smile. Every day that passed, though, the blurrier that memory became. Distorted, untrustworthy. But with this woman, I didn't want to take any chances.

> **E:** Remember when I told you that Alexa impersonated you this summer? Are you sure last night was actually her? How do you know?

J: Ok well tbh, I can't speak for her, but my dad, trust me, it's him. And nothing's changed in their interactions with each other, so... idk

Except, Julia had played her part as Alexa really well when they'd switched appearances. William hadn't noticed a thing.

The risk is too big, especially with Dad and Aunt Becca. I have to make sure.

> **E:** Okay. I have a big mission for you and it needs to stay top secret. Your parents CAN'T know about it or follow you.

J: Baby's first mission? On it. What do you need?

> **E:** I'm gonna send you Steven's number. I need you to get something that belongs to Alexa and meet up somewhere private with him, he and Cara just had their baby so not the hospital but

not their house, either. He can find out where
Alexa is with that, though

J: Ok then. 007 over and out

I looked up from my phone as if someone would arrest me if they caught me texting. With no updates available, I was afraid that Alexa and William would know that their son was onto them and they'd *purposely* do nothing to give him an update while working in the shadows on their real plan. Especially if that shadow was the size of a cruise—

I froze. A pair of dark-oak brown eyes stared at me from across the street in front of a restaurant. Spiky black hair, leather jacket. Familiar.

I've seen him before. Where have I seen him before?

Just as I took a step forward, a hand grabbed my wrist and turned me around. A brief second, I only glanced for a brief second at Breanne when she'd grabbed me and started saying something. When I looked back at where I'd seen the boy, he was gone.

I looked up and down the street, scanning for the black jacket he'd been wearing. Crowds of long-sleeved shirts, baseball caps, and sunglasses bustled by on each side with every jacket color under the sun but black. How had he disappeared into thin air?

"*Emmy*," Breanne snapped. "What's wrong?"

I wasn't sure what to say. I *know* I'd seen that boy before, but some kind of buried instinct was warning me that it had to do with magic.

"I thought..." I began, my mind split in two. "I thought I saw Jak."

Sarah snickered. "Oh, so she's using her phone to tell him how much she misses him."

The teasing was always easy to endure when it got me out of answering the difficult questions.

Alexa had done the same thing—appeared and then vanished. Was I *actually* hallucinating? Was Jak right and the Delphines really were back in North Carolina?

—*Hello?*— I called to the boy, but no response ever came.

⚓

I think seeing that boy had affected my subconscious greater than I wanted to admit, especially when we got back to the ship and he hadn't made another appearance. Well, maybe it was him *and* Jak's text saying that he'd scheduled a meeting with Steven for two days from now. The second I laid my head down that night, I was out—but the blackness only lasted for a few moments.

In the space of a breath, the cold of a cobblestone alleyway flooded my mind and body. A familiar-looking boy with spiky black hair stood in front of me.

Him!

"So you're her," he said in Spanish. "Adara—"

Flash.

"—that make you?" I heard myself asking in Spanish, now in the passenger seat of a black sports car. The windshield overlooked a body of water sparkling in the sun.

He ran a warm-brown hand through his hair. "I'm the mage."

Flash.

"—join you?" he asked with a devilishly charming grin.

I felt my lips curve upwards in a giddy smile. "Sorry. Girls only—"

Flash.

My fingers tightened around my phone as I held it up to my ear, my gaze desperately searching up and down the bustling street vibrant with shoppers, food, and photography. "That's not possible, Jak—"

"Find them," Jak said solemnly on the other line. "That's the only—"

My eyes shot open in a dark and silent room. The windows of our cabin silenced the lapping waves outside, leaving me in a fuzzy silence. My mind had to reorient itself with the fact that we were in Spain, the location of the vision trailing behind my consciousness.

That's *where I've seen that guy from!* I thought, my memories finally working together. *That same vision, he was—*

Wait. Who was he?

He'd spoken Spanish, he had Spanish features—but we were leaving Spain. If he was meant to approach me, why hadn't he done so while we were here? When he'd seen me right there in the street? Why had he disappeared? How was he going to find me in the future?

I had my theories, I always had my theories. This time, though, I couldn't formulate them alone; I needed as much backup as I could get before the consequences outgrew my ability.

Annisa. It's a slim chance, but she might—

Wait a second.

"Find them."

Find them? Who? Why had *Jak* been the one to tell me to

find someone unless... unless he were talking about his parents?

I swallowed and prayed that it wouldn't somehow wake up Breanne lightly sleeping in the bunk above me. Her breathing was deeper, but she wasn't doing her scratchy snoring; she'd just fallen asleep.

Okay. I'm gonna need Kamose, too.

C H A P T E R

TWELVE

Even though I knew nobody would come charging through the cabin door after I'd told my friends to go to breakfast without me the next morning, I stared at the door from the couch like my eyes alone could keep it shut. My phone screen was a little too warm against my cheek as I waited for Annisa's response to my question.

"No, I..." she began quietly, "I don't really get visions about you unless I'm—directly involved. That's usually how a druid's visions work. So I can't tell you who that guy is."

Wi-Fi calling was starting to come in really handy. I technically could've spent all of breakfast on the phone if I really had to. I prayed that I wouldn't have to.

"Kamose?" I said, bouncing my knee.

"Sorry, commander," he replied, his Egyptian accent stronger than Annisa's Indonesian. "If you want the answer to that, you will have to find a way to Aswan to pay the traditional nore's price. Unless you want to use your own nore abilities."

"I don't—well, my mom doesn't. Every time I've asked her to help me practice, she refuses to be my enquirer. And she doesn't want me using Mr. Dawson, either. I'm not like you, I can't know present circumstances at whim."

"I do often forget that other nores aren't as privileged."

Annisa let out a sweet chuckle, but I couldn't join her. My worried curiosity was starting to rain down on my mind.

"Neither of you can tell me a single thing about him? Just to ease my anxiety?" I asked.

"I only found you because of a vision," Annisa said. "Remember? And then my nore friend told me how to find you. But the price to know your number—it was big."

I internally grimaced, remembering the day Moren had asked me about who exactly Morgana and I were. I'd realized that every time Moren used his ability on me, he saw when Annisa had exposed herself as Morgana. I wondered if her friend had asked her something similar—if different countries were more familiar with other sacred identities, Morgana being Canada's and Ezranai being Egypt's.

"The only thing I'm allowed to tell you is that you are not in danger," Kamose told me. "But anything else, because it's your question, I will be put under the nore's truth curse until someone wants me to answer their question next."

I turned away from my phone, sighing. Kamose knew who the boy was, but he wasn't allowed to tell me. All I could know was that he wasn't a threat.

The circumstances kind of reminded me of when I'd met Annisa for the first time. Moren had told me that she wasn't a threat, either. He'd even called her an ally.

What if this boy is my next ally? If he was just like the three of us, I had the best-case scenario with a stranger for once.

"Okay," I finally said. I stood and started my way to the door. "Thank you, guys. You're able to get information more easily than I am. I'll see what I can do."

⚓

With the ship out at sea, we spent that day conducting our second hunt: avoiding a tail from our fellow Callistro Girls. It was another round of the basics, but we were definitely taking advantage of that to stay on top of our skills.

That night, Cara and Steven were finally able to video call me, Momma, and Mr. Dawson with their newborn son: Samuel Baelford. Named after the mage Caralyn Callistro allied with two centuries ago to bring forth the Callistro Academy and help the soul of unity—me—find her way when the time would come.

For once, though, the good things *didn't* have to come to an end: Jak texted me the next afternoon saying that he brought Steven one of Alexa's necklaces, and Steven located Alexa in Topa. I guess that was good news depending on how you looked at it: no Alexa on the ship, but I was hallucinating. Well, I definitely knew the lesser of *those* two evils.

Suspiciously enough, the goodness continued: it kind of goes without saying, but swimming in a heated pool on the sun deck was a fairly great way for the rest of my anxiety to melt off. A few Callistro Girls were cozy in the hot tub while Momma was having the time of her life soaking in her first tan since... well, I can't remember a time in my life when she'd tanned before then. But watching her lie in the autumn sun on a cushioned lounge chair, her chestnut hair pulled up in a bun and sunglasses concealing her eyes, I quickly noticed that I wasn't the only one stealing glances. Her one-piece lining her figure was probably not helping the case. (The Hunter career keeps you in shape even when you're just an instructor.)

"Told you you'd enjoy this one," Sarah said, leaning against the edge of the pool and basking in the sun. Karaoke had *sounded* fun until everyone remembered that Breanne and I couldn't sing, and bowling had gotten fatally competitive—so we were hesitant about the pool. "When's the last time we went swimming just to have fun?"

"It's cold." Opal shivered next to me, holding her pale arms close to her chest. "I'm sorry, I have to get in the hot tub."

Sarah pulled herself upright, adjusting her messy bun. "The water is a solid eighty-five degrees."

"And the hot tub's *warm*," Opal argued, turning to me and Breanne. "Do you wanna come—?"

"Watch out!" Elizabeth Moody called, pulling our attention to the transparent beach ball about to crash into us.

Telekinesis instinctually acted within me as I squeezed my eyes shut. A slap rang out, water splashing onto my face.

I opened my eyes to the beach ball floating in front of us.

"Sorry!" Elizabeth exclaimed as she swam toward us. Her black braids sat neatly on her shoulders, her dark-brown skin aglow under the sun. "You guys wanna play?"

"Let's do it!" Sarah tossed the beach ball up and hit it toward Amelia Baker, Ava Baleen, and Sloane Moore in the middle of the pool.

"She just made me colder," Opal said, shivering again as she stepped in slow motion to the ladder ten feet away. "Come with if you wanna."

Breanne stayed comfortable in her spot next to me, arms resting on the sunny edge of the pool as her eyes followed Opal. "Well, I guess now I have freedom of speech. You know what I find crazy?"

I met my back with the wall, sinking into the warm water. "What?"

"As long as we're not around the other girls, we can just stand here and talk about magic openly. We don't have to sneak around as long as it's just us."

"I can hear you," Momma said nonchalantly from her chair.

"Okay, and her." Breanne smiled, the ends of her blond hair swishing in the water. "But it's weird. It being a norm, I mean."

I noted how calmly the water rippled in front of me, trying to stop myself from saying the first thoughts that came to mind. The pool wasn't full, but it seemed like more people were out than in. I sank to chin level as an ocean breeze blew by.

"I wonder what it's like in other countries where magic is illegal," I mused. That was a question that had been buried in my mind for years. "If they're as bad as we are."

"Yeah..." Breanne shrugged. "What about Greece and Italy? They both have a few cities where magic is outlawed—but Athens and Venice were so..."

"Lively," I said. "Fun, rich."

"With everything," she added, like she was eager to take this load off her mind. "You know, ever since this summer happened, I've been thinking back to the beginning of the whole war. Way before it was waged in America. Someone *had* to have caught a couple of wielders in the act and blown it up into something bigger. Or maybe a group of wielders actually did do something, and it ruined their entire reputation for the rest of time. It's just... What's the difference between the leadership of legalized magic and the leadership of illegalized magic?"

"Everyone has a story," I said, the words sending a light shiver through me. I was grateful that Breanne could blame it on the water. "Everyone has a reason. Some people are just louder when they express how they feel, I guess."

"Yeah... I guess I should just enjoy the freedom while I have it. Wanna go join Opal in—?"

It was like Breanne knew: she saw it the instant my gaze froze on the other side of the pool. The redheaded woman in a flowy navy-blue cover-up standing next to her twenty-two-year-old son in a T-shirt and cargo shorts.

No. Jak said she was still there. The spell said—

Alexa's warm smile turned the water around me to ice. Breanne went rigid next to me with caution. I stared just past the top of Sarah's head as she threw the beachball back at Kimia, oblivious.

"Emmy?" Breanne whispered next to me. Her feeble, child-like voice shook my bones, infecting me with the venom of her fear. "Is... is that *her*?"

I nodded so lightly that I could barely feel it.

Those doe-like eyes latched onto our targets, who were walking along the edge of the pool until they came to the edge of the deck—the pool bar. Anthony allowed his mother a seat on the stool, his triangle-shaped jaw tight despite his sweet smile. Forest-green eyes landed on me as he sat next to Alexa.

—*Beautiful day,*— he remarked, signaling to the bartender.

I *hadn't* been hallucinating. Alexa had been following us in Athens.

But the spell, magic couldn't lie! And Alexa couldn't have dropped all this money, time, and effort—she couldn't have dropped her cover so hastily—for the sake of chasing us! And letting us *know* that they were here? Why?

The spell, if Jak gave Steven something that belonged to Alexa—

Unless he hadn't. Unless he'd accidentally given him something that belonged to the person pretending to *be* Alexa at Redway.

She's here.

"That's them, that's really them?" Breanne whispered, her sweet voice quivering in a way that was wickedly concerning for a Hunter-in-training. "What do we do?"

"We..." I used every ounce of muscle and courage to rip my gaze away from Alexa and Anthony. "We—"

A shadow loomed over us. Breanne and I spun around in the water as Momma bent to the edge of the pool, her gaze set forward as she lifted her sunglasses.

"That psycho was desperate enough," she whispered under her breath. Her eyes fell onto us with a resolve that I envied. "Okay. Remember your training. You both know she has no legal authority here, right?"

Breanne nodded. I didn't dare move. I don't know why, but any reaction felt unsafe.

"Mr. Dawson and I prepared for this," Momma assured us. "We're going to stay here for now to maintain our cover to the class and stay under the protection of the public. We can't talk about this now, so just trust me when I tell you to not worry. We have a plan."

"You knew this would happen?" Breanne whispered frailly.

"We prepared, honey." Momma's eyes softened just for her. "You know that every good Hunter prepares for the worst instead of expecting the best."

C H A P T E R

Thirteen

Unlike when Alexa had shown up in Athens, now they wanted us to *know* that they were here. That was the most chilling fact of all: a phantom circle could only be ruled out of possible tactics they were using if they didn't want us to know *yet*. Grand Hunters only expose themselves to their prey if that prey's been cornered with nowhere left to go, when it's too late for them.

My friends and I gathered into the small main area of our cabin after dinner, waiting for Momma and Mr. Dawson to get back from surveillance so they could tell us the plan. Meanwhile, I had to contact Jak ASAP and tell him that his parents were nowhere near in Topa.

"I have to call and tell him before they come back," I said in front of the couch, where my three best friends sat with no room for me. That was just as well, considering there was no way my panic would let me relax right now.

"Are you *sure* he's gonna be safe over there?" Sarah asked again, leaning forward. "What if we have the real Alexa, William, and Anthony and he has undercover agents ready to 'take care of him' if he finds them out?"

"Either way, we have a threat," I stated, hardening my stance as if to grab her attention with that alone. "A *breach*. It doesn't matter which one is the real one—what matters is that we're the partially trained targets of a hunt, each with a bounty over our heads. That means we have an obligation to respond accordingly. And if he does have the dupe, they're most likely Delphines, meaning they won't hurt him."

I'd learned all too well this year about the consequences of staying silent—trying to piece together a problem myself instead of arming my loved ones with the knowledge that there were broken shards everywhere. So while we were doing recon here...

"Jak needs to gather intel over there. And he knows how to be safe—"

I closed my mouth at the specific ringtone I'd set for him. *Look at that: he got the timing just right.*

I quickly picked up. "Listen up."

"Whoa, feisty Merlin," he said, surprise lacing his words. "Is now a bad time to update?"

I stilled, glancing at my best friends in my peripheral. Taking a deep breath, I held up a finger to them.

Let him know who's in the room so he adds a filter.

"No. Perfect timing. Tell us."

He paused like he was translating my code. "Great," he then chimed. "Yeah. They're still here."

I closed my eyes, like he could see me rolling them to begin with.

"No," I said, putting Jak on speaker, "they're not."

"Okay…" he said curiously. "Then where did *you* see Waldo, Merlin?"

My eyes jumped from each girl in front of me, the sole sight of me seeming to ensnare their attention. "We found Alexa and Anthony today."

"That's not possible," Jak finally said, wearing a serious tone I'd last heard when my family and I told him about the Delphines. "I pass Alexa at least once a day—"

"I need you to trust me on this," I told him. "We haven't seen your dad yet. Are you *sure* it's actually still him with you?"

"Yeah." A lingering melancholy in his voice told me everything I needed to know—that that was the truth, the whole truth, and nothing but the truth, and he knew it. "Trust me. It's him."

"My mom and Dawson are surveying before they come back and discuss the plan. Someone's a decoy, and we need to figure out who. Do you know what to do?"

A few moments passed before he said, "Yeah."

I could practically feel the knife in my own gut, the anchor of remembrance that had probably just fallen on top of him: the Delphines were magicians, and that fact was probably going to take longer than two weeks to fully digest.

I never got enough time to digest it, either.

Momma's three-point code knock rapped on the door, letting us know that it was her and Mr. Dawson on the other side. I hung up the call with Jak and hurried to the door to let Momma and Mr. Dawson in.

"We just updated Jak," I told them. "He's gonna investigate whatever's going on back home."

"Pray he isn't caught," Mr. Dawson said, staying by the door. "Especially if he doesn't have the real deal. We don't know what the pack would do to him—or even if they'll go against Alexa and William's authority—if he finds out and they need to 'detain' him somehow."

"We have too many unknown variables to take any unwise risk," Momma added, following me back to the couch. "So keep him updated as we go along so that he can stay as safe as he can."

"Did you find anything?" Opal asked in front of us.

"No." Mr. Dawson rubbed his sharp jaw. "Something tells me that they have our location but we don't have theirs. And without something that belongs to them, we can't find them with a location spell."

"Even then," I said cautiously, "Alexa might be the only dupe. Jak says he *knows* it's his dad that's at Redway, and Anthony doesn't really need to maintain a cover back home. So we just need to figure out where the real Alexa is."

"That means Mr. Dawson and I will be pretty busy with supervising you girls and conducting our own hunt." Momma rubbed my back like she already knew that I needed something to keep me anchored during this conversation. It was kind of embarrassing. "If we're going to be able to anticipate anything they have planned, gather any intel they leave behind, we need to find them first and maintain a status on them. They can't do anything to us under legal authority while we're here—which is all the more of a warning that they do have a reason for being here."

My friends looked at each other, their eyes charged with concern; worry; and, thankfully, fear. I needed them to be afraid. I needed them to be ready to protect themselves, protect each other, because I couldn't do it to the full extent of my ability. Not without telling them, without making them bigger targets. Right now, for all the pack knew, they weren't leads to the Ateras yet. If they knew Emmalynn Atera and the Delphines didn't get to me first, the Delphines would get another pack in on the hunt. Caldwell himself would get involved. I wouldn't be a Delphine target anymore, I'd be the entire country's. And so would my best friends. There was just no way for them to know without someone finding out *that* they knew.

Stop it. I took a deep breath to push away the emotion seeping into my rationality. *Focus. Your mind is the best weapon you will ever use against yourself.*

I cursed the fact that Alexa had been the first one to teach me that.

"Recon," Breanne suddenly said, pulling our eyes to her. She mindlessly stared ahead of her, at whatever her brain was projecting to her right now. "*Recon.* They can't do anything while we're here. They're doing to us what we're doing to them. They're doing it *first.*"

Weaknesses, vulnerability—potentially finding an open spot for them to extract Alexa's magic while we were here. But they couldn't arrest me or Opal here...

I looked slightly up at Momma, whose hand slowed on my back. If they were doing recon on one of us, they were doing recon on *all* of us—including her and Mr. Dawson.

"So we don't have to worry about them exposing us while we're here," Sarah noted, standing from the couch. "That negates the effects of recon. But all of this just to make sure we don't spill their secret?"

"Recon is the most realistic possibility," Mr. Dawson said after a second. "I think they're just figuring out how much Emma's been revealing, if anything at all."

That's all Alexa's been doing this year. He knows that's not it.

"But if that's the case," Sarah began, restricting her emphasis on the words, "my point is that doesn't that mean they've been watching us this whole time? Because then that means they've been hiding *really* well in Capperson. And like we just proved, they're able to hide on a cruise! Alexa and Anthony purposely showed themselves today, that wasn't for no reason."

The girl is too deductive for her own good. Because whatever that reason was, it was one she couldn't know about.

I think the rest of us more than knew that it had something to do with Alexa's magic in Breanne. But they knew that we couldn't discuss that openly in front of Sarah—we couldn't devise a plan against them as long as Sarah was around, which was always. But with them being open now, even making themselves known—

They *were* cornering us. Like telling her was our only choice to fight back. And honestly, I think part of me always knew that it'd eventually come down to that—I just thought we had more time.

I looked at Breanne, who met my stare with timidity. Opal's gaze started burning a hole through my head. Sarah glanced between us all.

Again, she's too deductive for her own good: "Okay, there's something I don't know."

Just like that, the timer went off.

Breanne shifted to the front of her seat, picking at her arms. Opal furiously fiddled with her thumbs. When I looked at Mr. Dawson next to the couch, he was trapped in a staring contest with Momma.

Breanne and Opal knew how to act better. They knew how to keep a secret; they wanted to tell Sarah, and I knew because I wanted to tell her, too. To give up.

"Breanne," Momma finally said, crossing her arms. "It's up to you."

Sarah's eyes widened, her gaze darting to the small girl sitting next to her. "You? This is *your* secret?" She looked back at Momma before Breanne could respond. "Wait—you know?"

The cherry of Breanne's now red nose twitched, her fingernails digging into her arms. A tear mixed with mascara rolled down her cheek. She sniffed, grabbing Sarah's attention.

"Hey—no, what's wrong?" She gently wiped away Breanne's runaway tear with her thumb. "Bre, no, I'm not upset, I'm just confused, what's wrong?"

"Please don't hate me," she whispered, wiping her other cheek dry. "Please don't hate me."

"Never, stop talking like that," Sarah replied, pushing a blond bang out of Breanne's face. "Tell me, you're scaring me."

"I'm..." She inhaled with a ragged, dry sob. "I'm... I'm—"

"She has Alexa's magic," I blurted before I knew the words were even in my head.

Breanne stayed in her position like she hadn't even heard

me, while the entire room glared at me with a scold. All except for Sarah—who, surprisingly, was the tamest.

"What?"

"Alexa's a magician but she doesn't have her magic, Breanne does," I forced myself to say before I could change my mind, building a mental wall to the harsh stares of everyone else in the room. "It's my fault. That bracelet she tried on this summer in my room was an enchanted bracelet Mr. Dawson got to extract Alexa's magic. I was dumb enough to leave it in my room the day we found out Alexa got her memories back, and then you guys came over and Breanne tried it on when I was in the bathroom."

Sarah's golden-brown skin paled. She stared back at me with stun, her posture frozen. "What?" she whispered again.

"Alexa's magic was in the bracelet when Breanne put it on. So it transferred to her."

Sarah looked back at the girl next to her, whose fair cheeks were stained with streams of transparent black and inflamed with red. Opal never looked up from her thumbs as Sarah's gaze returned to me. Then it switched to Opal, and then Momma and Mr. Dawson.

"You all knew?" she asked.

Silence is golden—and loudest.

Pained green eyes fell onto me, me of all people. "Everyone knew but me?"

For a girl that had revealed to me her greatest secret days before we left for this trip, it had to be the conflict of the century to decide if she could be angry because a life-changing secret had been kept from her.

I'd been there too many times.

"Why?" she finally asked. The white ceiling light above us betrayed her and exposed the glisten in them. "Did you not trust me? Did you think I'd turn you all in? Why was I the only one who couldn't know?"

"Your knowledge of Breanne solidifies your position on Alexa's list," Mr. Dawson replied, arms crossed. "They don't know you know yet. You wanting to protect Breanne specifically would tell them that you know she has a Delphine's magic. We kept it from you to keep you off the list for as long as we could."

"I don't care if I'm on some stupid list! I've been on it ever since this summer happened, and I'm supposed to be there for my friends!"

"Another reason we didn't want you knowing," Momma said firmly, finally removing her hand from my back. "Your emotions would cloud your judgment—like they are right now. We're training you for these exact types of situations, and anything you practice will reflect on your real-life execution."

"So I'm supposed to be okay with this?" Sarah snapped.

Whoa. Her judgment really was clouded if she wasn't even afraid to challenge Momma.

Momma cocked her brows to show it, too, her hands planted on her hips. "No," she stated, "but if you want to prove that you can be trusted with confidential information, you'd bite your tongue and *listen* for wisdom and guided instruction."

Sarah's breath tripped over the beginning of a hundred words until she grew desperate enough to rub her face. Her makeup barely even smudged as she stared down at the dark-blue carpet.

It was too quiet.

"I'm just... I'm confused and—I feel like..."

It only took one glance: one glance at me screamed exactly what was running through her head in that moment, because I'd seen those eyes before. I'd seen those eyes at the beginning of this semester in our dorm room, on a girl who'd revealed to me her darkest secret that not even our best friends knew...

She was the only one who hadn't known.

"I need a minute," she whispered.

She darted straight past me, past Momma, and grabbed the doorknob. Momma called after her as she threw open the door and bolted into the hallway.

I held out my hands when the room tried to move. "I know what's going on," I said.

I ignored the looks on Opal's and Breanne's faces, even the curiosity on Momma's and Mr. Dawson's, as I turned around and followed after Sarah.

At the end of the right side of the hallway, her black waves bounced as she charged for the lobby. I shut the cabin door behind me and rushed after her.

"Sarah," I called, dodging a couple entering the hall. "Wait."

She continued to the lounge chair in the middle of the nearly empty lobby. It was then that I caught her hand over her nose and mouth. I never thought I'd have to see her in that position again after she'd confessed her dyslexia. At least this time, though, her eyes weren't red. Her features were stolid. It was like her tears this time were too... angry.

"Hey..." I began cautiously, reaching the chair. "I know you can't be this mad that we kept the whole—magic—thing a secret."

She rubbed the cherry of her nose, denying me her eyes. They stayed on the orchid on the glass coffee table in front of her.

I kept my hand on the top of her chair, too wary of the atmosphere to touch her. "Sarah…"

Only a sniff in response as she rubbed her hands together.

I glanced around the lobby, then lowered my voice for her. "It's just like when you confided in me earlier this semester. You don't have to share every detail with me. Just—don't do this alone. Whatever you're thinking, whatever you're processing, please don't do it alone."

"I'm angry."

I stayed quiet, letting her open the gates.

"I feel left out. I feel like I didn't meet some kind of standard, I feel—ostracized."

"'Ostracized'—?"

I shut my mouth when her words fully settled. "Some kind of standard". Even her best friends had left her out. But it hadn't been because of dyslexia, it had been for a rather valid—

"Because I was gonna get caught in the crossfire anyway," Sarah said next, like she was reading my mind. "I live with you guys. I'm guilty by association. And honestly?" Hard eyes snapped up to me. "Who cares? What're best friends for if not to go through the hard times together? Why wasn't I ever good enough to be included in the hard things?"

"That's not true," I told her. "You know that's not true."

"But it feels like it, Em." She ran a hand through her thick hair. "That's just it. That's what it feels like. That's what my mind does with it. That's all that matters."

All I could do was listen. I wasn't sure that I had the words this time.

Maybe she didn't need to hear them from me this time.

"Breanne knows how you feel," I said. To my relief, Sarah didn't say a word. "She feels ostracized every day being a magician. A magician against her will. This isn't who she is, but she's taking it on anyway for reasons beyond herself. And she didn't want to suck you into it. She's wanted to tell you more than anything but she fought herself every time because she knew it was her best way of keeping you safe because she loves you."

Sarah looked up at me. The words found me in that instant: "Maybe that's all that matters. She did what she could with what she understood."

Sarah swallowed, rolling her lips together. After a few seconds, she stood up and wiped under both of her eyes.

"They can only understand so much without the whole story," I told her. "Only you can help them understand all the way."

"They won't judge me...?"

I couldn't help but smile. "You're in the wrong group for that."

"Your mom and Mr. Dawson—"

"—already think you're one of the brightest, most intuitive students they've ever had."

Her nose quivered as she inhaled and then released.

"But are you..." I began, putting a gentle hand on her arm, "ready? To tell them?"

She gave me an empty nod. Right now, I wasn't sure that I believed her, but I wanted to pretend that I did. Anything to make it easier.

"Sorry," she whispered. "This is the last thing I should've

done after..."

Oh. Alexa and William could be watching us. Even in the midst of her storms, Sarah Duncan is an intelligent Hunter. In that moment, I had to envy her for it.

We walked back into the hallway and opened the door of our cabin. Nobody had moved from their spot, Opal and Breanne on the couch and Momma and Mr. Dawson next to it. I held my breath with them all as Sarah stepped away from my side.

"Thanks for telling me," she began in a voice too soft to be hers. "I got upset—because—I have to tell you something, too."

With every sentence of her story, she gradually drew closer to the couch. By the end of it, she was sitting between Opal and Breanne. She didn't even cry like she had when she'd told me, and I took that as a relieving sign. Two simple words were exchanged between the four of us that brought us closer together than we'd ever been in our lives: "I understand."

Sarah stood, motioning for Breanne to do the same. That was when Sarah pulled her into a hug.

"This doesn't change anything," she whispered. "Nothing has changed. We haven't changed. Okay?"

Breanne nodded, exhaling with a sniff. "Right back at you."

"I'm glad we're all on the same page," Momma began, drawing me to her side, "because this is a serious matter that demands your greatest attention and care. If William is helping the Delphines now, he has to know about them."

"Meaning you've made another powerful enemy," Mr. Dawson added, leaning against the couch. "Recon is going to be our most valuable tool—as long as we're all in on it and we do it *well*."

—We need to figure out what their full plan is,— he told me. *—You*

know it has to do with your magic. Possibly even Adara.—

I immediately thought of Kamose and Annisa. I had to wonder what Alexa would do if she ever found out about them—about
how they were exactly like me.

"So, girls," Momma said firmly, regaining our attention, "stay
on guard. And promise me: no magic unless necessary."

CHAPTER

FOURTEEN

The vision about the Spanish boy came hard and fast that night, repeating details I'd already seen and taunting me with unknowns I was still trying to convince myself I didn't have to be afraid of. I was all the more confused on why he'd never approached me while we were in Barcelona. How did he expect us to meet in Spain if—?

Wait. No. That was it: the architecture was wrong. Pointed archways, stained glass windows, thin columns—the rich architecture of Spain—none of it had been in my visions. The architecture from my visions, on the other hand—high ceilings, intricate molding, decoration along the buildings...

...like the ones I was staring at now as I waited in line for the Louvre. French, Parisian. I guess there *are* perks to waiting in line and all you can do is observe the world around you. The down-side, though?

"Nice handoff, Miss Walker," Mr. Dawson said in my ear-piece. "It's your turn, Miss Marie."

Caroline smiled sweetly at me, strolling right on by in the packed square. I tightened my coat around myself and apologized to the people behind me in flustered French, using what Monsieur Goubeaux had already taught us in September. The silver band that Caroline had just pawned off to me warmed in my hand.

The only reason my friends and I were even allowed to be out and about by ourselves for this mission was that Mr. Dawson and Momma had a tracking device hidden in our coats to make sure they could get to us in time in case we were abducted. I stuffed the ring inside my coat pocket as the ticket agent handed me my entry ticket. The giant glass-paned pyramid sat before me in the midst of bustling locals and tourists, a medley of languages float-ing around me. I wanted to see the *Mona Lisa*, too, but that wasn't possible until I passed off the Minotaur's Ring to another Cal-listro Girl. That was why I'd followed Ava Baleen here—in case I'd need a target, and now I did.

I stepped through the entrance, entranced by the splendor of the main room alone. Tall walls of glazed stone stood all around me, a matching floor reflecting the sunlight casting its rays through the upside-down pyramid in the center of the room. The different sections spread out on four vast sides, transporting visi-tors to the different eras of the world.

My heart skipped a beat, and I grinned. *This is the Parisian Hall of Generations.*

Right—which side did Ava choose?

Recalling the girl's collection of Leonardo DaVinci prints she'd started collecting last semester, I decided that my safest bet was the Renaissance section.

Paintings by Raphael, Leonardo da Vinci, and Titian adorned the walls in neat rows all across the room. One line of people traced down the entire length of it: the Mona Lisa sat at the front of that line.

Hopefully I'll have time before we have to leave.

Most of these paintings, I was only familiar with because of Mr. Broadhurst's Renaissance module last year—but my awe and reverence was reserved for the textured details on the canvases now in front of me. I exhaled, gazing past the sea of shoulders and heads at the golden frames mounted on the walls. The Hall of Generations was a verbal tale of history, and the Louvre was its storybook pages. Almost literally: most of DaVinci's subjects were wielders. (Annisa was even able to confirm for me.)

A head of sunshine-blond, shoulder-length hair, with a fair face and baby-blue eyes, caught my gaze in front of *The Last Supper.* Ava examined the painting up close, her Tiffany-blue shopping bag hanging from her left hand.

Perfect.

I stepped forward. Ava turned around.

I paused, sighing in defeat. If I was going to get the ring in her bag without her noticing, the easiest way was with magic... and a distraction.

Sorry, Ava.

Weaving past a couple of people to have a clear view of her, I finally caught a glimpse of her feet. I waited until she was close enough to someone to trip her next step.

Her small frame flew forward. The black-coated stranger in front of her spun as she fell into him. The bag dropped with a papery echo lost to the waves of conversation and marveling.

With Ava lost in her superficial French exchange with the man, I kneeled to the cold stone floor and slid the ring inside her bag. The swarming crowd never ceased, letting me camouflage myself as I stood and Ava picked up the bag.

Her blue eyes rose to meet mine as she swept her hair to one side, pink lips that matched her sweater grinning. "Emma!"

"Hey, are you okay?" I asked.

"You saw that?" she asked awkwardly. "Geez. You're always coming to my rescue."

That night in the back alley of the mall with those three rotten teenage boys flashed across my memory. The leader, the leader who was a *wielder* and willing to...

I blinked it away before my rage could wake back up, maintaining my smile with Ava. "It's what I'm here for. Just wanted to make sure I could give you a hand..."

...off.

I gave her arm a gentle squeeze before continuing my walk. Mr. Dawson spoke proudly in my ear: "Smooth handoff, Miss Marie. Enjoy your time in Paris."

Sorry, Ava. No rescue this time.

I didn't risk a glance back at her. Now I could actually *enjoy* the Louvre; Ava couldn't pass the ring back to me, only to the remaining Callistro Girls who had yet to pass it off twice. Thanks to her, I was done with the hunt.

Finally—because a single painting in this section overtook an entire wall, and I'd spent all day needing a look: *The Wedding Feast at Cana* by Paolo Veronese, almost ten feet tall by almost forty feet wide. Approaching it, I could almost hear the clinking of glasses and faint echoes of laughter—probably thanks to the conversations singing all around me. A grand table, delicacies splattered across it, was the proud focus. From meats to fruits, my stomach growled and begged me to visit one of the cafés after this.

To have every moment of happiness frozen in time, I thought. *If only this trip could last. Without Alexa.*

I looked away from the painting and toward the *Mona Lisa.* A pair of dark-oak-brown eyes at the exit snagged my attention.

My heart skipped a beat. Spiky black hair, warm-brown skin, leather jacket. It was him!

I dropped the *Mona Lisa* from my mind and ran. With one tourist passing in front of me, he was gone.

I'm not letting him get away!

I weaved in and out of the crowd, barely able to excuse myself. The mural painted above me moved just as agonizingly slowly as I pushed my way to the doorway of the Renaissance section.

That head of black hair strolled down the main room of the Louvre, on his way to the escalators. He turned around and met my anxious gaze. His lips curved into a smirk as he turned back around and stepped onto the escalator. Next to him stood a large man in a dark-blue trench coat.

I muted my earpiece and pardoned myself in French as I made my way through, darting away from everyone accidentally shoving me to the side. When I looked back up at the rising escalator, I found the man in a blue trench coat. The boy, on the other hand, was gone.

Where did–? How?

I continued pushing forward in the crowd, begging to see the release of people in front of me. Finally, my foot met the bottom of the escalator, and I climbed on.

Every second dragged on like an eternity, one I had to restrain myself all the way through to not put a sleeping spell on everyone and climb the rest of the way up. I could only pray that the boy was still visible in Place des Pyramides as we arrived at ground level. I darted through the mob without another thought and to outside.

Okay. I know he wants me to follow him.

Those brown eyes struck me again at the end of the square. He was leaning against the corner of the building.

You're not going anywhere.

—Mira, amiga. Detrás de ti.—

I froze. Behind me? I turned, facing the Louvre.

Met with nothing, I spun back around to the edge of the square. The boy was gone.

My legs pumped across the square with new determination until I ran to the corner of the building he had just leaned against. It didn't matter that I hadn't seen him run down the sidewalk along the street; my instincts were on fire, and right now, in a battle of wits and magic, I had to trust those.

—Amiga, estoy detrás de ti.—

I skidded to a stop on the sidewalk just before colliding into a bicycle standing next to its owner, who was tying his shoe. I turned around, watching the corner of the building I'd just left, where the boy stood. Waiting for me with that cocky smirk.

How did he do that?

I started in his direction again, but then he disappeared around the corner in the Louvre's direction again.

–Detrás de ti.–

I mentally growled. *Again? How?*

I spun around. Past the bicyclist, the boy leaned against the building's crème wall. With his head coming up to the middle of the window, he looked to be my height.

Good. I can easily take him just in case.

I briskly began walking down the sidewalk, away from the square, when Mr. Dawson snapped in my ear, "Emma!"

The boy walked farther down the cobblestone and turned right, into what had to be an alley.

"What're you doing?" Mr. Dawson said. "It's like you're trying to avoid Alexa!"

"That's not funny," I shot back in a whisper.

"What're you doing?"

Well, I was going to tell him sooner or later. And if things went south, Momma would know not to pursue Alexa in trying to find me.

I started my way down the sidewalk and toward the alley. *–I think I just found someone like me, Annisa, and Kamose.–*

–What are you talking about? Who?–

–I'll tell you once I find out, if I may!–

I turned right into the cold alley the boy had disappeared down. He was gone.

How does he keep doing that?!

–Emma, if you're about to deal with a powerful magician––

I groaned to help tune Mr. Dawson out. *–If you don't trust me, trust Kamose. Moren told me Annisa was an ally. Kamose told me this* *boy isn't any different.—*

Nothing. I could only hope that meant what I needed it to as I left the alley and faced the direction of the Louvre again. Maybe I could catch the boy pulling the same trick, *whatever* he was doing.

There he was. Back down the sidewalk, smirking at me.

When I faced the alley again, a second later, he emerged from behind a pillar of decorative shrubs attached to the right wall.

That was it. *Twins.*

Looking behind me to see if anyone else had seen the cat-and-mouse game we were playing, and expecting the second boy to come up behind me, I stepped into the alleyway. The air immediately enveloped me in a humid, icy front, licking my skin with the cold. Cobblestone reflected the sound of my steps as the boy came to stand in the middle of the wide lane and faced me. The olive-green T-shirt under his leather jacket paired with his golden-brown skin in a perfect complement. His black ripped skinny jeans and black-and-red sneakers told me everything I needed to know about his style. Save for being a couple of inches shorter than me (and the fact that I couldn't look into his eyes without thinking about Jak), he was pretty cute.

Wait. I looked over my shoulder again. Nobody was behind me. Nobody that looked identical to him was approaching.

How did he do that...?

"*Entonces eres ella,*" the boy began in a silvery voice. "Adara."

This was him, the mage. But how had he managed to—?

I replied in Spanish, warily stepping forward. "Do you speak English?"

His grin softened with shyness, surprising me. "Not..." he said with a heavy accent, "not very well."

At least he knew the difference between "well" and "good" better than most Americans.

I stuck with Spanish. "No problem. So you're the mage. What's your name?"

"You don't trust me?" He gave me another cocky smirk, taking out a pair of black fingerless gloves and pulling one over his hand. "Didn't you have dreams about this moment, Adara?"

"You're stalking me?" I joked, crossing my arms. "Or is reading minds your impossible ability?"

He gloved his second hand, his smirk widening into a grin. "No. Let me show you." He closed the gap between us, holding out his hand and winking up at me. Never mind—he was two inches shorter. "If you can trust me."

Kamose had told me that he wasn't dangerous, and I trusted the nore—but I still needed information. "Before I go anywhere with you, I need a name."

"With pleasure." He squared his shoulders. Now the height difference tempted to amuse me; I'd never met a boy my age (assuming that he was) shorter than me—but I'd never met a lot of boys in general. "I am Azariah to the magic world. Alejandro Vidal to you."

Vidal... I'd never heard of his family like I'd never heard of Annisa's, the Mires, before. Needless to say, though, he was one of us—the most obvious reason being that he wasn't supposed to know who the name "Adara" belonged to.

It must've killed Kamose not being able to tell me why this boy wasn't a threat.

"Ready now?" Alejandro asked, shaking his hand slightly as if to remind me that he was still waiting for me to accept it.

"I know what to do if things take a bad turn," I told him, giving him my hand. The softness of his fingertips surprised me. I had to wonder if he was somehow *younger* than me.

"So do I," he told me, winking.

In the blink of an eye, when his ignited with amber, a sheer tunnel of magic enveloped us. Behind the wall of flowing waves and glimmering sparkles, the world whizzed by in a motion so fast that somehow showed the scenery yet blurred it all at once.

What was happening?!

After just a split second, we were in the front seat of a black sports car parked on a cobblestone street. This time, though, familiar Spanish architecture stood on both sides of us.

Not twins. Teleportation. No way. It's not—

I couldn't bother with that p-word again. We four were walking, living examples of impossibility.

"Do you like my magic trick?" Alejandro winked at me again, resting his hands on the black steering wheel. "How about we go for a drive?"

"I didn't say you could take me to another *country!*"

He chuckled. "Welcome to Valencia, Spain. Where did you think we would go when I took your hand? To our honeymoon?"

Oh no. He's as flirty as Jak, too.

I exhaled, gazing out the windshield. Pedestrians and tourists walked by, staring back at me for longer than any normal person would feel comfortable staring at someone; the windows were tinted. Dark. That meant this conversation was private, but the second it became *too* private, I was ready to wipe Alejandro's memory for the sake of stealing the car and driving to the nearest airport. (It'd be *pretty* cool to drive it, illegally or not.)

"We will make this quick," he began, leaning back in the fabric seat. "You seemed busy. Based on who contacted me so that I could find you, I want to see if you know how this conversation will go."

"Okay," I said, folding my hands in my lap. "You're Azariah, the magic world's mage, a one hundredth generation of your family and born into intense power. Your impossible ability is teleportation, and Kamose—I'm guessing—managed to get into contact with you and tell you that I'm here so that we could meet. You're destined to become the most powerful mage the world has ever seen. Am I missing anything?"

He nodded like he was satisfied with my analysis. "One of my friends knows who I am in the magic world. He's a druid and started having visions of the three of us meeting, sometimes in Barcelona, other times in Valencia, other times in Paris. Then we heard about the cruise stopping by in Barcelona, so I teleported us to where he dreamed of so we could find you. But you were with your friends, so it wasn't the right time to talk—and then when you left, I thought I'd lost my chance. When you told Kamose about your visions of me, he got my number with his powers, sent me the cruise's itinerary, and gave me your name."

I had to wonder if Kamose spoke Spanish or if he'd just used a translator, because I could see both possibilities. I also had to admit, the boy's powers were starting to scare me. He'd mentioned this summer that he had his limits, but I was starting to doubt if they were enough. What was stopping him from taking advantage of what he *could* do? What was stopping any of us?

"Well," I said, relaxing into my seat, "now that I've met you, we can add you to the group chat."

Alejandro's straight brows furrowed. "'Group chat'?"

I couldn't help but smile at the memory: "There's another one like us, Annisa. She and I started a group chat once we met Kamose. There's a clear pattern with us—we want to stick together until we figure out exactly what's going on."

"I'd be honored to join."

At the thought of my phone, the earpiece in my ear became twice as heavy—and I realized that I was *way* out of range for telepathy right now.

I took in a tight breath. "Okay, speaking of groups, I was doing a mission for my class, and my teacher is supposed to be able to communicate with me at all times. He's probably freaking out right now."

My main concern: getting back before Momma had a heart attack and *actually* started chasing me down. I highly doubted that my brief explanation to Mr. Dawson earlier would keep them both calm for long.

"This is an interesting school you go to."

I snickered. "I'll have to tell you about it sometime. Ask Kamose to add you to the group chat after you take me back."

Alejandro's gaze lingered on me for a second too long. "And here I thought we'd get to explore Valencia together. I'll take you back. Can I join your assignment?"

I rolled my eyes. "Sorry. Girls only. I don't think you'd fit in."

"They would like me, no?" he asked, rubbing his chin. "Maybe this trip is for new experiences."

"My mother is with us and happens to be the headmistress."

He laughed, running another hand through his hair. "Forgive me. I'll take you back now."

I gave him my hand at the same time my phone buzzed in my pocket. Through another tunnel of magic, we transported back to the cold yet humid cobblestone alleyway in Paris, a sharp difference to the car.

Alejandro released my hand, a little breathless. I was about to ask if he was okay, but he opened his mouth first. "You are an interesting girl, Adara," he said, smirking as he took a few steps back. "I hope to get to know you one day. I can take you anywhere in the world that you would like. Just let me know."

I wonder what his limitations are.

"'Emma'," I replied before he could teleport away. "That's my real name."

He winked. "I know."

C H A P T E R

FIFTEEN

Momma and Mr. Dawson sure had fun with their lecture about me going off to Spain with a total stranger—until it really settled in *how* I'd gotten to Spain. The only reason they weren't completely angry was because Alejandro was, we supposed, an ally—and we'd probably need to discuss things further with Dad and Aunt Becca, so getting upset right now was pointless.

The next afternoon passed in mostly a calm blur. My last memory as I lay on the couch the next afternoon was of the comforting presence of my friends while they chatted away about the plans for the evening. The quiet soon submerged me when their chatter eventually ceased and my mind slipped away. It reached a trough until a scream split it straight in half in my head.

"Leave me alone—!"

I opened my eyes. A haze settled over my dream-like vision. My head snapped in every direction, searching for something to help me escape the chair I was cuffed to. The cold of the empty concrete room swallowed me whole. I could almost hear a fuzzy static around me.

Flash.

The haze was gone.

"Wow."

That low, clear voice was sickeningly familiar. William Bleu strolled out from behind me. A pastel-yellow file rested in his hands. "Didn't mean to give you—"

Flash.

What's happening?

Alexa was pulling me through a fluorescently lit hallway resounding with screams and gunshots. Before I could hold a single thought, she threw me into a room on the left side and barreled after me, slamming the door shut behind us.

My voice was too afraid to be my own: "What're you—?"

Flash.

"I've sent as many targets there as we could," Alexa was saying, keeping a gun aimed at the door, "and if they—"

Flash.

Alexa's body slammed into me in the corner of the room as she kept her gun aimed. The door banged open. A gunshot followed. My body jolted. Another gunshot rang in my muffled hearing. Shouting ensued in front of me until—

"Emma!"

I shot up from the couch with a sharp gasp. Sarah jumped

back, retracting her hand. She was already dressed in jeans and her new winter coat she'd picked up in Athens.

"Are you okay?" she asked, dumbfounded. Breanne and Opal stood behind her, gawking at me with wide, concerned eyes.

Vision. Vision. That vision felt... familiar. There was something so wickedly familiar about it.

"Um..." I said groggily, wiping my eyes. "Thanks. I just had—the worst nightmare I've had in a while." I scanned my surroundings, orienting myself. "What time is it?"

"Time for us to go see Big Ben!" Sarah urged, taking my hands and pulling me up with little effort. "And Westminster Bridge! And the *London Eye!*"

Once again, she was way too excited on my behalf. Not even after today's mission could she bring herself to take a nap: Momma and Mr. Dawson had wanted to go all out and made all forty-five of us stop Momma from cutting off the propulsion and electrical power sources of the ship. We almost didn't make it because Teresa Darci forgot the thumb drive Breanne had programmed next to the devilled egg platter on the buffet in the main lobby. (It's a *long* story.) We had to conduct the mission relatively early in the morning to avoid as much foot traffic as possible, but that had left us with plenty of time to explore England.

The *Elina* was docked near Canvey Island, so those of us who wanted to visit London took the train. The girls and I only felt safe doing that because Momma was close to us the entire ride to the city. Alexa and Anthony had yet to make another appearance since the pool, which made our mission of spying on them—let alone conducting recon—a little more difficult than it needed to be. How were we supposed to spy on targets who weren't there?

They wanted us to know that they were there, yet they didn't want to show up to prove it?

The execution was too precise. Too intentional. If recon really was the only thing they were here for, there was something we were missing. They weren't doing it for *just* the sake of intel.

What were we missing?

"Did you know," Breanne chirped excitedly, snapping a picture of the clock tower looming high over us, "that 'Big Ben' actually refers to the bell *inside* the clock?"

Another pedestrian grazed shoulders with me, and I stepped closer to Momma. I almost wanted to believe that Alexa and William couldn't kidnap me here, but if they'd managed to do it at the carnival, London was probably not off the table.

"Cool, but we still need to go on the London Eye!" Sarah exclaimed, taking Breanne's wrist and pulling her close to avoid a little girl accidentally ramming into her. "The seats up there will be a *lot* less crowded than down here."

"I'd rather you all stay in my vicinity," Momma said, wrapping one arm around me. "The last time I let Emma out of my sight to ride a Ferris wheel..."

I hated that the same thing was on our minds. Because if Momma was thinking of it, too, I knew that I wasn't being dramatic.

"Then I'd rather go eat," Opal said, rubbing her arms as she hugged herself. "It's cold—and it's easier to see everyone in the room from the corner of a restaurant."

Agreed.

Big Ben inside the Elizabeth Tower struck two o'clock. The bustling tourists around us looked up in wonder.

"I've never heard a more beautiful ring." Breanne sighed wistfully, awe-filled gaze marveling at the clock. "I've waited my entire life to hear that."

Momma grinned, rubbing my shoulder. "Glad to have helped cross something off your bucket list. Opal has a point, if we eat right now, we'll still have time to walk Westminster Bridge."

Breanne gasped, her doe-like eyes lighting up. "Wyatt wanted pictures of that! Let's go!"

"*Food*," Opal whined, patting her stomach. "Please?"

Breanne politely rolled her eyes. "Fine. But I'm ordering extra dessert."

That meant that the girl was overly excited, but I couldn't blame her. I wanted her to enjoy every last bite of her chocolate trifle and custard crumble; as cruel as it sounds, I wanted her to savor every sweet moment of our time in London before it came falling down. I'd just had that nightmare of a vision a couple of hours ago, and Alexa had definitely been the cause of whatever had happened in it. I didn't like how many visions I was having this year that were coming true, because if that one was going to be one of them, I had no choice but to be ready for it.

But I *couldn't* be. We had a plan and it wasn't working because we couldn't even enact it—and just thinking those words made me realize that it was probably exactly what Alexa and William had planned on.

I couldn't stand being left alone in the dark. Couldn't stand how close we could be to figuring out what the pack was doing yet remaining so far from it. The sheer *need* to know was slowly consuming me, and fear trailed behind it as if trying to pull it back.

"You can prepare all you want for the end of the world, but it doesn't make it any less tragic. Sometimes there's more comfort in what you don't know than there is in what you do."

Mr. Dawson said that to me last year when he told me that he was a druid. The only thing that comforted me that afternoon as we walked into the nearest café was coming to understand in full what he'd meant. We were one in the same; at the very least, I wasn't alone in wanting to stay ignorant no matter how much I couldn't afford to.

CHAPTER

Sixteen

The Callistro Academy has classes on self-defense, MMA, coding and decoding, hacking, programming, overriding, advanced weaponry, nuclear chemistry, lock picking—everything a Hunter needs to know. The one class we *don't* have? Dance. Which really would've come in handy for the ball the *Elina* was throwing tonight.

Then again, I knew that dancing wouldn't be the point of tonight's assignment.

Nonetheless, thanks to tonight's royal ball theme, Sarah had us go all out. She'd slipped on a gown with a bejeweled bodice and red satin skirt. Her black waves were half up in a crown hairstyle, and she was four inches taller in her heels. If anything, I felt guilty that Adrien couldn't be there to dance with her tonight—it probably would've encouraged him to abandon the break they were on.

Breanne went much simpler despite Sarah's protesting with a yellow mermaid dress. Sarah did manage to put her hair into an elegant side bun, and Breanne and Opal got to match dresses, save for Opal's dark purple color and ornamented waistline.

For me, Sarah had picked out a white column dress with bedazzled sleeves. And then Momma made me curl my hair and gave Sarah permission to do a "tame" smoky eye on me. It was the most makeup I'd ever worn in my entire life, the most glamorous I'd ever looked, and I'd never felt more out of place. At least Breanne was more than happy to share the sentiment.

"Come on!" Sarah squealed, scurrying to the cabin door and pulling it open. Breanne, Opal, and I stumbled after her in our heels. "I wanna be the first one there before we have to start the assignment!"

"We have to wait for my mom and—"

"Wait for who?" Momma said in our bedroom doorway, right on cue with Mr. Dawson appearing in the cabin entrance.

And, well, I was thankful that my jaw wasn't the only one that dropped.

Mint is definitely my mother's color. A taffeta bodice met a bejeweled waistline transitioning to a lace skirt. Her brown hair was put up into a twist bun I'd never seen on her before. In fact, I'd never seen her look this... *hot* before. Forget the man in a navy-blue tuxedo standing in the doorway!

Full disclosure: I'd never seen Mr. Dawson in a tuxedo before this moment. Even on his date with Alexa this summer, he'd grabbed a casual suit—but a tux? With that jaw? With that gelled-back pompadour? Those bright yet deep-set eyes?

These two were going to have to stand far away from each other if they wanted to avoid dating rumors.

"You two look fantastic!" Sarah exclaimed next to me.

"So do you four." Momma grinned, strolling to the door. Mr. Dawson moved aside for her, and she nodded toward the hallway. "Shall we?"

⚓

A live orchestra played on the stage at the front of the auditorium. Round tables with white tablecloths lined the walls, and a yellow tint glowed around the room, probably because of the glazed wooden floor and mahogany paneling. A massive crystal chandelier almost too bright to admire hung in the center of the ceiling. There had to be at least three hundred people, each one dressed in either a gown, a tux, or waiter attire. The entire scene was a sight for sore eyes—and so were the Callistro Girls that met us at the back of the room a few minutes later.

"You all look stunning, ladies," Mr. Dawson began in the middle of the tight circle we'd surrounded him with. "Well done, that will help you with tonight's method acting test. In my pocket, I have an index card with a name, trait, and occupation. The second you get your card, you are no longer a Callistro Girl, but the girl in your hands, even to each other. Headmistress Marie, a few Hunters, and I will be monitoring you throughout the evening to keep track of your progress." He pulled out a deck of index cards from the inside pocket of his tuxedo jacket. "Once I hand you your card, the night begins."

One by one, he gave the inner ring of Callistro Girls their role. My friends stood next to me on the outermost circle, tightly crossing our arms over our chest—save for Sarah, who was ready to breeze through the night in a fantasy.

"I feel like such an idiot," Breanne whispered.

Sarah's perfectly shaped brows crinkled together. "Why?"

"I didn't even dress this glamorously for my aunt's wedding!"

"You look dazzling." Sarah lightly touched Breanne's exposed shoulder. "Wyatt would kill to see you right now. Just wait until he sees the photos."

"Stick to your role," Opal added, nudging Breanne's arm with her shoulder. "It'll get a lot easier."

"Good advice," Mr. Dawson said in front of us, holding out a card to Breanne. Immediately, he took our attention. "If you're fully invested in your cover, you'll forget how uncomfortable you are, Miss Shaw."

Breanne slowly released herself, reaching for the card.

"Don't show your friends," he warned, handing Sarah hers. "They should also forget who you are and learn about your new self as their covers."

He passed the last two cards to me and Opal. With a final smile, he ambled straight by us, leaving us to flip the cards around in our hands.

Carmela Jordan. Spontaneous. Private school teaching assistant.

I furrowed my brows and looked up at my friends, who were staring after the ballroom before us one by one. Did we really look old enough to have jobs and internships?

Sarah definitely does. But—

A blond boy with dark-green eyes approached Sarah, bowing

graciously once he stopped. "*Bonsoir, mademoiselle. M'accordez-vous cette danse?*"

Sarah's upturned eyes hardened on him, a frown pulling down her crimson-red lips. She held her head higher, turned to Opal, and then asked in an impeccable British accent, "Pardon me, miss, would you please take this for me?" She held out her notecard. "I've a gentleman requesting a dance."

"Oh, sure!" Opal exclaimed, eagerly taking the card from her. "Not at all, miss, go, have fun, dance!"

I almost forgot that the girl in the red gown was my best friend as she awkwardly eyed Opal. "Much appreciation, love. Thank you." She turned to the blond boy, whose narrow face highlighted the locked firmness of his jaw. "*Une danse. J'ai peur d'être occupé.*"

He *was* cute; there was no way that the real Sarah Duncan would give him just one dance. I was dying to know what was on her card.

Is she allowed to do this while dating Adrien? Or does being on a break let her dance as long as it's harmless fun?

Carmela. Right. Get into the mindset of Carmela.

Breanne briefly caught a glance with me before diverting her gaze, walking off to the side of the room with downcast eyes. Opal had already walked to a trash can by the back door, so I mindlessly searched for Momma as I walked deeper into the ballroom. I caught her mint dress in the shadows of the other side of the room. Against the wall, she held a glass of champagne. Her eyes eventually met mine, but she just as quickly returned to her evaluation.

Right. Proper mindset.

Tearing my gaze away, I took a deep breath. I faced the other side of the room. A tall, familiar man with dark hair sat at the table in front of me against the wall. He spoke to someone I'd never seen before.

Finishing his sentence, his round brown eyes landed on me with a smirk. My blood froze over.

No. Jak swore the real William was with him. He knew it was him, this can't be the real him!

But he was here—with all of my classmates.

My target was locked in sight for the first time in days and I couldn't grab my pack; the second I turned away, it was practically a guarantee, William would disappear.

He turned his attention back to the woman sitting next to him.

I felt myself backing away as if to take my opportunity to escape. *Why here? Why now? With everyone around? What are they planning to do?*

My training knew better than my heart did, which was booming across my torso and pumping blood so fast that I felt its rush under my skin. William glimpsed me again, and I took another step back. A tall man caught me when I stumbled, and I had to apologize to him in Spanish. He walked away with his company while I looked back at William and his. Who was sitting next to him? Someone he knew? A random passenger? Another Hunter he'd just happened to meet?

I needed a plan, I needed it now. Spy, recon, do anything that was part of the plan, grab the people who were supposed to spy on—!

Calm down. Calm down. They can't do anything, they wouldn't try anything here. We even have other Hunters watching, it's—it's fine...

Don't give them the mental victory, don't let them win. Don't let them break you. Spy right—

"Excuse me, miss," a Nordic accent behind me said. It took me a second too long to realize that I'd somehow meandered to the middle of the ballroom floor and bumped into someone.

My gaze met the one staring back at me. I stepped back. Those eyes were *purple.*

"I'm—so sorry," I said, forcing steadiness into my voice. "I wasn't looking, I'm sorry."

The boy lightly chuckled. "Round" encompassed everything about his face, from his jaw to his nose to his eye shape. "It's okay."

The second thing I noticed about him: he *towered* over me. The bottom of his chin was two inches away from the top of my head!

"The room is crowded," he said, helping me nail his accent: Swedish. "Are you on your way to take a break?"

Right. My friends were completely different people right now, and I had to be, too.

"No," I replied, monitoring my heart rate. Wait. Actually...

"Yes," I quickly said, "I'm—um, it's hot, I was... I actually don't know what I was doing. This is my first ball."

I didn't have a choice: I had to be Carmela Jordan while keeping track of William. I had two assignments over my head right now, and if I failed one, I'd fail them both.

I perked up, glancing all around. *Assignment. Mr. Dawson.*

—Can you hear me?—

"Welcome to your first ball," the boy in front of me said. "I have only been to a few. But I think it's a good warm in here, considering the weather outside."

—*Are you okay?*— Mr. Dawson replied.

I chuckled lightly with the Swedish boy, my mind conjuring a hundred different plans, each with a beginning but no middle or end. Hopefully the boy would leave after enough time spent in awkward silence.

—*William's here. Six o'clock from where I'm standing and facing now, I don't know if Alexa or Anthony are here.*—

"Sorry," I said, releasing an awkward laugh that was anything but fake. "I'm pretty out of my element, too."

—*I see him,*— Mr. Dawson said. —*Look, usually, I'd let you leave class and have myself or your mom escort you. But we need to play this carefully. You're the only one here with not just one, but two family members. We don't need the other girls suspecting favoritism. Focus on the assignment. I'll tell your mom and we'll keep watch.*—

That made me feel somewhat better... I was pretty sure.

"I understand," the boy told me in the same heavy accent. His purple eyes smiled down at me with his thin lips. "Well, you don't look it. You blend in nicely—um, in a great way, I promise."

The next laugh we shared made the situation feel *slightly* lighter.

Okay. Okay. Focus. Backup is on the case. Carmela. Carmela. Spontaneous. You're being graded.

I shrugged. "Well, that's relieving to hear. I wanted to try something different."

"You are doing great. Um,"—he extended a pale hand—"I'm Johan."

Carmela Jordan. Spontaneous. Wanted to try something different, prefers to go with the flow.

Got it. The second I opened my mouth to introduce myself, my rationality finally started overtaking me: "I'm Carmela. People usually call me 'Carmie'."

"That's a beautiful name," Johan said with a soft smile, sounding like he really meant it. He offered me his hand again. "Do you want to dance, Carmie?"

Every time I repeated the word "spontaneous" in my head, Carmela Jordan latched onto me a little more. In just a couple of seconds, I was able to grin and tell him, "Love to."

I took his hand, submerging myself into my cover completely. I had to, and not just for the grade: I needed to figure out how to switch between the cover and agent at the drop of a hat, to keep up the façade that could safe my life while also keeping tabs on the real world. This wasn't just an assignment, it was practice, and I was going to take advantage of that.

The song already playing faded to an end, and the audience applauded the orchestra. Johan leaned in to be heard over the clapping: "Do you know the waltz?"

"Show me," I told him.

As the applause faded, he took my right hand into his left. His other hand mindfully took my left wrist. "Keep this hand right here," he said, placing it on his shoulder. "His other hand rested on my lower back. "And take one step forward."

Emmalynn Marie could (vaguely) waltz. Carmela Jordan knew nothing about it. I did as I was told, allowing myself to fall under the hypnosis of Carmela's fascination with Swedish accents and purple eyes.

Is Carmela a magician? I asked myself. No, stupid question—

even pretending to be one would lead to unnecessary conflict with anyone from Callistro who might overhear.

"Follow my lead," Johan whispered. "Don't look down. Once you get into the rhythm, your feet will follow me."

The orchestra at the front of the room began a new song, and with it, we were waltzing. Our steps glided over the floor, like Carmela had a knack for picking up things quickly.

She does—I do. I'm a teaching assistant, after all.

I caught a glimpse of the right side of the room, at the table where I'd last seen William. There the man sat—observing.

"Isn't it easy?" Johan asked, a smile blooming on his face.

"Yeah," I replied thoughtfully, entranced by the purple that I'd only ever seen on one other human being in my life. "You're good at this."

"I've had practice."

I took a glance down at our steps and then at the table again before going back to Johan. William was still there.

—Jak would be disappointed, wouldn't he?—

Johan stumbled over my feet that had bolted themselves to the floor. Almost too late, I caught his arms and helped bring him upright. He asked me something that the man's voice echoing in my head blurred.

I can't explain how many thoughts, how many questions and doubts and fears, rolled through my mind like a car turning over and over again. So the man on the right side of the room *wasn't* William. I knew his voice, and I'd heard this telepathic voice before—

"Carmie?"

I blinked, my attention snapping back to reality. "Yeah, are you okay?"

"I was asking you that," Johan said. "Is something bothering you?"

A couple behind me grazed my back, which warned me to continue our waltz. I racked my mind for a response; that question had only one answer and a million reasons why it was "yes".

"It doesn't 'bother' me, but..."

Spontaneity. I had to keep up this cover for as long as the night lasted.

"Your eyes—you're a druid, aren't you?"

Johan grinned and took a quick glance down. "Yes."

At least he's supposedly safe here. Mom told us that the authorities wouldn't be necessary if we met wielders here.

"And the purple means you're gonna become a high priest one day, right?"

He shrugged with one shoulder. "I guess that's true. Why do you ask?"

"Just curious. Random question."

"You're from the United States, right?"

"Yes."

"Isn't magic outlawed everywhere there?"

"Yep. So any magician I meet, I never know I'm meeting one, you know?"

Johan hummed in thought, our bodies flowing effortlessly together across the dance floor as the song reached its second chorus. "So," he began, "you yourself are not one, I'm assuming."

I glanced at the people around us. Too many familiar faces nearby despite the vastness of the crowd, and I realized then how possible it was that they'd heard our conversation already. This lie had a bigger audience than just Johan right now.

I bit the inside of my bottom lip. At the table I'd last seen William—maybe Anthony—the woman he'd been talking to still sat, gazing at the dancing couples. "William", on the other hand, was gone.

"No, I'm not one," I replied, the lie all too familiar on my tongue. "I just—I, um, know about them, that's it."

With William's absence, anxiety was dismantling the wall of my cover story brick by brick. Never in my life had I fumbled that lie so dismally, but I didn't have time to pray that Johan hadn't seen through it.

—*Do you still have eyes?*— I asked Mr. Dawson.

—*He stood up and left,*— he replied from somewhere in the room. —*It's like he just wanted you to know that he was here.*—

—*Did he talk to you?*—

—*Made sure we made eye contact, but that was it.*—

Johan paused in front of me. "Are you actually a mortal?" he asked carefully. "Magic is legal here, you don't have to hide—"

"Shh," I instinctually mouthed, dropping Carmela from my mind like a rock in the water. I had to shut him up before anyone really did hear us, but there was *no* excusing that knee-jerk reaction with anything but the truth. My cover had been blown.

"You're trying to hide from someone, aren't you?" Johan whispered, a concerned divot bending his brows as he looked down at me.

Well, on the bright side, I didn't have to use my voice anymore: —*Yes. No one here can know I'm a magician.*—

Johan nodded, tightening his hold on me and reviving the steps of our waltz. —*Are you in danger despite magic being legal here?*—

—*The extremely short version is yes. I'm here on a class trip with my non-magician classmates. Someone I'd rather not meet is here, too. So can you keep dancing with me and avoid talking about... me?*—

Johan maintained his smile, lending me the courage to keep mine. "You don't typically like big parties, do you?" he said.

"Like I said, I wanted to try something new," I teased.

He promptly spun me, and I barely caught on in time. "You're picking it up well!"

Upon twirling back into our starting position, I caught a familiar figure in the corner of my eye: black hair in a crown hairstyle whirling as the French boy spun my laughing best friend. She said something about having a better time than she'd expected to have, and then she caught my stare. Those pear-green eyes didn't widen, but they were definitely demanding answers.

Before I knew it, Johan and I were coming to a stop. There were no lights directly on us, I wasn't wearing any tights or leggings underneath my dress, and my dress straps were only an inch wide, but another sudden wave of heat soared over my body. There's such a thing as too much blood in your head, and I was pretty sure that I was reaching that point as the auditorium clapped again for the orchestra and Johan took his hand out from mine. He brushed my hair out of my face, and I worried that he could feel the dewdrops of sweat beading on it. For some reason, his eyes kept glancing between mine. He placed his hand onto my waist, his eyes falling to my lips.

Oh no, I thought. *Please don't, no, don't*–

He cleared his throat, throwing on another smile. "You're a great dancer. Are you sure you haven't done this before? Maybe with someone else?"

It didn't take Hunter training to realize what he was really asking. It did take girl training to figure out how to reply to that—girl training that I did not have.

"Dancing closely with someone else, yes," I said before I could think about it. Which, I guess, meant that Carmela had said it for me. "Which is why I'm afraid that that has to be our last dance."

"Oh. I see," Johan said, at least *trying* to leash the disappointment in his words. He even smiled at me. "Well, you were a great dance partner. I hope we'll meet again before we arrive in Sweden."

He turned without another thought and disappeared into the crowd.

That was... different. The entire experience had been. It was honestly a little difficult for me to believe that Johan had been interested in dancing with me at all. Was the makeup really that powerful? I wasn't into him or anything, but I also couldn't help but wonder, what was he thinking right now? What did he really think about how I'd tried to keep a cover? What did he think about me lying to him?

Those questions were just easier to think about when a heavy hand landed on my back.

"2701 Cunningham Court, Forest City," whispered the same voice who had spoken to me telepathically tonight. That was Mr. Dawson's address.

Anthony. It *had* been Anthony.

A weighty, warm wool coat fell across my shoulders. He brought the hood up. "That's where we can find them if you don't follow me out to the deck, isn't it?"

—Mr. Dawson, he's here!—

—I know.—

What? He knew? Where was the man?!

—Just follow him, honey. Please.—

—Where's my mom, you have to get her!—

"Tick tock," Anthony whispered closer, "Miss Atera. Keep your head down."

—Just do what he says, Emma. You have to trust me, okay? All they can do is talk to you. Whether they realize it or not, they're giving you a chance to gather intel. You've trained for situations like this. Just stay calm. I know you can do it.—

Those words were all too familiar: the morning of the spring final, Momma had said something like that to me. She'd knowingly sent me out on that final because she'd believed in me. Mr. Dawson had that same faith in me right now—meaning he wouldn't send me out alone if he didn't believe I could navigate this and protect our family.

I have to do this. As much as I hated it, I had to do this.

My eyes fell to the wooden floor. None of my classmates were coming. Not even my best friends were coming. What had Alexa and William done? How had they managed to divert even Momma's attention long enough to—?

With a subtle shove from Anthony, my mind silenced every last question. I forced myself to take his offered arm and walk with him.

Just a few minutes ago, I'd struggled to successfully swap between the cover and the agent—yet in the space of a single breath, I'd gone from student to agent to hostage.

SEVENTEEN

"Thomas never disappoints," Alexa sang as I stepped onto the promenade deck.

A bolt of rage shot through me. I hadn't seen this woman since she'd bruised my arms, given me a concussion, fractured my ankle, and broken my ribs. Now she sat on a bench in front of me in a wool coat that matched the one on my shoulders, her gloved hands casually folded in her lap. Like old friends meeting for a chat.

Anthony's coat, as violently as it churned my stomach to know that I was wearing it, was the only thing keeping me warm in what felt like thirty-degree weather. That was probably the reason the deck was barren: no one in their right mind would loiter here in this weather, which made even more sense because neither person who had brought me here was in their right mind.

"Well, well, don't you look pretty?" Alexa's eyes beamed as they watched me approach, a puff of air betraying her every word. "You and I haven't gotten to chat in a long while, my dear."

"I was busy recovering after you hospitalized me," I spat, glancing at the empty bench across from her. I didn't want to sit and confirm my stay here; maybe if I stood, I'd leave faster.

I shook my head, scoffing. "I really wanted to believe you weren't psycho enough to follow us all the way here, waste all that time and money for the sake of a stupid chase."

"We don't need allies to have eyes." Alexa spoke innocently, like she was explaining who'd broken Mom's favorite vase. "All we need is intel. The day your tickets were booked was the day we booked ours. You should have known better."

"So, what, you wanna talk before William gets here?" I swallowed down the nausea that came from tightening Anthony's coat around me.

Alexa grinned like she was proud of me for figuring it out. To my disappointment, she gestured to the bench across from her. "Sit. Let me tell you about it."

I turned around, anticipating Anthony to shove me forward or pull me to the bench—but he wasn't there. How long had he not been there?

I forced myself to obey. Every resounding step on the deck was too loud, like it could alert any other Hunter in the area that I was here. Anthony's coat protected me from the cold wood of the bench as I sat, denying myself the comfort of leaning back.

"William isn't here," Alexa began, now situating her gloved hands between her crossed legs. She hadn't dressed up for the ball;

she had stuck with the coat, wedge boots, and dress pants. "He never was. You saw Anthony in the auditorium. William is stuck with one of my sisters, who's been switching appearances with me."

I was right. Jak had accidentally taken something that belonged to Alexa's sister.

And William had taken on Anthony's appearance at the ball when they'd switched—but the only way that was possible was if he had done so willingly. William was more than aware of the Delphine secret; he was flat out using it to his advantage. And he was maintaining his role as a behind-the-scenes Hunter. No wonder Jak couldn't tell the difference between the real and fake Alexa and William: he had had his real father all this time, the person he knew the best out of the entire pack and could actually pick up tells from if it wasn't really him. They'd picked the right Hunter to stay home.

"But William *can* hear you." Alexa smiled like she missed talking to me. "He says hi."

"Why is Anthony acting so shy now?" I said, restraining my bare, cold hands from stuffing themselves into the pockets of his coat.

"You wanna know a secret?"

I barely suppressed a scoff in time. It felt like we were talking in circles. She was replying to me, but she wasn't answering me. I wanted to turn around and go straight back into the auditorium, but Anthony's threat crawled in my mind: Mr. Dawson's address. They'd known it was a safe place for the Ateras since this summer, but now they were weaponizing it.

"He's staying in the shadows," Alexa told me. "You can't see him, but you know he's there. He's ready to do whatever he has to according to the circumstances. You know that, too. You just don't know when he'll attack or even if."

An anxious frost spread out from the center of my chest. That was exactly what *she* was doing.

"Do you get it now?"

She knew the answer to that. Why was she asking? Just to patronize me?

"I think we both don't have a lot of time," I stated, forcing steadiness into my voice. "My friends are gonna know what's up when they find my mom and Thomas. What do you want?"

Alexa grinned, the kind of grin I always saw from Momma whenever I did well on a practice hunt back at Callistro, or whenever I'd raised an A- to an A. "You've grown up so much. Smart girl. Fine, you win. You want to protect your friends, right?"

My mouth stayed shut. She already knew too much about my mental state regarding our cat-and-mouse game. She didn't know the extent of my desperation to protect my friends, and I definitely wasn't going to be stupid enough to give it to her.

I knew I'd made the right decision when she smirked: she could even read my silence.

"I can't help but be proud of you sometimes," she said, tilting her head. "You're right, that was a stupid question. What I meant was, let me give you the chance to protect them."

The uneasier I became, the stiller I remained no matter how deeply the cold was penetrating into my bones.

"It's the simplest hunt in the world," Alexa began. "When the prey gives way to the hunter. Sometimes the prey is even set free if they don't have anything of value to the predator. And all it takes is examination."

"Kidnapping," I said, correcting her.

She shook her head. "There's really no difference here."

I knew that all too well from the first week of my sophomore semester. My body succumbed to a shiver. I convinced myself that it was the breeze that had just blown past.

"So you want my friends to just give themselves to you?"

"Simple memory wipe. That's *all*," she said—tapping the air beside her right ear. A signal. William was listening in, and he wasn't supposed to know that Breanne and Opal were wielders.

So this call is part of the mission William thinks they're on. But why would Alexa protect my friends from him? He wouldn't actually send them, mere teenagers, to their deaths, would he? And if he wasn't supposed to know about my friends' magic, did that mean that he didn't know about mine?

"Their minds will be wiped of the Delphine secret." Alexa lowered her hand back to her lap like she had seen my understanding transpire. "And then they can carry on with their lives."

My rationality snapped back into focus: "they". *Their* lives.

"And your plan for me?"

"One step at a time. We're talking about your friends and how to protect them right now. I'm giving you a fair deal. What do you say?"

I say you're not telling me the full plan because William's on the other line. Which was too big a risk to gamble on: whether or not Alexa had been forced to have him listen in or if she wanted him to be. And as tempting as the offer was—a simple memory wipe—I knew that Alexa Delphine's magic wasn't safe in her own hands. As for Opal's magic... How was I supposed to trust what Alexa would do with that? How was I supposed to decide my best friends' fates for them?

Even if it was the right decision to make, it wasn't *my* decision to make.

"Just because I'm not fully trained doesn't mean I'm ignorant," I said. "It's not that simple. You're wasting time, what do you want? Why am I out here on their behalf?"

Alexa's eyes shed their softness, their pity for me. "You're not acting smart. Take the deal while we're being nice."

—*Take it,*— Anthony hissed, —*for their sakes. All of theirs.*—

For my family and my friends.

"Why am I out here and not any of them?" I asked again, my anxiety starting to chain my rationality.

"You're not in a position to ask questions, Emmalynn," Alexa replied, pushing her shoulder-length hair behind her right ear—the one with an earpiece. Another signal, a reminder. "I'd make sure that we're your friends' first stop when we get back to North Carolina. Am I understood?"

"Tell me why I'm making this decision for them." Somehow, despite his position in the shadows, I could feel Anthony's hands on my shoulders, holding me down on the bench as my feet itched to stand. "Stop treating me like I'm a dumb little girl, I know better!"

"If you did, you'd be on your way back downstairs right now," Alexa snapped, cold and firm in her position that hadn't shifted. "Are we seeing your friends at the airport in a few days, or is William sending out a team for—?"

"Time's up," boomed a deep voice that had pulled me out of the water more times than I could count in the last year. "Get up,

Emmalynn."

I looked to my left just as Mr. Dawson strode up, taking my hand and pulling me off the bench. His gaze, stuck on Alexa, burned with the same anger he'd had that early morning at the beach house.

Alexa leaped to her feet. "Where is my son—?"

"Sleeping spell, he's fine." Mr. Dawson pulled me behind him. "Your five minutes are up."

"I should've taken her stubbornness into account." Alexa stared straight at me from over Mr. Dawson's shoulder. "You've rubbed off on her."

"I gave you that time for both our sakes," Mr. Dawson stated, one arm partially barring me from stepping forward. "Now you're gonna leave us alone for the rest of the trip like you said."

I gawked. "She has an entire team ready to swarm your house for—!"

"She also knows they're not there."

The stream of tension was practically crackling between his and Alexa's eyes. I couldn't stop mine from glancing back and forth between them, daring either one to acknowledge me— acknowledge how lost I felt right now.

"I think William knows it, too," Mr. Dawson said.

—*He can hear you,*— I told him, whispering it as if Alexa could hear our telepathy.

—*I know. Or so she says. But I don't think they're actually ready to dox Tristan and Becca. The only way they could've found them at this point is with magic, and that would expose them as much as it would expose us.*—

Well, that offered me a *bit* of peace, but Alexa couldn't be bluffing about William listening in. Whether she was recording the whole thing or had Wi-Fi calling, she wouldn't have made sure that I didn't mention a word about Breanne's and Opal's magic.

Or was she just pretending...? Would she really go that far to make me believe such a small lie?

Alexa's gaze took another chance on me. Maybe she did see how lost I felt, how hopelessly desperate I was for any answer, because she sighed. Emerald-green eyes glowed with a softness I'd actually seen before—like she pitied me. I once made the mistake of calling it "compassion". That was before she sent me to the hospital.

"That was your plan?" I asked her. "Blackmail him into letting you take me so you could have some time to make your demands? You've been stalking us this whole trip just for this?"

"Here we go," she said tiredly, "the *mind games*. Don't you ever get tired of playing them, Emmalynn?"

"Don't you ever get tired of doing them?" I shot back. Mr. Dawson wrapped his arm around my shoulders like he was ready to run with me at a moment's notice.

"You know better. You should." To my surprise, Alexa lightly shook her head as if she couldn't believe that I'd even asked the question. Her gaze floated back to Mr. Dawson. "Tell me you still know me, Thomas. After high school. After this summer." She stopped. Like she really wanted him to hear her heart and soul when she said, "Tell me you still know me."

Either he didn't know what she was saying—or it was exactly because he knew that he didn't reply.

Maybe that's why Alexa gave up on him and came back to me. "Do you know me, Emmalynn?"

I thought I did. I thought Alexa was whoever she'd exposed herself to be behind the mask of Julia—she'd been doing recon on me back then, too. I thought Alexa was whoever she'd exposed herself to be on Mr. Dawson's sofa in his living room—that had been pure, unadulterated Alexandra Delphine, stripped of her past and decisions. At one point, I think those two people *had* been who she was—but she was far from both of them now.

"You know what?" she said, snapping back into her cover story. "I feel terrible. I want to give you some advice. Listen to me *very* carefully."

Mr. Dawson's grip on my shoulder never wavered, like he was warning me to be just as firm and resolute no matter what was about to come pouring out of this woman's mouth.

"The sheer *mental torture* of this industry is never in vain, no matter how long it lasts—as long as you follow its every rule. They always say to keep your friends close but somehow your enemies— our enemies—closer: in your circle of friends, even in your own *hometown*, you name it. Honestly, that didn't make sense to me for a while, until I became part of a pack: it's because your enemies in this industry always have all the answers. They have exactly what you're after. Keep your enemies close, get them right where you need them, win the prize. Wasn't even Robin Hood, a thief, con-sidered a hero by the people who really knew him? And the second you have your gold, you protect it, you store it somewhere not even your allies know about—because somehow, the people we trust most in this world with our money are complete strangers: at a bank, of all things. No matter how far away it is. For some people, it's not even in the *country*. Isn't that funny? But that's how it is. And it's not changing for anyone or anything. The sooner you accept that, the easier life gets. Trust me."

I hated it: I hated the instincts her words were raising up in me, the fact that the Hunter in me was telling me that she had embedded a code in there for me to decipher. She had the art of manipulation mastered to a fault. That was why she'd pretended to help me in the past, as Julia and even while trying to convince me that Opal should know the truth: to make me doubt what I knew. She wasn't my ally. She was my enemy, and she was keeping me as close as she could.

There was no code. She was laying her traps.

"You don't get it and you never will," Mr. Dawson said. With one step, he swiped his foot, tripping her and catching her arm as she fell. He threw himself over her body and twisted her arm behind her back, her other catching her fall. Mr. Dawson used his left knee against her back to pin her to the deck, using his free hand to pin her free arm.

I never thought the man had it in him after falling back in love with her this summer. But then again, he'd confessed to me in the hospital that he'd lost her all over again. Maybe that loss had been the one to break the chain.

"Listen to me, and listen closely, because it's the last time I'll ever speak to you," he spat. "As long as you and I are alive, this will never end. I've dedicated my life to the Ateras, you've dedicated yours to their end. Tug-of-war only ends when the other side falls. Let's both be wise enough to realize that and remember that I make good on my promises. I told Emma and Tristan to trust me in that beach house, and I flat out came back from the dead to fulfill that."

"Not the most traditional way to propose, Thomas."

Alexa winced as he shoved her arm farther up her back.

"I promise," he hissed, "the next time I see you around my family will be the last. I'm done being merciful, giving you every chance in the world to"—he scoffed, laughing at himself—"redeem yourself. You're a different woman from the one I could forgive. This is the last time I let you live. Trust me."

He shot to his feet, but Alexa didn't move. For some reason, I couldn't tear my eyes away from her as Mr. Dawson came to my side and wrapped his arm around my shoulders again, ready to pull me away. I didn't move. He said my name as if to signal me to go, but I stayed staring, watching. Waiting.

"You know me, Emma," Alexa said. She dared to look up at me, even as she lay on her stomach and at our mercy. And somehow, those emerald-green eyes sliced straight through a heartstring. "Don't you?"

I think they sliced me that night because there was one thing not even Alexa Delphine could feign: sincerity. That was why I'd believed her care when she was Julia. I'd believed her heart when she was memory rid.

But I didn't want to make the mistake of believing her again.

"Enjoy the cruise and leave us alone," I said. "Or you'll be flying back in the same state you left me in."

Turning around with Mr. Dawson, I shoved off Anthony's coat and let it fall to my feet. The frigid-cold air struck my skin like a knife blade, but neither I nor Mr. Dawson spared Anthony a glance as we walked past his sleeping body and started down the staircase below deck.

EIGHTEEN

Imagine having to break *that* news to your friends, who were already hesitant about spying on your mortal enemies because of how unpredictable they were. Especially since tonight in Sweden was our last night on the ship—as if Alexa was just waiting for the right time to strike and had saved the climax for the finale. For all we knew, she planned on taking over the farewell dinner tonight.

"Do we see them?" Breanne whispered that afternoon, glancing all around her as we entered the Blue Hall of the Stockholm City Hall. "Are they in disguise? Are they part of the group?"

The girl was doing little to satiate my anxiety—especially considering I'd had that vision again last night where I was somewhere underground with William, Alexa, and a hundred gunshots going off. Alexa was the last thing I wanted to think about right now.

"Bre," I whispered as the tour guide stopped the group in the middle of the ballroom. "You're drawing attention by asking."

"Okay, I'm sorry." She sighed, picking at the hair on her arms and staring back at the front of the group, where our tour guide continued citing facts about the Hall. Opal touched Breanne's shoulder as if to tell her that it was okay.

"...where the Nobel Prize Banquet is held. Over a thousand guests, including the Swedish royal family, are seated in this room, where they partake in one of the world's largest and most significant feasts of all time."

The floor was made of all sorts of different tile and stone, large crosses scattered throughout it. Archways supported by stone pillars lined the room, and we had been standing underneath a balcony with a stairway that ran half the width of the room, leading to the Golden Hall, our next spot on the tour. Small square windows sat below skinny rectangular ones and above the archways, an entire row of windows lining the top of the room. Our group snapped pictures, fantasized about eating at the Nobel Prize Banquet or holding their weddings there, and asked questions about the history of the architecture—and, finally, my friends and I were part of that normal group and doing the same thing.

"Ragnar Östberg," Breanne chimed, walking up to our tour guide. "He was the designer of the City Hall, right? And he designed the spire with the golden Three Crowns?"

Nothing, not even sweets, can distract the girl better than trivia.

"Correct!" The guide beamed, nodding curtly at her. "Did

you know that the Hall is built from approximately eight million bricks?"

She gasped, doe-like eyes widening. "You're kidding! So, would *you* say it's the quintessence of Sweden's national romanticism and prime example of the country's architecture?"

Sarah shook her head next to me and rolled her eyes. "Great to know she's easily distracted," she said, a chuckle escaping me and Opal. "But seriously, can you imagine having your wedding here?"

Wedding? I'm not entirely sure that Adara will have time for romance while trying to unite the world in an everlasting peace and acceptance, much less getting married.

"You're already thinking about that?" Opal asked.

"It takes a lot to plan," Sarah said defensively, "so I'm trying to make it easier on my future self."

"Aren't they supposed to be a two-party agreement thing?" I asked, subconsciously twirling my locket.

Sarah politely rolled her eyes. "I'm giving my fiancé *options*."

"Any more questions?" the tour guide called from the front of the group. When nobody raised their hand, he smiled and began walking to the stairway across the Hall. "Great. Please follow me, we will now explore Stockholm's municipal center, the highlight of the tour: the Golden Hall."

We walked up the steps and then down the balcony. I looked down at the main hall: the edges of the room were dark, hiding more doors and hallways that led to other rooms and areas of the building. I thought about how the place, as somewhat morbid as it sounds, would make a great venue for a murder-mystery party, maybe even a murder-mystery-themed wedding...

How did Sarah get me to start thinking about weddings?

A few more tourists were entering the hall out from under the archways that lined the room. It was just like Momma had taught us last year: sometimes, part of blending in is standing out—I couldn't help *but* notice the tourists who stopped in the archways and stood next to its side, some leaning against it, looking out at the Blue Hall and those of us on the balcony.

"Em?" Opal said, bringing my gaze to the side. "You okay?"

I inhaled, taking one last glance around the room. "It always feels like they're watching."

"Well, even if they are, they can't do anything," Sarah said, turning toward me and resting her hand on the stone banister. "We're untouchable even off the ship—"

"It doesn't *feel* like that," I said, facing her. "It's not like they'll stay away just because I told them to."

"Okay, and what will they do even if they do take us?" Sarah replied flatly. "Talk? Threaten us? If they want us to come with them after the cruise, that means they wanna keep us for more than a few minutes. William's in on things but doesn't know Bre and Opal have magic, so they need to follow protocol for a basic memory wipe anyway. That alone is gonna take a few hours. And then they have to extract their magic somehow without William knowing. Unless they found a much faster way to do it, they have no room to act while we're here."

"She's right," Momma said, gaining our attention. She came up the staircase sitting along the width of the room. Part of me couldn't help but relax a little. She was supposed to be tailing us to make sure that Alexa wasn't about to kidnap us; if she was walking up to us right now, we were safe. "You're virtually untouchable right now. Mr. Dawson is keeping track, too. Just stay alert like you're already supposed to be and keep your covers. We're okay."

Even though my mother had broken promises to me before, one thing still stood: she only ever made promises she knew were true. I had to trust her.

CHAPTER

NINETEEN

Before we knew it, we were getting ready for the farewell dinner for our last day in Sweden—our last night on the ship. We were almost done packing up, and we were getting ready to say goodbye to the *Elina*.

Momma left with Mr. Dawson while the girls and I took the "scenic route" to get to the dining hall. We wanted to enjoy our last walk to dinner on a cruise ship before we stepped off for the final time tomorrow morning. As we linked our arms into each other's and our dresses flounced with our every step, all we could focus on was the lavish architecture, furniture, and décor of the ship and the comforting company of each other.

Sarah sighed contently on my left. "I could've never pictured something like this for our junior trip."

"We're really going back to Capperson tomorrow," Opal murmured as we entered a foyer bustling with conversation and formally dressed passengers. "Do you know how many questions we're gonna get when we get back to the school?"

"Stop," Sarah said, holding up a hand, "my mind has forbidden school as a topic until we're back in North Carolina."

"We've had lessons for, like, a majority of the trip," I said flatly, enjoying how the plush red carpet carried each of my steps. "They just picked up school and put it somewhere else—"

In a snap, my group stopped in the dead center of the foyer—or, at least, Sarah, Opal, and I were pulled back when Breanne froze in her spot.

"What?" Sarah asked, but when she saw Breanne's stiff body, she followed her gaze to the left. That was where Anthony Delphine sat in a red armchair against the wall, dressed in a white button-up shirt and black slacks.

What is he doing here?

I looked ahead, trying to ignore him and force my friends forward. I wasn't allowed a single step before a woman rounded the corner of the entrance and strolled into the foyer.

The shoulder-length red hair that sent a chill down my back. The emerald-green eyes that had the power to freeze my blood. The smirk I hated with a passion that burned so strongly, it could start a forest fire.

In a navy-blue evening gown and clutching a golden handbag, Alexa strutted with poise. Her every step in our direction sucked me dry of confidence and let her absorb every drop for herself. She was taunting me with her title and power, daring me to move from my spot. Then, she stopped in the middle of the path. A sweet yet daunting smile played on her lips. I could practically hear what she was tacitly saying: she was calling me "darling" or "Atera", asking some kind of icebreaker that she didn't mean, trying to convince me that my family wasn't safe—or, more likely, that *we* weren't safe.

But we were in public. We weren't at their base. They couldn't do anything.

Alexa glanced in Anthony's direction and then nodded her head toward the exit of the foyer, where we'd just come from. I felt my friends stumble into me, sandwiching me as Anthony stood from the armchair and followed Alexa. She walked out of the foyer with him, leaving the four of us standing in the dead center of the room.

—*Enjoy your evening,*— said a familiar male voice. —*It's been quite the trip.*—

Sarah, Breanne, and Opal stayed silent beside me. Nobody knew how to move on. That was just as well.

—*What was that about? Just trying to scare us?*—

A couple of seconds ticked by. I could almost hear him chuckle. —*If you really think Grand Hunters will just tell you what or even if they're planning something, you have a lot more to learn.*—

"Now they're getting on my nerves," Sarah snapped, pulling us along with her down the foyer. "They know they can't do anything here!"

"*Here,*" Breanne urged. Sarah stopped to look at her—like she really wanted to hear Breanne's feeble voice whisper, "But we won't be here tomorrow."

⚓

"I encourage you, ladies," Mr. Dawson announced from the head of our table in the dining hall, "tonight, put school far out of your minds, eat, drink, and be merry. You've earned it." He raised his flute of sparkling cider, Momma following suit beside him. "It's been a fascinating couple of weeks, and I hope they provided an unforgettable experience—both personally and career-wise."

That was definitely one way of putting it.

"Cheers."

"Cheers!" my classmates chimed. My friends and I held up our own glasses of cider with them.

I set down my flute onto the dark-red tablecloth, grateful that I'd managed to grab the seat beside Momma tonight. (She was popular with our class, and understandably so.) Sarah sat next to me with Opal next to her and Breanne next to Opal, but while the rest of our class dug into the asparagus wrapped in prime rib on their plates, the four of us stayed tensely still in our cushioned chairs.

"Eat, honey," Momma whispered to me, picking up her golden fork and nudging my arm. "It'll get cold."

Evidently, seventeen years on this earth wasn't enough to convince my mother that I understood how leaving hot food out would cause a decrease in temperature.

I forced myself to pick up my fork. It wasn't right. Why had Alexa and Anthony shown up tonight in front of us? Pettiness? If they kidnapped us tonight, we'd be held hostage in Sweden, where magic was completely legal. They couldn't do anything to us here, only back home, where we were *heading*. Had it been just to ruin our night? Remind us of our place?

She wouldn't've given us a warning. I tried raising my bite to my mouth, but the mere smell of steak and asparagus swirled my stomach with nausea. I swallowed, setting my fork back down.

It hit me like a train that we'd technically had two carefree weeks of vacation available: Alexa and Anthony knew that they had no grounds, they always had, they'd known that while booking the tickets! Yet they'd booked them anyway? They couldn't have waited just two weeks for us to come back, when they could actually hunt us? They needed two weeks of recon? Since when? Why would they—?

—*Stressed?*—

The anxiety bubbling in my stomach rumbled into a boil. He was watching me right now.

I've already given too much away, I thought. If I did take this bite of grilled asparagus, I was going to gag it straight back up. Not even after the night of the dance did I know anything for certain. Nobody would tell me. Not unless I forced it out of them. But there was no way I could do that without exposing myself.

Why can I feel her staring at me right now?

—*Stop watching me.*—

—*Scared?*—

I gripped my fork, clenching my teeth. He knew was he was doing, and he was succeeding. I was giving him his victory.

—*Let's go for another round of magic, just you and me,*— he teased. —*It wasn't fair last time. Remember?*—

"Eat, Em," Sarah whispered beside me. "Someone's gonna ask what's wrong."

People are watching.

I shut my eyes. Forty-five pairs of eyes were on me. Forty-five girls were looking at me. The entire room was looking at me. That was what my mind kept telling me. Something was wrong. I couldn't stay here. I was too exposed here.

Momma's whisper warmed my ear. "What's wrong?"

Sarah was right.

I kept my eyes down. "I don't feel good."

"Do you need to go back to the cabin?"

I nodded.

She stood from her chair, allowing me the room to stand and walk away from the table with her. The only pair of eyes I caught was Mr. Dawson's, but I was pretty sure that even Sloane Moore, who was sitting all the way down at the other end of the table, was able to see us get up and start walking to the doors.

At least nobody else in the hall cared; everyone was dressed formally tonight and people came in and out all the time. It was my classmates I was embarrassed in front of. It was my friends I was worried about.

As we reached the ornate doorways, I felt Momma's hand land on my back. But as my mother guided me down the carpeted hall, a hundred red flags waved furiously in my chest. The way back to the suite was a blur. Muscle memory walked the way for me, Momma's guidance providing little assistance, until I tripped in my two-inch heels.

Why would you make me wear these, Sarah? I thought, ripping them off my feet in the main lobby. Momma continued her string of questions, every single one eliciting the same answer from me:

"Did the girls say something to you?"

"No."

"Do you want me to bring you something to eat in the room?"

"No."

"Are you okay?"

"No."

"Do you need me to stay in the room with you?"

She didn't stop asking questions until we reached our cabin's hallway.

I anxiously swiped my keycard, jiggling the knob until the light finally flashed green. Shoving the door open, I barreled into the room and furiously rubbed my eyes.

I just left them with Alexa and Anthony.

They're safe with everyone else, Mr. Dawson's there.

Does that mean I'm not safe here once Mom leaves?

My hands trembled in front of me as I brought them to my face. Every breath was echoing. My steps were mindless as I walked to the couch. What was happening? It'd been weeks since I'd last felt this, what was going on? Why was everything crumbling apart inside? What was happening?

I've felt this before.

I turned, my back sliding down the side of the couch. I don't know why, but the carpet was comfier. Sarah's hard work on my makeup was ruined almost instantly as tear after tear streamed down my cheeks and I continued rubbing my eyes.

Is this what they wanted? For me to snap? Was this what they were waiting for?

"Emmy," Momma said. I heard the door softly click shut behind her. "Come on. Talk to me."

Talk to her, tell her the truth. That was what I was supposed to do, right? Tell her that I'd seen Alexa and Anthony and didn't feel safe because their restrictions were coming to an end?

Why is this happening again?

I pressed my hands harder against my eyes until a throbbing pulsed under my palms.

A presence approached in front of me, kneeling down. Gentle hands took mine and slowly pulled them away from my face. I raised my gaze to a worried Momma, honey-like eyes red and shiny.

"You worry me when you act like this," she whispered. "And I don't know what to do to make it better."

I wished she *had* the ability to make it better.

I shut my eyes, embarrassed to face my mother in this state. I was bigger than this. I was better, stronger, I'd learned too much just to fall apart at the tiniest little thing!

"I haven't changed," I cried.

"What?"

"I'm still the same." Breaths came in gasps that threatened my tear-soaked words. I rubbed my eyes again before opening them to Momma, because I don't care if she sees me with mascara and eyeshadow streaked down my face, but I care if she sees me weaken. "My stupid—emotions got in the way of—my rationality, and... I couldn't—I couldn't stay—up anymore!"

"Honey..." The word sounded like a lullaby from her lips. She reached for my hands, taking them into hers before I could wipe away more of my makeup. "What are you talking about?"

"I saw them, we saw them tonight," I rasped, "and I don't know why, and we're going back home tomorrow, where we'll be vulnerable to them again—"

"No, sweetheart, stop thinking about that," she told me, squeezing my hands. "You've been strong for a really long time, okay? You've thought like a Hunter during this entire trip, you've stayed calm and rational throughout every encounter we've had with them. You've grown up a lot since this summer. Do you hear me?"

I did; I just wasn't sure if I believed her, if I could see everything she was saying.

"Did you see them while we were eating?"

I nodded. "I don't know why—just that—that one thing—sent me over the edge."

"You've been keeping strong for too long," she murmured, her thumbs rubbing my hands. "Everything was stacking and building up without you realizing it. It's okay, Emmy. Not even the best Hunter in the world is strong all the time. They actually choose not to be—because it's a death sentence."

The gentle words tried to land like a blanket over my mind, but too many wrinkles were left behind. The friction almost burned.

"Look at me."

I slowly dragged my eyes up to her nose.

"You don't have to be strong all the time," she whispered, slowly shaking her head. "Promise me."

For her sake—and mine—I forced myself to nod again.

Momma moved beside me and turned me into her. Her arms encompassed me in a firm, tender hug. And I sank into it.

Finally.

Finally. They were working again—her hugs, her arms of comfort. I could lean into them and hold her tighter and tighter until my strength gave out and my tears finally stopped. She could hold me for as long as I needed her to. And I really needed her to hold me.

"No matter what they want you to believe," she whispered, "you aren't helpless no matter where you are. If they're ready for us once we get back to Capperson, we'll be ready for them."

In that moment, it didn't even feel like I knew self-defense. I felt useless crying in my mother's arms, needing her to tell me that things were going to be okay—all the while my instincts told me otherwise, that things would only be okay if I knew how to fight back. But I didn't. Not in that moment. And that was why I resented my emotions and had suppressed them for as long as I could: they made me doubt what I knew, what would win the fight.

"Don't leave me," I managed to whisper. "Don't go."

Momma kissed the top of my head. "I won't. I'm right here. You have me for as long as you need me."

"I love you."

She rested her cheek against the top of my head. "I love you, too, honey."

CHAPTER TWENTY

You can hear things in the silence—it's a paradox, and it's true. I know because of the happy, soothing silence among our classmates as we drove back to Callistro, leaving room for thoughts about how excited we were to be home. Those happy thoughts turned into verbal cheers the second the vans parked in the driveway and we were all invited to take our suitcases from the back and walk inside from the cold afternoon.

The silence from my best friends, on the other hand, was anything but joy. Gratitude to be back in a battlefield that was at least familiar, more like.

I did see why Momma had left her final words to me at simply "In my room when you're done." After I stuck my suitcase in my dorm with Sarah, Breanne, and Opal, I went one floor down to meet Momma. Then, she quietly led me to the elevator—where she proceeded to take us down into the Hunter's Room.

At least it was afterschool hours; otherwise, it would have made sneaking into the secret underground passageways behind the Atera family tree in the Hall of Generations much more difficult.

"Dad!" I cried as Momma slid the opening behind us closed. I ran into his arms, wrapping mine around his neck.

"I missed you, kiddo." He regained his balance, reciprocating with equal affection and his famous dad quality. In the frigid underground passageways, they were that much more comforting.

"I thought..." I whispered. "I thought I was gonna—lose you."

"Lose me?" he asked, first to let go. "Why would you lose me?"

Because they had a team ready for you. Supposedly.

"I just..." I took a few seconds to gaze into his icy-blue eyes, to study his square chin and rugged features. For a second, I almost saw the man who'd just freed himself from the zip ties down in the beach house basement. "I always think I'm about to lose you. Alexa and Anthony were on the ship, I didn't know if they'd come for you guys while we were gone or if they planned on taking you—"

"No, honey." Dad soothed me with his signature fatherly tone. "Nothing happened."

"Your auntie's still alive, too, by the way," Aunt Becca said behind him, holding out her arms. "Any day now."

In all honesty, I didn't even remember seeing her when Momma, Mr. Dawson, and I first walked in—but I didn't dare bring it up as I reached for her arm. I yanked her toward me, pulling her into a tight embrace.

"All right!" she exclaimed. "I could get used to this, you should go away more often."

"I was worried about you, too," I told her with squished cheeks.

"Uh huh," she teased. "I could tell from the hundreds of messages you sent me. Especially about the evil woman and her little boy on a leash."

"Becca." Momma rolled her eyes. "I kept you guys perfectly updated."

I didn't—that was what Auntie was complaining about.

Looking back, it felt like a lot more had happened on the cruise than I'd initially thought. Meeting Alejandro, Sarah getting onto Alexa's list because she knew what the rest of us did, Jak's family stalking us for the entire trip—but I didn't have to rip off the Band-Aid alone this time, and that offered a lot more courage to hide in the background and let Momma and Mr. Dawson take care of it.

What tripped up Dad and Auntie the most, surprisingly, wasn't Sarah knowing about the Delphines, wasn't Alexa stalking us, but Alejandro.

"I'm not the only one thinking how freaky this is, right?" Aunt Becca remarked, crossing her arms. "Is it not a little terrifying to anyone else that we officially have a group of kids doing impossible things with magic because they were born with these superpowers?"

"No, it's definitely freaky," Momma replied, nodding like she'd been thinking about this for the better half of her life. "Even freakier that Emma's just collecting them like baseball cards."

"I guess it—makes sense," Mr. Dawson remarked, taking our attention. He shrugged. "I never said Emma was meant to 'save the world' on her own."

The pause in the room swelled with realization.

"Okay," Dad said after a couple of seconds. "So these kids are good."

"As long as they believe in what they're meant to do," Mr. Dawson replied.

The words landed heavily on me for some reason. It was hard to believe that our world, full of people ready to jump the gun—literally—and kill anyone they didn't trust, could possess people who believed in a cause for good. People that weren't us, at least.

"The Alexa thing still throws me off," Dad began. "Especially since Jak saw his parents walking around like normal and talking to him the same way. But if Alexa knew she was going to reveal herself to you guys, why would the decoy need to be so convincing to Jak?"

"Correct me if I'm wrong, but…" Aunt Becca mused, like she couldn't even believe herself, "it almost sounds like it was a ploy for *Jak*, if nothing else."

The words curdled in my mind: something about them was so vaguely, so discreetly familiar, but why? Some kind of connection was hanging off of them, missing the other link. Why did a hypothetical situation sound so familiar?

"How much did they get out of conducting recon?" Dad asked, holding himself next to Momma and not daring to lean against the frigid cobblestone wall.

Mr. Dawson sighed through his nose. "Just about everything

they were looking for."

Auntie tightened her cardigan around herself like she'd been exposed. "What about on us?"

Nobody wanted to answer that. If we were right about Alexa and Anthony conducting recon in Europe, it was the perfect distraction while William and the team back home gathered intel on the family. Which they seemed to do when they had a team ready—that was the hardest part to confess.

"Did you ever use the safe room at my house?" Mr. Dawson asked. "Or my house at all?"

"Didn't have to, no," Dad replied.

"Alexa did threaten to send the pack after you both," Mr. Dawson said. "But it was specifically to my house. So she had to be bluffing. "

"But why?" Momma asked, scoffing. "It's so... pointless."

A lot of things Alexa had done over the trip seemed that way. I think everyone's minds were echoing that, because silence trailed after Momma's statement for longer than I was expecting.

"What do we do?" I asked.

"Move again?" Dad replied tiredly, wrapping one arm around Momma's waist. "Are we really safe staying at the apartment? Threatening Thomas's house could've just been a bluff for knowing our actual address."

"So we continue staying in one place without ever seeing the light of day," Aunt Becca mumbled bitterly, her eyes downcast. "Got it."

Mr. Dawson released a heavy sigh. "I know you're tired of the living situation, but it's temporary. And we're making the absolute most of it until you can settle."

"Right." Auntie kicked at an invisible stone on the concrete, meandering to the left side of the passageway. "Sounds like a plan. Make the most out of the most dangerous situation of our lives."

Mr. Dawson could only manage a shrug. "Happy Halloween," he muttered.

⚓

It unnerved me, but I had to be grateful that all was quiet the next day. That wasn't just because Momma and I had to be quiet as Steven guided us down the main hallway of his house because Cara had just put Baby Samuel to sleep. I cringed with every step that seemed to resonate throughout the tall ceilings of the house, almost anticipating a fragile cry after each one.

The hallway opened up into the large space with the kitchen on our left and the living room across from it. Cara sat on the white leather sofa, holding her sleeping newborn.

I whispered my awe, tiptoeing closer like any one of my steps would shatter the scene in front of me. "I can't believe it."

"I know." Cara grinned at us before taking her tender gaze back to her baby. "He's so perfect."

"He's amazing," Momma crooned, her hands resting on my shoulders as we came to stand at the sofa. "Congratulations, honey. How are you feeling?"

Cara's body shook with a quiet laugh. "So exhausted." Her arms gently rocked the baby as I took a careful seat next to her, Momma sitting on the arm of the sofa. "I barely have an idea when breakfast, lunch, or dinner is anymore, haven't slept for more than two consecutive hours in two weeks, and—I'm mentally all over the place right now."

"The warning *definitely* would've been nice," Momma teased, squeezing my shoulder. "But it's always worth it."

"It is." Cara used a slender hand to brush her fawn hair out of her face. Then her gray eyes met me, and my heart skipped a beat with anticipation. "Do you want to hold him, Emma?"

Up until that point, I'd *never* held a baby before; it's not like I'd had any chances to (I'd never even been outside of Capperson before last year), but I'd always been curious about what it was like to hold someone so... small. Needless to say, I was nervous as I glanced between Momma, Steven, and then Cara before asking, "Can I?"

Cara sat up a little straighter and brought Samuel away from her body. She slowly put him into my outstretched arms.

"Support his head," she told me as Momma positioned my hands and arms. Samuel's head rested on the crease of my arm while his tiny, warm body lay against my chest. He was even smaller than he looked, smaller than I could've prepared myself for... He *was* perfect.

"There you go, honey," Momma whispered.

With smooth brown skin and puckered-out cheeks, he had a full head of dark-brown hair, and his closed eyes highlighted how long and thick his eyelashes were. "Adorable" didn't begin to describe him—and I felt something brand new awaken in me the longer I stared at his face, the longer I felt his weight in my hold.

"Momma," I whispered, "I want one."

She gently smacked me, shared a subdued laugh with Cara and Steven. "We're not having this conversation."

"In ten years, sure," Steven said, walking to stand next to

Momma. "We'll let you, um, babysit Sam until then. Then you can decide if you still want one."

"Babies are adorable and fun as long as they're not yours," Cara added. "He's the best thing to ever happen to me, but I know the road is long from here on out."

Samuel made a few coos as he slept, and I realized that that was the only thing I could hear. Everyone's eyes were on him, on me holding him, and I'd never felt more like a little kid in my life.

I loved it; it was the most normal I'd felt in a *long* time. The most normal anything had felt in an even longer time.

Even though little Samuel couldn't understand telepathy yet, it felt like instinct when I told him, —*I promise I'll make this world a better place for you.*—

Never before had I believed in myself more than I did in that moment. Never before had I so desperately wanted to accomplish my fate as Adara. There was something about Samuel's clean slate, about his lack of exposure to the cruel truth of the world regarding what he was, that restored my determination and belief. If anything, especially after everything swarming me and my family then, he was a reminder—a much-needed reminder of who *I* was and was working harder and harder every day to become.

CHAPTER

Twenty-One

It'd only been a couple of weeks since I'd last seen him, but Jak still sparked something in my chest when I found him sitting on a bench in the pristine lounge area behind some of Capperson's stores and businesses. I didn't want to admit to myself the last time I'd been here—with Nolan—so that spark shared an equally exciting and nauseating burn.

"Hey."

He looked over his shoulder, his smile lighting up the air. I instantly shared it as he got up and met me at the bench. My arms reached up for his neck, and his wrapped around me in a comforting warmth I hadn't realized I'd craved throughout the cruise. Firm and snug against my body. Subtle, musky cologne piqued my nose, and I held on tighter to him, letting the butterflies have their fun in my stomach.

"Next time, take me with you," he said, letting me go. He took my hand and led me to the bench. "How was it?"

"Well, awesome. Fantastic. Except for—what we're here for."

Jak leaned back in his spot, hanging an arm over the top of the bench. "Yeah. If only we were normal. I could've invited you over to my place to have this conversation."

I realized then that he was in the exact same seat Nolan had taken the night he'd confronted me about me stringing him along—the night he'd seen through every lie I'd ever told him and uncovered my identity as a wielder.

I twiddled my thumbs and bit my lip. For some reason, the situation just felt too familiar to that night.

"Apparently my place would've been a better option," Jak added curiously, leaning forward to better look at me. He softly nudged me. "What's wrong, Merlin?"

Even though I was there to update him over what had happened the past two weeks with the whole Alexa-cloning-herself thing, I wasn't nervous about that. I couldn't be nervous; with Jak knowing as much as my family did, I couldn't help but... adopt him somehow into a deeper part of my life beyond friendship. We could talk to each other openly, and he was the only one who wasn't a family member that I *could* do that with.

"Bad memories," I admitted, gaze stuck on my thumbs. Because Jak knew, and that made me completely vulnerable to him. "I haven't been here since... the last time I talked to Nolan."

In my peripheral vision, Jak's brown eyes stared carefully, thoughtfully. "I haven't heard about him in a while," he finally said.

It's been almost three months.

The beginning of November so far had been calm. Too calm. It gave me too much time to soak in what memories I'd yet to fully process.

"You're not gonna hear about him again," I eventually said, exhaling as I straightened and resting my hands on my knees. "Go ahead, give me your updates from last month."

"We don't have to talk here, Merlin," Jak murmured, eyes as soft as his voice.

"No, we do." My frustration—and, for some reason, helplessness—was mounting. "We can't go to your place and we can't go to mine in case someone wants to track you there and find you-know-who, and it's private back here."

"You're not comfortable here," he replied, like he was insistent on convincing me. He held out his hand. "Don't do this to yourself, come on."

I stared down at his offer. Just stared because I couldn't take that.

When Jak saw that, he laid his hand on the center of my back. "What's wrong?"

Because somehow, Jakson Bleu knows me to the extent that he can read when I actually do want to open up—no matter how hard I try to shut myself off.

"I erased his memory here," I finally said, slouching and twiddling my thumbs. "I made him forget me."

Silence prevailed for a few excruciating seconds.

He finally asked, "It was... easier?"

"He figured out who I was."

Jak's hand on my back flinched for a split second. Then, like he'd recovered, his thumb started rubbing me.

"I didn't even have the ability to lie to him anymore," I said, tears impeding on my voice. "He saw straight through them. He wouldn't believe any of them. He just knew. And he didn't... *care*."

Despite how a tear was rolling down my hot cheek, despite how red I knew my eyes were, I still raised them to meet Jak's. "I made him forget me like I did with Alexa."

Accidentally, I didn't add. Because I honestly believe that a part of me *had* done it on purpose because it was easier, even if just subconsciously. Especially in that moment, I was torn on how to interpret that.

"We don't have to stay here," Jak repeated softly.

He dropped "Merlin".

My eyes traced the way his dark-brown hair went down to his ears and curled upward at the tips. I'd become so fond of that signature trait, so fond of everything unique about him and just— him.

A shaky breath went through me. "I wanna replace it with a good memory."

He breathily chuckled. "I'm not sure this conversation is gonna lead to a good memory, Merlin."

There it is. Good. Okay.

"I know it's not gonna end in an argument. Or me erasing your memory of me."

A smile parted his lips. "Have you ever made me forget anything before? Is that why I fall for you as if for the first time every single day?"

This boy managed a stupid giggle out of me with that one, no matter how ridiculously cheesy it was. And yet, anxiety bred like bacteria in my chest at the words, my knee instinctually bouncing, like I *needed* him to know that I hadn't and would never do that to him.

Now I didn't know if his question was genuine or just part of the pick-up line—which made it easier to answer seriously.

He's good. He knows what he's doing.

"I've wanted to," I admitted, gripping the edge of the bench. "But obviously my mom told me that that's a spell I have to have strict self-control over. I don't... we don't like to invade someone's boundaries like that unless it's life or death."

Like Opal finding out about me in the forest. Or Nolan knowing about me with his father being a Hunter. Or Alexa being... Alexa.

"And you can't say things like that anymore," I said, returning my gaze to Jak. "You know—"

He held up a light-brown hand, nodding. "I know."

I took a deep breath. "Tell me what happened."

He shrugged. "Alexa and William did quite literally nothing the entire month except logistics and paperwork."

I turned my body to completely face him. This story would be long, but I needed the results. I ran through Alexa and Anthony watching us the whole time, them confronting us that night demanding that my friends come back to North Carolina with him, and even (as terrible as my recap was) Alexa's bizarre riddle speech—which Jak straightened for.

A divot formed between his brows. "That sounds like... code or something."

I paused, questioning if I'd actually heard the words or if my brain was only giving me what I wanted. "Really?"

Because I knew better: if those words were code, they were a warning. They were too kind to be anything but, but the Delphines didn't warn their prey. No Hunter did.

"Maybe to my dad," Jak mused. "If he was listening in."

I tried to translate the words as such, but the pieces didn't fit. Right puzzle, wrong pieces.

"But why mess with us at all, like you said, if they were just gonna reveal themselves?" I asked, grabbing the reins. "Why would they need to trick you if they knew they didn't have any power overseas? Why *did* William listen in if the conversation wasn't gonna have any results, why did they need to tell me that they wanted my friends to go with them after the trip was over? What was the point of them coming at all?"

Maybe I'd knocked down his pride or something, because all I could hear in his silence was hesitance to say anything, like he didn't want me to prove that he'd been wrong about something.

"I don't know what to say," he told me.

"Alexa says they bought their tickets when the junior class's tickets were bought, so they had this planned from the get-go. But was the *point?* Why would they just stare and make us think in circles and... do so many things that were just pointless?"

"I don't know."

It was the least I'd heard Jakson Bleu say in a two-minute period, and yet it was the most he'd ever told me before. Slowly but surely, he was becoming more and more like me the deeper he was integrated in the situation: worried. Maybe even scared. The one mole we had, that we depended on for insider intel, was defenseless against the unknown.

Yet at the same time, it had never felt more like we were in it together.

"It's—torture," he said next, almost surprising me. "You know it's not for nothing, but that's the only piece you have. Piecing it together is just mental torture."

Mental torture.

The very first sentence of Alexa's riddle resonated in my memory like the metal keys on a vibraphone. Code. But code for what? There wasn't *any* alternate universe or dimension where this woman would try to warn us, let alone *help* us! Had it just been for William, after all? Some kind of plan she was initiating phase one of—?

Had it been for both of us?

This is *torture.* I couldn't take it, and I definitely couldn't figure it out on my own; I turned to Jak. "Do you think...? Is there a way for you to get answers? Any kind of answers, anything?"

He released a heavy sigh and leaned forward, folding his hands together. "I'll definitely try."

Without a doubt now, it was the most he'd ever told me before: saying he would try instead of giving a definite answer meant he was intimidated. Jakson Bleu simply doesn't get intimidated unless he's convinced that the situation is slipping out of his control—which, I'd realized, was just as important as mine. We needed to hold on for as long as we could.

Twenty-Two

"Now that we're on the second week of November," Mr. Dawson announced from the front of his classroom, "we're roughly halfway through the semester. That means your training advances from here on out."

Our classroom of nine remained still and untouched.

He folded his hands in his lap. "It's finally time that you ladies start fully submerging yourself into the mental aspect of hunting. Your physical training was easy and only half the battle. After the cruise you had to relax your mind—"

HA, right. That's what it did.

"—you're hopefully prepared for the next part of your training. Which is, arguably, the most grueling part of it."

He stood and turned to the whiteboard behind him. Picking

up the dark-blue marker, the tapping of its tip softly pattered across the crimson room as he wrote.

"Today, ladies, I want to dive deeper..." Mr. Dawson began, blocking whatever he was writing, "into the art of recon."

I remembered him saying back in September that this was his lesson plan for this month. Still, I regretted that he couldn't have pulled this up *before* the cruise.

He set down the marker in the silver lip of the whiteboard, stepping aside. The word was written in all caps in the center of the board. "Reconnaissance is often interchangeable with spying in the Hunter game—except it's conducted on a much more individual and, therefore, mental level. It's the very first step you'll take for every single mission you're assigned, hence your first lesson in mastering the mental training of the industry. And the best way to master recon on your targets is to master your mental game to play *with* your targets.

"Let's talk about the Faddian case." Mr. Dawson walked down from the platform and to the right side of the room. "Miss Baker," he said, passing Amelia's seat in the first row, "remind us what happened to the Faddian family in April this year."

Amelia straightened in her seat, keeping her eyes on the whiteboard. "The Faddians were arrested in a magician hideout they'd built in Kingsport."

"How, Miss Moore?"

Sloane, on the other hand, stayed slouching as he passed her in the last row. She pushed her black hair behind her ear, brown eyes on the table. "I'm gonna propose through recon."

Mr. Dawson raised his head, clasping his hands behind his back. His eyes closed in disappointment at Sloane's usual apathy, but he continued strolling down the back wall of the room. "Care to elaborate for her, Miss Shaw?"

Super natural way to have this conversation.

"Establishing operatives at frequented locations to gather intel on the target's vulnerabilities?"

It was one of the only times in her life that I'd heard Breanne Shaw answer a teacher's question unsurely.

"And when Dante Faddian found out that he'd been followed into the hideout that morning to be captured, what Grand Hunter tactic did they use against him and why, Miss Marie?"

"The phantom circle because they found out he was superstitious and terrified of ghosts. When he realized it was a trap, it was too late."

Something about my own words resonated across my head. I think that was why Mr. Dawson reserved a few seconds after my answer, because all I could hear was the echo:

When he realized it was a trap, it was too late.

The trap. When Grand Hunters are conducting recon, they're laying a trap. We had to find the trap.

Mental torture... Alexa had specifically alluded to that—flat out stated it—on the cruise. Like mental torture was...

I looked up from the dark-gray table as Mr. Dawson walked down the other side of the room now. He eyed me for only a moment.

—*Understood?*—

—*Loud and clear,*— I replied, glimpsing Breanne beside me as if for confirmation.

I was sick of waiting for the pack to give us something to react to—sick of doing *nothing*. We were back on hunting grounds; they were free to do whatever they wanted, but so were we. And we were going to use *our* medium for recon. With Mr. Dawson's lesson and what Jak had already said, I was pretty sure I knew the first step of the pack's game. The second Jak gave us our next piece of intel, we were going to fight first.

That's the only thing we're allowed to do at this point. No exceptions.

It was like Alexa and William had been secretly listening in on the class—because after that, a whole week passed without any sign of them. Or, rather, I should say that *another* week passed without any sign of them. But if their first step was playing a mind game, my group agreed that fighting back at the first lick of intel was best.

Unfortunately, that was just the problem: Jak didn't have anything to report back on. And it wasn't like we were going to barge into Redway Academy and demand what was up. According to Jak, their biggest concerns that week were filing paperwork from their last hunt, communicating with the agency for their next one, and making sure that Jak didn't get in the way.

Obviously, we all knew better than to believe that—especially since, at this point, we were pretty sure that *most* of the pack was made of Delphines.

I knocked on Momma's office door Friday afternoon. I would've complained more about the "no phones" rule at Callistro if it weren't for that meaning I had to go see her every time I had to make a call. Jak had left my emails un-replied to for three days now; I didn't feel that guilty this time around.

"My favorite Callistro Girl." Momma smiled from her desk as I walked into her office and shut the door. "Who do you need to call?"

I gave her a tight smile. "Jak."

"You're not secretly dating, are you?" she asked in a warning tone, picking up the office landline and holding it up to me.

I rolled my eyes. "No. We already said we wouldn't."

Until this all blows over, I didn't add. Because she'd probably never let me hear the end of that.

"Good. Do you want privacy?"

I shook my head as I dialed his number. "It's nothing that I wouldn't tell you about later, anyway."

She turned to her desktop monitor and rested her hand on the mouse, back to work.

I waited for several dial tones before getting Jak's voicemail. Then I pressed the hang-up button and redialed.

At the end of the third round, even Momma looked up from her work. "He's certainly busy."

"He usually isn't..."

"The boy has a life, Emmy," she assured me. "Come back in an hour."

That was one of the reasons I *didn't* like having to go to Momma to make a phone call: when the person I was trying to contact didn't pick up. Especially when it was so out of character for Jak—he never took longer than half a day to get back to me, *one* time a day, forget three. And to not even pick up his phone anymore...?

My fingers were almost tempted to dial again—but according to Sarah, four times is clingy even when you *are* dating.

Except, she had that same opinion for me going to call him at all today, as she made obvious when I came back to our dorm faster than expected and she said, "Decided to take my advice, after all?"

I rolled my eyes, leaning against the closed door. She braided Opal's hair on her bed, and Breanne sat typing away at the desk. "You wish. He didn't answer. I called, like, three times."

"And now Emma's gonna be waiting all night for her mom to knock on the door, telling her she has a call from Jak," Opal teased from the foot of Sarah's bed.

"Am I really not allowed to be impatient?" I asked, crossing my arms. "Is this normal?"

"For a seventeen-year-old boy to have a life?" Sarah remarked.

"No, for *Jak*, of all people, to be radio silent with me for three days on email and now phone."

Now the room was still. Now my friends were pausing in a way that even changed the quiet of the atmosphere—from fuzzy to soundproof. They needed the reminder that I'd emailed him twice over the last three days and nothing.

It's so easy to think the worst-case scenario, and I don't even have anything to tell me that the worst-case scenario hasn't actually happened.

"He's busy," Breanne said, setting down her pencil. "He'd never ignore you."

That's why I'm scared. Because what could Jak possibly be so busy with that he was ignoring my requests for updates and valuable insider information?

That's another thing he wouldn't do: deprive me of details or at least the update that there aren't any.

"Do you think," I caught myself asking, "something's off?"

"What do you mean?" Breanne asked without a glance in my direction.

"What if *this* is our smoke signal? The intel we've been waiting for to investigate?"

Sarah's eyes met mine as she started tying off the end of Opal's onyx braid. "I think you're stretching it a bit, Emmy."

"Am I?" I was genuinely asking. "Something just feels off. It's too convenient and coincidental of a time for this to be an exception to his usual routine and nothing else."

"You emailed him over the *weekend*." Sarah released a disbelieving chuckle. Opal kept her eyes on her fiddling thumbs. "He has other friends and homework, too, you know."

"Well," Breanne started cautiously, standing from the desk, "we're dealing with a group of people who *are* more trained than even Mrs. Marie. And we know they're currently purposely keeping their plan as vague as possible just to mess with us."

"But Jak isn't supposed to be involved," Opal said as Breanne stepped up next to me. "If they do anything to him, they're cluing him in on their secret. What other reason would they have for—?"

"Getting information on Tristan's descendant out of him," Sarah said behind her, her hands dropping into her lap. Realization stung her face, and Opal turned around to look at her. "If they know more about that than we do, then..."

The pack had every motive in the book—even from a perspective that was limited.

"Okay," I began, trying to keep my voice afloat, "I have—a really bad knot in my stomach. It's not Hunter instincts, but I can't shake the feeling that something's not right. And it's not like I can go to Redway to find out the answers for myself."

"Okay," Breanne stated, like I'd lent her my confidence and that was where it had disappeared to, "it's fine, I can email Wyatt about it just to double-check."

I nodded gratefully, and she went to her laptop and started clicking away. The rest of us hovered around her as her delicate fingers flew over the keyboard.

To: Wyatt Zhang
From: Breanne Shaw
Hi, hi~ How's the week been so far for you three?

"Okay, but what boy regularly checks his email?" Sarah asked dully, standing next to me and resting her hands on top of the desk chair.

"He does," Breanne replied. "He's involved in a lot of organizations and is a freelance programmer, so he's always in contact with someone important. He should only take ten minutes tops to reply."

We had our reply in two:

To: Breanne Shaw
From: Wyatt Zhang
Hey :) The week's been busy, everyone's prepping for Thanksgiving break next week so the instructors are extra hard on us rn. Jak and Adrien are doing okay, just catching up.

There was a red flag waving in my chest. Two, three, but my mind couldn't place a single one in the ground.

He's not ignoring me. He'd never ignore me. Something was still off, a detail was askew somewhere.

Breanne didn't need to turn around to read my mind:

I didn't like this: my paranoia having no grounds to breed, my rationality storming the capital, yet the red flags flying even higher on their masts.

"Okay," Sarah said with finality, standing up straight. She faced me. "So he's fine. Just busy."

There's something not right. It wasn't exactly like I could ask the group chat for help, either: it turned out that Alejandro's teleportation ability took a lot of energy like Annisa's time traveling, and having him teleport *overseas* was a significant ask—especially because he needed to know where he was teleporting to at all. Annisa could potentially travel into the past and figure out something, but it would be next to impossible for her to find the right date and time to travel to that would *happen* to offer her a piece of the puzzle.

And as much as I despised it, I couldn't ask Kamose for help and pay his price because, sure, I'd know exactly where Jak was—but if he was in trouble, I'd need to explain to these three how I'd known to save him in the first place.

And according to Wyatt, Jak simply wasn't in trouble.

I bit my lip. *Don't be clingy...*

"Give it two days," Opal told me, sensing my unease and touching my shoulder. "That's enough time to get back to someone to at least tell them they're too busy to reply."

For now, I had to trust in the girl who was an expert socialite and the girl who was an expert in all things about boys. I was getting better, but in no way was I an expert in either.

He'd never deprive me of his help. That was my only hope right now.

Twenty-Three

"Don't be clingy" meant waiting until Sunday to go to Momma's office to call again. Still no response. And that was when I reminded Momma that the pack's plan was most likely to psych us out so they could nail us when we least expected it.

"Do you want me to call Redway?" she asked simply, folding her hands on top of her desk as I set down the office phone. "Ask William if I could speak with Jak directly?"

That could work; William's response would at least hint at what was actually going on.

I nodded, handing her the phone.

A handful of seconds passed, and Momma took a deep breath in with the phone still pressed against her ear. That was a good sign.

"Headmaster Bleu, this is Headmistress Marie of the Callistro Academy, how are you?"

Forget the formalities. He doesn't deserve the formalities.

"Right..." Momma slowly nodded like he *wasn't* a sworn enemy whose downfall she was planning. "Right, I'm sure. Listen, may I speak with Jak while I have you on the phone?"

I really hope you have an excuse for that.

"No. No problem waiting at all."

What?

I gawked at Momma and her smug smile, her defined eyes glinting at me. "Relax," she said, "I'm on hold. He's calling him into his office right now."

Is Jak... mad at me? Was that even remotely possible? Had I done something stupid without knowing it?

I scoffed, sitting on the edge of the desk. "Since when can William get an easier hold of Jak than I can?"

"Since he's the headmaster requesting a student's presence," Momma replied dully, arching a brow at me. "Are you *sure* you're not secretly dating?"

"I wish we were," I replied, sending her a cheeky smile.

She slapped my arm in a scold, then pointed at the chair in front of me. "Get off my desk" in other words.

An excruciating couple of seconds passed before Momma finally smiled. "Hi, Jak, it's Headmistress Marie. You mind talking to Emma for a bit?"

Thanks for the heads up! Right now it felt like Jak and I were standing on thin, unfamiliar ice, and I at least wanted a moment to decide if I was upset at him for blowing me off for almost a week!

Momma went to hand me the phone before pulling it back, her smile slightly shrinking. "Just for a minute, honey."

Did... did he not even want to talk to me?

I finally took the phone. My chest burned with an anxiety that *was* familiar, just not with Jak. And I hated that it was probably about to control my end of the conversation.

"Jak?"

"Hey," he said, my chest deflating with relief. He was okay. He was just... not replying to me.

"Busy week?" I asked lightly.

"You have *no* idea."

Okay. That was said more casually. It didn't *sound* like he was mad at me.

"I don't wanna be 'that' person, but is there a reason you haven't been getting back to my emails? Or why your dad had to get you for you to finally pick up?"

"Okay, I *am* sorry about that, it's just—I'm doing my best. Seriously, I just need more time, if you can trust me on that."

He's being pretty open about what he says in front of his dad... William's definitely gonna ask questions.

"You need more time?" I asked, my brows furrowing. "For what? Did you find something—?"

"Trust me, Merlin. Please."

Before realizing it, I exhaled. That was all I needed to hear. "Okay. I trust you."

"Good. Now isn't really the right time to talk about it, you know?"

Because his dad was still in the room. *I really hope you can excuse all of this to him.*

"Right, okay," I said. "Just keep me updated when you can."

"I will. Stay safe."

I found my hand slightly shaking as I handed Momma back the phone. Like... like relief and worry were violently combatting each other, warring for my body.

Was I just being paranoid? After everything that had happened?

"Em," Momma said. I realized that she'd been speaking and hung up the phone, and I'd tuned it all out. "Go take a bath or something. Use my lavender salts. You need to relax before going into this week."

I mean, that was true. And I was starting to convince myself that the "paranoia" was really just a fear that Jak was upset with me.

"Thanks for calling him," I finally said, standing up.

The great thing about having good best friends in the face of uncertainty? Being able to count on them not saying "I told you so" when you come up to them saying you were wrong.

Especially because I wasn't sure how "wrong" I actually was.

⚓

The only reason I was able to somewhat relax when Mr. Dawson told me to meet him in his classroom the next day was Momma meeting us a minute later, just as unknowing as I was. In other words, I probably wasn't in trouble this time. Unfortunately, I knew how these meetings typically ended; my relief probably wasn't going to last long.

Behind his mahogany desk, Mr. Dawson leaned back in his desk chair. Okay. Maybe things *hadn't* fallen apart just yet.

"Opal just asked me if it's possible for a druid to have visions while awake because she keeps getting 'flashes' of a night in the forest with Emma and Alexa."

My body stiffened against his door. *Things are definitely falling apart.*

"What?" Momma said next to me, narrowing her eyes. "Her memories are resurfacing?"

"Trying to," Mr. Dawson said. "I put the memory-wiping spell on her again. But we need to be honest with ourselves, Amy, how long is that gonna last?"

Or what if she pulls an Alexa and pretends she doesn't remember when she actually does? I really hoped that Opal didn't know her own tell for lying, because that would be the only thing to tell us if something like that actually happened.

"I can't put the spell on her every day just to make sure," Mr. Dawson added flatly. "We've always known that this is a really temporary solution. We also know that she isn't the best liar to people who know her. She'll tell Sarah and Breanne sooner or later, and we're not in a position for them to know yet."

It was strange—anxiety breeding—referring to the inevitable as a "yet" instead of "inconceivable". I think that was part of growing up in the last year, too: realizing that it never really was inconceivable just because I was afraid of the consequences.

"Then what are we going to do?" Momma said, the two of them locked in each other's gazes as if I weren't in the room. "Right now, things are way too complicated for us to even think about the risks and possible rewards of exposing Emma, especially with Tristan 'dead' and Becca a month away from following suit. No, we just can't do it right now. Please, Thomas, keep this under wraps and make her forget if things come to that. For just a little longer, like you said, it isn't the time right now."

He sighed curtly. "The point is that you and I both know we're running out of time with this. Look at me, Amy."

It was like they really *had* forgotten I was in the room; Momma's eyes never strayed to mine once as she obeyed.

"We need to stop figuring out how to hide the truth longer and start figuring out how we're gonna reveal it."

I opened my mouth, but Momma beat me to it, scoffing. "You're insane. Are you seriously—?"

"Not right now," he said, holding up a hand in defense. "But after this year—maybe even this school year. We need to start facing reality."

I dragged my eyes to Momma standing next to me, stripped of any rebuttal. Hers met mine, and she seemed to remember that I was there. She started twisting the golden band on her left ring finger. I kind of wished that her ring from Jak could've accompanied her right hand.

"Em, you..."—she spoke softly, like she was afraid that the words would break me—"you know that, right? You know we can't keep this a secret forever."

The words were heavy on my tongue and no lighter in the air: "I always have."

Honestly? Sometimes it felt like I knew that better than she did.

"I had to let you both know that first." Mr. Dawson sighed, resting his chin on his hand. "Because then she talked to me about

Alexa. She was pretty freaked out."

"I'm pretty sure freaking us out is what they're *trying* to do," I said, strolling over to the whiteboard, "based on your first lesson about recon and laying the trap."

"You have an idea for what the trap is?"

"After Jak and I talked about it. He said it was 'mental torture' trying to figure all of this out. And I remembered,"–I turned to Momma to include her—"that's what Alexa said to us that night on the cruise, about the hunting industry. She'd emphasized it. Like she was trying to tell us that that was exactly what they were doing."

The atmosphere shifted, still as if a hundred laser beams had activated and if we made one wrong move, we'd disintegrate.

"That implies that Alexa was warning you," Momma said, wandering away from the door. "Give me one good reason she would do that."

"I don't know." I dropped my head against the whiteboard. "There has to be a clue or something in what she said."

"Could be that William is planning something a lot worse than what Alexa was offering at the time," Mr. Dawson said. "Or based on how he was listening in and this case isn't federally appointed, maybe they wanted to give us the chance to come willingly before they did something worse."

That didn't... *sound* like them. Did it? Would they? Could they have been?

"What else did Alexa say, Em?" Momma asked.

I recalled the next bit of info Alexa had given us that night: "Something about keeping your enemies closer because they have what you want."

Her back straightened. "*That* makes sense. Enemies close—she kept you guys close during the entire trip."

Mr. Dawson peered at me in the corner of his eye from his chair. "And she keeps you close now through Jak."

The statement fell onto me like an anchor. Jak's number one fear, what he'd even addressed when we first told him about the Delphines: that they would bar him from protecting me.

Son or not, Jak's relationship with me makes him their enemy.

"What does that mean for us now?" I dared to ask.

Momma and Mr. Dawson shared a glance. I think they were waiting for the other to speak, and she took the chance.

"Mental torture has always been her tactic. So has been keeping you close, we don't need a reminder of that. You have exactly what she's looking for, so if anything, we're nowhere different than where we began. Do not let her convince you otherwise. Know your enemy, Em. You need to keep her just as close."

Know your enemy. Know her.

"Do you know me, Emmalynn?"

"You know me, Emma."

I froze. The detail. Against Momma's lesson in this very classroom last semester about catching the smallest detail that could reveal the entire picture, I'd missed that detail. Alexa had always refused my nickname until she was memory rid, where she even called me by my fake nickname I'd chosen as a cover. Until she was memory rid. Until she'd been forced to be genuine. *Sincere.*

She had never called me "Emma" in the entire time that I'd known the real her until that night.

"You know me, Emma. Don't you?"

If Alexa Delphine was being sincere that night, if she had

already exposed the mental torture part of her plan, her speech hadn't been a taunt. It hadn't been a mind game or some random moment of reflection. It had been a warning—maybe a warning she didn't want William knowing about.

That doesn't make any sense. Since when on this planet would she help us? Was Anthony in on it?

I didn't bother asking those questions; I needed more first. I needed more pieces than what I had right now, because my only conclusions would just land us back where we started at the beginning of this conversation: a hundred questions we flat out couldn't answer yet.

CHAPTER

Twenty-Four

Sarah scoffed, walking with us out of the Dining Hall. "We deserve a *day* of relaxation! Tomorrow: spa. They finally opened one in town for a reason, you know."

"You're paying?" Breanne asked cheekily.

"Duh," she replied, matching her attitude in full.

"You guys! Emma's getting away!"

Thanks, Opal. Thanks a lot.

I stopped my way to Momma's office on the other side of the Grand Foyer. Despite his reassurance on Sunday, Friday had come and Jak still hadn't gotten back to a single email. "It's been three days!" I said. "I'm just gonna make sure he's okay—"

"He's *fine*, Em, just busy." Sarah rushed up to me and grabbed my arm, encouraging me toward the Main Stairway. "This is why you need a spa day."

"Just come with me." I pulled her back in the direction of Momma's office. "Really quick."

She rolled her eyes, but Breanne and Opal strolled up to my side, and she caved. "If he's fine, you're paying for your own spa day, Em."

Fine by me—Momma would probably be in support and chip in, if not join altogether.

She didn't even question us waiting by her office door when she came down the right hall with a stack of papers; she just cocked her brows in a here-we-go-again kind of way before taking out her keys and unlocking the door.

"Will William even be in his office right now for you to call him?" Breanne asked skeptically, taking a seat on one of the white couches with Sarah and Opal.

"William is my last resort," I replied as I went to the desk. "He's only if Jak doesn't answer his personal phone after three times."

"You really have this down to a science," Sarah noted. "It scares me."

"Me, too," Momma added from the door, drawing our attention. She set down the stack of papers on the glass coffee table between the couches. "Look, I've had to use the bathroom since dinner was halfway over, but Professor Gene wouldn't stop ranting about the chemical mutations he's conducting on Breanne's serum. Thanks, Bre. So be good, I'll be back in five."

We each offered an innocent smile, Breanne's the proudest, as Momma turned and closed the door behind her.

I grabbed the office phone and dialed Jak's number.

"We should make Jak pay for the spa," Opal said from the middle of the couch. "For *causing* this in the first place. He couldn't even say he'd get back to Emma later after, what, almost a week?"

"Agreed," I said as the dial tone rang in my ear.

"Even perfect boys need help sometimes," Sarah said wistfully, her manicured fingernails gently combing through her hair. "Believe me."

The next dial tone was cut short. Jak had picked up. I smiled, straightening and opening my mouth to tell my friends—

"Emmalynn."

Who... who was this?

How did they know it was me calling?

The girls stood from the couch when my brows scrunched together.

"Who's this?" My eyes jumped to anything in the room like each surface was made of lava.

"He lied to you," the voice replied. Male. Most likely older than Anthony, possibly as old as William... and someone who knew Jak? One of his instructors? "He has all the answers."

Someone who knew the secrets he was harboring?

"He has all the answers everyone's looking for. And he won't tell anyone."

"Who is this?" I repeated, firmer this time. The girls around me stayed noticeably still.

"He's a liar and a traitor."

Stun stretched like a tightrope across my body.

"Now he'll reap everything he's earned."

A low buzz vibrated against my ear as the line clicked.

He was taken.

The phone was being ripped out of my hand. Hands were landing on my shoulders, trying to shake me. People were surrounding me.

He's not okay.

"Emma!" I heard Sarah urge as I tried to blink myself back into the passing reality in front of me. "What's wrong?"

"Em," Opal said next to me, hanging up the phone and then turning me to face her. "Talk, what happened?"

"They said he knows and he'll face the consequences," I whispered. "They have him, they know he knows, they know he knows—"

—everything.

"Tristan's descendant," Breanne said, freezing me in Opal's grip. "He's only a few months away from being eighteen, they can detain him until they're able to try him as an—"

"No," I snapped, jerking out of Opal's hold. "I don't care what they *can* do, we're getting him out of there before they do!"

It can't be too late, I refuse to wait!

"Em," Breanne said softly, "this is officially a Hunter matter. We have to get your mom—"

"And wait for her to have time to find him?" I snapped. "Even when she does go after him, she won't let us come, and I'm not staying here!"

"You expect *us* to get him?" Sarah gawked at me, wide-eyed and in disbelief. "Us, the girls who are Alexa Delphine's biggest targets right now, who've barely gotten halfway through our *high school* training—you want us to step into a Delphine trap? You know they're behind this, and you wanna walk straight into their plan, that's what I'm hearing?"

"We said we'd fight," I stated. "We know he's in danger right now, and I'm not waiting to get him out."

"Em," Opal began, fiddling with her thumbs, "it's too dangerous, we can't do this alone."

I gestured loosely to her. "You have your magic, so does Breanne. It's not like we'll be going purely off of physical skill, we'll have an advantage!"

Three, actually!

Sarah's eyes dulled, her stance relaxing as she crossed her arms. "Are you seriously forgetting everything about this *whole* career this mission revolves around?"

Okay. Stupid suggestion.

No—desperate suggestion. I was spiraling, going too fast for my logic to keep up. Every part of me knew that my friends were being rational, but I almost trusted myself to get Jak out more than I trusted Momma: after what had happened with Marcus Greenwell the last time she'd taken a "solo mission" upon herself, the last thing I wanted was to continue minimal training in the walls of the school. Especially if it was for the sake of saving Jak—someone who deserved my willingness to take risks and fight my worry to get him back.

He deserved my rationality, every instinct my training had already instilled in me.

"Fine," I said. "I have a plan. You can come with me or just stay in contact, but either way, I'm getting him back."

Sarah's jaw dropped. "Give me *one* good reason you should go—"

"Because if it were any one of you, you wouldn't think twice."

One by one, the girls backed down. I swallowed, keeping every word steady. "None of us would hesitate to come after each other if one of us were taken. Jak..." I realized the words as I spoke them. "Jak is one of you to me. I can't even *hesitate* to go after him."

The quiet that trailed after was fragile—but I knew my friends. I knew that it was fragile in the sense that if it went on for much longer, my friends were ready to agree to *let* me go.

Good. Then I'm–

As if the woman had actually heard us and wanted to disrupt any plan we could think of next: Momma pushed the door open and stood in the doorway.

"I don't like this." She shut the door behind her like someone was waiting to eavesdrop. "What happened?"

You know what? I'd snuck out before; if she wanted to bar me from saving Jak now, she couldn't.

"Jak was kidnapped," I said, pushing past the girls. "It wasn't Alexa or William or Anthony on the phone, I don't know who picked up and I don't even know if I know who has him, but they called him a traitor and said he was gonna pay the price."

I'd never been more grateful to watch Momma's speculative face meld into her Hunter face, to watch her eyes harden and brows bend in determination. A plan was forming.

"We waited until they struck first," I said. "I'm done waiting to react. I say we find him and get him back. Now."

Momma continued thinking, still determining our steps.

"Who do you propose we involve in this?" she asked—but it wasn't a question. It was a test.

"You and I are definite," I said, then glancing around at the girls. "Anyone else?"

"No," Mom said. "We know they want you all together. I can almost guarantee that Jak is bait right now to get that."

"It wasn't Alexa or William on the phone—"

"They're not the only members of their pack, Em. We don't know how many of Alexa's family members are in it, but that could've been any of them. They're in on this, no other way around it."

"What if I come with you for added security?" Opal said. "Magic to protect you—"

"No, I'm not taking an undertrained magician," Momma said without missing a beat, holding up her hand. "Then we'd be putting a target on your back for Caldwell to shoot at. It's a miracle I'm taking Emma as it is, but I know she won't listen and *stay put* just because I tell her to."

I was glad to know that Momma did know me that well.

"What about Mr. Dawson?" Sarah asked.

Mom shook her head. "It's too dangerous to involve a magician period. You're gonna have to trust me, girls. Just because we're going after Jak doesn't necessarily mean we're saving him." This, she looked at me for. And I'm glad she did, because I needed the reminder. "You *never* run into a mission without assessment, you all know that. Best-case scenario, Jak is in a position where we can grab him at all. Stay here and close to Mr. Dawson until I say otherwise, am I understood?"

I wished the girls could know that she'd have a hybrid wielder to protect her. Still, Breanne nodded obediently. "Okay," she said. "Then even if you don't grab him, stay in constant communication with me." She looked up at me with doe-like eyes. "Promise."

I took her small hand and squeezed it. "Deal."

Twenty-Five

inutes later, we were in Mr. Dawson's classroom down in the Hunter's Room. I was pretty sure that my will to know where Jak was would easily give the nore part of me the answer. That, and I wanted to see for myself where he was, to at least be in control of that.

"I can't waste time trying to wake Kamose up right now," I told Mr. Dawson in front of his desk, "but I don't have anything that belongs to Jak to use a locator spell, so if you're willing to pay the price, I need to use the nore part of me."

He sat perfectly still in his chair, glimpsing Momma at the door. Looking back, those wary eyes were knowing—like he knew that she'd rejected to pay the price with me but had been forced to agree to let me use him. I was glad that Jak was worth it to her.

"Okay," Mr. Dawson said, returning his attention to me, "but I don't like you two going alone—"

"Someone needs to stay with the girls," Momma told him. "In case the pack is waiting for a portion of us to go and the rest to stay behind. Nobody can protect them like you can."

Exhaling, he gave me his hand. I placed mine under and on top of his. This was my first time ever using the nore part of me for a reason other than training. Now it was real life, which meant I couldn't afford the mistakes.

I inhaled and closed my eyes. *Not your regular magic, your nore magic.* Moren's words echoed in my head from every lesson we'd had up until that point. *Let it reach in and...*

There.

I opened my eyes as the events of Mr. Dawson's life flew through my mind. How ignited my curiosity was, how tempted I was to ask about these flashing images where I heard clues that he was referring to my parents or me, when I saw frames of what were younger versions of my parents—but Jak was too present in my own mind, shattering the possibility of distraction.

I raised my eyes to Mr. Dawson's. "What would you like to know?"

Hang on—he wasn't just looking at me. He was *gazing* at me like he could see his life's memories rolling across my eyes, back and forth between both irises, his lips partially open.

Moren told me when I managed my first-ever successful question that my eyes turned blue. That must've been it.

He better hurry before I lose—

Mr. Dawson lightly shook his head, finally just looking at me. "Where is Jak right now?"

A white burst flashed in my mind, fading to a golden light as a dirt floor shimmered into view. Stone walls on both sides of my peripheral. Black sneakers... dirty, dark jeans... Jak's perspective.

In a room that's... familiar.

Jak didn't raise his head to look at anything. His vision stayed down.

Something's wrong.

The internal knowledge of the nore floated to the surface, a reverbed whisper echoing across the chasm in my head: in *Capperson.* At—

I stumbled backwards. Momma managed to catch me before I could trip down the step of the platform. Calling my name, Mr. Dawson sprang from his chair and ran out from behind his desk.

There was no way.

"The mine hideout in Capperson!" I exclaimed as they pulled me up. The man's words on the phone pounded in my head, the pieces falling into place too quickly: "He—they're—they trapped him down there!"

He'd been right there the whole time, only twenty minutes away from the school this *whole* time.

"Was it just a voice you heard, or did you see something?" Mr. Dawson urged, locking his eyes with mine.

"In—in the room we fought in during the final." The words continued repeating with a cruel taunt. "Something's wrong with him, he's... I—"

"Emma, breathe," Momma commanded, a firm hand on my shoulder as she locked our eyes. "Focus, don't let your mind work against you right now."

"You'll stay under the nore's truth spell until you ask me a question," Mr. Dawson told me. "You need to ask me something before you go anywhere, just calm down and think."

With my breath hitching in my throat, I remembered all of the moments that my emotions had cost me the hunt before. When fear and paranoia and anxiety had kicked me down a flight of stairs and given my enemy the time they needed to advance and take me in.

You've learned too much by now. You have too much training.

You don't have to be strong all the time...

Right now, you do. For him. He needs you at your best.

Jak needed me to be a Hunter right now.

"I'll make this easier," Mr. Dawson said next, noting the slight ease of my body. "Pick the first question that comes into your head when you think about what you saw in my life."

Like he'd said, I was under the nore's truth spell. That was why the question flew from my lips without needing a second thought: "You were fourteen when you first dreamed about me. What was your first thought?"

Somewhat to my relief, the corners of his mouth turned upward. "You were what told me that the guy I was rooming with was actually Tristan Atera. I instantly knew how special you'd be. I was excited. If anything, I was grateful."

Just like that, the weight of the truth spell lifted. I exhaled again, trying to reset myself. Calmer, yes—but fear was still threatening the dam of my mind that I'd already rebuilt so many times, and I refused to have to build it up again.

Now this was officially wielder business. Why else would Jak be in the abandoned wielder hideout with someone who knew that he knew wielder secrets?

"Are we good?" Momma asked, ready to jump into action—and I was right there with her.

"Yeah," I said, my breath steadying. "We have to go, right now."

"Stay safe," Mr. Dawson told us as we bolted for the door. "Emma, contact me the second you need backup."

—I will,— I said as Mom shut the door behind us. We started racing across the crimson rug of the Hunter's Room.

—I guess sapphire is the color the nore part of you activates,— he said as Momma pressed the elevator button. —You're a magical marvel, indeed.—

⚓

We needed to give ourselves time without the girls interfering; that meant telling them that we were going to Topa an hour away because it was "the most logical place to start looking". Since they weren't tracking us on GPS, they couldn't see that we'd be in Capperson the whole time.

"We don't know how many people we're dealing with," Momma began, hands firm on the steering wheel as we drove down Main Street. "Do you know what to do?"

"Lookout spell. I'll knock out anyone on the spot if I have to."

"Good girl."

Minutes later, Momma parked the car along the sidewalk by the field where the historical mine entrance sat. I swallowed down another ball of nerves as we walked up, the sun just beginning its descent. It wasn't the torture Alexa and William had inflicted on me threatening to incapacitate me now; it was the torture that Momma and Mr. Dawson had inflicted on me during the spring final. It was how, when I *had* managed to come back here while on a date with Jak, Alexa and Anthony had stolen this hideout from me by burning it down. And now I was back to rescue a boy I cared about without knowing if he'd even still be in one piece when I found him.

He needs you to be a Hunter right now. Don't use your own mind against yourself.

I took another step on the grass, toward the mine entrance, when Momma took my arm and Breanne started speaking in my earpiece.

"Emma?" Her sweet voice was cautious. Overly cautious—in its analytical register. "I know you need to focus right now on the drive, but—new email from Wyatt."

"I'm guessing it's important," I said, approaching the entrance. Breanne wouldn't have interrupted otherwise.

"So, we were talking about homework, schoolwork, the chaos of Thanksgiving week—and then he said that he really wanted to exchange notes with Jak..."—Breanne spoke slowly now, like she was reading the message in front of her but didn't believe it—"but he doesn't know when Jak will be back."

I paused, Momma's gaze turning just as pensive as I asked, "What do you mean he doesn't know when he'll be back?"

"That's what I asked. To which he replied that Jak has been gone since last Friday. To visit his sick uncle. Obviously, his dad couldn't go, but Jak's been gone for a week."

Sensation drained from every muscle in my body. My knees turned to slush under me. Jak had been missing since last Friday, yet six days ago on Sunday, he'd spoken to me on the phone. He'd assured me that he just needed more time, he'd called me "Merlin"!

That wasn't Jak. Wyatt and Adrien hadn't been rooming with the real Jak for almost a week and half.

Breanne had pieced it together. She'd been there during that call on Sunday, and she wasn't telling me that it was okay to come back now.

It made so much more sense: Jak's hesitance to be on the phone with me, his avoidance on that call, why we *really* hadn't been able to reach him. And for someone to have pretended to be him, it was all the concrete evidence I needed. William Bleu didn't just know the Delphine secret; he was working with them because he now knew *my* secret, too.

Twenty-Six

Momma thanked Breanne for the update before assuring her that we'd come back as soon as we could. In actuality, I wasn't sure if I could face my friends once I learned what had really happened to Jak; Wyatt's emails had confirmed my greatest nightmare as of now, and it was threatening to send my mind spiraling.

But I reminded myself that I couldn't afford the distractions. I went to address the rusty lock before my eyes snagged on the side of the door: it was already ajar.

Sloppy. Especially for a Grand Hunter with magic.

If Momma was thinking about it, she didn't show it as she slithered inside first. I stuck close by the entire time as I carefully pulled the door shut behind me, submerging us into pitch-black darkness.

I pictured the lanterns that probably no longer hung above us, wishing that I could turn them on; I doubted they'd survived the earthquake Anthony had inflicted on this place this summer. Even if they had, though, turning them on would alert anyone down here of our presence.

I grabbed my phone and turned on the flashlight, Momma following suit. The white lights illuminated the old wooden steps in front of us. Sure enough, glass shards and the frame of a vintage lantern sat at our feet.

"Em," Momma whispered, so softly that she'd practically mouthed it, "assess. Lookout spell."

I closed my eyes. *Prospectus.*

The spell illuminated an otherwise pitch-black bird's-eye view of the tunnel in my head, leading my vision down into the space where the five main tunnels stretched out. All empty, and the spell wasn't detecting movement.

"We're safe," I whispered.

Momma eyed me, her brow arching slightly. "Do you—feel anything?"

"Feel anything"? I just said we're safe.

"What do you mean?"

"No one's down here?"

As much as I wanted to question it—because there was no way that something wasn't underlying what she actually meant—*Jak* was down here. He needed us, and there was nobody stopping us from getting him.

Hang on. What?

That's *what she's asking.*

"No one's here." I tried to make sure that she heard my doubt, even in a whisper. "No one's moving, at least."

"Something's off," she replied, keeping her flashlight steady on the ground. "Stay focused, get your sleeping spell ready, and let's go."

We traveled through the cold, damp tunnel before reaching the first staircase. Strangely enough, the steps weren't burnt as we crept down.

Anthony's fire didn't reach up here. How much did *he burn?*

At the bottom, Momma and I faced the dirt room that branched off into five separate tunnels. "He's in the room we fought in for the final," I whispered, taking her hand and pulling her to the center passageway.

"Emma," she hissed quietly, pulling me back. The darkness wasn't enough to drown out the scolding I already felt from her hard gaze. "You *always* double-check when you can afford to."

I internally groaned and then performed another round of the lookout spell. "Nobody's in the tunnels right now, I know that."

"Something's not right..." She glanced around, still careful of her flashlight. "Or we have even less time than we thought."

"Then we need to *hurry*."

She sighed, following me down and to the end of the middle tunnel. We now stood at the top of the wooden stairs that ultimately led to the cavern—or what *used* to be the stairs, each step now charred to the ground.

This was going to take a lot longer than I wanted it to.

Momma guided us down the incline, my steps threatening to push away too much of the dirt and send me tumbling. We used the walls for balance, inching our way farther down and staying alert for any sounds beyond the draft and shifting pebbles.

I didn't waste a second when my feet landed on solid, mostly flat ground. *Prospectus.*

Another X-ray view of the cavern projected itself in my mind. I homed my focus on sensing movement. The lake that made up most of the cavern space was next to silent—because it was mostly gone. All the majestic stalactites from above had fallen into the water and crumbled apart, half-sunk in the water. Some boulders had rolled off the second-floor ledge.

It's almost scarier being down here now than it was during our final. Probably because it wasn't a test this time.

"Nothing?" Momma whispered.

"No." I shined my flashlight on the steep incline that led to the second story. It all but called me to run up and grab Jak as I moved my light to the intimidating, jagged walls of the cavern: not a single lantern had survived the earthquake. I furiously rubbed my arm for warmth, my phone's light falling to the placid water in front of me. Particles of dirt and rock floated in the white light, reminding me that I had anything but time to stare.

"Let's go," I whispered shakily to Momma, skulking to the incline.

The metal room where the Callistro Girls and Redway Boys had been locked in, Jak was inside. As Momma and I crept up to the second floor, it felt like he was getting his turn in that room after we'd both somehow managed to be the only two to evade it that morning. And I hated that it was exactly what Momma had said earlier that semester: now it was life or death. Now we were out there.

I did it once, I thought as we reached the entrance of the cave. *They tried to make it as real as possible for a reason.*

Jak and I had walked down this same tunnel and met a disguised Mr. Dawson and terrified Momma at the end. But now, when we stepped into the dirt room, it was... empty. Only a chair had been here before, but I'd expected at least some kind of debris from the damage Anthony had inflicted.

My flashlight landed on the metal door in the right corner. I stopped myself from shouting Jak's name and leaped across the room, Momma close behind. With my eyes set on the lock, I pressed myself against the wall beside the door. *Exsolvite procul!*

The lock clicked, in sync with my pounding chest. The heavy door swayed open with an old creak, fluorescent light pouring into the space.

One more round of the lookout spell showed me that there was only one person in that cold room, and he sat in the dead center of it, needing me.

I threw myself into the doorway, Momma right on my heel. There Jak sat tied to a chair with disheveled clothes and his head hanging down—bruised, bloodied, and all.

"Jak!" I cried, darting to the chair and taking his face into my hands.

I barely suppressed a scream in time. *No. No.*

An inch-long cut ran vertically under his right eye. A stream of dried blood followed it all the way down his bruised cheek. Purple and yellow against his light-brown skin—it was at least one or two days old. His swollen bottom lip had been busted open, barely having scabbed over. Something had struck him on the left side of his head, matting a chunk of his hair on his hairline with blood—and pebble dust.

They threw a rock against his head.

His eyes widened before he jumped in his seat, breathily gasping. Then he sank in my hold. "Emma…" he whispered, eyes dazedly closing. "You…"

He'd lost weight. Too much weight in a week.

This wasn't right. Not even Alexa and William would have done this to him. William couldn't have been that far gone. Jak had said himself that besides the "hunting his would-be girlfriend" part, Alexa treated him almost as if he were her own son. They wouldn't have done this. They couldn't have done this.

How are they making me consider the possibility that they weren't the ones who did this?

"It's me, Jak," I cried softly. Momma moved to the back of the chair, kneeling to untie him. "I'm here. I'm right here, it's okay."

"I thought"—the words were so quiet that he was practically mouthing them—"you were them…"

A long cut ran from his left cheekbone down to his chin. A clean slice, like a knife's.

Mom stood up with a switchblade in hand and tossed aside a raggedy, bloodied string: butcher's twine. Torture around the wrists.

But Jak was so dazed that his hands merely fell to his sides, his body slumping forward. His forehead landed on my shoulder, a sharp grunt escaping his lips. Momma's stunned eyes met mine, both of us asking a million questions as if we had the answers. My hands hovered over Jak's arms, afraid to touch him, like he'd turn into sand if I did. Even his head felt lighter. He had to have lost at least ten pounds. He didn't smell like his usual sweet musk. If anything, I doubted that he'd been allowed to bathe even once in the time he'd been gone. And for some reason, I couldn't have cared less.

"Jak—" My hands rested on his upper arms. He cried out, his body shooting up.

Tears had never brimmed my eyes faster. "I'm sorry! I'm so sorry, I'm sorry!"

No response. His eyes stayed closed. His nostrils flared like he was struggling to breathe properly. For all I knew, he was.

That looks like what it felt like for me when my ribs were healing...

I could only see the external damage—did I even want to know what they'd done to him internally?

"We need to get him treated," Momma stated, sliding her switchblade back into her pocket. "Em, do a lookout spell, make sure we're still alone."

I wasted no time and shut my eyes: *Prospectus.*

I demanded my magic to extend throughout the cavern—throughout the mines, a protective instinct stretching my abilities for me. Silence. Not another presence. It was the three of us in this entire mine.

I opened my eyes, but Momma beat me to it: "Nobody's here?"

"No."

"We need to leave ASAP," she said, kneeling next to me and in front of Jak. "No Grand Hunter would leave their target for the taking. This could be one of the most basic traps in existence, we need to leave."

Something is wrong. This was too easy. The words pricked my mind with unnerving truth. All of it had been way too easy, like someone had *wanted* us to find him.

Urgency sprang to life like a fountain in my chest. I carefully rested my hand on Jak's knee. "Jak, can you hear me?"

"Yeah," he mouthed.

"Do you know when someone will be back?"

His lips stayed parted, but they never moved to form words. For the first time since I'd known the boy, I couldn't read his answers and it *wasn't* because he wasn't letting me in.

"We're gonna help you, okay?" I silently begged his eyes to meet mine, but he kept them closed. "You're safe. And Alexa and William aren't getting away—"

"No," he said, the first hint of his voice seeping in. It was scratchier, rougher. More desperate. "No. Them."

I blinked, begging my understanding to click the pieces together. Based on Momma's tightened lips and firm gaze on me, she wasn't comfortable with taking our time just because we were alone. She was right: the entire situation screamed "trap". Anyone could be on their way, we could've tripped a silent alarm—but Jak had my full attention right now, and I needed him to know that I was there for him.

"What do you mean?" I asked.

"Not them," he said, trying to raise his head.

I stood and carefully took his face into my hands again to support him. My right thumb stayed light on his cheek because of the bruises, and my left was careful to avoid the long slice on that cheek. "What's not them?"

Finally, his lids dragged themselves open. Rich-brown irises met mine, but I'd never seen them so bereft of the light and charm that made Jakson Bleu so perfectly him. My heart sank a little lower in my chest, and I swallowed down another threatening wave of tears.

"Alexa and—William," he whispered, "Delphines—didn't do this."

C H A P T E R

Twenty-Seven

There Jak lay in his hospital bed asleep. Finally asleep despite the agony racking his body.

Wait—I thought he didn't want to go to the hospital. Didn't we take him to Mr. Dawson's house?

Early morning dimly glazed the room through the window behind me. As I lay on the firm couch, Jak's eyes fluttered open. They stared without his usual smile, eyeing me. In contempt. In scorn.

"Why did you let this happen to me?"

I sat up. "What?"

"I thought you loved me."

What?

I blinked, brows furrowing in bafflement and worry. "What

are you talking about—?"

"This wasn't my price to pay. It was yours."

I shut my eyes, shaking my head as if to change the picture. Like I could change his mind, change his words.

Jak was gone. The hospital bed was made.

I stood up. "Jak?" I called across the cold, empty room.

My feet pounded against the white tile as I ran across the room to the heavy door and swung it open. I took a step before realizing too late the navy-blue void stretching out below me.

My body hurtled down, my stomach left in the hospital room now miles above me. I screamed. I screamed and screamed for Jak, for the boy I'd involved, the boy I'd hurt by asking for his help in the first place. I screamed until I couldn't hear myself anymore, until my throat was straining just to produce my voice at all.

Help! I shouted in my head, a hole burning inside me where my stomach should've been. *Stop! Stop it, stop! Please, Jak!*

My jaw dropped open in a silent shriek as belligerent ocean waves thrashed below me. I crashed through the icy surface without a sting. Arctic cold swarmed my body, depriving my lungs of the air I needed to recover from trying to scream.

I can't breathe, I can't breathe!

I tilted my head back. The ferocity of the waves battered against me on all sides even under the surface.

Surface, surface, surface!

Let me go, please!

I furiously grabbed at the water above me. A burning ache ignited throughout my arms as I flailed about. Everything I'd ever learned about swimming, about surviving, dispersed when I called on it.

With another blink, my head finally broke the surface of the waves. I coughed up the water, suffocating every time I tried to inhale. A storm blared above me, a violent shiver racking my body. Thunder rumbled in the distance through the screaming rain. Water sloshed into my mouth as I tried calling out to Jak again.

Get me out, get me out!

Hot tears streamed down my cheeks, mixing with the prickling raindrops pounding on my face. Terror billowed in my chest, anticipating an attack on all sides.

Nothing could have prepared me for Jak in his blue Redway uniform rising, face-up, to the surface in front of me.

Drowned.

My scream echoed across the ocean, startling me awake.

My wide eyes met the white ceiling above me. Short, shallow breaths gripped my chest. My hand flew to my eye, fingertips pressing against a fresh tear and wet lashes.

Was it real? Is it actually happening?

I looked next to me in the yellow light. Mr. Dawson's living room. A red mug, emptied of hot chocolate, sat on the coffee table right in front of me. Momma always said that sugar before bed gave her nightmares—I guess I inherited that.

I must've screamed in just my dream, because nobody came to my rescue in the seconds that followed. Considering how quiet the house was, Momma and Mr. Dawson must have been in the backyard.

Right—Mr. Dawson's house. We *hadn't* taken Jak to the hospital. He'd begged us not to for reasons he wasn't able to explain but we were able to infer: his parents. He'd sworn up and down that they hadn't done this, yet he didn't want them involved. At least, not yet. Which was fine, because I didn't want them involved, either. I knew better: they had to have known about this. They were too good not to, which meant they'd *allowed* it.

Besides that, though, whatever Jak was enduring mentally and emotionally had to be taken care of just as much as his physical state. And if we took him to the hospital, even if we made up a story about what had happened, the first people the doctors were calling were his parents. Mom and Mr. Dawson had enough medical training and knew what to do; Mr. Dawson gladly took him in as soon as we told him that we'd found him like that.

I groggily sat up and moved my legs over the cushions of the sofa. Against my initial judgment that I wouldn't be able to sleep tonight, I'd fallen asleep as a last resort; I didn't know what else to do. I couldn't stand the sight of Jak in Mr. Dawson's bed, but I also couldn't stand talking about the situation with the adults. I didn't know what to do.

I ran my hands through my hair, brushing out any potential imperfections. There was only one other person in the house. If it were me—and it *had* been me three months ago—I wouldn't want to be alone right now.

I stood up, crept out of the living room, and turned into the hallway splitting the house in half. The carpet cushioned my steps, but that didn't deter my awareness of each one. Especially as I neared Mr. Dawson's open bedroom door on the right side of the hall and peeked through the doorway.

There Jak lay in bed, eyes shut with his mouth partially open. Bandages covered his left cheek, under his eye, and part of his hairline. His screams and cries of pain as Momma and Mr. Dawson had assessed him—and treated him, stitches and all—blared their echoes like a torrent in my memory. It was so painful for him to breathe from the broken ribs Mr. Dawson had felt for that his chest barely moved. Every breath he took was uneven, labored.

I knew that. I remembered that.

He's alive. But injured.

The tip of my nose stung, twitching as a fresh wave of tears burned my eyes. My nightmare pulsed in my head like a migraine. He was alive, but how close had he been to…?

I closed my eyes, rubbing one with the heel of my hand. My chest rapidly rose with a quivering breath. I allowed myself one sniff, hoping it wouldn't wake him. He needed all the rest he could get.

I'm sorry. This shouldn't have happened. All because of me.

I'd never seen a dead body before. If the dream version was any resemblance to the real thing, I was nowhere near ready for the real world.

You're the last person he needs to see right now.

I swallowed, turning away from the door. One step was all it took to sound a feeble, cracked "Merlin?"

That nickname. That nickname had been desecrated—violated by a sinister imposter. But coming from Jak's lips right now, I couldn't help but run home to it.

I spun back around, wiping my eyes dry. "Jak?"

All he did was blink, but I took it as an excuse to come to his side. I laid my hand on top of his. "Are you—how are…?"

I swallowed, a failed attempt at quelling another round of crying. My hand tightening around his fingers on the navy-blue comforter. His right cheek boasted the purple-and-yellow bruises and knuckle scrapes, gauze plastered down his left. The short cut under his right eye had been bandaged, as had both of his wrists. Stitches stuck out on his head where his kidnappers had used a rock against him. I couldn't stop the raging sea of nausea in my stomach every time I looked at him now. Able to piece together so easily what had been done to him. Knowing that I'd been the cause of it.

"Come here," he whispered.

I leaned toward him like my very presence would break him. With a grunt, he frailly raised his hand that mine lay on top of. His thumb softly swept under my eye, taking a tear with it.

I took his hand into both of mine, placing a soft kiss on his knuckles. Thankfully, that earned his faintest shadow of a smile.

"What's wrong?" he whispered.

"Nightmare," I replied, to name one of them. "Just a nightmare."

At least this one had been unrealistic enough for me to know that it *wasn't* a vision predicting the godforsaken future.

"You stayed?" he whispered.

"I can't believe you're asking that."

All we'd told Sarah, Breanne, and Opal was that we'd found Jak and had to "lie low" until we came back. Thankfully, that was enough for them. It was definitely after midnight now, yet we were still safe—which all the more fueled my determination that Alexa and William really had done this. If they'd been heartless enough to allow this, they were heartless enough to abandon him.

A lump passed in Jak's throat as he stared at his hand that I held. I'd never seen him so dazed. So... not there. Lifeless.

"Do you need anything?" I whispered.

He shook his head. "Just you."

He pulled his hand to himself, slipping out of my grasp. With eyes still stuck on my hands like they were the greatest marvel he'd ever seen, he took my right and gently pulled me closer against the bed with a wince.

"You want me to...?"

"Please?" he whispered.

I wanted to hug him. All I'd wanted to do was hug him since we'd found him, and this was the only way I could.

I rounded the bed and climbed on like the mere shifting of the mattress would send a bolt of pain through him. As I reached his side and lay down, Jak's arm somehow knew to wrap around my shoulder, encouraging me to twist to my left side. I kept my hands to myself. With a couple of broken ribs, he also had severe bruising on his chest and stomach. It was a miracle he wasn't internally bleeding—according to Mom's and Mr. Dawson's best inference and Jak's symptoms. Placing my head on the edge of his chest was daunting, but after a grunt and then an exhale, he relaxed.

"Are you sure this is okay?" I whispered.

He hummed his verification. His bandaged wrist rested around my right shoulder. The butcher's twine had left them raw and blistered. The fact that he was breaking past the barriers of his suffering just for me, just to show me that he still cared about me... half of me crumbled. My enemy had wanted his answers, and he had suffered for protecting me.

We lay there without a single word passing between us. His breathing was too weak, too uneven, for my liking, but at least his heartbeat was in my ear. It reverberated against the nightmare of his body in the water—assuring me that he was alive.

Thank God.

I'm so sorry.

I closed my eyes and exhaled, embracing the warmth of his chest underneath his T-shirt, which Mr. Dawson had lent him. Jak kissed the top of my head with another wince of effort. From what I could feel, his nose stayed resting on my head.

All I could think about was how real he was right now and how close he'd been to dissipating. How much I wanted to wrap my arm around him and squeeze him. How badly I wanted the story, to hunt down the dead men walking who had done this.

"Better?" Jak asked.

"Yeah."

It was as good as it could be, because until he was ready, he was safe in this room with a wielder protecting him. I didn't need the story yet. I just needed him like he needed me.

Twenty-Eight

Saturday morning arrived with no uninvited guests or parents looking for their recently tortured-and-starved son. Despite who those parents were, my heart couldn't help but break for Jak nonetheless. He deserved better. More. Infinitely more.

As noon approached, we were back in Mr. Dawson's room to give Jak the "bad news". Momma and Mr. Dawson took a comfy spot standing next to him as I sat at the foot of the bed. One thing I was grateful for was the fact that Momma and Mr. Dawson weren't afraid of ripping off the Band-Aid, of talking about the hard things—especially when I couldn't.

"I know this story is the last thing you want to think about," Mr. Dawson began, resting a hand on the post of his bedframe.

"I'm not gonna force you to remember it. But we do need to talk about what we're doing next—where you're *going* next."

Jak said nothing, staring down at the lump his feet made under the covers. His silence had never been so eerie and unfamiliar to me.

Mr. Dawson didn't let it faze him. "Obviously, we're not letting you go back to your parents. You're still a minor, but no matter what any Hunter says about Caldwell's laws, this will be classified as child abuse in any courthouse. They can make up whatever story they want, but you can testify against them—if things were to escalate to that."

Jak negligibly shook his head. "It wasn't them. They didn't do it."

"You saw who kidnapped you?" Momma asked in a strictly professional tone.

Jak blinked a few times, his brows slightly furrowing. "No—but... but it wasn't them. It was a man and a woman, they had the bottom half of their faces covered. Brown eyes on both of them. They were strangers. I just... The pack didn't do this."

"Didn't you say you don't know what the whole pack looks like?" I asked carefully, my fingers around my locket.

"I don't, but—" Jak swallowed. It was as if the foot of the bed was playing his memory for him and only he could see it. "The Delphines have green eyes. And they usually have red-toned hair. The guy had blond and the woman had black."

Confusion knit my brows together. Neither of those descriptions were familiar to me...

"Jak," Mr. Dawson began skeptically, "your parents know this house. If they didn't know anything about your current state as a result of what happened, your father would've at *least* come break-ing down my door by now. I say this for your sake and just your sake: the only people who came for you when you went missing were Emma and Amy."

Even I wanted him to stop talking. To stop slapping me across the face with the truth.

"Involved or not, do you really feel safe being around your parents right now? Around the pack period?"

Jak's mindless daze persisted as he reserved a few seconds for himself. "I've wanted to leave for a few years now."

"Thomas," Momma said, wrapping herself in a loose hug, "we don't have the grounds to keep him for any longer than we already have. Logically speaking, someone should've come for him by now, either his parents or the police. The pack has one reason or another for not stopping by yet, but the longer we wait..."

Mr. Dawson ran a hand over his face, sighing. "I know—but you can't honestly tell me that you think they didn't do this. Es-pecially after everything they've already done, the sheer lengths they'll go to for deception."

"Like when they had someone pretend to be you when I called last Sunday," I said to Jak.

His eyes moved to mine. "What?"

"We called Redway after you still didn't get back to my emails. Your dad put 'you' on the phone, and you told me to give you more time. You even called me 'Merlin'."

That daze transfigured into stun. "No—n—no, I didn't, that wasn't me."

To hear him confirm that felt like an anchor being dropped on my chest. The pack knew way too much, and they were taking advantage of *all* of it. Our enemies had stolen and violated something sentimental that was supposed to stay between me and Jak.

"Honey," Momma told him softly, resting a hand beside his legs on the comforter, "I think you know that means that they *are* involved. William wouldn't have grabbed Alexa or Anthony or whoever to disguise themselves under an appearance spell unless he knew that you'd been kidnapped. They used a small detail like that to make sure Emma stayed away long enough for them to get what they wanted out of you."

"I'm sorry, Jak," Mr. Dawson added, "but I really do think the pack had something to do with this. Even if you didn't recognize the members."

"No," Jak said a little more firmly, like his disbelief found the mere notion stupid. "They didn't do it, they wouldn't do this to me."

"We're not saying they did," I told him, "it's just possible—"

"He didn't do this to me!" he cried, furious, teary eyes grabbing mine.

The room halted. Jak's jaw clenched tightly, fighting a tremble. He just as quickly tore his eyes away. He'd let us read too much.

Oh... I realized. *That's what this is about.*

In his defense, I'd never be able to digest one of my parents having the ability to consent to my physical torture, either. No matter how terrible they'd been to me in the past.

Maybe I was still too naïve, because I still couldn't imagine it for William, either. Or maybe I just had too much hope.

"We don't want to put you in danger." Mr. Dawson spoke softly. "I get it, this is... Please. Let us help you, Jak."

"I don't wanna talk about it." Jak's eyes returned to his feet. "I don't want to remember."

I'd been in that exact position: he didn't want to give it any more thought in fear of the truth trumping his ignorance.

Just when I thought my heart couldn't fall any lower.

First mental torture. Now physical.

If only Alexa had warned about *this* in her plan. My biggest regret was how Jak had been right under our noses the entire time—almost literally—and we'd never known. I could've saved him a week earlier if I'd just known. He'd been so close. He'd been kept close the entire time, tortured right in my own hometown—why?

Right in my own hometown.

Those words... were echoing with something beyond regret. Familiarity. A sinister taunt whispered in the corners of my memory as the pieces faced each other.

Mental torture of this industry. Enemies kept close—in your hometown, even.

"*In your circle of friends, even in your own hometown*". Jak was in my circle of friends, but he wasn't my enemy. He was theirs. He was their enemy they'd kept close to their lair right here in Capperson, my hometown.

Alexa had *warned* me about where to find him. She'd known this was going to happen. She'd planned this.

I'd been warned and could have saved him.

"I get that remembering is the last thing you want to do," Mr. Dawson replied gently. "But we *need* to know one thing, especially if it actually wasn't them: were these people magicians?"

"The pack did this."

I'd earned Momma's and Mr. Dawson's scolding glares in my peripheral vision, even the pang in my chest from the betrayal on Jak's fallen features. I'd earned Mom's reproachful "Em" and the crack in my strength to stay put together, but my anger and regret were filling it straight back up.

"Keep your enemies closer—our enemies, of all people." I forced on my mother and godfather to avoid Jak's hurt as much as I could. "Alexa warned us about the mental torture of this industry. Then she flat out said the best thing you can do is keep your enemies close, in your circle of friends"—I gestured loosely to Jak—"or 'even in your own hometown'. Because they have what you want. Jak has information, they know that. They knew *we* would come after him because we would be the only people who would. The pack did this."

I'd become well acquainted by then with the silence that followed: defeat. A suffocation of wisdom that forces you to know the truth, to face it. I'd faced it when we'd realized that Alexa was conducting recon on the cruise, and I'd faced it when we'd correctly theorized that mental torture was the pack's game.

But this time was different. This time, I was hated for it.

"I should've known," I said, too late for Jak's eyes, which had fallen to his lap. That was just as well: no heart would've been able to survive the storm of anger, of resentment, raging in his irises right now. Like he regretted having me in the room, like he couldn't stand that I was there. And that crack that anger and regret had filled melted into hot guilt, stinging tears pushing against my eyes.

"Jak, I'm sorry—"

"They didn't do it," he snapped—with a crack in his voice that

I hadn't heard since the night he confessed his mother's story. "Just—please get out."

It was the first time Jakson Bleu had ever kicked me out. But that wasn't what bothered me the most: what bothered me the most was that, in my mind, he had every right to.

The three of us left the room and went into the hall without saying a thing. We knew what had really happened, after all—but we had to leave it at that for now, until Jak was ready. I think that was why Mr. Dawson simply passed me and Momma and walked into the kitchen to start making tea.

I opened my mouth, but Momma held up a finger and shook her head. She gently guided me into the living room, across from the kitchen.

"I should've known," I said as we sat down on the sofa.

Momma looked at me. Just looked at me. Like she wished she had the answer.

"I was warned," I whispered, desperate for her to say otherwise, for her to tell me that I was overreacting and that it wasn't really my fault. Then I could spend however long we had not believing her but at least having those words in my real memory, not my fictional wishes.

"You didn't do this, Em," she said, smoothing my hair. "This is not your fault."

"She *warned* me," I told her, locking every muscle in my face in a dying attempt to cage my tears, cage myself from falling apart.

"And she let this happen," Momma stated, resting her hand on my thigh. "She told you about a wicked plan knowing that you wouldn't have decoded it in time. She wasn't warning you, Em. She was taunting you."

Her hand rose to my chin, guiding my eyes to hers. "This is not your fault."

Without warning, she leaned me into her and embraced me—because my mother probably knew that I needed it. She knew me. She knew I was falling apart. And despite how often my emotions and breakdowns had weakened my ability to survive in the past, I sat there in her arms and cried. This time, though, I could excuse it; my heart wasn't the only one I was crying for.

C H A P T E R

Twenty-Nine

Momma took a "sick day" on Monday to stay with Jak, who'd been moved to our house the day before just in case. She more than had the training to keep him safe in case anyone uninvited or soon to be dead tried to walk in.

Sarah, Breanne, and Opal had been all but threatening me for updates, but I didn't know the full story, only who was at fault. I did know one thing, though: with how Alexa had "warned" us about her plan, we now had every reason to investigate everything else she'd said that night on the cruise. If she'd really left her plan behind like that and was letting it slowly unravel, then I'd gladly accept the gift and send a little "thank-you" while I was at it.

Today, though, my nerves buzzed a little more than usual; it was the first day we'd be visiting Dad and Aunt Becca since the whole Jak situation. In full honesty, I didn't want to relive the past weekend with a long recap and discussion, but Mr. Dawson stuck me in his car after school anyway.

"You doing okay?" he asked as we drove onto the main path of the forest—probably because I hadn't said anything since we'd walked out of the school.

I leaned my head against the cold, moist window. "Yeah."

"You don't have to lie."

I lightly shrugged. "I'm not really thrilled that Jak has to go back to them when all I wanna do is rip out their eyes."

I never thought I'd hear Mr. Dawson *chuckle* at me threatening someone.

"Out of all the ways you could be handling it," he replied, tapping the steering wheel, "I have no problem with that one. Honestly, I'm almost surprised at how well you've been carrying yourself during the whole thing."

After I'd just sobbed in my mother's arms because of how small and helpless I felt?

I left it alone, watching the trees of the forest glide by. "Thanks."

"You've grown a lot."

"I've heard."

The engine purred beneath us. I closed my eyes. I'd have to spend this entire drive convincing myself that there was nothing to do except hope for Jak's safety. And persuading myself to sit and look pretty when all my magic wanted to do was strangle Alexa and William. That was *tame* compared to what they'd done to Jak. And they still had the audacity to ignore him, to pretend that their plan had failed.

The situation had become so twisted, so disfigured from what it was supposed to be.

"I'm serious," Mr. Dawson said after a silence I hadn't expected. "I think you've honestly proven this semester that you're not the same young woman you were this summer. Far from it. You haven't just learned a lot, you've learned a lot from yourself."

I narrowed my eyes at him. "Are you dying?"

"I know I'm not your mom or dad," he said next, ignoring me, "but *I* think you're ready to know about your identity as a sorceress."

I froze. I'd been waiting for months to hear those words. Sure, he wasn't the one with the final say, he didn't even believe in keeping it from me at all, but it was a step. A step I'd earned.

"Thanks," I said, meaning it this time.

"Especially with how you handled the rescue mission," he added. "Your mom told me how proud she was that you kept your conduct, even when you found the room Jak was locked in."

I twisted my locket, my memory sparking. "She asked me something weird before we found him. I did a lookout spell to make sure we were alone. And when I told her we were safe, she asked if I could 'feel anything'. Like—I'm pretty sure she doesn't know that lookout spells let you detect movement. *I* didn't even know until you did an in-depth lesson with me this year. So... what brought that up?"

Mr. Dawson's fingers tightened around the steering wheel. Then, he straightened in his seat and drove with both hands.

He knew how to lie a *lot* better than that; it was how he managed to switch through three different agencies without ever being caught or suspected before he took a job at Callistro. (He even managed to lie about having a photo of one of the head agents participating in a romantic scandal with magician Nanteeka Kenzy.) He really didn't want to keep this from me to the extent that he was willing to be lazy with his cover.

"Oh," I said in realization. "It has to do with that."

"Yep."

I paused on the words, my brows furrowing. "How? A lookout spell, of all things?"

"Can't tell you," he said.

Which was a cruel response, because I just couldn't figure it out. *Did I feel anything during the lookout spell?* Why would I feel anything unless someone else had been with us besides Jak? How had she known that I could feel movement? Was movement even what she'd been referring to?

She said "anything"…

I crossed my arms for warmth and leaned back in my seat, suppressing a huff. The sun was already low in the sky; winter was fast approaching. Mr. Dawson had the car heater blowing at half power, and it was just enough to stop me from shivering.

It was going to be a brutal winter.

Mr. Dawson's finger brushed my shoulder, calling my attention. My thoughts had distracted me long enough for me to miss the drive to Main Street. "Want me to talk to her?"

I gazed ahead at the road, remembering where we were going and why. How much bigger it was compared to a little secret my parents were keeping. Maybe it was too exhausting to care about something else right now, because I shook my head.

"It's annoying not knowing, but—there's too much else I'm

worried about right now. That doesn't really matter to me in the current grand scheme of things."

Mr. Dawson smiled at me, turning on his blinker to turn right. "You just brought yourself one step closer."

⚓

Mr. Dawson pushed open the front door, and I stepped inside. There Jak sat on the sofa with my parents, never glancing up from the mug in his hand.

"Hey," I said, sliding off my jacket.

"Hey." Jak glanced up at me from the seat in the middle. Stitches kept the long cut on his left cheek sewn together, bruises still marred his right cheek with a cut under his eye, bandages wrapped around both of his wrists, and I could see the end of his stitches on his hairline. It was just as hard to look at him now as it was two days ago.

Momma rested a hand on his knee, pushing a wave of her hair behind her ear. "He's been through more than you can begin to imagine, Em."

Mr. Dawson hung our jackets on the head seat of the dining table as I bit my lip, only brave enough to look at my parents sandwiching Jak. "He told you what happened?"

"Yeah," Dad replied, leaning forward in his seat, "and it turns out that he's safe with us for now. Whether or not the pack was responsible for this, if they make an attempt to contact the authorities and pin kidnapping on us just because we have their son and we're magicians, *they'll* be interrogated because they never came for their son after he went missing. Or put out a missing person's report.”

Just like the cruise, their tactic was too intentional. They’d arranged his kidnapping, they’d allowed his torture, and they weren’t coming for him for a reason. Whatever it was, it was too buried this time in the layers they’d laid down. Mental torture didn’t really fit in this time.

“Right now, *they’re* the perfect suspect,” Momma added. “And if Jak pressed charges, it would get even uglier.”

Somehow, I highly doubt he would.

“Is that a good-enough explanation for you?” Mr. Dawson asked me casually as he strolled to the armchair next to the sofa.

Which reminded me… “Where’s Aunt Becca?”

“Napping in your room,” Dad said, locking his fingers together. His silver ring that Jak had gotten for my birthday glinted in the natural daylight despite the closed blinds. “She hasn’t been sleeping well lately.”

My fingers found my locket as I bit my lip. “I’m glad you’re both still safe.”

Momma lightly nodded in agreement. Jak was quiet again, staring down the drink in his hands.

I hate this. This isn’t who he is. He shouldn’t be…

…everything he refused to be a year ago. Afraid. A pawn. A victim.

I licked my lips as if I were preparing dangerous words, hoping my eyes were gentle on Jak. “I’m glad you were able to open up about it.”

He nodded. To my surprise, I wasn’t upset that he’d trusted my parents before me—because all I knew was that at the end of that conversation, he had to be at least a *little* emotionally lighter than he'd started the week as. And he'd found someone safe.

More than anything else, I just wanted to comfort him. Show him that I cared, I cared more than I could put into words.

"Jak," Momma murmured, her hand on his back. "Do you want to tell Emma and we leave you alone?"

His swallow was the only part of him that moved. Seconds passed that made my heart pound just a little harder with every one. Then, he finally nodded.

Relief coated my stomach as my parents and Mr. Dawson stood from their spots. They each eyed me as they walked by and down the hall—not like they were telling me no funny business, but like they were telling me to be careful with him.

I approached the sofa with muted steps once Momma's bedroom door closed. The coffee table was the only thing separating me and Jak now.

"Hi," I said.

Some say silence is golden, but Jak's was nothing but fatal in that moment. It was foreign territory, waters that I was alone in because his head was probably torturing him with a thousand nightmarish memories that he couldn't just shake away and erase. I knew because I was still living like that. Except, I go so far as to immortalize every experience in a journal, hoping that pouring it out onto a page will keep it there and out of my head.

"Can I sit?" I muttered.

"Yeah."

I took Momma's old spot next to him, slowly setting myself down like he'd shatter. The last thing he needed was for me to say anything, I knew that. I knew that the quiet was the only thing that would lend him the courage and words for the conversation about to happen. I couldn't interrupt that.

He released a shaky breath. When I looked at the coffee in his hands, my own craved something warm to press against.

"Wednesday, I..." he began, my heart tightening with antici-pation. "Wednesday night—middle of the month—one of the teachers caught me on my way to my room. My favorite, Mr. Hollister. Just standing there by the entrance to one of the secret passageways. He told me he had to talk to me about my dad. The way he was acting—I had a feeling like he knew who my dad really was. He asked me to follow him into the passageway so we could talk about it. I figured the most I'd do was convince him my dad isn't who he actually is." He shook his head. "Protecting him ended up being the biggest mistake of my life."

Those words plunged a knife straight into my stomach. Whether with vengeance or secondhand regret, I didn't know.

"'Mr. Hollister' and I went inside the passageway, rounded a corner, and I was attacked. Like, immobilized. Mr. Hollister disappeared and those two agents that took me to the hideout came out. They used—you as leverage. They threatened you if I didn't comply and go with them. So I left Redway behind, was drugged, and then woke up in... in that room."

He'd been in that room for a week and a half...?

Jak swallowed hard as if he'd heard my exact thought, remembering every second of each of those days. "They knew. They knew I knew something... They—threatened me to confess that I knew anything at all. Beat me for it—" He took a deep breath, grunting in a pain I felt too clearly from memory as he brought his hand up to his ribs. "They never... they never stopped... kicking and punching and—bashing—" One hand rose seemingly on instinct for the back of his head. "Stones. Small enough to hurt but not kill me."

The cherry of my nose stung, twitching.

Jak's thumbs rubbed his mug. "I wanted to die, Em."

Hearing those words from Jakson Bleu obliterated the brick wall I'd built behind my tears. I couldn't understand how he was being so much stronger than I was about this. I couldn't understand why something that had affected him this much was dragging me down with him, why we both seemed to be crumbling but in different ways. Why I hurt *this* much with him. For him.

I covered my mouth and nose with one hand, desperately trying to keep my tears to whispers. I couldn't hug him, and that pushed my cries into sobs. They were all trapped in my chest, pounding to be let out. I just couldn't process the fact that another loved one had been caught in the crossfire because of me.

Like in the forest in August.

All for me.

"You shouldn't've done that," I cried. "You shouldn't have done that."

"Protected you?" he asked dully, like I was stupid for saying so.

"Been ready to die for me." I refused to meet his eyes, pressing the back of my fingers to my nose. "Been *tortured* for me! You shouldn't've been—you shouldn't have known anything they wanted, you shouldn't know the truth at all!"

He took my hand like it didn't hurt him, making me look up at him. His eyes were finally saying something: his determination despite his brokenness, despite the price he'd paid for my sake.

"I know because I love you."

I froze, the words piercing my ears. They boomed across the walls of my memory, daring me to believe that I'd actually just heard them. He loved me. Jak just told me that he *loved* me.

The world around me stopped, but not in the way everyone always said it did for this moment—with time slowing and fireworks exploding. It stopped in a way that constricted my breath and crushed my lungs, because that love was too heavy. That love bore a weight I couldn't live under and I would never force him to carry.

But he didn't give me the chance to respond, his grip on my hand firmer than ever. "I chose to tell you I know because I love you. I go through all this because you are more important to me than any rule or law. I didn't think I'd get through that week, but I did, and you were worth every second of it."

"Stop it!" I said, tearing my hand out of his. "Stop, you can't know that. How can you know you love me after all of that?"

"Because that was how I found out," he told me. "I knew it when the pain got worse and the days got longer but I didn't hate you for it. I knew it when I was *grateful* for every second because I was going through it and you weren't. You weren't why I was suffering, you were why I was able to get through it."

Don't do that to me. I can't take that, I can't handle that!

I wanted him to forget. I wanted to make him forget the last week completely, I wanted him to stop caring about me. If he forgot, if he stopped caring, I wouldn't be hurting this much right now.

"You wouldn't want me to feel guilty if you did the same thing for me, would you?" he asked.

It's not the same. The inch-long slash under his right eye was a sinister reminder of that, forget the one on his left cheek that ran almost the entire length of the side of his face.

"I did this to *avoid* you getting hurt." A light tremble shook his melancholy voice. "Please don't let that be for nothing."

He knows exactly how to reach me. It's a blessing and a curse.

"Are you really gonna go back to your parents after this?" I muttered.

He closed his eyes, surrendering to stillness. I remembered that his ribs were stifling his breath, shooting bullets of sharp pain in his chest if he didn't breathe the right way. He didn't deserve this. All just for me.

I scooted closer to him and placed a hesitant hand on his back. With more caution than I knew what to do with, I gave him a peck on his cheek. "Thank you."

A tight, negligible smile touched his lips as he looked back down at his mug. "What are friends for?"

THIRTY

J ak had to go back to Redway eventually, if nothing else than to make sure that his parents wouldn't actually come for him. For our sakes—and I had to physically bite my tongue to restrain my rebuttals—he picked that night. He was still being our mole, gathering intel.

But after Momma brought him to the school, he came back out ten minutes later with his phone and some extra clothes. Apparently, when he found his father, William blatantly ignored him.

And despite everything that had happened in the last two weeks, my jaw still dropped.

That was when Jak made the decision to come back to Capperson with Momma until Thanksgiving break was over. He'd stay with us until Wednesday and then with Adrien "just in case".

That was what made Wednesday afternoon so interesting: the girls coming over before he went back to Topa so that we could finally decode what was going on.

I was hesitant to let them in at first; I didn't want anyone probing his brain, but there wasn't really any way to have this conversation otherwise. So Momma told them to be mindful, and the first thing they did was join him on the sofa, sitting down as if they weren't allowed to leave a dent in the cushion.

"Hey there," Sarah softly sang next to him. "Long time no see, stranger."

"Mrs. Marie is taking him back to Topa after this," Mr. Dawson said, coming out of the kitchen with three strawberry smoothies. He handed them to the girls. "We won't get to see him for a while after this conversation. Make the most of it."

I'd rejected a smoothie earlier, and Jak's appetite still evaded him. That was making it next to impossible for him to gain back the fifteen pounds he'd lost, but all Momma could do was make him eat once a day. That was all his body—his mind, more like—was allowing him.

"Em told us how Alexa said something about this on the cruise," Breanne said next to Sarah, stirring her smoothie with a straw. "Keeping your enemies close, right under your nose in your own hometown. And the whole mental torture thing. I hate it, I *hate* it, but it makes sense. Torture is all they've been doing since Emma and Opal were hospitalized. Alexa waited to attack them until just before the school year, which left them physically incapacitated and all of us on alert. They knew that doing nothing on the trip would put us even more on the defense."

"Until they did do something," Opal muttered on Jak's other side, pushing her straw up and down in her smoothie.

"Which Alexa *possibly*"—Breanne glimpsed me—"warned us about."

"Why would Alexa Delphine *give* us her plan?" Sarah asked flatly, setting her glass down onto the coffee table. "Unless it's part of her sick torture game."

I could find comfort in the fact that my friends were almost as angry about all of this as I was.

"I don't want to think about motive right now," I said. "Whoever picked up the phone the night we found him said he was a liar and a traitor. It wasn't Alexa, William, or Anthony. They may have planned it, but whoever took him had to consider this as bigger than just part of a plan. So I'm gonna say we're right about Alexa warning us about it, because..."

I still couldn't shake the sincerity I'd seen in her eyes that night. "*You know me, Emma.*" I didn't know why, but she *wanted* us to know what they were up to. Which made her entire speech on that deck code.

"What did she say after alluding to Jak?" Momma asked from the recliner, glancing between me and Mr. Dawson in front of the window.

He leaned against the sill. "Robin Hood. To this day, I can't figure out why she mentioned Robin Hood."

"The prize," I answered, straightening with remembrance. "She said something about winning the prize when you keep your enemies close. And Robin Hood was considered a hero by people who actually knew him, what he was really doing: stealing from the rich to give to the poor. Wrong thing, right reasons."

Mr. Dawson rested his sharp chin in his hand. "When you have your prize or whatever you're after, you protect it by keeping it someplace safe. Where... not even your allies know about."

"A bank," I said, the words bubbling back to the surface of my mind. "Where strangers protect it, but we trust them with our money anyway. And sometimes that bank is really far away, even outside of the—country."

Our words sounded insane, no other way to put it. I more than understood the furrowed brows and frustrated glares from each person in the room.

"The beginning part about mental torture didn't make sense in context until it actually happened," I began. "I'm not gonna wait until these next parts unfold: if Jak is the enemy Alexa was referring to, then the 'prize' has to be his intel on Tristan Atera's daughter."

"Did they... *get it?*" Sarah asked Jak cautiously.

"No," he said, left with nothing to do but fiddle with his thumbs.

"But why *Robin Hood* specifically?" I asked, eager to keep the conversation away from his memories. "He wasn't really a 'bad' guy despite theft. He was the hero to people who knew him..."

Knew him.

Know your enemy.

"You know me, Emma."

"So Alexa Delphine is trying to tell us..." Opal said skeptically, arching a brow, "that she's a hero for murdering her own people?"

No. Not possible. Was she seriously trying to tell me that she believed ridding the world of wielders was for the greater good?

Sarah echoed my thoughts almost exactly: "It doesn't matter if she's one of them. What matters is what she thinks of them."

"Robin Hood," I repeated, testing the name. "Who stole for the greater good. Alexa is stealing her victims' lives for what she believes is the greater good."

Mr. Dawson exhaled quietly, lightly shaking his head. He'd said that night that he was done believing in this woman, that she could ever become someone redeemable. I was pretty sure that not every part of him had been convinced of that yet.

"But then what about the—bank part, you said?" Breanne asked, swallowing some of her smoothie. "When you get your prize, you store it someplace safe that not even your allies know about, even if it's far away."

The prize... Storing it somewhere... I didn't even want to think about what that could mean. Storing bodies in one collective space wasn't exactly the easiest image.

"Her money?" Momma answered, dropping her hands into her lap. "Any reward she gets for doing this job is plausible."

The Delphines were following in Henry Callistro's footsteps to become more powerful. So if Alexa were to finally get her hands on us, on Breanne and Opal and even Mr. Dawson...

Sarah and I gasped like Breanne had revealed the plan in its entirety, riddles shed and all. With a glance at each other, not an ounce of doubt lay in those bright-green eyes.

I had to formulate this like my life depended on it; the girls couldn't know what I knew about Henry and Caralyn Callistro.

"Magic," I began, looking at each person in the room—even Jak, who kept his eyes on the coffee table. "The Delphines are wielders in a Grand Hunter position. That alone doesn't make sense, not even when we try to justify it with Alexa's story. What if it's really because she's using this as a means to get *more* magic?"

"For power," Sarah added, like we had practiced this speech a hundred times beforehand. "And she's storing it somewhere not even her allies, William and her nonfamily pack members, know about to protect that power."

"Out of the country," Mr. Dawson said. "Now it sounds like we have something."

"But she picked Robin Hood specifically?" Opal asked, leaning forward again to look at her uncle. "The guy who did the *right* thing for the wrong reasons?"

"Maybe she believes that she and her family are the only ones who can have it," Breanne said, her brows scrunched in doubt at her own words.

"The woman's psycho enough to," Mom muttered.

No, something still wasn't right. One piece still didn't fit. Or we were missing one.

"If she was warning us about their plans," I mused, "then why would William be helping her get stronger? And what does that mean for the rest of the pack?"

"What did she say?" Sarah asked, gaze locked on me as firmly as her body remained still. Her Hunter instincts were officially aflame. "This industry is mental torture, keep your enemies close to get what you want out of them, and then protect your prize?"

"Yeah."

"Hello?" She gestured to the five teenagers in the room. "Jak isn't her only enemy."

It fell into place with that one sentence: Jak had been the precursor. An *example*.

"You're saying," I said, "that we have a choice to either turn ourselves in, or…?"

No one stopped me. No one told me I was wrong or crazy; the woman had authorized the torture of her own stepson. Why were we any better to keep around?

"How?" I stated, daring anyone to answer. "We're protected at the school all day, someone is bound to notice our absence, and Mom and Mr. Dawson would know immediately!"

"They're smarter than that," Mr. Dawson said, his arms crossed over his chest like he was protecting his answers. "They probably only took Jak because they *are* his parents and they had someone to substitute for him so nobody else would notice his absence. But dealing with the four of you one at a time would be, for lack of better words, way too messy. So they're likely waiting to get all four of you at once."

"Like…" Breanne said, her grip on her straw tightening, "Thanksgiving break?"

"No," Momma said, shaking her head. "You'll all be with your families and separated, Sarah's even going to a different state. Not even they would be able to pull that off. If they wanted to, they could've grabbed you guys today."

"Which means, dare I say, you're safe over break," Mr. Dawson added hesitantly. "That gives us a few days, at least."

There was still a piece that didn't fit: Alexa's sincerity. Why she had practically begged me to understand what she was really saying in those moments. She'd been playing a part somewhere, but I didn't know whom it was for.

But I could find out. Now I had enough pieces.

I glanced at Mr. Dawson next to me in the corner of my eye.

—*You think Mom would let me use her for nore practice for this?*—

He released a deep breath and cast his gaze down. —*Nope. You can pick anyone else, though.*—

Perfect. Timing was everything; as long as we had break, I wasn't going to risk a critical piece of the puzzle yet and disrupt the peace. We were going to get answers by the end of this week even if it killed me.

C H A P T E R

Thirty-One

I was so close to having a normal Thanksgiving with my family. It'd been perfect until I fell asleep that night and a white flash burst through my subconscious.

Concrete walls surrounded me on all fronts in a big, empty office. Cold handcuffs bound me to a metal chair.

"We finally found her, you know." William Bleu smirked as he stood in front of me triumphantly. "Tristan Atera's—"

Flash.

"Emma!" Breanne exclaimed as she ran toward me and threw her frail arms around me. We stood in a damp hallway, the urgency of being chased surging through me. "Thank God, I—!"

Flash.

I was running down the hallway—alone. My gaze was set on

one door at the end. I had to get there for some reason. That was my end goal. I needed to get there. Someone needed me—

My blood went cold as a cold hand clamped over my mouth, an arm sliding around my waist. Alexa kicked open the nearest door and dragged me inside.

Flash.

Tears soaked my lashes and cheeks. Alexa was gone. I was alone, back in the concrete hallway, stumbling into the wall. The wind had been knocked out of my chest. My mind was playing a sick, fresh memory that the vision couldn't invade.

Flash.

My eyes could barely capture the person pulling me through a cavernous room.

I should be dead, I thought, the word being the only thing I could see in my head. *I should... We were almost—*

With another flash, I sat in the back of a car with people I couldn't see yet knew were my allies. People I loved more than anything in the world.

"Emma?" a frail voice asked, terrified.

"No, they're..." I whispered, so quietly that even I couldn't hear it. "They're dead—"

I shot up in bed, already gasping.

Next to my bed, my bedroom window provided just enough light for my eyes to focus on the comforter. Early morning. Momma was sleeping soundly in her bedroom on the other side of the hall. I wasn't alone. I was okay.

No, I wasn't. Nausea itself was swaying my body. I kept one hand on my heaving chest. Fear mingled with anxiety and bred biting mites of dread.

No. No, no, no. It can't be, it can't be, don't let it be, not that one.

August. That was why the vision had been familiar on the cruise, that same nightmare had plagued me in August. I'd thought it was just my subconscious still recovering from the horrors of when I'd first had it—living out whatever effects were still lingering. But now? I wasn't going to lie to myself again.

I leaned myself back down in my bed. My mind tortured me over and over again with paranoid theories and sick possibilities. For some reason, I could only get enough breath from my mouth as I stared up at the ceiling. I strained to keep my breathing quiet enough, as if it'd be enough to wake up Momma through my closed door.

My visions were trying to tell me something. Warn me about something. As if even my magic itself knew what Alexa and William were planning and was trying to prepare me in the way that it could.

Like I couldn't help but feel Alexa doing.

Right. The nore in me was ready to grab answers as soon as Sunday hit, when I'd see Mr. Dawson again. I just needed *exactly* the right question for him to ask...

⚓

Like all students on break, private school or not, by Saturday afternoon, I was already dreading coming back. All there was left to do was enjoy not having homework to stay up until midnight finishing, and look forward to one more morning of sleeping in tomorrow.

From the living room window, I watched Momma reverse out

of the driveway, on her way to the store. The first snowfall of the season lined the street, gleaming in the sun. Winter had come early this year. My breath collected in a fog on the window, the house kept at a toasty seventy-six degrees from the overactive heater. I almost wanted to draw a smiley face on the glass.

I was almost tempted to get my phone from my room and see if Jak had replied to my texts yet, but based on his messaging pattern of the last week, he'd probably be getting to them later tonight. The girls were usually my next option, but Opal was at Mr. Dawson's for mentoring, Breanne was staying in her aunt's snowy mountain home until tonight, and Sarah wasn't going to be back from her grandparents' in Florida until tomorrow.

Maybe the group chat is up. Early afternoon here meant Alejandro was almost definitely still up if he didn't have a healthy sleep schedule.

It only took one step toward my bedroom for a knock to rap on the front door.

Despite the fact that I wasn't an infamous face to the U.S. Government and the Delphines *wouldn't* knock, my nerves burst into flames. I turned to face the door.

Not the government. Not the Delphines. Not the school.

But also not my parents, Mr. Dawson, or the girls.

I crept to the door. My mind repeated that first thought over and over again to keep my nerves steady. There was a peephole, and nobody was barging in. If it was anyone dangerous, I could knock them out with magic and climb out my bedroom window.

In case an enemy was on the other side, I didn't need a creak telling them that someone was home. I leaned on my toes slightly to peer through the peephole without having to lean on the door.

No way.

I unlocked the door and carefully pulled it open. "Jak?"

The long scar that ran down the left side of his face glared at me, along with the one under his right eye and on his hairline. The bruising on his right cheek colored his skin a jaundice-like yellow. Although he was physically healing, it was still nowhere near any easier to look at him.

"Hi," he said, his hands in the pockets of his black purple-rose hoodie I'd gotten him for his birthday. "Can—can I come in?"

I opened my mouth to reply, but a lightning bolt of paranoia struck me first. And I'd already opened the door.

Jak doesn't stammer, but my Jak was just recently scarred for life.

He's wearing the hoodie. That's a good sign.

But he never texted me that he was coming. He always warns me when he's on his way.

I bent my head and swallowed. Then, I closed my eyes. If the Jak in front of me was fake, which not even "Merlin" could determine anymore, they couldn't see me use magic if this interaction was being recorded. Only a truth spell would let me know.

Veritatem dicere.

I brought my head back up. "Is it actually you?"

He nodded quickly, troubled brown eyes locked on me. "It—it's me. I promise."

"Okay." I opened the door all the way, letting him step inside and releasing him from the spell.

Mere moments before I shut the door, already, the silence was fuzzy. Already, the air was awkward and—foreign. In no way had I expected Jak to bounce back to normal after just a week, especially since he'd had to go back to his parents after everything he'd gone through—but that's what made it all the harder to be around him. Helping him heal while I was why he'd been broken in the first place.

"Was Thanksgiving okay?" I asked.

"Yeah." He nodded, rubbing his palms against his jeans. That was a new habit. "Adrien's was nice."

With another look at his twisted scars, the way his face still hadn't completely filled back in after he'd starved off fifteen pounds, the question shoved its way out of my mouth: "I know this is a stupid question, but—are you okay?"

He scoffed, his gaze stuck on the wooden floor of the entryway. "Yeah, that... that is a stupid question. But I'm fine, I guess."

I pressed my lips together, crossing my arms over my chest. No, I realized, the moment wasn't awkward. It was... fragile. Too still for my liking, like there was nothing I could say to make this moment right. Like the balance between us was... wrong.

"Jak, if... if you wanna talk, you can."

He stuck his hands back into his pockets, breathily chuckling. "You could've warned me it was no picnic in the park."

Joking. But this wasn't Jakson Bleu's usual banter. I knew him too well by then; this was Jakson Bleu trying to avoid the truth of the matter, trying to avoid how he really felt—convince himself that he *wasn't* rattled, disturbed, hadn't been shaken like a ragdoll into cold reality.

"Sorry," he said. "That was stupid, I know—"

"You don't have to pretend like you aren't affected," I told him, intently staring at his downcast eyes as if I could make them meet mine. "Don't do that to yourself. Do you know how much I wished I had someone to open up to, someone who wasn't an adult to talk to about this? And—ha—where you've been? So much further than I've ever been. You can talk to me."

Then his eyes rose to meet mine. They were empty. I couldn't help but feel like he was trying to find something to fill this moment with, too. Everything just felt too off balance for us.

Everything in general did lately. And with him being as constant as he used to be, I didn't want him falling into the pile of things that had changed too quickly.

He took a step toward me. "I felt hurt. I felt betrayed by my own family, which I didn't even think was possible, considering everything my dad's done to me since my mom died. And that angered me, because for me to have felt betrayed, it meant that I'd been stupid enough to still have hope in him to begin with."

"You weren't stupid—"

"Yes, I *was*," he said, clutching his chest. I cringed at the bruises he was probably touching. He took another step up to me, causing me to walk backwards and into the door behind me. "After he emotionally abandoned me when I was seven, after I'd just been kidnapped and watched my own mother get shot in front of me, after he went off and married a stranger I'd never even met until their engagement, after he completely detached himself from me and fails to live up to my mom's honor every single day he plays his stupid role at my school to hunt—I *still* had hope, Emma! I had hope he could get better, and I was the one burned in the end. Again. My own dad *authorized* my torture. And then he pretended nothing ever happened when I came back to him. And I still believed in him. So yeah. I was an *idiot*."

Don't talk about yourself that way, I wanted to say. But my criticism was the last thing he needed right now.

He rested his arm against the door, next to my head. His forehead fell to rest on his fist. I didn't step away. I just stared at those eyes as they closed and a heavy sigh left him. I hated seeing him beat himself up over things that were out of his control—especially when I was the one who'd been "warned" about it ahead of time.

They've managed to break a new boundary with me. Too far.

I didn't understand this new depth of connection I felt with Jak—felt toward him, and sometimes felt *with* him. I just knew that his happiness, his safety, was as important to me as anyone else's in my family. Except, for some reason, he was in a different league. Like... like I wanted to be the warden responsible for guarding all of those things for him so that he wouldn't have to. Yet none of those things had been protected.

"I wish I didn't love him," he muttered.

"It's not your fault that you do."

He matched our eyes.

"He's your dad," I told him. "You need time to adopt someone as a father figure into your life. And sometimes you need time to detach from them when they've hurt you like that."

He lifted his head, his arm still on the door.

"How long did it take you?" he whispered, looking down at me. "To adopt Tristan?"

My mind was buzzing like a wire had been cut in it. "I... I don't remember."

"Does it get easier?" he asked, leaning in. His eyes fell to my lips. And stayed there. "Waking up every morning thinking you're gonna end up back where you were? Never knowing when someone's gonna take you again?"

"Eventually," I replied in a shaky whisper. I couldn't tell if it was his proximity or my sheer anger of what had been done to him, physically and mentally. "It will. It'll get easier."

A tense second passed by, one I knew he could feel.

He leaned in close to my ear, the words tickling it. "Does this get easier?"

His breath sent an electric jolt down my spine. *Resisting you. Pretending I don't feel this way toward you. Holding up our understanding that if I'm with you, it's a death sentence for both of us.*

That was what I imagined him saying after that question. And I wanted to believe that I was right, because it was what I would've been saying to him right now.

"No," I whispered.

He brought his free hand up to my jaw, his fingers tracing down it until he reached my chin. Gently, he tilted my head up, his gaze darting back and forth between my eyes and my lips. His were almost brushing against mine—like they were daring each other to be brave.

The tension in his fingers slightly tightened his hold on my chin. His lips grazed mine, as if he were reminding himself of every reason that this was a bad idea.

"It never will." Then, he pressed a lingering kiss on the corner of my mouth. He was teetering on the border itself.

He was giving me the power to demolish it completely.

I closed my eyes and turned my head to meet his lips where they were. The communication between us was painfully explicit as Jak pressed his lips to mine in a familiar kiss, a familiar desire to be close. His hand that was holding my chin dropped and slipped around my waist, pulling me away from the door and closer to him. With us lightly pressed against each other, his other arm fell from the door and rested on the other side of my waist. My hands found a careful resting spot on his chest. He grunted in pain, and I remembered his ribs—and yet the more he seemed to hurt, the deeper he kissed me. We were both giving ourselves up to the emotions swirling in a roaring blizzard between us, and that was when I realized something: those brown eyes weren't just empty. They were empty and starving like the rest of him.

I wanted to do anything to get his mind off of what had happened—get *my* mind off of what had happened. I wanted to forget the rules and laws and wisdom and remember him, just him. Just for this moment right now. He was okay, he was distracted, I didn't have to think about the world outside of us. We were okay. We were being what the other needed—weren't we?

The kiss still lingered, but Jak pulled back ever so slightly, our foreheads resting against each other's. "It hurts," he rasped, wincing between each breath, "but I don't—I don't want this to stop."

"Then"—I placed another peck on his lips—"don't let it."

He pushed me back against the door with another pained gasp, deepening the kiss like he was savoring every taste he could get off just my lips alone. His hands tightened around my waist as mine rose up to his neck, all too aware of the injuries on his face. Every touch of his fingers sent another bolt of electricity through me, every single kiss a reminder of—

Another excruciating reminder of everything we weren't supposed to be. But I didn't care. Not right now.

Jak broke away nonetheless. "I shouldn't—be doing this," he whispered with a higher pitch—every rapid breath labored now, a wince hiding in the back of his throat. His hands strained against my waist like they were begging to hold me tighter. "Wow, this—

this hurts... Em, you shouldn't—we shouldn't—"

"We didn't," I said, my voice matching his. "We haven't been—"

"We need to keep—doing that." He swallowed, then exhaled like he'd been holding his breath. He pressed his hand against his chest. I knew that gesture, I'd lived it almost every day at the beginning of the semester: he was trying to control his breath to stop the pain in his ribs. "Look, Emma, this isn't worth sacrificing your family. Nothing is worth giving up their safety—or yours." His breathing began to slow, his eyes trained on the floor before he shut them tight. "Following your own advice—is one of the hardest things—you ever have to do. But the reward's always greater than the struggle, you know that. I know—you know that."

But I also know that I want something with you. So badly. And him being so wise and mature right now wasn't helping the situation any. In fact, unintentionally, Jak was being the worst solution possible.

I had to help myself and break away completely, striding from the door and to the living room behind him.

"Em—"

"I know," I said, resting my hand against my forehead. I closed my eyes, taking a few disbelieving breaths before turning around to meet him. "I know that, I know."

Silence.

We shouldn't have done that. We shouldn't have done any of that.

Against my pride, I forced myself to look him in the eye. "I'm sorry. I—I took advantage, you're still shaken up and I don't know how to help, I just wanted..."

He turned to the door and rested both arms against it now.

Why does he have to be taller than me? Why does he have to be so cute? Why does he have to be so right?

His hand fell to rest on the doorknob. Part of me begged him not to twist it.

"I'm sorry," I said again, like he hadn't believed me the first time. And I really didn't know if he had or not.

"It's okay," he replied simply.

Too many seconds of silence passed.

"I'm gonna stay with Wyatt for a few days," he finally said. He never looked at me. "Just—don't worry about me for a bit. I'm gonna... I'm gonna be okay on my own for now. Please."

He wasn't assuring me. He was asking me. He couldn't be around me.

As much as my selfishness wanted to say otherwise—as much as my gut twisted with disappointment—I wouldn't let them rule what came out of my mouth next: "Okay."

Jak opened the door. The subtle ambience of the rural street outside flooded into the house. Without another word, he walked out and shut the door behind him.

The heavy silence he left behind seemed to cushion my every movement as I mindlessly made my way to the sofa. It wasn't until I felt myself plop down that my head fell into my hands, helpless sobs racking my body at my own stupidity and greed. Jak had never taken advantage of me any of the times I'd gone through what he had. The first time it was his turn in the chair, I'd used it as an excuse to satiate what I'd persuaded him to help me bury in the first place—as if it *were* an excuse.

Why do I want to be with him so badly? Why does it hurt to not have him around when he's hurting? Why do I want to be his and him to be mine this *badly?*

Why did I hurt him like that just now?

Every question had the same answer: *I am such an idiot.*

CHAPTER

Thirty-Two

"Are you ready?"

That was a question I never thought I'd ask Thomas Dawson. Nonetheless, there his hand lay in mine as he sat across from me at the dining room table Sunday evening. Momma sat next to us in the head seat, observing.

"As ready as you are," he replied.

I'd spent all weekend trying to find this question, which meant I wasn't going to lose this opportunity for anything. I reached into myself for my nore magic, willing it to reach into Mr. Dawson's mind and transfer his life's memories to me.

There they flashed: images I'd seen a couple of times before, blurring in my head yet whispering their contents to me.

"What would you like to know?" I asked. I prepared my mind

for whatever answer my magic was about to give me.

"Are Alexa and William on the same side for this mission?"

A presence swirled in my brain, magic flowing through my veins and beating with life through my heart. It was like the nore's magic had transported itself to Alexa and William and then back to me as my mind flashed a foggy tapestry of the two—arguing in a dimly lit, gray debriefing room. A pastel-yellow file sat on the table beside them.

The Atera file.

The image faded into another second: the last second of Alexa ripping the file in half.

This is an event past. Her true motive unveiled.

And there in the center of my mind, my answer lay, spoken to me by the nore's magic: "Alexa Delphine isn't William Bleu's ally in this mission," I said, my vision held by what I'd seen for only a second. "William wants the Ateras' downfall, but Alexa—"

My magic's answer jolted my conscience awake. It wasn't possible. It went against everything she had done, everything she'd ever wanted—everything we'd already fought!

"Emma?" I heard Mr. Dawson ask, his hand remaining between mine.

Somehow, my magic was deep enough in that it never deactivated, not even when I said, "Alexa's mission is the Ateras' protection."

Stillness zapped the air like a scorpion's sting. Even I wanted to doubt my own ruling, to deny it as even a possibility—but a nore's answers aren't speculative or inferred. They're whispered to us in a still, small voice that knows infinitely more than we do. It's magic.

But I had to be misinterpreting something this time—Alexa wanted to *protect* my family? Since when?!

Despite his lack of ignorance about a nore's magic, Mr. Dawson still asked, "Are you... are you sure?"

"It's what the nore knows." I fought to keep a grip on my words, my mind still running. "I can't change it."

But I wanted to. There had to be a loophole of some kind, because if there wasn't, we'd been fighting wrong this whole time. Alexa's mission was our protection? How? Had my magic *somehow* lied to me?

Momma's presence was heavy between us. I knew she probably had a hundred questions, a hundred angry exclamations at how magic could possibly dare to propose something like that—frankly, I was right there with her—but none of it mattered. What mattered was what we knew: Alexa's alliance with William Bleu was a cover.

She tore up that file to protect us. I knew that. But figuring out her excuse to stay undetected was a whole other ballgame. Grand Hunter versus Grand Hunter is a match where not even the laws of probability can determine either side's chance of victory.

I don't get it. My magic said it, but I can't... believe it.

"Okay," Mr. Dawson began warily, "then what's your question to me?"

It was right there: *What are you keeping from me about my identity as a sorceress?* But there were two other things right there in the room just as quickly shoving it out: my mother, and my respect for her.

So I settled on a question I'd wondered the answer to ever since he told me that he was a druid: "What boundaries are you willing to cross to protect your family?"

I don't know why he had to think about it first; a nore's magic puts our enquirer under the "truth spell" when we ask our question. Then again, maybe Mr. Dawson wasn't thinking about it; maybe he wanted just the right execution when he replied, "Any moral boundary I've ever laid out for myself."

I paused as I released his hand, my magic retracting into the shadows of my mind again. Neither of us were under the influence anymore, but I still had the courage to ask, "Lie? Steal? *Kill?*"

He chuckled—whether out of embarrassment or amusement that I'd ask, I was almost too afraid to know. "Not sure I wanna have this conversation with your mom in the room. But—yep."

"I agree," Momma, to both of our surprise, said, her chin resting on her locked-together hands and her elbows on the table. "I want Em to be willing to go to any reasonable lengths to protect those who deserve it."

Yeah, exactly: reasonable!

In full honesty, half of me could and couldn't believe that I was hearing the words—but it was my mother after the last year had happened. It was the Master Hunter reacknowledging the world we lived in and respecting its rules; that was why the other half of me more than believed it.

But even kill...?

"Especially if this woman is only pretending to protect us," she added, arching a brow at me.

I shook my head, not knowing what she wanted me to tell her. "I have no choice but to believe it, but I can't. Like... *how?*"

"But we know a nore is never wrong," Mr. Dawson mused. "They physically can't be."

"I don't understand a single thing about it," I said, leaning back in my chair. "I don't even feel like we're dealing with the same woman anymore. But for one reason or another, she's protecting us right now."

"That's the key phrase," Momma said, twisting her wedding ring. "'One reason or another'. Just because she's protecting us in no way means she's on our side. William flat out wants us dead, but Alexa probably wants to preserve you to get your magic and whatever you have on Adara. That's the only plausible reason for her mission to be our protection."

Mr. Dawson looked at her for only a second, but it was enough for me to read: neither of us were convinced that Momma would believe it no matter how many pieces of evidence she was offered. If Alexa's mission was protection, that made her coded speech on the deck a warning—not a taunt, not even a riddle. And she had coded it because William had been listening in. He couldn't know.

I froze in my chair, swallowing the shock down. *That* was why she'd seemed so sincere that night. She had been. Maybe she actually had temporarily reverted back to the woman who'd spoken to me on Mr. Dawson's sofa, doing my makeup. Just for a second— just to show me who she really was in that moment. In this mission. Our protector.

It felt way too much like we really *weren't* dealing with the same woman anymore. Or even that we'd never been dealing with that woman in the first place like.

⚓

Needless to say, that wasn't the best piece of news to come back to school with on Monday. Sure, my family was "safe" from the Delphines, but my friends still had every reason to be on their list. And it wasn't exactly like I could *tell* them that.

Breanne was anxious enough for reasons she refused to tell us until Sarah came back. In the classes I had with her, she'd spent them bouncing her knee and tapping her pencil eraser against her paper for every second she wasn't writing. And she kept quiet despite my and Opal's perpetual nagging all day until the door to our dorm finally swung open that afternoon.

The three of us jumped, looking up from our game of Uno on the purple circle rug. A grinning and glowing Sarah skipped inside the room, reaching out her arms.

"Hello, my loves!" she chirped, dropping her white purse onto the carpet as we stood. "I missed you so!"

"Someone's in a good mood!" Opal remarked as we joined together in a tight group hug. "What's your secret?"

"Notice how I'm the only one who took an extra day off," Sarah sang, taking off the sunglasses perched on her head. "How were your Thanksgivings, my dears, tell me, I wanna hear all about it!"

As she walked past us and to the walk-in closet, the three of us spared each other baffled glances. What had her in this great a mood?

"Nobody's talking!" she said, coming out of the closet with her sunglasses put away and white coat from Greece taken off. "What? Was it that bad for all of you?"

"Mine was great," I replied, sparing Opal a glance.

"Same. I got to be with my uncle and biological parents."

"Wonderful, I love it! Well, dinner with my grandparents not only allowed me a trip to a heated pool afterwards, but I also met the *cutest* boy there—who's also Egyptian, like me!"

Kamose? I immediately thought, but even I knew that that was (close to) impossible. Then Sarah's words had a chance to fully land.

"What about Adrien?" I asked before Opal, mouth open, could get the words out. "I thought you guys were on a break!"

Sarah's eyes dulled as she leaned against the doorway of our closet, crossing her arms. "We've been 'on a break' for months now. I think you guys know what that means."

Something sank into my stomach like an anchor to the bottom of the ocean, but I couldn't name it. Sarah and Adrien had been a thing since September last year; the problems had begun this summer (as far as we knew), but Breanne, Opal, and I had been so sure that they'd get past it...

That was it: disappointment, grief for what was familiar. The world was changing again, yet Sarah didn't seem fazed one bit. Maybe she'd already coped on her own.

"Besides, this guy—his name's 'Ziyad'—not only was it an instant click, but it was instant *friendship*. We texted for the whole weekend, he's the sweetest and most respectful guy I've ever met."

For some reason, that felt like a punch in the gut.

To my fear, an awkward air settled over the room—but I definitely didn't want Sarah to feel our caution, especially if it was being interpreted as judgment.

"I mean, that's awesome," Opal said for us, "but are you gonna tell Adrien it's over?"

"Next time I see him." Sarah shrugged with her hands on her

hips. "I'll tell you guys why it didn't work. Eventually."

The room's eyes fell onto little Breanne, the only one who hadn't said anything since Sarah had walked through the door. She avoided our gazes, furiously picking at the hairs on her wrist.

"My Thanksgiving was good," she muttered.

Sarah scoffed, tossing her hair over her shoulder. "You need to get better at lying. What happened?"

Breanne looked up at her. "No, I just—you're happy right now, I don't want to ruin your mood—"

"You already are by scaring me," Sarah told her. "What happened? Don't tell me you're freaked because midterms are this month."

"I think it's about Alexa," I said the second the thought formed in my brain.

Breanne dished out a glare at me. "Emma!"

"What? It is?" Opal asked, Sarah sparing her a pensive glance. Sarah was definitely observing again, something that I really had to learn to start doing.

Breanne took a tentative step back. "Look, I just... I've been thinking, and—and with what happened with Jak and—what we talked about last week—"

"Wait," Sarah said, holding up her hands. "Wait, wait, wait, calm down first. We're all gonna sit down, eat some candy, and talk about this, okay?"

"No."

Breanne had never spoken with such authority in her life—at least, not for anything that wasn't an academic decathlon, spelling bee, or public scholastic performance of any kind. Maybe she was even more exhausted from our situation than I thought, because that's the only way I can explain the courage she had in her eyes then—how hard they hit when they landed on me. "Emma—we have to talk to Jak about this. Can you ask him when he can meet?"

I restrained a tight swallow. *This is gonna be worse than I thought.*

No, she just has a theory, right? Who's to say it'll come true?

That was foolish thinking—this was the same girl who solved one of the seven Millennium Prize problems, the hardest math problems in present existence, in eighth grade. (She refuses to let us tell anyone about it because she believes it'll be the demise of our country's social hierarchy and mathematical construct.)

I nodded, going to grab my phone off my bed. "You got it."

C H A P T E R

Thirty-Three

My head swam with exhaustion and dizziness. I recognized the feeling of my body sitting upright, chained to a chair with cold handcuffs.

A haze settled over my vision. Dizziness was too powerful to allow my eyes to focus, stirring my stomach with nausea. The cold gray room, besides an oak desk in the left corner, was practically empty.

"Emma?" a familiar, comforting voice asked on my right. I whipped my head in its direction. A man stood on the other side of the room.

"Dad—?"

Flash.

A gloved hand covered my mouth. That sweet, sympathetic

voice was whispering into my ear again. "Shhh, darling. It'll be over—"

A flash before I screamed, "Stop it! Dad!"

Before I could react, another blinding flash burst in front of me.

"—woke up." William Bleu stood in front of me. The haze was gone. "I have a few surprises—"

Flash.

Alexa...?

She stood against a heavy metal door, her chest heaving. For some reason, I was standing right in front of her.

"What do you want?" I furiously exclaimed.

Her hauntingly emerald-green eyes locked onto me. "You don't get—"

Flash.

The familiar gray hallway in front of me was narrowing. There was one door dead ahead of me. All I knew was that I had to get there, I had to—

Why were there tears streaming down my face? Why did my chest hurt?

I spun around. A gunshot went off.

My eyes shot open with my gasp. Pitch black surrounded me on all sides, unable to swallow my rapid, shallow breaths. Memories of the vision flashed in a replay.

No, I shouted in my head, grabbing it. *Stop it, stop it, stop it!*

That same vision. The one I was terrified of, the one that was similar to every occurrence of it and yet never had identical structure. Nothing was solid. Nothing was set in stone.

The nightmares were officially torturing me. The visions were overwhelming. My future was racking my mind more ravenously than any Grand Hunter I'd met in the last year.

Stop it, get out of my head!

I buried my face into my comforter, trying to silence my breathing before the girls woke up. Did Opal ever get these visions? She'd been in one of them, wasn't she getting what I was? If she was, why hadn't she said anything yet? Was she scared to worry us because there was only a chance this would happen?

Get out! My cries in my head gradually grew weaker. *Stop it...!*

My magic had been cruel to me before. But right now, it had never been so sadistic.

How many times had Mr. Dawson foreseen his goodbye with Dad when he first left? How many times had Opal received a vision she was scared of? Did Annisa ever have dreams of a terrifying future?

Torture. This was complete and absolute torture.

⚓

I followed my friends to a red vinyl seat at a table in the middle of Waverly, all the more on edge. Even though Sarah had insisted on paying, and despite the corny beach decorations reminding me of my childhood, I was still stuck in a numb daze. Even Breanne was stressed because, thanks to the Grand Hunter drama, midterms in a couple of weeks really were starting to freak her out. She wanted to get back to the school to study ASAP.

A few minutes later, Jak walked into the restaurant.

I really hope that's him.

I hated looking at the boy and never really knowing if it *was* my Jak. Especially because now he had a long scar on his left cheek, a cut healing under his right eye, and faded bruising across his face. This wasn't supposed to be my Jak.

Our last encounter burst through the doors of my head. It'd only been a few days. That was nowhere near enough time for me to forgive myself for my selfishness with him.

I shoved all of that far down; the conversation Breanne wanted to have was priority right now. After all, it was serious enough that she needed Jak in on it.

I couldn't let that conversation happen if this wasn't actually Jak.

I stood from the table and strode to the front of the restaurant. "Hey."

His eyes, marred by his experience two weeks ago, stayed dull yet careful. "Hey."

Has he chosen to forget what happened, too? Did I hurt him that badly? Does he want to forget it?

We stepped aside so as to not block the restaurant entrance. Even though I didn't know if this was the real Jak or not, I still wanted to take his hand. I restrained myself for that one reason of last Saturday.

"Um..." My mind reeled from everything that had happened in the last year—almost a year and a half. "Do you remember what I told you when Redway left Callistro? In the passageway?"

A slight furrow knitted his brows together. "You mean about"—he leaned in, lowering his voice—"'her'?"

I mentally facepalmed, realizing how I'd asked the absolute worst possible question I could've. "Yeah."

"Yeah. His 'daughter's' name, why?"

Okay. So it's him. And for now, I was going to pretend that he thought I'd randomly made up that name.

"We..." I glimpsed the front doors of Waverly, trusting Jak to tell me if any of the girls were coming up behind me. "We need to think of a codeword or something so I can know that it's actually you. Since 'Merlin' isn't gonna work anymore and I won't be able to use a truth spell every time."

My heart twinged at the possibility that Jak was never going to call me that again; it'd been used as a weapon against both of us in a way that we could never erase.

He nodded slightly, thinking on it. After a couple of seconds, I realized that I should probably think of some options, too, just as Jak said, "How about 'anchor'?"

I tilted my head. "Why that?"

"Like on your cruise," he replied simply, shrugging. "Might be just random enough to work."

That was the biggest glimpse into his old self I'd gotten yet.

"Okay. Let's do it."

He followed me to the table and took a seat next to Breanne, who had Sarah on her other side. Soft greetings were exchanged as he scooted in, folding his hands on the table. Nobody found his timidity strange, his mellowness out of the ordinary despite how it was everything not Jakson Bleu.

But despite the arrival of our guest of honor, Breanne refused to open her mouth until after we ordered and received our food fifteen minutes later.

"You wait until we get our food," Sarah began, stabbing a scallop with her fork, "so you could tell the story and not be able to eat?"

"Why do you think I got a salad?" Breanne deadpanned, not even picking up her fork. "You guys eat. I'll talk."

Jak sat there without a word, sipping on his mango smoothie—the only thing he'd ordered. It was at least an improvement from the last time the five of us had met up, where he couldn't stomach a strawberry smoothie yet. Any relief was welcome even though I wasn't the one actually receiving it. I just wanted it for him.

Breanne leaned in, gaze steady on him. "Jak, your parents—"

"Alexa and William," he stated. "What about them?"

Not only was it the first time anyone who wasn't an instructor had ever been brave enough to correct Breanne Shaw—but it was also the first time I'd ever heard Jak so firmly refer to his father by his first name.

"Um..." Breanne staggered, and I couldn't blame her for it as her gaze shifted to the rest of us. "Well—I wanted to meet up today because I think... I think I finally figured something out about their plan. And why"—she glimpsed Jak for only a shadow of a second—"*that* happened."

Whether we were too scared, too patient, or too tired to move, I couldn't tell, but we let her continue.

"Break gave me too much time to think." She leaned in closely, dropping her voice to a whisper. "How long did it take for the bracelet to drain Alexa's magic? Did Mr. Dawson ever say?"

"I think—a few days," I replied. "But it'd be hard to tell the exact moment every last bit was gone."

"Exactly. Knowing that they want us for a few days, a bracelet can't be their new plan. Unless—they kept us hostage until the magic was all gone."

Across the table, the girls and I exchanged wary glances, all except for Jak. Silence. Maybe we *were* too naïve, because it felt like none of us wanted to believe that we lived in a world evil enough to try something like keeping a teenage girl against her will for the sake of magic. Despite the boy sitting with us.

"It put me in a cycle of sheer mental torture trying to figure out what they *could* be planning," Breanne added, timid like we were classmates she was meeting for the first time. "But when I almost broke down from the stress, it hit me. I don't think they just want us on edge, I think they're trying to *break* us. That's the point of the mental torture, because when they have us right where they want us, they can act. In the end, they kill four birds with one stone."

Chills crawled down my torso. I could almost feel the words themselves slink down from the top of my skull to the heels of my feet.

"So," Opal said at the end of the table, "in the end, that means..."

"Whatever they have planned, not only do they need us as mentally weak as possible, they need more time to do it." A hard lump passed in Breanne's throat. "And they know how to break us in time for it."

Even if we didn't have the proof right in front of us with Jak, that was just wisdom. We didn't have a choice but to believe that.

"Okay, say they do," Sarah stated with authority. "Then what? What do they actually *do* when they have us?"

"Take Alexa's and Opal's magic, for one," Breanne replied softly. "But after that... They can't just erase our memories. They're too entangled with them, we'll have triggers everywhere reminding us of them and who they are—if they use magic to make us forget. So I know they have a plan, that's obvious, but I don't…"

Breanne's lips physically quivered with the words. She couldn't look at any of us as she squeaked, "I don't know what it actually is."

If the words were as terrifying as they were to hear from Breanne Shaw, I couldn't imagine how they felt to say them.

I glimpsed Jak staring down at his smoothie. I knew why he was staying quiet, but I didn't *want* him to—I didn't want him to verify that he was still as hurt, that he was mentally still in worst-case scenario. And now so were we, if not even Breanne could dare imagine what his stepfamily had planned.

I can't sit here and do nothing. I grabbed my phone, opened up my messages, and started typing.

Please still be up, Kamose, please.

> **E:** We're in trouble. The Delphines are planning something huge for us and we can't figure it out unless we pay some kind of price, but I'm reaching that point. Just yes or no, since you know all present circumstances, do you know what they're planning? And do you know WHEN they plan on attacking?

I looked up at my friends as I shut off my screen. The atmosphere would've swallowed us whole if not for the clanging silverware and conversation drifting around the room. I envied those people more than I ever had in my life. Sure, this was the life I'd spent seventeen years preparing for, but now my friends were trapped in it because of me. Maybe not because of anything I'd done directly—and even then, that wasn't completely true—but because of me nonetheless.

How much worse would it be if they knew and then the world had three more leads to the Ateras—and Adara?

"How does what happened tie into all of this?" Jak said in an unfamiliarly deep tone. Then I remembered that he'd gotten the worst of what we were talking about.

"That..." Breanne rested her hands in her lap, her salad untouched and lettuce probably getting soggy. "Okay. Jak was starkly different from anything any of us have been through since finding out about the Delphines. What happened to Emma and Opal this summer was Alexa threatening them to stay silent about it. With Jak, though, they wanted *results* out of it, out of him. If he'd ever trusted Emma with what he knows, Alexa would've gotten it out of her by now. So they know that he knows something and *hasn't* relayed it, but the question is why they waited so long to act on it. And why they did it this conveniently close to when they're carrying out their main plan with us—at the exact same time as their mental torture stage."

The table's eyes were on her, but hers were on me. So help me, every ounce of paranoia was telling me that she knew what I was really hiding under the surface.

Despite being the smallest one at the table, her voice had never been bigger when she said, "I think they're after the people you love most. That's how they're going to break *you*."

If that was true... if that was what they were doing, my friends were in *immediate* danger. I needed a defense against them as soon as possible, I needed an absolute answer *now*.

Breanne took a deep breath in. "Which means Jak had been bait. They want Emma to know that they still have all the power and will cross any line to get what they want. That, in turn, makes her feel guilty and pressures her into giving up."

It's almost a miracle the girl hasn't figured out that I'm Tristan Atera's descendant.

An unspoken message seemed to pass between us four girls as we glanced at each other: one that warned us not to look in Jak's direction. We'd spoken way more on this than we were supposed to, theorized past the boundaries that had been set.

And yet, I spared him a quick glance. He was still staring down at the glass in front of him.

Like a miracle, my phone buzzed in my hand.

K: I'm hesitant and remorseful to say that the
answer to both of those is no.

They've managed to keep their plans internal.
Unless one of them asks me a question and al-
lows me to see the past events of their lives, I
can't access their plans.

No—how could they keep everything *internal?* That meant *no nore* could tell me what they were actively planning if I asked; the Delphines had somehow managed to formulate it and then keep up with it without ever revealing it externally. How?

Internally. Like our minds.

Like telepathy. We were at a dead end.

But then how does Alexa know about them if she's without her magic?

I put my phone to sleep again and looked up, collapsing against my chair. "So that's it?"

I'd surprised everyone, even myself, with the question. I didn't know I was desperate enough to actually voice how my brain wanted more than what we'd already given.

"Jak,"–Breanne rested her light hands on the edge of the table–"all of this is just a theory based on speculation. If you can tell us what the kidnappers said or did the very last time you saw them, that might solidify some answers. It could give us another piece, at least some insight."

Jak blinked a couple of times before resting his folded arms on the table. A light-brown hand ran through his hair. "They came back–what felt like hours before Emma came. That was when they cut me." His thumb traced the slash down the left side of his face, but his gaze never wandered. "Here. They said that was it."

"What was it?" I forced myself to ask.

"The last thing they told me, specifically, word for word: 'This is'"–his eyes rose to meet mine–"'your last warning.'"

"And then they left," I whispered. "For good. Left you to us."

Which couldn't mean anything else: the pack was determined to get what Jak was harboring out of him one way or another. At just the right time.

And yet, I couldn't feel like those words had been for me instead of him.

C H A P T E R

Thirty-Four

"**D**ad?"

"How did you get here?" he asked, kneeling down next to me as I sat in a cold chair. He cupped my face, but the feeling of his fingers against my skin was blurry. There was even a haze over my vision.

I felt the answer drown in the sea flooding my head as the scene flashed.

"You can't leave me here!"

"There's nothing I can do, sweetheart," he said in the most defeated tone I'd ever heard him bear.

Flash.

The haze was gone. William Bleu stood in front of me. Anger carved his square features as he marched toward me. "You better shut—"

"And you *punished* him for knowing! You—!"

A blinding flash swarmed my vision.

William and Alexa brawled on the floor. A small key clattered at my feet, cuffed to the legs of the chair. Alexa growled as she threw William off of her and into the adjacent wall.

Flash.

"Listen to me, Emmalynn." Alexa spoke harshly yet lowly. Her eyes pierced the metal door in front of her. A gun was pointed at me. "You and your family—"

Flash.

I heard the door bang open, but darkness had swallowed my vision. A gunshot followed. I gasped as something banged hard against me. Another gunshot followed as I screamed—

Flash.

My feet rested heavily on the floor of a car. My hands trembled in front of me. Tears left them both shiny and wet.

"They're..." I whispered, so airily that I barely heard myself, "they're dead."

The world shut to black, thrusting me awake. I sprang up in bed with a ragged inhale, immediately covering my mouth with my blankets. I couldn't wake the girls, I couldn't let them know why the tears were pouring down my face—

A gasp across the room cut straight through my own breaths.

I turned my head to the left, smothering myself with my blankets to stay quiet. Opal was sitting up in bed, too, Sarah sleeping soundly between us.

"Opal?" I whispered.

Her breathing almost instantly slowed. "Sorry, did... did I

wake you up?"

"No," I said before I could think the answer through. Saying that she had would've meant I wouldn't have to lie about why I was already awake.

"Are…" she began shakily, her voice hollow, "are you okay?"

I know that reaction. A vision. A nightmarish vision.

"Bad dream. What about you?"

"Same," she said in a whisper that was all too high. "Stupid nightmare."

No—just tell me it was a vision, I almost told her telepathically. Because in all honesty, the last thing I wanted was my friends pretending to be okay when we needed each other's strength now more than ever.

"Are you sure?" I whispered.

"Yeah—it's fine," she said quickly, maintaining that high pitch. I watched her silhouette lie back down on her bed. She stayed on her back as she pulled the covers up. "Nightmares have… kind of become regular."

Those words settled into her regular register. If she was anything like me, her visions had become synonymous to nightmares. A desperate part of me wanted to believe that she'd had a vision of the same scenario I had just now.

"Can I ask you something random?" I whispered.

"Sure."

"How often do you get druid visions?"

An uncomfortable silence settled over the room. In the dead of night, it almost felt threatening.

"Um… not often. Maybe once every few months."

Lie. I didn't even need her tell to know that; this summer, when Alexa's memories were still gone, Opal had had a whole conversation about Adara with me and Mr. Dawson in his living room and about how her visions were getting more often and clearer. Why didn't she want me knowing how often she had visions?

"I don't like talking about them," she added. "Not after—I had one on the cruise about what happened to Jak."

My gaze hardened on the girl's bed. Anger curled my fingers and tightened my grip around my cold comforter. I felt my mind physically restrain itself from screaming telepathically, *How* dare *you lie about that?* Spinning Jak's story into a tall tale?

"What're you talking about?" I was brave enough to whisper.

"I never said anything because druid visions don't always come true, and I didn't want to stress you out even more. I really didn't think it would happen, especially since I only ever got it once."

Every word was in that wicked high pitch.

Druids don't get visions about other people unless they're directly involved with them. It seemed like the only exceptions to that so far were any visions about Adara, maybe even Morgana, Ezranai, and Azariah.

Did this girl really think me so ignorant to the laws of magic?

"Don't withhold your visions," I managed. "Not right now, please. We need all the help we can get."

"I didn't have a vision," she said in the same voice.

I let a couple of moments tick by, trying to gather my calm so I could ask the question gently. "You didn't?"

The quiet shifted. It felt like our previous atmosphere had paused, like I was persuading it in my favor.

"No. I did," she finally said. "It was dark."

So I got her. She really doesn't know her own tell.

"'Dark'?"

"I really don't wanna talk about it."

"Was it about Alexa and William's potential plan?"

"I don't wanna talk about it."

I didn't want to pressure her, I didn't want to press her—but this was my hunt, and she was the only one who had an answer that I'd been searching for, for months.

"You don't have to explain it," I whispered, "just a yes or no can—"

—Just leave it alone!— her voice shouted in my head. And if not for the dark, my jump would've exposed me in full.

But I had to pretend that she hadn't just snapped at me despite her not realizing it, so I asked in the dark anyway, "Opal?"

"Good night."

I heard her turn over onto her side. Knowing her and how she was feeling now, her back was to me. Good. That meant she was trying to ignore me. It meant that she was blocking out everything the atmosphere was exposing: my anger. The tension in my body, the urge to demand the truth, to even cast a truth spell no matter what it exposed about me—if only she weren't familiar with the weight of a truth spell as a wielder.

I chained every thought to myself; I couldn't risk telepathy after her mistake just now.

The weight of my own vision fell straight on top of me like an anvil from the sky. Then I realized, I'd been feeling this dread for a bit now with my visions—but I'd never felt this much of it: a subconscious knowledge. It was as if my magic knew the context of my visions and was pouring it into my gut, and I was feeling the weight of its tragedy despite not knowing the circumstances surrounding it. I only knew that a deep sadness, a deep horror, was devastating my mind and chest. It was happening more and more often—

No. This one can't happen. I need to stop this one.

I didn't want to know the unknown details of this vision, I didn't want to know if it'd even come to pass for sure. I wanted to know that I could *prevent* it! That I could override the word of my magic! That I wasn't stuck helplessly falling into it again!

There has to be something I can do about this.

I didn't get much sleep after that. And because that pattern started repeating, the days following only left all the more room for fear, anxiety, and paranoia. We only knew one thing for absolute certain: that we had to be at our mental best, we had no choice but to be.

The only reason I didn't lose my mind at the morning news on Tuesday was that I'd known beforehand that Aunt Becca was going to fake her death. Lunch was ablaze with the topic, and the one who had to feed the school's appetite for gossip? Opal Dubois. Who, for the first time in her Callistro Girl history, was out of gossip.

Or, rather, she just couldn't bring herself *to* gossip anymore. Despite how that cover was protecting her—us. It was finally past outside gossip and now inside our actual lives, and I don't think Opal had it in her to glorify the drama of it anymore.

"Once every few months". Yeah, right. Not only had she had a dark vision the same night I had, but the night before today, she'd woken up with another vision, based on her furious and hollow

panting. I'd only caught her because I was dealing with another horrible case of insomnia.

"Nothing?" Teresa Darci asked next to her, resting an elbow on the table anyway despite Mrs. Durrett's scolding five minutes ago. "You always have something! Hasn't your mom said anything?"

Opal mindlessly stirred her beef stew, staring it down like she'd lost something in it. She shook her head. "Been too busy to pay attention."

I wanted to scream at her. Sure, midterms were only a week away and we were all busy studying, but she wasn't acting well enough. It was like she *wanted* to get caught, like she wanted people to ask what was wrong and why she hadn't been paying attention. Did anyone else know her tell for lying?

"Babe, do you even realize what this means?" Sloane Moore asked dubiously on her other side. She rested her folded arms on the crimson-covered table. "The last remaining Ateras are dead, one of the most important magician families that've been hunted for CENTURIES, and you have no reaction? No details?"

"They're both dead, what else do you want?" Opal exclaimed, her spoon clattering against her bowl. She drew every pair of eyes at the junior table, but she didn't regard any of them. "I'm not your only source of info, can I just eat for once?"

Silence ensued across the long table almost the length of the Dining Hall. The curious whispers from the sophomore table behind Opal and the senior table behind me quickly transfigured into regular chatter.

I looked over at Sarah and Breanne next to me. Sarah's gaze was caught on the other girls while Breanne bit her lip, scared eyes on the girl in front of us.

But the table rested after that. The Callistro Academy gossip girl had nothing to say, no chatter for hungry ears. For the first time in the time that I'd known her, since orientation just before sophomore year, the girl was too afraid to speak, to grant any input about the hottest topic of the year. Of the decade.

The pack had broken Opal.

CHAPTER

Thirty-Five

Dad turned forty-one that night. Walking down Mr. Dawson's hallway and toward his bedroom, I hoped and hoped that the present dangling in my hand would be enough.

I pushed open the door. My parents lay peacefully in each other's arms on the bed, gazing at the Christmas card Cara and Steven had sent us of them with Baby Samuel. Their first one as a family.

"Hey, kiddo," Dad said, looking up. He set the card onto the nightstand next to him. "What's that?"

"Oh." Momma's realization caused a nervous thrum in me, but she smiled. "You wanna give that to him alone?"

I nodded.

She kissed Dad's cheek. "I love you."

"I love you, too," he said as she slid off the bed and strolled in my direction. She placed a gentle hand on my shoulder before leaving the room, shutting the door behind her.

I took her spot next to Dad on the bed. The two of us sat up, and I handed him the gift bag. "Your last present for the night."

"Did you really buy this for me?" he asked, taking it.

"No—I didn't buy it."

He pulled out the white tissue paper, immediately pausing. He brought out the small wooden jewelry box sitting in the bag, gawking at it as though he hadn't seen it in years. After he'd come home last year, I'd brought it from my dorm to the vanity in my bedroom, so that wasn't true—but he hadn't *owned* it since he'd given it to Momma as a wedding present almost twenty years ago.

"Honey," he murmured, "why are you giving me this?"

"I've kept my most valued possessions in that box ever since Mom gave it to me for my tenth birthday." I stared at the reflection in his bright-blue eyes, wanting him to know how much I meant it when I said, "It sounds cheesy, but—well, you obviously can't fit into it, but if you have it, that's what it'll feel like."

"I get what you're saying." He smiled, twisting the box in his hands. "I really appreciate it, kiddo. It's the only thing I have left of *my* grandparents, and it'll be one of the only things I have of my parents when Grandpa passes." He wrapped an arm around my shoulders and kissed my head. "Thank you."

"I also want you to be the one to give it to me on an important day of my life," I said. "Like my twenty-first birthday or something."

"Oh, I see." He chuckled. "You're giving it to me so I can give it back to you?"

I grinned at him. "I'm giving it to you so you can have the joy *of* giving it to me. So technically, you get two gifts."

He squeezed me. "You're awesome. I love you."

"I love you, too. Happy birthday."

He rested his head on top of mine. "It really was. Wanna know something crazy?"

"Duh."

"December 17 has always been a special day for me—and it has nothing to do with my birthday."

I curiously furrowed my brows, tilting my head. "Why?"

"It started my first year of middle school, when I had the best dream of my life about being the main character in my favorite book series at the time." He chuckled hysterically to himself, closing his eyes. "I kid you not, Em, it was so real and I was so naïve that I thought, if I could just have that same dream again, I'd actually *become* that character."

"And December 17 played a part in that?"

"Yep. That was the night I had the dream. And I really thought I'd have it again on that same date just because it was that special to me. Then, the year after, the author of that series released a surprise spin-off—the best, albeit only, spin-off I'd ever read. And the year after that, my parents told me that I'd be going to Redway for high school."

I propped myself up on my elbow, interest fully piqued now. "That wasn't scary to you?"

"*No*," he replied, like I couldn't have been further from the truth. "Far from it, that was some of the most exciting news of my life. Even if it meant Becca was upset with our parents about it for as long as she was."

"I still can't believe you went there at all." I bit my cheek in thought, trying to picture a younger Dad walking the halls of Redway Academy—Jak's school. "I just can't see it."

"One of these days we'll have to visit the campus together. I'm really curious about how much it's changed... If it's ever safe for us to visit, of course."

Invisibility cloaks would be great, but there's only so much they can protect us from.

With that, though, curiosity had lit a fire in my head: "What was it like going to Redway? Like, how did people *not* recognize you? How were you able to convince everyone you were just like them?"

He set the jewelry box down onto the nightstand. "Well, it was probably like you going to Callistro. Went under a fake name, and back then, people didn't know my and Becca's faces—they just knew our parents'. Nobody had a face to our names until after I graduated."

"*How?*"

He shrugged, pursing his lips together. "The same way you have even *with* modern technology."

Fair point.

"Were you ever scared that you'd be found out?" I asked.

"It's really hard to pretend you're not scared. So I convinced myself that everything was okay. I had things under control. You can't be nervous if you believe there's nothing to be nervous about."

I took a deep breath and sighed, Dad's arm resting around my shoulders as I lay back down. "How many friends did you have?"

"A decent-sized group. But Thomas was my first close friend there."

"Really?"

"Yep." Dad stared at the wall in front of us, his thumb mindlessly rubbing my shoulder. "All my close friends from high school are now either Hunters out for my blood or normal people *hoping* for my blood."

I wanted to shudder—was that how it was going to be with me and my best friends? Were they going to grow up to become Hunters while I was exposed to the world as the next generation of Ateras? Would they start wanting my blood?

My voice dropped with sincerity. "I'm sorry."

"It happens. You lose friends and then you gain them. Hey, the only one I ended up needing in my adult life was Thomas, anyway. The most important ones will still be there when you need them."

Well, that made me feel slightly better, but I still had the rest of high school to go before I reached the point Dad was at when he lost all of his friends.

A knock sounded and the door eased open. Momma poked her head into the room. "How's it going?"

"Great." Dad nodded to my other side. Momma got the message and rounded the bed, climbing on and lying on my other side. I turned onto my back.

"Did he like it?" she asked, tracing soft patterns on my arm.

"I think so."

"Sure, I did," Dad replied, but then his eyes locked with Momma's, softening his smile. "But I like this better."

Momma wrapped her arm around my waist, leaning her head against mine. Dad took her hand and kissed the top of it. Then he kissed the side of my head. I sighed out of contentment, closed my eyes, and told myself that it was okay to fall asleep now.

I liked this a lot better, too. So much better.

C H A P T E R

Thirty-Six

When that Hunter vision happened again early Thursday morning, I realized that the only thing there was to do about it was tell someone. That didn't make approaching Mr. Dawson in his classroom after school any easier.

He's never failed me with his advice before. He'll make it... okay.

No one else was there to talk to him as I walked through the doorway, and it was the one time I cursed that there *wasn't* a wait to talk to one of my teachers. When those diamond-blue eyes rose from his laptop and landed on me, it was anything but comforting. In fact, I felt more like I was serving an afternoon detention sentence.

"Pleasant surprise," he began all too casually, lowering the lid of his laptop. "What's on your mind?"

"I have to talk to you about"—I closed the door behind me—"a vision."

He paused, arching a brow. "You're actually seeking out my counseling on a vision?"

I couldn't tell if he meant it as even a partial joke until he spoke again: "This is bad, isn't it?"

I stepped up to his desk on the platform. "I think so. But this is the druid in me acting, so there's a chance we can avoid it."

He leaned back in his black desk chair. "How many of your visions have been wrong?"

Not many. Not many at all—and even a majority of the ones that were wrong just had the wrong setting, the wrong dialogue, a few details askew. I don't really write about the ones that don't happen, but I'd even had a vision during the cruise where Anthony had kidnapped Breanne for Alexa's magic. It was only once and obviously never came to pass. But in general, the main event almost always takes place.

"That's what I thought," Mr. Dawson said, reading me again. "I think that's because you're part seer. The two parts can't help but meld together, directly pit against each other. If I had to venture a guess. So"—he leaned forward in his seat—"what was the vision?"

I swallowed, the nerves prickling me. *That* was a lovely preamble to everything I was about to say. "I've been having this one for... since this summer. It's been getting more and more frequent—twice this week, and I swear, I feel it coming, like it's about to happen tonight or something. It usually starts with me inside this concrete room, with either Dad or William in front of me.

Sometimes I hear—voices, but nothing's... it's cloudy, it's foggy, I can't see clearly sometimes. But then it'll cut to Alexa taking me, or a couple of nights ago it was her with a gun aimed at me, I... And then it'll cut to—gunshots and screaming and—"

"Calm down, calm down," Mr. Dawson said, holding up a hand. "Catch your breath. What's actually happening during that?"

The context—the grief—was threatening my rationality again. I blinked those images away, trying to shake off the tease that this would be reality soon. "I don't know. It's a lot of gunshots, and I'm running until I'm finally—I'm finally in a car, yours or Mom's. And I'm sobbing, and every single time, I always say—"

I cut myself off. I couldn't speak these words. I couldn't make them real. I couldn't set them in stone.

"What do you say, Em?" Mr. Dawson gently asked.

"I'm saying..."—I fiddled with my locket, gaze locked on his laptop—"'They're dead.'"

Silence rang throughout the room. I couldn't look up. I just needed his advice, his word.

"Every time?" he asked.

I nodded. A stray tear rolled off my cheek and onto the mahogany of his desk. "And... I'm pretty sure Opal is having similar visions. But every time I ask her about it, she either lies or changes the subject." I scoffed. "She had the nerve to lie and say she actually had a vision about Jak's torture."

A familiar disappointment pulled down his sharp features. Part of me pitied him; the other part was still too angry to sympathize with anyone.

"I don't know why she isn't telling me what her visions are

actually about," I said. "It's like she wants to keep what might happen all to herself. Has she said anything to you?"

"Nope."

What is going on? Nobody could read the girl, and I couldn't help but wonder if she wanted it that way.

"The seer part of you," Mr. Dawson said next, "can it sense how close that vision is to happening?"

"No."

"So the next time Alexa and William plan on kidnapping you—based on its frequency."

My heart skipped a hard beat. We had no idea when that would be. We didn't even know if they were standing in the shadows or just making us think that that was where they were. They had every angle under the sun they could attack from; all they had to do was wait for us to look in the opposite direction.

"Okay," Mr. Dawson said with finality. "I'd tell your mom about all this and then leave as soon as midterms are over."

I nodded. That was the word I'd come in here to get, and the only thing I had time for now was to obey it. "Thanks," I said, turning to the door and stepping off the platform.

"Emma," he called, turning me around, "I'll talk to Opal and see if she'll tell me about her visions. But if you have one again—remember when I shared my vision about William interrogating you last year?"

What a fantastic introduction that was to visions. "Yeah."

"The next time you have a vision, anything, share it with me if can."

I paused, facing him better. "How do I do that?"

"Well..." His features scrunched together in thought. It took a dozen starts to a sentence before he eventually exhaled and passed his hand over his face. "Okay, when you start dreaming, harness your focus on me. You have to realize that you're having a vision first—that's the hardest part. But as soon as you do, think of me. Your magic will maintain the vision for you while you concentrate on the person you want to share it with."

I nodded for his sake, because actually executing that was a completely different story. That, and now I had to have this same conversation with Momma. And finish packing for break.

⚓

With the last day of the semester tomorrow, the girls and I were practically walking on nails. In some ways, we were more than ready for break, and in others... it sounds dramatic in writing, but I was genuinely wondering if I'd make it back next semester. But break did leave us a lot more moments to stay on alert with abandon—no need for a cover.

"Bre," Sarah said from the bathroom, tying off the end of her long, thick braid. "Stop eating those, you're gonna make yourself sick before the last *two* tests of the semester."

"I can't," Breanne said in the middle of the room. Colorful and silver wrappers sat scattered around her on the purple rug, and she was already dropping another to pop a Twix into her mouth. "This is the only thing keeping me calm right now."

Yeah. "Calm".

Opal and I glimpsed each other from our beds. She'd been quiet for a majority of the week—not just at lunch the day Auntie was found "dead". And I think it was starting to infect me.

"You'll be fine," Sarah said, shutting off the light in the bathroom. She came to Breanne's spot and knelt down, grabbing the fabric box. Breanne slouched, her chewing slowing. "Remember? You're coming straight to New York with me right after, and Alexa can't get you on a plane."

There were a hundred rebuttals to that statement, but I don't think any of us had the energy or capacity to bring them up.

Opal was going to Washington, and Momma, Mr. Dawson, and I were dedicating all of break to making sure Dad and Aunt Becca stayed safe in their apartment. It was the only thing we *could* do—and hopefully my friends and I being in other states would postpone the Delphine agenda if they were planning on trying anything over break.

As Opal crawled into bed, Breanne picked up her empty wrappers. "I won't get to do anything in New York until I figure out their stupid plan. I've been trying since Thanksgiving!" She stood up and went to the trash sitting next to the desk. "Why can't I figure it out? It's like they poisoned me! What am I supposed to do until I know what they want with me?"

I took a deep breath in. Breanne didn't deserve this.

Pulling back the covers of my own bed, I knew I had now or never to ask this. Opal had one more chance to get it right:

"Opal," I started tentatively. "Please, tell me you've had a vision about this, anything about what they're doing."

"No," she said—in that high-pitched, airy voice. Yet her purple eyes bored into mine like they were standing on a foundation of rock-solid truth. "That's why I'm so scared, I have *no* idea what to expect."

So that was it. Her "dark" visions really had been about this, and she wasn't going to warn us about it.

My blood boiled under my skin. Not even after the first day of school, when we'd met at the bottom of the Main Staircase and she'd challenged my argument against there being an Atera descendant, did her words ignite such resentment in me. I was ready to telepathically talk to her then and there—call her out, demand answers, *anything* to make this girl cough it up. Breanne needed the context more than I did! Why would Opal subject her, any of us, to that? Or was she thinking that if she kept things to herself, she could handle it on her own?

This feels familiar.

"You're sure?" I dared to ask, fighting the urge to narrow my eyes. I kept them wide to portray worry against doubt. "Nothing?"

"No," she said again, still lying. "I've been waiting for any vision to make sense at all. If I did even get one about this, I doubt I'd be able to make sense of it. I just—I'm sorry, I don't know, I don't."

So she rambles when she feels cornered.

Why would she hide her visions about this if she was so scared?

If I tried to comfort her that she wasn't alone in this, none of us were, she would know that I knew her tell—she'd at least be given a hint that I knew. And for some reason, I felt like I needed that secret under my belt for now.

"I hate this whole thing," Breanne muttered, following suit with Sarah climbing into bed. "My parents still don't know about me. I hate keeping something so big from them, from my brother, and now I have to keep it in front of Mr. and Mrs. Duncan. I hate this so much. It's getting harder every single day."

Yeah. I swallowed a hard lump in my throat. *I know.*

"We'll find a place for Alexa's magic," Opal assured her. "You won't have to do this forever."

"How are we gonna do that?" Breanne asked flatly, lying on her back and propping herself up. "It's been almost *half a year*. I've had to go an entire semester as a wielder! Where are we gonna put Alexa's magic where they can't get it?" Her small voice grew bigger with each sentence. "We hide it somewhere, I'm still a target because I know where it is. They use a forgetting spell on me, I'm still a target because you can reverse it. I give it to someone else, I'm still a target because I know who has it! How do *you* suggest we figure this out, because I've been trying for five months with *nothing*! Just waiting for them to give us a weakness!"

It was the most Breanne Shaw had ever said at once in her life that wasn't an academic speech.

"And now Christmas break," she said with just as much firmness, "you really think they're gonna let us go that easily just because we're gone? You think they won't find us when they want us this badly and they have a plan?"

I opened my mouth to argue. I wanted to argue so badly, but she was saying what we were all thinking, what we already knew. She had the rebuttals we hadn't dared bring up earlier.

"We don't fight, we lose. We fight, we expose ourselves. We pay a price either way. They have us"—she sharply inhaled—"right where they want us. I can't..." She fell onto her back, voice falling to a tear-stolen whisper. "I can't solve this."

In all her life, not once had those words ever fallen from Breanne Shaw's lips. The pack had broken Breanne.

CHAPTER

Thirty-Seven

I've had weird dreams before, but that night took the cake regarding the strangest this year.

There I stood at a grocery store check stand as a bagger when Dad came through with his two kids: Jak and Opal—and Momma was the cashier. As if all were normal, I bagged his groceries and asked if he wanted paper or plastic, how his day was, and if he wanted any help with carryout.

The first red flag should've been how suspiciously normal everything was.

Then my manager—Alexa—came up to me and asked me to start serving coffee at the Joe's House kiosk in the store. With one turn of my back, I stood behind the counter of the Joe's in Publisher's Ink, serving pastries and drinks to strangers. William and

Aunt Becca came up next, but now they were old friends that I hadn't seen in years. Then Becca held up her left hand to show me the engagement ring on her ring finger.

The real me knew how much of a train wreck the whole situation was, but Dream Me was ecstatic for them. Two conflicting realities tried to co-exist and somehow make sense together, but not even my subconscious had the power as Sarah came up from behind me and tapped my shoulder.

"Hi, Emma," she said.

"Hey! How are you?" I asked.

"I'm good, Emma. Emma!"

She said it again and again and again. My name echoed in my head like a curse. Sarah grabbed my shoulders and shook me.

"Emma! *Emma!*"

The world around me went dark. Even the bouncy surface under me shook as I opened my eyes and looked around for the voice. There Sarah Duncan stood on my left side.

"What? What's wrong?" I whispered sleepily, propping myself up on my bed and rubbing my eyes.

"They're gone!" she whispered hollowly, an unfamiliar high pitch piercing her words. Unfamiliar because that pitch belonged to terror—and Sarah Duncan isn't easily terrified.

As the rods in my eyes adjusted to the dark, I saw it all over her face: she was petrified. And then her words shattered the glass wall that had stopped me from understanding the first time.

They're gone.

"No," I said, immune to volume as I jumped from my bed. "No, but—!"

I glanced at the clock on the nightstand: 6:07. I will never forget that time.

I strode past Sarah and to the closet. "Get your shoes," I urged, fighting the strain in my voice, "we need to get my mom."

I didn't have a plan. I didn't have a single coherent thought finishing itself. I knew almost nothing for certain about the world around me except that two of my best friends had been kidnapped and nobody had taken me or Sarah with them.

"Why did they take just them?" Sarah whispered as she slid on her flats, reading my mind exactly. It sounded more to herself than anything as we rushed to the door. "Why did they take them, why not us, why not all of us—?"

I spun on her. "You need to calm down. I know that's not what you want to hear, but we're about to pass the entire school sleeping in their dorms, you can't wake them up."

"They *took* them!" she whispered-screamed. "The only two with magic, the smallest two in the group!"

There was definitely a reason they'd taken Opal and Breanne specifically. That reason was bubbling, coming to fruition, but in no way did I have time to play detective right now.

"Calm down," I told her firmly. "For their sake right now."

She reserved a couple of seconds, taking deep breath after deep breath. Finally, she nodded. I wasn't sure if I wanted to know what had her so panicked—because the girl knew better probably than any of us that freaking out is the *last* thing you do on a mission, especially a rescue mission.

I turned the doorknob, needing to put my own mind into focus. The absolute worst part as Sarah and I leaped down the hall? Being able to do something—to get their location with a locator spell, tell them that we were on our way to get them—while knowing that if I actually went through with that, my head would be next on the chopping block. Momma and Mr. Dawson were our only hope—

Mr. Dawson. Mr. Dawson!

I telepathically called him our entire way down the stairs to the staff dorms. It wasn't until we rounded the corner of the hallway with Momma's room that he finally replied.

—Are you okay? What's wrong?—

—Opal and Breanne were kidnapped, meet us at Mom's dorm!—

Silence. Good. He was jumping into action.

Wait.

With Sarah and I suppressing our rapid breaths, I stared at Momma's door. There was absolutely no way she'd left it unlocked, but there was also no way to unlock it quietly without magic.

"Say a prayer," I whispered, placing my hand on the doorknob. I gritted my teeth and closed my eyes: *Exsolvo.*

The door swung open.

"The stress must *really* be getting to her," Sarah whispered behind me as we crept inside, "for her to leave the door unlocked."

Yeah. You can go with that.

I ran to Momma's bed against the wall across from us as Sarah closed the door. The window in front of me provided scarcely enough moonlight to see.

It didn't take much shaking to wake Momma up. Upon Sarah coming up to her bed, Mom's lips parted with realization.

"No," she whispered. She flung the covers off of her, jumping up from bed and tightening her ponytail. "What happened?"

"I woke up and Breanne and Opal were gone," Sarah said uneasily, like she was trying to sound steady. "I just—I don't know, I think it was the anxiety, I kept waking up throughout the night and then—and then the room felt empty, and—"

"What do we do?" I asked.

"We find them," Momma stated, rubbing her arms. That was when I realized how cold it was in her room—or maybe that was because we were standing right by the window and it was past mid-December. "Come on."

Halfway to the door, Mr. Dawson slipped into the room in a loose T-shirt and sweatpants. Not an unfamiliar sight for me, but definitely one that caught Sarah off guard—not to mention the fact that the man had just entered my mother's, the *headmistress's*, dorm room without knocking. Like the girl needed another reason for shock.

I didn't think this through. I really hope I don't have to explain—

"Opal just telepathically called me," he whispered anxiously, shutting the door. "They're gone."

Thank goodness.

For the first time in her life, Sarah Duncan had nothing to say and only everything to witness.

I looked from her to Mr. Dawson. *—Did she really?—*

—No. I needed an excuse because of Sarah.—

Hang on. Why hadn't Opal or Breanne *actually* called out to him yet for help?

Unless... I thought. *No. Are they out of range?*

"Come on," Momma said, pushing us toward the door. "We need to get something that belongs to them for a locator spell."

Sarah was wordless the entire time Momma and Mr. Dawson

followed us back to our dorm. Moments passed before I heard her swallow next to me, but not even a whisper passed her lips as I opened the closet and grabbed Opal's and Breanne's blazers.

She was tightly holding herself when I handed the clothes to Mr. Dawson. He closed his eyes and submerged the room in the most nerve-racking silence I'd ever experienced in it. And that's saying a lot.

"South Mountains State Park," he said too simply, opening his eyes. "That's almost an hour away."

"Okay," Momma replied, taking the hair tie out of her ponytail. "Then that's where you and I are going."

"What?" I asked, Sarah sniffing next to me. "Just the two of you?"

"South Mountains State Park is a Hunter hideout, Emmalynn," Momma said. "You are *not* coming with us. Thomas and I have completed our training, you're both halfway into your junior year, and this is a *Grand* Hunter mission! I'm not risking your life on a hunt Alexa Delphine and William Bleu are leading!"

"They're my best friends!" I snapped, uncrossing my arms. "I already went on a mission with you this semester—"

"That doesn't count for anything." She stood up taller, growing her confidence and authority. She was assuming her mom role all over again. "That's actually an even *bigger* reason you should stay here: four of you are at risk, but two of you are in danger. We're going to keep it that way."

"The longer you stand here arguing, the less time we have to save them," Mr. Dawson told me. "You're staying here, that's that."

"No," I stated. "How do we know this isn't their plan?"

Mr. Dawson sighed next to Momma, who closed her eyes in the way she does when she's trying to regain her patience. "What are you talking about?" she asked.

"How do we know they're not trying to lure *you* and Mr. Dawson out there so they can take me and Sarah when nobody's here? How do we know they're not waiting until we're alone to come and get us next?"

I could practically *hear* the mental click in the room, and I was pretty sure a part of Momma was mad at me in that moment for being right.

Even Mr. Dawson rubbed his face with his hands. "What're we supposed to do, Amy?"

Momma crossed her arms at me. "So you're suggesting I take two under-trained teenagers who also happen to be my enemy's targets?"

"They want me more than anything." That was part of the real truth, but I was reaching the border of not caring anymore; as long as Sarah stayed with a Callistro Hunter instructor today, she'd be fine long enough for us to grab Breanne and Opal. At least for the school day. Besides, Sarah was still a wordless stick next to me, hugging herself and sniffing every once in a while. I wondered if she was even listening to a word we were saying. "If I come with you while you're trying to take them down, it's gonna throw them off. The last thing they're expecting is for me to come charging at them."

Momma heavily sighed and took a good, long look at me. I could almost see the tug-of-war happening in her head, but she wouldn't let me see which side was winning.

"Get dressed," she eventually said. "We'll wait outside.

Scream the second something happens."

The words honestly struck me with a blow. Part of me had been convinced that she wouldn't let me come, and now that it was happening... I was facing Goliath head-on.

Mom and Mr. Dawson closed the door behind them. I finally faced Sarah next to me, touching her shoulder.

She sniffed, her eyes unable to connect with mine. "You can't go."

But my mind and heart were aligned with the truth—and fear had no room in the face of instinct, of a year and a half of training. "I have to."

"I trust your mom and Dawson," she said, tears seeping into her voice. "You're outnumbered. You're a partially trained Hunter, you can't even knock them out with magic or anything!"

I can. I wish you could know that I'll be okay.

At least, for the sake of my sanity and rationality, I had to believe that I would be.

"Sarah." I took her arms. "Come on. You know I have to. They need us and they can't have both of us."

"So I stay here and be useless?" she snapped, wiping an invisible tear from her cheek. "I don't even get to save my best friends? The one thing I'm best at, I have to just sit with some teacher all day and hope you guys are okay?"

I had to convince her that this was safest. Momma and Mr. Dawson knew that my magic would defend me, but Sarah had to believe that I had *something* other than my wits and hands to protect me.

"I'm staying by my mom's side," I finally said, tightening my grip on her arms in a promise. "But if I have to worry about you the entire time, I'm not gonna do well. Please. For me, for them. Stay here, stay safe. For us."

She swallowed again. Sniffed again. Exhaled. Then, her body started shaking in my hold. Sarah Duncan wasn't the brave, fearless Hunter I'd come to know her as since starting the Callistro Academy last year. She was different. Her attitude was foreign. I was speaking to a new girl right now.

"Sarah, please."

"I'm scared," she whispered. "I'm really, really scared. I don't know what to do."

She didn't need to say anything else. I knew then and there that the pack had broken Sarah.

Thirty-Eight

The most excruciating wait of my life: waiting until 7:30, when breakfast started, for Momma to drop off Sarah at Mr. Broadhurst's classroom and give him the cover story. There was no other way to make sure that Sarah would stay safe unless we saw her to drop-off—but that meant all that time that Breanne and Opal needed us and we weren't there.

Mr. Dawson sat in the passenger seat as Momma drove through the Callistro Forest. A terrified burn flared in my chest as Momma drove down the main path. The sun had finished its rise, but that didn't make the drive any less unnerving: this exact spot was where Alexa had sent me to the hospital. And this was all too similar to exactly what Momma and Mr. Dawson had gone through just to find me and Opal lying on the forest floor.

I'm sick of this woman. I'm sick of her hunt. I'm ending this today.

"Emma, call your dad," Mom told me, sparing me a glance in the rearview mirror. "Update Becca, too."

There was no way that Auntie was up at almost 8 in the morning. Dad, on the other hand, preferred waking up with the sun.

—Dad, are you up?—

No response. *The one time he sleeps in.*

—Dad, please wake up, it's important.—

No response. But there was no point in giving up.

It was when I could see the end of the Callistro Forest that I resorted to waking up Aunt Becca. And it was when it only took calling her three times to wake her up that my heart skipped a beat, because why hadn't that worked on Dad?

I could practically hear her groan. *—Why am I awake right now?—*

—Where's Dad?—

—Huh?—

—Where's Dad, go look!—

The silence was numbing. The seconds were excruciating.

Becca's response shattered both: *—He's not here.—*

The words flew out of my mouth. "Dad's gone."

The car screeched to a halt just before Momma could turn onto the main road, throwing me into Mr. Dawson's seat.

"What?" she hissed.

Mr. Dawson whirled around to face me. "Wake up Becca—"

"She's the one who just looked for him, he's not responding to me!"

—Dad,— I called. *—Dad!—*

My chest was on fire, my heart rolled like a snare drum, and my throat was in a knot.

—Emma!— Becca cried in my head. *—He's at South Mountains State Park, you have to get him!—*

A locator spell. Dad was with Breanne and Opal.

"He's there," I said, fighting to stay present, "State Park."

The car thrust forward, but the world in front of me had gone blank, not a detail to be remembered. Some subconscious part of my brain kept me aware that I was still breathing. Panic roared in my chest, demanding that my body and instinct bend to it—but I needed to breathe. I needed to stay present, stay out of my head and in my training. I needed to fight harder than ever for myself right now for me to be able to fight for them.

I spent the entire drive in review, recalling past hunts and my enemies' motives. By the time Momma pulled into the parking lot of the park, my panic and fear had transfigured into resolute fury—determination to get this done right once and for all.

Momma gave me an earpiece before we each jumped out of the car. Not a single other sedan was parked. Then again, it was almost 9 in the morning with five days left until Christmas.

Worst start to Christmas break ever.

I steadied my breath as we began our march down the asphalt path leading to the first trail. *—We'll find you, Dad.—* I couldn't help but try one last time. It was wishful thinking at this point, and not even the snow-dipped forest standing tall all around us could temporarily distract me from things. *—I promise.—*

—Emma?—

I froze, grabbing Momma's and Mr. Dawson's attention.

"It's Dad," I said, "he's nearby."

—Dad, it's me!—

His voice was too afraid to be my father's: —*What are you doing here?*—

—*We're here to get you and Breanne and Opal!*—

A brief pause. —*Alexa and William brought them here?*—

—*Where are you?*—

—*The hideout, one of the debriefing rooms. Nobody's come by since they stuck me in here.*—

And yet, as far as we knew, news hadn't broke out across the country yet that Tristan Atera was alive. What were they planning on doing with him? Why had they taken just him and not Aunt Becca, too?

—*We're coming,*— I told him, —*and we brought you an invisibility cloak. Just hold on.*—

—*Emma. Do not. Get. Caught.*—

"Where's the hideout?" I asked, my breath clouding with every word.

"Off of Headquarters Trail," Momma said. "Half a mile from here."

I didn't have time to scoff at the name—or how the builders of a Hunter hideout could've been so blatant. I guess that's what hiding in plain sight is all about.

"We need to plan our moves right now," Momma said next, continuing our walk down the asphalt. "The wisest thing to do would be to split up: Thomas, you find Tristan, and I go with Emma to find the girls."

"And when and where do you suggest we reconvene?" he asked sarcastically.

"Give the cloak to Tristan when you find him and get him to the car. Emma will put a sleeping spell on the girls, and we'll drive home together."

"You *really* think splitting up is wisest—?"

Momma's eyes were intent on him as I walked between them. "Better for them to catch one target instead of all three."

⚓

The earthy aroma of the forest left a cold trail in my nose as I inhaled and climbed down the snowy boulders beside the wooden bridge. According to Momma, the entrance to the hideout was a sewer-like door under the highest bridge on the trail. It was only a five-foot drop, and the entrance was maintained to constantly stay hidden—which meant we had to go digging through the snow.

This is why she reminded me to wear gloves.

Mr. Dawson kept watch on the bridge; we highly doubted any hikers would pass through, but we were anything but safe with Hunters.

Finally, part of a manhole cover appeared under our gloves. Momma and I furiously shoveled away the surrounding snow, my breath clouding my view.

"We got it," she quietly called to Mr. Dawson, signaling him to come down. They pulled off the cover, revealing a concrete tunnel underneath with a ladder leading down.

"I'm going first," Mr. Dawson announced, already crouching in front of the entrance. "Then you, Emma. Then Amy."

Light glowed at the bottom. I cringed the entire climb down, every movement echoing. Whoever was down here could definitely hear us coming.

Pray that nobody's down there...

Mr. Dawson stayed right where he landed as Momma and I stepped down. Concrete surrounded us on all fronts. The room was almost twice as cold as outside, which had already numbed my toes. Unfortunately for us, our path was already illuminated: fluorescent lights hung in vertical rows across the large entry room. Crates and boxes sat scattered across the floor, and two doors sat on each side with one directly across from us.

My eyes mindlessly dragged to the corners of the room before blinking in surprise. *No cameras?* Why wouldn't a Hunter hideout have cameras on the entrance, of all places?

I released another foggy cloud of breath. —*Dad, we're at the entrance.*—

—*Every Delphine is here with William. If any of you are caught, it's over.*—

I wanted more than anything to hear a pep talk. Anything to hear my father's usual consoling words, but unrealistic expectations right now were fatal.

"Dad says every Delphine is here with William," I said.

Momma double-checked that her belt was secure around her waist. "Okay. We just need to grab everyone and get out of here."

Mr. Dawson brought out the folded-up invisibility cloak from his jacket. "Em, you need to be the one to wear this. The pack knows your dad's alive and he has enough training to get him by, so we're gonna get out of here the old-fashioned way. You, on the other hand, *need* to stay hidden for as long as possible."

I faked my confidence as I took the cloak. "Thanks."

"Wait," Momma mused as I threw it over my shoulders and clasped it together. "If Emma's invisible, she can split from us and cover more ground. Breanne and Opal won't suspect a thing since anyone can wear those."

It felt risky, it felt like we couldn't get away with it, but I don't think a single Hunter mission *doesn't* feel like that.

"I'll go straight," I said before I could change my mind. The frigid air was starting to penetrate my bones, and I silently begged that we'd leave before I started shaking.

"I'll take the right," Mr. Dawson said. "You take left, Amy. Use your earpieces, stay in constant communication if you can, no matter what. Especially if..."

He glanced back and forth between us. I knew exactly what he was alluding to, but it felt impossible to believe in. It didn't matter that Dad, America's most wanted man for the last eighteen years, was here, too, and now so was I. It didn't matter that Momma and Mr. Dawson were accomplices to the greatest felony in the country. We were the good guys—something like that "if" wasn't possible for us. Was it?

"If things come to it," he said, squeezing my shoulder, "we promise each other that we escape no matter what."

A single glance at me was all it took for me to know that Momma didn't want to discuss this here, not with me. But this wasn't a test in either of their classrooms. This was life or death, and the best way to protect me from it was to make sure I knew that I was potentially staring death in the face.

"No matter what happens," she finally said, "escape is our priority."

She looked down at me, her index finger grazing my cheek. "I know this is the biggest thing you've ever done. But you're gonna do great. Okay? Stay focused."

The second I nodded, my mother punished me for it: she

wrapped her arms around me and rested her cheek against the side of my head. She hugged me. She swayed with me. And when she pulled away, she cupped my face and kissed my forehead.

"I love you, baby girl." Not a tear glistened in her honey-like eyes. My mother has more strength than anyone I know. "You can do this."

"I love you." Call it survival instinct telling me not to use my own mind against me, but I refused to believe that it would be the last time I would see her. But if it was, those would be the last words she heard from me.

She nodded at me and at Mr. Dawson, and then darted to one of the doors on our left.

Right as I turned to him, he pulled me into him and embraced me, too.

I paused until that same survival instinct told me to wrap my arms around my godfather. Around the texture of his coat, around his rectangular, toned build that was trained exactly for a mission like this. I let the side of my face warm against him as he squeezed me and then kissed the top of my head.

"I love you, Emma," he whispered. "Thank you."

I pulled away just enough to look at him. Somehow, even in this moment, gratitude and warmth radiated in those deep-set eyes. "For what?"

"For making me a father."

Survival instinct wasn't enough to prepare my heart for the hard beat it skipped at those words—hearing how deeply he knew of the possibility that one of us, maybe even more of us, wouldn't be walking out of this base today.

I hugged him one more time. "Thanks for being my first

dad."

He kissed my hairline before stepping away. "They should be able to hear a pin drop," he said, jumping straight back into teacher mode—headmaster mode as he approached the far-left door on the right side of the room. "Keep your training. And your mentoring."

I nodded. "Stay safe."

It wasn't until he opened the door and disappeared behind it that I finally threw on the cloak's hood. I stepped deeper into the fluorescently lit room, the heavy metal door at the end glaring at me. I glanced at my surroundings as though I were touring the Callistro Academy for the first time. I tried to force activity through my brain, to make it process whatever my eyes picked up. Then my focus shifted to that heavy door, my main target. I glared back, hardening my resolve with every step, every step, every step.

It struck my mind like an arrow, and my feet tripped. I suppressed a gasp as I tumbled to the freezing ground.

I'd seen that door before. I'd seen this concrete, these walls, even these crates, I realized. I'd felt this exact dread before.

My visions. I *had* had visions about this. Since August, I'd had—

I threw off my hood, desperate to see where my arm was so I could press my head against it and try to grab my focus. Not this vision, not this one, I'd take any other over this one!

You're being too loud, you're being too loud.

I couldn't help the panicked gasps clogging my lungs.

Get up. Get up, get up, get up. It matters more than ever now!

Past visions raced through my mind. The flashing between each scene pulsed in my vision. Truth bragged its presence, boasted that my nightmares had been right before. My magic was doing it again. My magic was tormenting me. My magic was pushing me into the arms of my enemies.

Get up. Find them. Get up.

I forced myself to my knees and then my feet. The room in front of me stretched out what seemed like a hundred feet.

One. Two. Footsteps—behind me.

I spun around. An unfamiliar man with a strong nose towered over me. My foot shot backwards when his hand caught my neck, the other clamping over my mouth.

His emerald-like eyes flashed amber. My body crumpled in his hold as the world around me faded to black.

C H A P T E R

THIRTY-NINE

Morning. I remembered that much. I'd walked half a mile through South Mountains State Park, and we'd found the Hunter hideout to get Dad, Breanne, and Opal back. And—

And I'd still managed to get kidnapped.

This had happened enough times for me to instantly recognize the feeling of my upright body cuffed to a chair. My head, though, had never felt this heavy, had never swum and throbbed like it was underwater. I pried my eyes open to a hazy filter over the cold room. Fog? Was there fog? Was this real?

I was too dizzy, too nauseous, to focus on anything in front of me. Not that it mattered: the large concrete room, besides a desk in the left corner, was practically empty.

"Emma?"

My head moved to the right, where I'd heard my father's familiar, comforting voice. There he stood. "Dad?"

"How did you get here?" He kneeled down next to me, cupping my face. His fingers against my skin were blurry—like they were there but not connecting.

I felt the answer to his question drown in the sea pounding against my head. It was all I could do to not lean mine against his.

"We have to go," I urged. "You have to do something."

"I know, honey, I wish I could."

"Why can't you?"

"I'm sorry."

I closed my eyes and tried to blink away the exhaustion, the hazy filter, but to no avail.

"Emmalynn, they have it," Dad said, on my other side. "They won."

"No, you can't give up!" I cried, struggling against my chains holding me to the chair. "I never gave up on you, don't you *dare* give up on me!"

I blinked. Now he was standing in front of the door dead ahead of me.

"Don't leave me here!" I exclaimed.

"Keep trying," he said in the most defeated tone I'd ever heard him bear. "Keep trying, we'll get there—"

The door flew open, knocking him to the floor. The man in the doorway wasted no time in handcuffing my father, bringing him up and dragging him out into the hall.

"NO!" I screamed, leaning as far forward as I could against the handcuffs. I blinked again. For a split second, I could've sworn that my dad and the man were already gone. "Dad, please—!"

A gloved hand slid over my mouth. That nauseatingly sweet, sympathetic voice whispered into my ear, "Shhh, darling. It'll be over soon."

"No!" I shouted, jerking my head away. "Stop it! Dad!"

I opened my eyes. Alexa stood in front of me now, cupping my face with a soft smile.

"It's okay, my dear." She held me still and waited patiently as my body slowly but surely started to relax. "You're okay. See?"

"Dad..." I whispered, my eyes trying to shut again.

"No," Alexa crooned. She wasn't in front of me anymore. "It's me."

What's happening? What's going on?

"See?" I felt her hand rub my arm, but my brain was the only thing telling me that she was there. "You're fine."

I didn't know where the sudden burst of rage erupted from, but the handcuffs jerked my hand back when I tried to throw a right hook—even though I didn't know where she was. Or if she was even there anymore.

You need to pay! I screamed in my head. *For everything! Let me go!*

My eyes finally closed. A ringing overcame my ears, tiredness swelling in my head. I was exhausted. I was done fighting. Somehow I knew that nobody was there. And yet, the voice behind me wouldn't leave me alone.

"You can't keep it forever."

"Leave me alone," I spat, as if I knew whom it belonged to.

"You can't hide anymore," it hissed, closer now, but I couldn't determine the direction.

"Leave me alone!"

"*Everyone* knows who you are, little girl."

"Shut up!" I shouted, twisting my head every which way as though the person would appear. "Stop it, leave me alone!"

Silence boomeranged.

"Leave me alone...!"

I kept turning my head, searching for anything to hold on to, to grip. I could almost hear a fuzzy static around me. The cold room stayed empty, hazy, freezing me—

My breath hitched as my gaze landed on the black security camera mounted in the left corner. I looked at the right: another one.

Cameras... Hunters, Dad...

I shook my head one last time, as if to shake off every last mental shackle. The more I blinked, the more I regained. Finally, the room around me became crystal clear. I'd released myself from a nightmare and come back to reality, this was real.

I was hallucinating, I realized. *They drugged me.*

It didn't matter now. *Exs—*

"Wow."

I knew that voice. I *knew* that voice: the same one I'd woken up to in that underground lair after the carnival last year, the same man who'd drugged me that night, too.

William Bleu strolled out from behind me. A pastel-yellow file sat in his hands.

His eyes, matching Jak's brown without discrepancy, watched me carefully, all the more intense with his square jaw. The faintest smile twitched on his lips. He tapped the file once against his palm as he faced me head-on. "Shouldn't've given you so much. Sorry."

Too much clashed inside me: terror, survival instinct, anxiety, confusion.

"Please..." was all I could afford to whisper. "Stop."

"Don't worry. It's over now. You're done." He subtly cocked a straight brow. "Tristan's daughter is finally in our custody."

Those words were familiar. Those words were sickeningly familiar.

He scoffed lightly to himself, shaking his head. "You actually had me fooled, Atera."

I swallowed hard. The words stung me like a scorpion, paralyzing me with fear. Knowing is one thing; experiencing will always be another. William Bleu knew who I was, and right now I was staring up at him like a child begging for mercy.

"Really," he added, too casually for this conversation. "But you have Jak to thank for that. He was why I couldn't believe it. Him and Alexa, actually."

My lips parted without my control. "Alexa...?"

"Yep." That faint smile cracked into a smirk. "She protected you. She kept your secret safe for almost an entire year. Then I learned why. She told me the same day she told me about you. Then it all made sense. Magicians stick together, don't they?"

Finally, my anger had a wave to ride, and it jumped onto it. "She put me and my best friend in the hospital! She's hunted me for almost a year and a half! You call that 'sticking together'?"

"When you should've been dead by Caldwell's law a year ago, *yes*," he spat, leaning in toward me. "You've had the entire world protecting you. Meanwhile, people like my wife were thrown on the line and *killed* for your sake."

I lunged forward in my seat, but the cuffs threw me back

against the chair. So twisted. His view was so twisted!

"*Mortals* are the ones who killed her!" I retorted, my fingers digging into the armrests. "Aastha was killed because of Hunters like you—!"

"You will not speak her name!" William snarled, gripping my face with his fingernails. "Don't you DARE speak her name, do you hear me?"

"I'll say whatever I want to you," I spat. "Why would I listen to a man who authorized his own son's torture?"

His fingers dug into my jaw, his nails piercing my skin. "For the sole reason that I can either shoot you dead now or with your father," he hissed, every consonant harsh and throwing spit onto my face. "Your choice."

"But *we're* the monsters?" I exclaimed, willing my magic to throw the man across the room. Instead, William's cold fingers tightened around my face as his nostrils flared.

My anger was at the control center of my mind, and I gave it full control: I pictured the handcuffs around my wrists. *Exsolvo!*

Nothing.

What? No!

I jerked my wrists and ankles like that would wake up my magic. *Exsolvo!*

A wicked grin slithered to William's lips. "Why do I feel like you're trying to cast a spell right now?"

I willed my magic to throw him across the room again. Nothing.

It wasn't possible. They couldn't have, not yet, they couldn't—

"What did you do?"

"You really thought we were stupid enough to detain you

with normal handcuffs?" He dropped my face, stepping back. "Your magic is neutralized with those on."

Why did they never use these before? Whenever Alexa cuffed me, I had my magic, as far as I knew.

"What're you even here for?" I snapped. "To brag?"

"Anything but." His gaze hardened on me, his other hand tightening its grip on the yellow file. "I'm here for closure."

I knew what that meant. He wasn't going to release me. This was a man too far gone with vengeance. "Closure" meant something darker than any of the nights I'd woken up from this vision.

"Your family has been the bane of my existence since I graduated from Redway," William said. "I finally have the last of the Atera line and the most wanted man in America, and I'm gonna make sure you see just *how much* I enjoy that."

"And you wonder why it took you so long to figure out," I sneered. "When your own son knew the whole time. Did you know that? Your wife told Jak to *protect* my family right before she died. She hated what you did, that's why Jak's always been against you!"

He took a hard step toward me. "You better shut—"

"And you *punished* him for knowing! You sent him to suffer for what not even your own wife trusted you with, he wanted to *die* because of you!"

The back of his hand flew across my cheek. A hot, tingling sting radiated on my skin. My numb gaze fixed somewhere on the empty wall.

It was the first time in my life that someone had ever slapped me.

My jaw trembled with rage, my teeth chattering and hands

balling into fists.

"He was *never* supposed to suffer!" William snarled, gripping my face and forcing me to look at him. "They were *never* supposed to hurt him! That's why they were transferred!"

Transferred? The two members Jak didn't recognize had been *transferred* to a new pack?

They couldn't have been Delphines... They had to be non-family members; if Alexa and William had only authorized them to interrogate him, *they* were the only ones in the pack capable of torturing him. Alexa had warned us where to find Jak, but she hadn't known how far things were going to go. She *had* told us the plan. Outright. Informed us!

But why?

No, none of that mattered right now, because in no way did that excuse *any* of it.

"He was gone for over a week and you never came for him." I fought against the cuffs with every word; it was the only thing I could do when I couldn't strangle the man in front of me. "You've forced him to be involved in this since he was a *little boy.* And you don't even care! You don't even know that he doesn't blame magic for what happened, he blames you! Because it shouldn't have been Aastha, it should've been you!"

"Then I'll see you and your family in Hell!"

William raised his trembling hand again when the door slammed open. A gunshot banged before I could process who'd burst into the room. William cried out, crashing to the floor and holding his shoulder.

I looked up. Alexa Delphine was standing in the doorway with a gun aimed at him.

C H A P T E R

FORTY

I'm gonna die. I'm gonna die. I'm gonna die—

"Why haven't you unlocked yourself yet?" Alexa snapped, keeping the gun aimed at a grunting William on the floor.

She just shot her husband. For me. For me? Was it for–?

Wait. What? She's mad at me for not escaping?

"Emmalynn!" she growled, eyes darting back and forth between me and William. Leaning on his good arm and holding his shot shoulder, he glared at his wife with the same hatred I'd only seen in him once: moments ago, when he backhanded me.

Alexa's gun stayed aimed at him and only him.

She protected you. She just saved you.

Who was this woman?

I swallowed, reviving my words: "I can't, the cuffs—"

She growled, reaching into her back jean pocket. After a second of digging, eyes firm on William, she pulled out a small silver key.

William grunted as he leaned forward to stand, but Alexa took a hard step forward and tightened her hold on the gun. "It is solely my mercy stopping me from shooting you dead right now for what you did!" she snarled. "Try to stop us and the next bullet goes in your leg!"

Realization jolted through me: I'd never once seen Alexa Delphine and William Bleu interact, not until this morning. And now that I was seeing it, she had shot him and he had—*betrayed* her? William? How?

"Alexa Delphine isn't William Bleu's ally in this mission."

"Alexa's mission is the Ateras' protection."

Magic itself had spoken the words to me, yet not even seeing it right now was enough to make me fully believe it.

Alexa strode up to me, kneeled down, and stuck the key into the handcuff. "Can you do it on your own, fast?" she urged, twisting the key and unlocking my right hand.

Not fast. Not right now. Not with you looking at me like—

Like she wanted to save me.

The second I opened my mouth, she went to undo my other hand anyway. She knew better.

"Alexa—!"

The name left my lips without my control, but she'd seen William lunging for her first. She raised the gun just as he tackled her to the floor. The small key clattered onto the concrete as the two of them brawled next to me.

Focus!

Conflicted flashbacks ran across my mind as I reached down and fumbled with the key. The night William had interrogated me in the underground lair after the carnival, when Jak had come to unlock me before fighting his own father, when I'd watched in disbelief as they fought. Right now Alexa had replaced Jak in those memories. It couldn't be, this wasn't her! This had to be someone pretending to be her! Momma? Had Mr. Dawson cast an appearance spell—?

Under William, Alexa grunted as she threw him off her and into the wall. I snapped myself out of my head and undid my ankle as she grabbed the gun that had fallen next to my feet. She fired again, leaving a ringing in my ears. William's cry accompanied it. Undoing my other ankle, I forced myself to look up at the same moment Alexa grabbed my wrist: William's hand had been shot, hovering over his knee, like he'd tried to block the bullet.

I didn't have time to process anything before Alexa dragged me out of the room.

Pounding throbbed in my chest with our steps, my every breath shaking with terror and confusion. Alexa pulled me alongside her down a concrete staircase, the brutal cold stinging my hot cheeks. All she had on were her black jeans, boots, and jacket.

Her gaze stayed dead ahead as we ran down the hallway. "Truth spell, now!"

Actions speak louder than words, yet she knew I still didn't trust her. I obeyed.

"Why're you doing this—?"

"William ruined everything," she said, coming to an abrupt stop at an intersection and glancing left and right. "He sent

Breanne and Opal home before we could get their magic because he thought they were just bait to lure you." Before I could think, she pulled me left. "When you got here, he called in backup. Now Caldwell's best Hunters are swarming the hideout, all looking for you and your family."

Breanne and Opal are safe–?

Gunshots echoed throughout the base. Shouting followed in their wake. There were too many people here. There was no way we could outrun all of them.

My feet slammed against the ground as Alexa pulled me right and into a wide hall, lined with cabinets and shelves. It was too brightly lit for anyone to feel hidden.

"But," I began, "the Delphines want to steal—"

"Caralyn was only right back then," Alexa said as we passed a staircase leading up. She pulled down every metal rack of equipment along the wall. "Caldwell's following in Henry Callistro's footsteps now, that's why he's continued the hunt for Tristan's descendant under the table. That's why I've kept tabs on you, I've used whatever excuse I could to stay close to you while keeping William away, because William *will* kill you."

My thoughts reeled as we barreled through the hall, passing doors and tables and cabinets. Why she'd waited a *week* before getting me right where she wanted me the first time she hunted me—when it would be too late to erase my memory after William deemed me innocent. Why she'd been so kind to me as Julia, why she'd spent months "collecting information"—undercover from even William. Why she'd held off her pack for as long as she did when she got her memories back this summer...

The truth spell. *She's telling the truth.*

"Every reason we've ever had for coming after you," Alexa said, shutting the office door at the end of the hall, "the hunt, my magic, our secret—all real excuses, but primarily a cover. It was always a cover first."

Protection.

Her cold grip on my wrist tightened as she pulled us right and ran harder with me at her side. On our left we passed where the hallway broke off and led to downward stairs, and then another open door that Alexa slammed shut. A large metal door stood at the end of the hallway. Instinct roared in my gut: the door in my vision. We had to run to that, if we could just get to that—

Alexa stopped at the next door on the left and threw me inside in the room. The last thing I expected was for her to dart in after me and push the door shut behind her, locking it.

She raised her gun and shot the camera mounted right above the door. The bang sent a ringing through my ears, practically bursting my eardrums in the acoustics of all of the concrete.

I stepped back. My breath collected in front of me with every pant. Alexa's matched mine as she stood against the door, her chest heaving. Despite the numb tip of my nose, my cheeks burned with terror, with the wicked thought that this was my final moment on this planet. The gunshots and shouting were muffled—like they were in a nightmare. Except this was anything but a nightmare. This was worse. I couldn't wake up from this.

She saved me.

Alexa pushed herself off of the door and stepped closer to me, her breath huffing like a dragon's. I stepped back. "I have to explain before someone comes bursting through that door," she said, jabbing a finger at the right corner of the room. "Stand there so I can keep watch and shoot when they do."

When they do. The words sent a bone-chilling shiver through my body.

I obeyed, maintaining my eyes on her as she aimed the gun at the door. "Your message was code," I said, holding myself up against the frigid wall as if to draw strength from it. "What—what were you saying that night?"

"It was our plan," Alexa said. "The part William didn't know. 'Mental torture' to weaken you; keeping your enemies—our enemy by law, Jak—close in your circle of friends or your hometown; and 'Robin Hood' to tell you our main plan, which was to extract the Ateras' magic—"

Yeah, I know!

"—and then send it to a magician's security base to keep it safe from Caldwell."

My back met the corner of the empty room. Caldwell? *Caldwell?*

Alexa continued before I could process the words, her eyes keen on the door. "We take our targets' magic and then send them both to the base. We entrust that magic to an international 'bank'. Their existence is erased from American records, and no one innocent is killed."

I don't know if we would've ever figured it out, because it had one prerequisite: we would've had to believe that Alexa Delphine wasn't the bad guy.

It fell on me like an anchor: she was still under the truth spell. I had no choice but to believe every word coming out of her mouth.

Wait. "Was torturing me and *hospitalizing* me part of your

plan to 'protect' us?"

"I'm protecting your magic, not you," she snapped, briefly breaking her staring contest with the door. "I had *every* right that night to be angry! Believe me, just because I don't want to kill you doesn't mean I'm your friend. But the agency, William, and Caldwell *all* had to believe that I was a ruthless Grand Hunter, and there was only one way to keep that cover."

"So when you said you had the entire fight on camera—"

"I was bluffing." She narrowed her eyes at me, like I should've known better. "And believe it or not, telling William about you was key to this plan. Unfortunately, he figured everything out too early."

The words ran in my head like a treadmill on the fastest speed. Even my stomach was turning over and over, unable to keep up.

"Emma, if you remember nothing else, just remember that it's Caldwell, it's all Caldwell," Alexa said. "We've only ever killed the magicians who were *real* criminals, people like Anthony's father. Another reason I made sure William worked off field—so he couldn't interrupt that."

People like Anthony's father. That was it, the other part of the story, *her* story: Alexa *wasn't* killing our people in the name of revenge. She was killing the villains of our people and giving the rest a way out.

Is... is this why she let me go so many times when the pack first started hunting me? She was protecting me from Caldwell's investigation so she could figure out how to protect my magic privately?

"One more thing." The hard lump that passed in her throat warned me to brace myself. "I need you to tell Jak I'm sorry for killing his parents."

I stumbled into the corner. No way. God's honest truth was staring me right in the face, aiming a gun at a door when she'd used one just like it to kill Jak's mother.

Wait—"parents"?

"I didn't mean to kill his mother." Her voice moved into a foreign deeper register. "She suddenly moved and my bullet landed wrong. But I have every intention to kill William, that man is too far gone."

A sharp pound banged down the hall. Alexa solidified her stance and her grip on the gun. Shouting ensued, not one voice familiar as they all blended in a medley. I couldn't hear Momma's, Mr. Dawson's, or Dad's. My heart dropped to the center of the earth, frozen six feet underground.

"I need you to get to the base under Mount Steele in British Columbia," Alexa said with an authority I couldn't help but respect. "Tell them what happened here, who you are, and who sent you. They'll answer your questions I can't answer right now, they'll protect the Ateras from Caldwell." She swallowed. I don't know why it felt like a goodbye. "The Delphines are setting you all free. After tonight, we're on the run. You'll never see us again, nobody will."

"But why now?" I forced myself to ask. "Why did you wait a year and a half—?"

"Mount Steele will tell you. You and I are out of time."

The pieces were falling together too quickly. They were fitting too perfectly. Everything Alexa had ever done to me, she'd had another reason for. Her wickedness had always been a cover first.

She was the reason the federal government had never caught the Ateras in the last year and a half.

Even if she weren't under the truth spell right now, Alexa Delphine was too raw, too vulnerable in that moment, to be the same woman I thought I'd been dealing with all this time. And I think that was why I believed her.

"Whatever you do, do not let Caldwell catch you," she told me. "You can do this, Adara."

It clicked like a battery in a remote. *That* was why she'd been so desperate to find Adara: to keep her away from the president.

Footsteps echoed down the hall outside. Doors were slamming open. I cried out as Alexa ran to me in the corner with the gun still aimed at the door. She wrapped one arm around my shoulders and pushed me into her, then pressing her hand hard against my ear. To my overwhelming surprise, I curled into her hold—and went rigid when something banged next to the door.

It slammed open. A gunshot followed. Alexa's body jolted against me. Another gunshot submerged my hearing. Alexa jerked again as she released a gurgled cry. Someone shouted down the hall. A third gunshot rang out. Then another.

Silence crackled all around me.

A hot tear rolled down my cheek. My heart beat with a numbing buzz in my ears. Alexa's heart, I faintly felt against me.

She dropped to the floor.

I cried her name, cringing at how it echoed off the walls and probably down the hall, alerting anyone else on their way over here. In my peripheral, two men lay in the doorway. Dead.

I'd never seen a real dead body until that morning.

"Alexa?" I rasped, my hands hovering over her. The side of her throat, close to her collarbone, had been shot. Blood gushed from the wound that the bullet wasn't clogging well enough. I couldn't tell if Alexa was even paler than usual because of the cold or because of the wound or both.

"Steele," she whispered, so airily that I had to depend on reading her quivering lips to know what she was saying.

I moved my hand to the back of her head. Her hand pressed against the left side of her chest, a crimson shadow staining it. Her heart. Another bullet was too close to her heart.

I brought her head up, my vision fading into nothing but a hot blur. "No, it—I can't, without you, it—!"

"Adara," she mouthed. Blood relentlessly surged from her wound. "Save them."

"No, Alexa, please—!"

Her head fell limp in my hand. Those emerald-green eyes glazed over with death's hold.

Forty-One

She's dead.

I called out Alexa's name over and over again. Some cruel part of me kept shaking her head. Some sick, manipulated part of me kept begging her to wake up.

She's dead.

She's dead, she's dead.

"Emma!"

Despite the depth of my stun, a familiar, comforting voice broke straight through it with my name.

I jolted upward, setting down Alexa's limp head. My numb hands furiously wiped at my stray tears as I tried to get back in touch with the reality in front of me. I forced myself to my feet, but Alexa's body lay like a barrier in front of me. I couldn't take another step. I couldn't break past her.

She's dead.

"Emma!"

That was... Wait, that was—

"Mr. Dawson!"

My brain blocked out the body on the ground. I darted around it, over the two bodies in the doorway, and into the frigid hallway. Mr. Dawson was running around the corner far down on the other end. He jumped over two bodies lying in front of him.

"Go!" he screamed, furiously gesturing toward the door behind me as he sprinted. "Go now, run!"

Why didn't he warn me telepathically that he was coming?

I turned around. It was the heavy metal door I was meant to go through when we first got here. We were almost out.

I trusted Mr. Dawson and sprinted the rest of the way to the end, barreling my shoulder into the door. I stumbled into the entrance of the hideout, the ladder dead ahead.

I bolted forward. My mind throbbed with a hundred memories, a hundred theories, a thousand echoes of the cold environment. Something was wrong. Only my subconscious could detect it, but my survival instincts were raging and overcoming it. I climbed up the ladder, Mr. Dawson right behind me.

She's dead. My body started falling limp at the thought as my head broke through the surface, the air turning crisp. *How many else? Who else that I know is—?*

"Come on!" Mr. Dawson urged as he scrambled to his feet on the snow, grabbing my wrist.

I looked down the manhole. Nobody was following us up.

That was it: Mom. Dad. My parents, where were they?

With my emotions blinding the world in front of me, I pulled back on Mr. Dawson. "Mom and Dad—"

"Your mom's fine, we need to get to the car!"

My legs all but gave out under me as he yanked me again, to the snow-covered boulders we'd climbed down to get here. "Where is Dad?"

"We need to go, Emma!" he retorted, grabbing my waist.

"NO!" I screamed, kicking in his hold and writhing every which way. "He's still down there, where is he—?!"

Mr. Dawson let me go, only to grab my shoulders before I could slip and hold me in place. "It's me!" he exclaimed, his diamond-blue eyes aflame with desperation. "It's me, honey, it's Dad."

No. No. He's saying my dad is dead. He's saying he's the only father in my life now—

"We used an appearance switch spell, it's me. Tristan."

For a split second—because that was all I had—I looked past his eyes, deeper into his irises. That inflection on "Tristan", how it had slightly faltered the way it only does when someone says their own name—it was Mr. Dawson's hands squeezing my shoulders, but it wasn't Mr. Dawson standing in front of me.

I threw my arms around my father's neck in another blind surge of emotion. My relief fell in a heavy breath and pulled my hot tears with it. My father was alive, we'd rescued him—

Wait. Then where was Mr. Dawson?

"We have to go," Dad said, pulling away and pushing me toward the boulders again. "We'll be shot the second someone finds us here."

"But Thomas—"

"Emmalynn, now!"

My father wasn't giving me a choice—and I especially didn't have one with Mr. Dawson's commanding voice. Climbing up the boulders and onto the hiking trail, I forced myself to pump my legs with Dad's. Our feet pounded on the dense dirt. My mind was turning numb in the cold. Every part of me was going limp, shutting down.

Don't. Maybe he's already in the car, Dad wouldn't leave his best friend down there, not unless he was safe.

Or there'd been nothing else Dad could do for him.

Momma was already in the car when we ran into the parking lot. I nearly doubled over with relief but didn't stop until we got to the car and my hand grabbed the door handle. We were okay. We'd made it out—

I shut my door with the most deafening thud of my life. Mr. Dawson wasn't here. He was still at the hideout, we were leaving him behind.

"Wait," Momma said from the passenger seat as Dad threw the car into reverse. "Wait, where's Tristan?"

The car jerked to a stop. Dad's eyes snapped to me with the same headmaster authority Mr. Dawson always carried. "Sleeping spell, Emma, now."

"What?" I said just as Momma grabbed his arm and made him look at her.

"Where is my husband, Thomas?!"

"Emma, I said now!"

Fear bowed to discipline—especially with Mr. Dawson's voice giving the command—and I obeyed. Momma sank in her seat as she fell asleep.

My breath tightened when Dad turned to face me. His eyes glistened with a deep regret I didn't know they were capable of.

"Cast it on yourself, honey," he told me.

I opened my mouth to question him again—but with all of the evidence around me, I was pretty sure that I wasn't ready to face the full scope of reality head-on. And the only way to wake up from the nightmare it had become was to escape it by falling asleep.

Dormio.

I felt my body sag as my world went black.

CHAPTER

FORTY-TWO

When I woke up, rubbing my eyes to clear my groggy vision, the car sat parked on the shoulder between an empty highway and a forest. I jolted upright in the backseat, my memories whirling alive in my head.

The left door opened. My mother climbed in, muttering for me to slide into the middle seat. Dad—still disguised as Mr. Dawson—opened my door as I did, taking my original spot.

Relief wasn't an option yet: when a wielder dies, their magic dies with them. If Dad was still under the appearance spell, that meant either he had been the one to cast it—or Mr. Dawson wasn't dead.

I held my breath as Dad shut the door. The early morning's ambiance fuzzily trailed after, but I refused to stay trapped in it for long.

"Who cast the spell?" I demanded.

Dad nodded, like he knew what I was really asking. "He did. He's not dead."

My breath flooded out of me, tears brimming and overflowing beyond my control. Momma hugged me from the side, and I clung to her arms like they were the rope above a chasm.

"Yeah," Dad breathed, rubbing his chin. "He told me to wait until he switched us back."

"What happened?" Momma said.

His throat bobbed, eyes hardening as if they were the only shield against his emotions. He wrapped an arm around my shoulder, gripping Momma's hand. "He found me. Then he told me the plan and about—Em's vision."

I immediately denied the self-imposed guilt saying I'd somehow caused this, forcing myself to listen in full.

"He said it was stupid to assume all four of us would make it out untouched. If worse came to worst... he got to watch Emma grow up. I didn't. I had a life to live after it was stolen for all those years. I was their target, not him. So he switched our appearances to buy us—me—time, just... just in case. To take my place if—"

I wanted to scream as my father cut himself off, to demand for what had happened next. If he wasn't dead, where was he?

"William was on his way to kill Emma," he whispered. He squeezed Momma's hand. "Thomas ran for his life to save her. William only had to look at 'me' to change directions and—give Thomas the chance he needed to kill him."

The words slammed into my chest like a boulder. Kill. *Kill.* He was dead. Thomas Dawson *killed* William Bleu.

"He was just as quickly caught," Dad breathed. He looked down, closing his eyes. "That was when he told me to run and I grabbed Emma."

—*Why didn't you fight back?*— I demanded to know. I didn't trust how those words would come out if I'd spoken them. —*Did you even use your magic?*—

He didn't respond.

Grief and relief warred against each other in my stomach. Relief that it hadn't been my dad, after all, I still had him after less than a year and a half with him. I'd get this year's Christmas with him, too.

But for the first time in my life, Christmas with Mr. Dawson wasn't happening. I didn't know if it ever would again; he'd been caught by the federal government as Tristan Atera, which was a death sentence alone. Even once he exposed himself as Thomas Dawson, he'd still be killed for being a wielder. And an accomplice. The man was as good as...

I clenched my teeth, unable to care if they shattered. He had to come back. He was stronger than a Hunter's trap, stronger than death, he'd been stronger that morning on the beach house. If Dad told the story again, gave him more time, he would show up. Maybe he would already be waiting for us at home once we got back. He could do it. He had to. He had to.

"Why didn't you warn me?"

The words escaped without so much as my permission. At their release, I knew that my emotions had taken full reign over my tongue, and it was the biggest relief I could find in those moments. It wasn't like I would've been able to do anything, but I could've tried. Maybe I could've tried to help—

"He knew you'd want to help." Dad squeezed my shoulder, rolling his lips together. "You would've tried to help. But you were the only one who *had* to escape from that place. He wasn't going to risk your life—"

"Why didn't *you* warn me?" I snapped. Mr. Dawson's appearance speaking about the man felt like a sick joke.

Dad took in a breath I couldn't hear, only see—see on the face of a man that I still had to remind myself wasn't actually here. "My magic," he muttered, like his voice was trapped in his chest instead of his mouth.

Mount Steele.

No. That was why he hadn't replied to me telepathically just now.

I cursed the connection. Despite all that Alexa had revealed to me—despite the good I could even see in it—rage bent my fingers into fists and mind into an asylum for vengeance. If everything Alexa had told me was true, my father's magic was supposed to be on its way to Mount Steele right now. But only if it had a deliverer. Caldwell's team had swarmed the hideout—all the more reason Mr. Dawson had wanted to be the one Caldwell grabbed instead of the real thing...

A sinister voice whispered to me that he wouldn't come back this time like he had from the beach house. He *wasn't* coming back this time. Not on his own.

Coming to terms with the way things are—accepting that you can't change them no matter what you're willing to do or offer—is the first step toward recovery, toward healing. I know that. But not one part of me believed that for the rest of the morning as I mindlessly stared through the windshield while the car flew down the freeway. I didn't want to heal; I wanted to act. It wasn't right. I'd finally been set free from my heaviest chains of the last year, but it didn't matter. In the wielder world, it never does, because once hunted, twice goodbye. That's the rule. And this time, it had been goodbye to the two allies I needed the most.

Last year on my birthday, I'd sworn to never let a single power on Earth rip apart my family again. Months later, I'd told Moren how I regretted making that promise, for the exact reason of this morning: I'd broken it because it was outside of my control to keep. Mr. Dawson had sacrificed himself for my family's sake, and we couldn't do the same for him without invalidating it.

There was only one thing to do: save ourselves so we could save him.

FORTY-THREE

Dad still hadn't switched back to his own appearance by the time we grabbed Aunt Becca from their apartment. Mr. Dawson was still alive, and that was the only piece of news holding us all together at that point.

Not once in my entire life was getting back to my childhood home more of a relief than it was that late morning. Not once. Because now it was safe. Now there wasn't an enemy threatening to break down our door. And yet, somehow, the thought had never been more suffocating.

She wasn't my enemy. The woman sacrificed herself for me. To *protect* me. She was not my enemy.

I silently carried that with me for the rest of the day. It wasn't hard, not when we had one topic and one topic alone to keep us all busy: we had four people in the house, but it was too empty. Somebody was missing, and we were the only ones who could change that.

Dad didn't switch back until that night.

I refused to think the worst until I knew—until Aunt Becca paid the nore's price with me and asked if he was alive. He was— in custody. With that, all I had left was a forest fire ablaze in me to get him back dead *or* alive, because neither was guaranteed for when we'd find him.

"Okay," Momma muttered next to Dad on the sofa. "We need to leave."

Those words were no less wicked coming from her. I froze next to Auntie's recliner with my eyes on the tall Christmas tree in the corner, next to the sofa. Its lights were the only ones we had on; we didn't feel safe turning on anything else, which was a sign in itself that Momma was right. We couldn't get Mr. Dawson back until we were safe. Not only was it a matter of time before Caldwell's agents did locate our house, but it'd be all over international news soon that the Delphines and William Bleu were dead. Mr. Dawson's face would no doubt be plastered all over the news, announced as yet another prize of Caldwell's hunt. The world would soon know him as Thomas Dawson, junior-class Hunter instructor at the Callistro Academy—and a wielder.

This morning had changed our lives, but that news report would single-handedly uproot them. Mr. Dawson was the reason Momma had a job at Callistro at all; the school board was bound to question her. Then her daughter. The entire school was practically destined to know everything the second that report was released. We didn't have time for Christmas Eve, Christmas, forget

New Year's. We had to leave.

I knew that there was only one place safe for us.

"Where do we go?" Dad asked, his hand resting on Momma's knee.

"As far away from North Carolina as we can get," she said. "As long as it's not here."

Mount Steele.

I needed to tell them. But how could I do that as fast as possible and without falling apart at the memory of who'd told me about it?

"And we need to move fast for the head start," Momma added. "The sooner we leave, the more likely we'll have a clean getaway. That's all I'm hoping for."

Not even Aunt Becca in the recliner had anything to say in protest. The white Christmas lights softly illuminated Dad's hand patting Momma's knee.

"Okay," he whispered. "Let's start—"

A knock on the front door cut him clean off.

I know what it's like to be so paralyzed with fear that you physically can't move—and yet, despite every survival instinct screaming at me otherwise, I couldn't tear my eyes away from the door or my body from the sofa.

Momma stood up, already knowing that she was the best candidate to check. She walked over and looked through the peephole. I wasn't sure if I was all the more terrified or relieved when she turned to us with wide eyes and then unlocked the door.

When she pulled it open, she gave just enough space for our guest to slip in. "What are you doing here?"

Jak stepped inside.

Jak. Jak?

My brain couldn't grasp it. Not when he was standing there in a hoodie and sweatpants like nothing had happened today. Not when he was breathing through his mouth with shallow breaths and the Christmas tree exposed the wet tears on his scarred cheeks. Not when he was looking at me like I was an oasis in a desert, and then running to me. Not when I was running into his arms before my mind could help me realize it.

That moment of contact, the instant our bodies pressed together as our arms wrapped around each other, was what unleashed a wave of tears. Maybe Momma had been right, maybe I *was* too strong; I'd held it all together perfectly until now. I don't know why seeing Jak break—when he hadn't even broken down the night he told me his mother's story—was what obliterated my resolve. Right now, as we fell to our knees in each other's hold, everything I had poured straight onto the fabric of his hoodie.

"Anchor," he whispered in my ear.

I don't know why—maybe it was out of sheer relief that I'd never have to worry if someone was impersonating him again, or because that single word had unlocked some kind of cell in me—but I squeezed him tighter and sobbed in my Jak's arms.

And because I wanted him to feel just as safe, I whispered it back to him.

"I'm sorry," he rasped. "It's all my fault, I'm sorry. I'm sorry."

He knew. How did he—?

I don't care. He needs me.

That was why I'd broken: because he was broken. Because he had nothing, no one, and I was breaking for him as if it could give him enough strength to stay together for just a little longer.

And maybe, just maybe, I hated our circumstances more than I was admitting, and I found the strength to break down in his surrender.

I could only squeeze him in response. Holding him tighter was the only way I knew how to tell him that I didn't blame him. There was too much to say and not enough ways to say it all.

"It's not your fault." They were the first and only words that had broken the murky surface of my mind, and I lunged for them. He needed to know.

Somehow, his grip on me tightened. His cries became nothing but air as his body shook. I squeezed my eyes harder shut.

"I'm an orphan, Emma."

I stilled. Amidst everything, even William's death itself—those words had never once struck me.

"I need you to tell Jak I'm sorry for killing his parents."

My head resting on his shoulder, I opened my eyes. I couldn't tell him that Alexa killed his mother, had even planned to kill his father before she was shot dead. I couldn't add to the grief already devastating us, not right now, not when he was hurting—

It hit me, the reason he was crying despite the man William Bleu had been to him: he hadn't let go of his dad yet. He'd been trying since last month, and he'd lost him before he'd gotten anywhere that mattered.

I couldn't do it again. I couldn't stand watching him suffer again because of me. What was I supposed to do other than live vicariously through him and ask, "Do you want to forget?"

His grip loosened around me. Mom said my name, but Jak looked up. The dark mercifully obscured the long scar on his left cheek as confusion stitched together his features.

"What?" he whispered.

I took his tear-soaked face into my hands. "I can make you forget. A forgetting spell, you don't have to remember today, yesterday, the last month, this whole year, you can forget!" I glanced around the room, at Becca and Dad sitting behind me and at Momma standing behind Jak. "We can't. We have to remember everything to get Thomas back, even if he dies between now and when we find him, we have to remember all this—but you don't. You don't have to suffer if you don't want to, just tell me!"

Jak's hands slid from my back to my waist as he exhaled. "No," he whispered, cutting off Momma's breath in behind him. "No, don't—"

"Why not?" I cried, letting go of his face. "Why would you ever wanna remember this morning, everything you've gone through?"

"Because I can't—I won't, I don't want to."

"Why?"

"Because I don't want to, Emma!"

I realized it then: I wasn't asking even primarily for his sake. I was asking for mine. I did want to, and Thomas Dawson was the only reason I couldn't.

Jak's grip on my waist loosened. "I wanna remember what I lost, I wanna know why I am the way I am moving forward. I know you wanna forget, too, but that's the worst thing you could do to yourself. Everything in the world is gonna remind you of what happened, of him and what might or might not happen to him. You're gonna remember everything in one go. And it's gonna be a vicious cycle where you never overcome it, just forget it."

I hated him. I hated him for how my family had nothing to

say because he'd said everything on their minds. I hated him for his rationality, his stability despite the hurricane, his capacity for thought when I was crumbling apart in front of him—everyone. He'd become an orphan, but I was on the verge of losing someone I was deeply connected with. Jak had lost his parents, but I'd lost family. I had to cut myself something, yet losing my rationality when Jak simply hadn't felt like another stab in the gut.

"What're you gonna do?" I whispered.

"I don't know." His cold hands cupped my neck. "I just know I never have to leave you again. So the last thing you're ever gonna be, no matter what, is alone."

But Mr. Dawson isn't here. He needs us, he needs us now.

"I told you,"—Jak brushed my hair out of my face—"I know what it's like to lose a parent."

He knew what it was like to lose family.

He rose to his knees and reached out his hand. I used his help to stand with him. Maybe all he needed was to confront the fact that he'd lost his father to realize that he'd already suffered his greatest loss ten years ago; now he could breathe through this, even though I still couldn't. Soon I was crying and numb with anger all over again, but in Jak's arms this time. My parents' arms. My family's. If anything, I just needed to be held, to just find a shelter to wait out part of the storm in. It was rest. I didn't have to feel anything because Jak and my family already knew. That was something only they could give me: a source of steadiness, my only anchor now in the raging sea.

⚓

After that, I told them all about Mount Steele—and with that, we had somewhere to pack for.

It almost goes without saying, but we didn't touch our Christmas presents. We didn't know when we'd ever be back, in full honesty, but presents seemed frivolous when we were facing an emergency evacuation—from the country—because we were harboring Tristan and Rebecca Atera and Caldwell no doubt knew it. Alejandro had already been warned that we needed his "services" and would meet us in an hour, so my priority right now was packing.

Then Mom and Dad pulled me back into the living room and sat beside me on the sofa. Which jumpstarted my anxiety as much as anyone can imagine it did at that point.

"Emma," Momma began, the decorated tree standing tall on her other side, still the only light source in the house. She reached down for the wrapped present on the outskirt of the pile under the tree and handed it to me. "We think you should open this one before we leave."

The shape alone gave it away: a book.

I took it from her. "Why?"

"It's from Mr. Dawson."

I turned my head to Dad beside me, like I needed him to verify that Momma was telling the truth. He looked back at me with soft eyes, waiting for me to turn back to the present.

From Mr. Dawson. I almost felt like I had to preserve it for that reason alone: this could be the last present that Mr. Dawson would ever give me. But that was also the reason I had to open it.

I ripped the red Christmas wrapping paper away, exposing a soft, smooth, dark-blue cover underneath. The corners poked through the paper as I tore it off. Golden corner protectors gleamed at me as I crumpled up the paper. Momma took it from me, letting me hold the journal in my lap.

Mr. Dawson got this for me?

"He thought it'd make the perfect gift after this semester," Dad said. "Since you filled your last one."

His firm hand rubbed my back as my eyes glazed over the present in my hands. From Mr. Dawson. Something to record this semester in, to tie my sanity to while we approached the new year. Something to remember him by.

This could be the last present I'll ever get from him.

"Thank you," I whispered, wiping away a tear that had just escaped. I stood, gripping the book, because my determination had been fully restored—just as much as my grief. "I need to pack."

My parents didn't say a word as I strode past the coffee table and into the hallway, toward my room. Aunt Becca was packing a single duffel bag on Momma's bed in her bedroom, but she never spared me a glance and I passed.

I set Mr. Dawson's journal onto my bed and grabbed my suitcase from my closet. Determination pumped through me, but I needed to keep that at the front of my mind. If I thought about the journal, my drive would pull me out; if I thought about Mr. Dawson, my grief would pull me under. I threw my suitcase onto my bed. I glimpsed the book every time I felt my control slip as I tossed my clothes inside. As long as I remembered the situation and not the reason, I could move forward.

"Hey."

I turned around. At the sight of Jak standing in my bedroom doorway, I had to confess something to myself: I missed hearing

"Merlin" at the end of his greetings. Technically, it was safe again—just a vile reminder.

"Hi."

With his hands in his hoodie, he meandered to the hanging chair in the corner of my room. At least—on the very dimmest bright side—I didn't have to worry ever again if the Jak in front of me was really my Jak.

When the pack hadn't returned by tonight, Jak had broken into the basement's lair and grabbed the body cam footage each member had. He'd watched every Delphine get shot down—and Alexa and William.

But he hadn't asked about Adara yet despite Alexa calling me that just before she died. I think watching his father and step-mother die, no matter how detached he was from them, had hit a little harder than another secret identity I was harboring.

"Do your friends know yet?" he asked.

I stared down at the open duffel bag in front of me. My feet were practically glued to the carpet. "They're meeting me at the gazebo when we leave so I can tell them."

Needless to say, after Momma, Mr. Dawson, and I had prac-tically gone missing this morning, my friends hadn't gone to New York or Washington for Christmas break. Which was a blessing and a curse.

"Do you want me to come with you?" Jak asked.

I turned around to face him, sitting on the edge of my bed. "No. I have to be the one to tell them. I have to leave them with a letter explaining everything, anyway, I might as well knock it all out in one go. And if you come, they'll just ask why you're going with us. They have every right to."

I hugged myself, rubbing my arms in the cold. Jak was getting to come with us to Canada and they weren't. But if they knew why, they couldn't hate me. Could they?

How would they look at me if they knew? How would they treat me if they knew what really happened this morning? Would they be the ones comforting me right now instead of Jak?

Comfort. Jak...

It was the one question I'd blatantly forgotten to ask him in the last hour: "Are you okay?"

He scoffed, shaking his head as he swayed in the chair. "I just wanna survive. Now I can... We both can."

It felt like our stares grew cautious together the longer they remained with each other.

"They're both gone," he murmured. His swaying stopped. "We're free."

Free. Free from Alexa Delphine and William Bleu.

From Alexa.

"The Delphines are setting you all free."

My body tightened, eyes squeezing shut. I stood from my bed and turned back to my suitcase, straining to breathe the thin air.

"Emma?"

I took a sharp breath in and opened my eyes. "She protected us."

"Who?"

"She was trying to protect my magic, my family's magic, from Caldwell. She didn't want what William did, she was trying to protect magic, and she—"

The words slammed into my chest. I had to take another breath to carry them past the guilt and regret. "She died protecting me!"

The chair creaked as Jak stood. He appeared beside me, sitting on the edge of my bed. "What're you talking about?" he asked lowly, like he was daring me to repeat my blasphemy. And I couldn't blame him with that scar on his left cheek contradicting my every word.

"She wasn't the bad guy," I cried. "She was gonna take our magic and send it to a magician facility under Mount Steele to be protected. William wanted to kill us because we're wielders, but Alexa wanted to protect our magic from Caldwell. *He's* the one that wants it!"

"Calm down," Jak told me, holding up his hands. "You need to calm down and tell me everything from the beginning, because none of this makes any sense. You're telling me Alexa was the *good* guy?"

"No," I said. "She was a protector."

For the first time since they'd happened, I recalled the morning's events. I remembered them in full and relayed the information Alexa had given me. Saying it all out loud threatened my faith in her words—but she'd been under a truth spell. That, and someone who was lying about that simply wouldn't give their life for you if they didn't want you setting out on it. If the truth spell alone didn't do it, that was the only other reason Jak had for believing me—believing her.

The woman had shot her husband—twice—for the sake of helping me escape.

"This whole time," he whispered under his breath. He slouched in his spot on my bed. "She couldn't've told you sooner?"

"No. William—and Caldwell. Caldwell had a harder grip on her than William ever did. William was just an annoying fly she couldn't get rid of."

A long sigh left him. "Sure would've been nice if she liked you as much as she liked your magic."

That night in the forest in August almost felt *too* long ago now.

"So we're going to Canada," Jak said.

I nodded.

"On the other side of the continent."

"Yeah."

He scoffed softly to himself, but I think he was trying to convince himself that it was our only option—the best one we had—rather than convince me or anyone else of every reason we shouldn't be doing this. And it was in that next breath that he straightened, his dull eyes widening.

"What?" I urged, stepping back.

"You said William called in backup knowing exactly who he was dealing with?" he began, all traces of grief absent from his voice now. "Both the Delphines and you, and that's why he wanted you all dead?"

"Yeah..."

He tilted his head. "How do you know he never told backup who you really were?"

I froze. Just as with the fact that Jak was now an orphan, this had completely evaded my mind.

"He definitely didn't want to protect you," Jak said. "He wouldn't have kept your identity a secret. But if that's the case, backup definitely relayed it to Caldwell, too. There's no way your name and identity stayed unknown."

I relayed the events of the last few hours in my head in one quick, excruciating blur. We'd been fine so far. Momma had even checked the house for bugs and cameras, and we were clean, but that was why we were trying to move as fast as possible. If Caldwell knew who the Atera descendant was...

"Caldwell—can't know," I finally managed, my words tripping over their own validity—considering they probably didn't have any. "He would've sent someone after me immediately, he never would've let me go just like that."

"I'm saying this for your own good." Jak's eyes darkened, peering at me from the top of them in the dark. "There is no way that the President of the United States does not know who you are."

The words were as solid as steel when he said it. Because actually hearing them, hearing them in reality, put me face to face with the truth, the odds. I'd experienced far too much by now to stay naïvely ignorant. There was no possible way that Caldwell—and the alive Hunters from this morning—didn't know my full name.

"Why hasn't anyone come after us?" I dared to ask.

Jak lightly shook his head. "I don't know. I wish, I *wish* I knew."

Mom. Maybe Momma would know, maybe she—

Footsteps padded behind me a second later. I spun. Momma stood in the doorway with her arms crossed over her chest. She'd definitely been eavesdropping: slow movements, cautious eyeing, the fact her mind was turning when she hadn't said a word yet.

"I feel like," she began, stepping into my room, "you've seen this situation before."

Alexa. Alexa had known who I really was and taken forever to attack because she wanted my magic and was planning strategically in the quiet.

Except Caldwell actually wanted my magic to inherit, and he had the power of an entire federal agency *and* the whole country to get it. Why wouldn't he strike? Why would he postpone getting what he so easily could...?

There was no way that strategic planning was the excuse this time. Could it be?

"Then what do we do?" I asked my mother. "This is a new enemy, we don't know him. We don't know his methods and he's more powerful. Do we wait it out? Are we supposed to attack before he does?"

Believe it or not, that morning was not the most terrifying event of the month; instead, it was watching my mother's lips purse and her eyes, devoid of comfort, pierce me like I was her target on a hunt as she said, "No. We leave as soon as we can."

CHAPTER

FORTY-FOUR

The wind scraped my cheeks with blades of ice as I approached the gazebo in the dark, empty park. Snow crunched beneath my boots, my hands barely sustaining their warmth in my coat pockets. As much I wished otherwise, the cold wasn't enough to drown out the tension in the air that was so thick, it was hard to breathe.

My best friends stood together from the outdoor sofa in the lit-up gazebo as I climbed up. It was as if they *wanted* me to feel interrogated, but I knew this was their greatest attempt at trying to keep things "normal" while waiting for the most anticipated answer I'd ever had in our entire friendship.

I wanted to cry at how I didn't have to tell Opal that her uncle had been kidnapped by the U.S. Government and was most likely being held captive, tortured, something along those lines—and we couldn't even grab him until we had somewhere safe to plan. I wanted to cry at how my lips didn't have to bear those words, and at how I wouldn't be here to comfort her.

"Thank God you're alive," Sarah murmured between Opal and Breanne, like that was what mattered the most. I wondered how she'd be able to hear us with those fluffy white earmuffs on.

Right—the last time she'd seen me, I'd abandoned her at the school. And her teacher and headmistress had never come back.

I nodded, self-conscious of every puff of air that left my lips. "Yeah. You, too."

"Are you okay?" Opal asked, tilting her hooded head in my peripheral vision as I stared back at Sarah.

Opal Dubois. I couldn't look her in the eyes. I couldn't look her in the eyes without remembering, without that same blinding rage toward Caldwell gripping the control center of my mind.

"No," I replied, clenching my gloved fists tighter in my pockets. "But it doesn't matter, I'm gonna be."

"'It doesn't matter'?" She spoke to me with the same skepticism she had after the first day of school on the Main Staircase. "Like you don't have a right to be affected? Of course you matter, even more so when you're not okay. Breanne and I were terrified enough when we were taken, we didn't even want to *begin* to imagine what you were going through. We skipped our flights, waiting for news, and then all we hear is that you're okay but you 'have to talk to us'."

"Look, it's—" I cursed the tremble that had already gripped my voice, ruthlessly fighting an uphill battle to control it. "That's not why I'm here."

Breanne glanced next to her, toward the main road across the dark, snow-covered field: Momma was parked along the curb with Dad and Becca in invisibility cloaks and Jak in the backseat, the headlights gleaming against the winter haze. "You guys drove here?"

I didn't know what to say that wouldn't pull the loose thread and unravel me altogether.

"We're leaving."

Yet somehow, the Band-Aid was getting easier to rip off now.

"What?" Sarah asked, stepping forward but stopped by the table in the center of the gazebo. "For Christmas?"

No, I thought, but I wasn't ready to say it without falling apart. I did the only thing I could: I took the envelope out from under my scarf and held it out.

Opal took it for Sarah, who almost seemed to know what was in that letter: the exact story of what had happened at the hideout, and that being why we had no choice but to go (with me knowing too much about Tristan's daughter replacing me *being* Tristan's daughter). Sarah's scrunched brows glared at me like I was playing a sick joke on her.

"Don't open it here," I said when Opal moved her finger under the lid of the envelope. "Read it when we're gone."

"Why?" Sarah stated, shifting her weight to one side. She wasn't my best friend right now: she was a Hunter interrogating her target. "Where are you going?"

"It's in the letter."

"I don't want to hear it from a letter," Breanne told me, stepping around the table and past Sarah. Her brows furrowed like a child who'd just asked her separating parents what "divorce" meant. "I wanna hear it from you."

"Just—trust me," I said, holding up my hand. "Please. You'll understand why. Please, trust me. It's the last time I'll ever ask you to."

My best friends stared at me like they wanted to, like they really wanted to—until that look at me became a look *into* me, and they seemed to realize that they didn't have any questions worth forcing my memory of the morning out of me.

"I'm sorry," I whispered, my eyes taking turns with each of them: Sarah, Breanne, and Opal. "I'll be back as soon as I can."

"What about school?" Opal asked like she was determined to find any excuse to anchor me to this town. "Your mom's the *headmistress*, you're in the middle of—"

I shook my head and nodded to the envelope in her hand. Mom had already resigned as headmistress on "emergency", and I was officially a high-school dropout. It's hard out there. We couldn't care, we couldn't afford to. It was life or death.

"Em, no," Breanne cried, her doe-like eyes slightly looking up at me. The glisten in them was strong enough to combat the darkness trying to swallow the one light hanging from the ceiling. "Please, what's going on, why are you going?"

The girl is the smartest student in our school—one of the smartest in the state—but she has moments where the student is stripped off her and you're just left with the girl.

I softly shook my head, closing my eyes. A sniff escaped. "I love you guys. I really do."

When Opal came, they all came. They walked over to me, hugging me, squeezing me when I couldn't squeeze back. To my greatest surprise, besides me, the only other girl maintaining her composure and not bursting into tears was Sarah.

"We love you, too," Opal whispered with a tear-soaked breath.

And we stayed there for every second I knew I could afford with them, because I'd have to survive on these seconds for at least the next few weeks.

Few *weeks*.

I don't want to leave them. I'd never spent longer than four days away from Sarah and Breanne in the last nine years we'd known each other. For all I knew, after what had happened at the hideout... I *wasn't* coming back. Or I'd be coming back to an empty dorm.

You can't think like that. Don't.

Breanne's and Opal's smiles gutted me with a knife as they broke away. They were sincere despite their hot breaths clouding in front of them, their hands wiping their tear-streaked cheeks.

Breanne rubbed her arms. "Can we still text and call?"

I pressed my lips together in a tight smile as a final resort to cage the tears. "It's in the letter."

The answer to that was no. Not even email this time.

I don't want to leave them.

"I have to go," I whispered, wiping away the tear pooling in my eye. I turned around, stepping down from the gazebo and waving at my best friends.

To my relief, they waved back. I don't know for how long because I couldn't spare more than a glimpse back. I kept my fists firmly in my pockets and gaze glued to the icy field.

I think I didn't allow myself to think too deeply into the situation because I knew the consequences. At this point, there was nothing keeping my heart in one piece except my own two hands pushing it together. As soon as I released, whether by choice or force of tears, I knew where I'd be: here, still in Capperson. I'd never leave, not even for my family. Because I had family here, too, family that needed me.

Family that I'd already left behind at a Hunter hideout.

I walked and walked and walked across the park, desperate to make it to Mom's car before I broke down and fell to my knees in the snow. I'd lost too much. I'd lost one of my greatest allies; a father, a mentor, my teacher; and now my best friends. I'd lost too much with nothing but my own strength holding myself together, nothing but my own hand patting my shoulder in comfort.

Someone was running after me in the cold.

I paused. The crisp footsteps behind me slowed before stopping completely.

"Don't leave like this," Sarah said softly behind me.

I turned around. Her white-gloved hands hung at her sides. Her striking features now drooped, matching her tone as her heavy eyes stared at me.

"I can't talk about it, Sarah, that's why I wrote it—"

"Okay," she said in that same gentle voice. "You don't have to tell me what happened. That's not what I wanna know, I'm not scared of that."

What?

"It's what I see it *doing* to you that I'm scared of."

I swallowed. She couldn't do this to me right now. Not right now.

"I know about reading people." She took off her earmuffs and let them hang around her neck. "And after our talk where I told you about my... you know... after you helped me get the courage to tell everyone else? I think I know exactly how you're feeling right now. Like—you wanna talk and tell someone what's going on, but you wanna forget reality exists at the same time. You wanna let the world know how you feel but you're terrified of what it's going to do with that knowledge. You can't have both and you're hating and cursing and screaming at that fact. Leave what happened behind, fine, but now you don't even get what it did to you? What it *does* to you on a daily basis? I get it."

Stop. Stop it. You aren't supposed to know that. You aren't supposed to see through me right now.

Was I letting her?

She walked close enough to rest a hand on my arm. "I don't even want to *begin* to imagine what happened this morning, Emma, it was just *this morning*. Part of me honestly hopes I'll never have to hear about it. I'm not gonna force anything out of you. Just like you never forced anything out of me. But whatever you do wanna talk about, you decide what or even if you do. It just scares me because—this might be your only chance to decide."

A stray, hot tear was already falling down my cheek. My body had stiffened like a board.

"Would you hate me?" I whispered. "Would you still be my friend if you knew?"

A divot formed between her brows. "I could never hate you for that."

"No," I said, my throat tightening. "If you knew what the last year actually looked like."

"What I *hate* is that I can't take away what's hurting you, what's *been* hurting you, and now you're leaving with it instead of leaving it here. That hurts—I'm your best friend, and I can't help with whatever's caused you so much pain and... and has probably left you feeling as alone as I did."

My nose twitched. The tears were streaming down from both eyes without any help from a blink, whether I screamed at them to stop or not.

I turned around, facing Momma's car against the curb and squeezing myself tighter. Shutting my eyes, I took a sharp breath in, covering my mouth.

I'd known. I'd known it for a long time, for too long for me to bear the burden alone anymore.

"Yeah," I whispered, eyes piercing through the stream of the headlights too far away. "Yeah, I'm alone, I feel alone. I've been alone this whole time. There's never been *one* person I could immediately tell everything to without being scared of some kind of consequence. I've been shouldering them, being hunted for the last year and a half, lying to you guys and Jak and my parents because it's the only way to keep myself and everyone safe! I can only protect everyone if I lie, if I keep everything to myself, there's no other way to keep everybody safe!"

"Emma," Sarah whispered behind me, rubbing my back. "You should *never* carry your problems alone, especially just because of us. We would've figured out something together like we always do, there's always another way—"

"No, there's not!" I whirled on her, my voice stuck in a high-pitched whisper I couldn't bring down. "If I don't lie, if I don't keep EVERYTHING a secret, you guys pay the price, everyone pays the price, I pay the price, just like...!"

Silence lay beyond my gasping cries.

"Like who?" she asked.

The Delphines.

I didn't answer. I couldn't answer unless I was going to answer her and break. And I couldn't answer her without telling her the truth.

"Emmy..."

My body stilled at the tears I heard stuck in her throat.

"I can't stand this, I hate seeing you like this," she urged. Her hand grew heavier on my back. "Don't leave like this. Please, don't leave like this. You're not alone, okay? Don't tell me whatever's hurting you, just—please, *please*, tell me what to do to make it easier before you go. Anything."

I wanted to. I'd wanted to trust all of them with the truth back at the gazebo. If I was going to leave them without knowing when or even if I'd come back—I felt like they deserved to know.

But I didn't trust Opal as long as she was a liar, Breanne was only keeping Alexa's magic for the greater good and not because she was comfortable around magic, and Sarah—just wasn't a wielder. Not to mention that she was the greatest Hunter out of all of us.

And finally? I'd witnessed firsthand what being my ally in magic did to a person. A whole family.

I had every reason not to tell any of them, but I wanted to. I wanted to be a *real* friend to them. There was a reason I'd lied about everything. There was a reason I'd had so many "mother-daughter" dates that first week of sophomore year. There was a reason Thomas Dawson had been captured.

I took in a ragged breath, stuffing both of my hands back into my coat pockets. My cries were settling. The guilty fog of my mind was gradually lifting. "Would you still offer that if you knew?"

I needed to know before I went.

"Whatever you've gone through the last year and a half, I'm here for *you*." Sarah pressed her hand harder against my back with each emphasized word. "I will *always* be here for you because I'm your best friend. Nothing's going to change the fact that I'm your best friend."

"And I'm—"

I stared Sarah right in the eyes, my cries finally stopping as the waves ceased. Because she was also the strongest out of all of us: mentally, friend-wise, Hunter-wise. She was my best friend. And wielder or not... she understood me. Wielder or not, she loved *me*.

I swallowed my final burden. "I'm Tristan Atera's daughter."

ACKNOWLEDGEMENTS

I had some pretty wonderful alpha readers *transform* this book from the terribly rough third draft it was—Amelia, McKenna, Grace, and Bryce. And then I had some just-as-incredible betas—McKenna, Bryce, mc, Sabrey, Bella, and Ja (Jack only had time to get through half of it so he only gets half his name)—who polished it up in ways I desperately needed. (You can thank mc pending that OHTG is 103k and not 116k.) They each squeezed this book into their insanely busy schedules when it was the size of a brick and I had no one else. And they kindly left me alive when I offed a beloved character long enough for me to save that character. Thanks, guys.

OHTG would quite literally not exist, though, if not for MiblArt, the cover designers who did four whopping book covers for me in *two months* because I'd decided to breathe new life into the series and really get it out in the world. MiblArt, thank you for your endless patience and understanding with the chaos of my brain. And for all of the revisions. Y'all are real ones.

Susan Markloff slapped on the ISBNs for me when I started freaking out about cover quality—so thank you, Susan. You're my anchor in the publishing world in more ways than I can ever express.

And to everyone on Instagram who not only waited for this book, but encouraged it, who bought the series even five years after it began—thank you, thank you, *thank you*. You are the main reason I do this in every sense of the word, and I wouldn't have *anything* I do today without you.

We'll see you in 2025!

About the Author

Ariana Tosado is a 22-year-old author, musician, university student, book editor, and content creator for teen and young-adult audiences. She started pursuing her passion of writing novels in middle school. Today, she's homed her focus on the *Emmalynn Atera* Series, marketing *Thy Kingdom Come*, and producing music. She aims to create relatable and encouraging content through her platforms, all with her cat, Sophie, in one hand and an iced vanilla latte in the other.

You can find out more about what she's up to on her website (www.arianatosado.com) or on Instagram (@thearianatosado).